...in Afghanistan. *The Gunner Girl...* ...
by her mother-in-law's experiences during ...
in Nottingham with her family. Find out more at her
Facebook page: www.facebook.com/clareharvey13

Praise for *The Gunner Girl*:

'Clare Harvey's fast-moving debut novel, *The Gunner Girl*, will
delight all those who love a good wartime story' **Dilly Court**

'This is an irresistible tale of friendship, love and heartache
during WW2 that had me enthralled. Joan, Bea and Edie are
ordinary young women with extraordinary courage, who put
their lives at risk each day on the anti-aircraft guns. Wartime
London has never seemed so real. Clare Harvey's research is
intimate and impressive – I loved all the details of daily life.
She captures the dislocation, both mental and physical, that
wartime imposes, and I was gripped from the first dramatic
page. A vivid and beautifully crafted read that will captivate
hearts' **Kate Furnivall**

the GUNNER GIRL

Clare Harvey

**SIMON &
SCHUSTER**

London · New York · Sydney · Toronto · New Delhi

First published in Great Britain by Simon & Schuster UK Ltd, 2015
This paperback published 2016
A CBS COMPANY

1 3 5 7 9 10 8 6 4 2

Simon & Schuster UK Ltd
1st Floor
222 Gray's Inn Road
London WC1X 8HB

www.simonandschuster.co.uk

Simon & Schuster Australia, Sydney
Simon & Schuster India, New Delhi

A CIP catalogue record for this book is available from the British Library

Paperback ISBN: 978-1-47115-054-8
eBook ISBN: 978-1-47115-055-5

This book is a work of fiction. Names,
characters, places and incidents are either a product of the author's
imagination or are used fictitiously. Any resemblance to actual people
living or dead, events or locales is entirely coincidental.

Typeset by Hewer Text UK Ltd, Edinburgh
Printed and bound in Great Britain by CPI Group (UK) Ltd, Croydon CR0 4YY

For Chris, of course.

Chapter 1

She was almost home when she saw a swish of blue-grey as the airman rushed towards her up Western Way. The wind lashed a strand of hair across her face. It caught on her mouth and she spat it out.

He was barrelling towards her, arms outstretched, mouth wide. He was shouting something, but the wind took his words and hurled them down the street, towards London, the Thames and away.

Then she heard him: 'Get down! Get down!' The airman hurled himself at her, rugby-tackling her, pinning her down.

She began to scream, but before the sound escaped her mouth, the explosion lifted them both off the ground, tangling their limbs before throwing them back down. His knee was in her groin. The buttons on his uniform dug into her cheek, her breast. In her mouth, the damp-cloth-sweat smell of his clothes. The juddering weight of him on top of her and the sound: deep, loud, painful. Sudden and hard:

her skull whipped back against the pavement. And then it was over.

Black, and then everything concertinaed. Colours blurred and separated. She tried to breathe, couldn't, choked, shoved at the smoke-coloured weight on top of her. A brass button grinding into her cheek; acrid smell in her nostrils. Cloth, hair, flesh, grit. They rolled together, slow-motion wrestlers in the settling dust. A sound in her head, bomber engines thudding like bluebottles buzzing inside her skull.

Then they pulled apart, limbs dragging against each other.

He sat up. She looked up at him. There were patches of grit and mud on his uniform and a cut on his cheekbone, spilling blood.

'Are you all right?' he mouthed. She couldn't hear him properly, her ears still filled with that sound.

'Fine, I think,' she said, feeling the words, but not hearing them. She pushed herself into a seated position and rubbed the back of her head.

The pavement was cracked, slabs ripped apart to reveal tree roots and dry earth. The air smelled metallic, dark, burnt.

He staggered slightly, getting up, then he held out a hand for her. She took it and struggled upright, bare legs scraping the broken ground. As she stood, the world span, and everything blanched, momentarily white. There was gravel on his palm and there were little hard points of contact between their two hands, and she focused on the sharpness of it, holding his hand while the spinning slowed and the colours returned. The ground shifted; tarmac seeming to undulate like waves. And they stood holding hands as the world stopped turning.

'You're hurt,' she said, pointing at the cut on his face. He put a hand up to check.

'It's nothing,' he replied, his voice tinny and far away. He felt the wound, brushed a lock of dark Brylcreemed hair away and rubbed the dust out of his eyes, then noticed that his RAF cap was missing and let go of her hand as he turned to search for it. She watched him, the blue-grey figure, searching for his cap by the unravelled kerb. Her eyes followed him find it, pick it up, brush it off and shift it onto the correct position on his head – the missing piece of the jigsaw puzzle found and slotted in.

There was dust up her nose and in her mouth. She wiped her lips on the sleeve of her coat, but succeeded only in pushing more grit into her mouth and leaving a smear of red on the beige wool. As he began to walk back towards her, brushing the dust from his jacket, she looked beyond him, at the place the bomb had struck.

'Well, we were lucky, weren't we?' said the airman, as he drew level. 'I don't hold out much hope for the poor blighters at number thirty-two, though,' he continued, following her gaze. She looked past him to the smoking pile. It was like a giant's game of spillikins, a mess of sticks and rubble. She could hear the sound of the belated air-raid siren starting its slow wail. 'You're a bit shaken up, I can see that. I'm not too chipper myself, to be honest. Let's get you home. You'll feel better after a cup of tea,' he said. He touched her lightly on the forearm. She turned to face him.

'Now, where is it you live?' he said. There were specks of gravel on his cheeks, and the livid slash of blood. His eyes were blue and round, like a child's.

'I live at number thirty-two,' she replied.

Looking back, she thought the day ought to have felt more important. She looked for signs – she should surely have been able to sense that something life-changing was about to happen? But she hadn't. Life-changing things had been happening to everyone else since the start of the war, but not to her, not to Vanessa Tucker from number thirty-two. Everything that day felt so very normal.

That afternoon, there was a new Pathé newsreel in. The hazy swirl of the smoke curled up past the flickering screen at the cinema, as the afternoon crowd sucked on Capstans and Woodbines in the fuggy darkness. It had the usual jaunty music and newsreader with a voice like blocks of wood being tapped against each other: tap, tap, tap-tap. The Queen had just visited the Auxiliary Territorial Service depot, the voice rapped out, and black-and-white figures scurried on the screen. The Queen smiled, sweetly interested in the busy lives of the ATS, a piece of fondant icing among the dense fruit cake of uniforms and guns. Mary Churchill, the Prime Minister's daughter, was there, making a wobbly curtsey and smiling a sad smile. And Vanessa thought about her sister, Joan, who was about to turn eighteen and was joining the ATS. She wondered if Joan would be billeted with the Prime Minister's daughter – what a lark, if she was!

After that, she lost interest. She had to count up her change and make sure she wasn't even half a bob out or Mr Evans would be on at her, again, the old goat. He made no secret of the fact that she'd only got the job because her dad was a mason, too. And once, he touched her behind as she bent down to pick up her refreshments tray.

All her friends thought that being an usherette must be a terrific job: getting to see the flicks for free every day. But she never got to see the whole film because of stocking-up and checking her change and there was always some joker who came in late and had to be shown to his seat. She wasn't allowed to sit down, either, not in the public areas, which wasn't easy, what with these blasted shoes that would always be – whatever Mum said about the leather giving with time – a size too small.

Usually, Vanessa stayed after the matinee, had a cup of tea and a bit of bread-and-scrape in the office with Mrs Evans, because there wasn't quite enough time to get home and back before the evening show. But today, she had the night off. Today, Dad was off duty and Mum had been saving her sugar ration for weeks for the cake, and they would celebrate Joan's birthday. And tomorrow, Joan would be taking the train to London to join up.

On the way home, she imagined them all, waiting for her at the table: Dad puffing on his pipe, Mum bustling about in her pinny and Joan sat next to the wireless, listening for the news, clutching the call-up papers that she hadn't let out of her sight since they came in the post last week.

Vanessa tried not to listen to the wireless, if possible. The war had been going on for so long that the best thing was to try to have a good time and forget about it, in her opinion. Having a good time and forgetting about it often got her into trouble, but she didn't care.

It was nearly dark, the winter evening creeping in like a cat, and her legs were freezing in the breeze. If she had stockings, it wouldn't be so bad. But who had stockings any more? All anybody had was a line of black pencil up the back of their legs, which fooled nobody. To have stockings, you had to be really rich, or the sort of woman who wore red lipstick: fast. And she wasn't fast, no matter what anyone said – it was only the once, and she hadn't even wanted him to.

The airman faltered. 'Then . . . we should get you to the first-aid post,' he began.

'No,' she said.

The ground was still shifting, unsettled. She put out a hand – wasn't there a lamppost here? The airman caught her arm under the elbow as she stumbled. People were pouring out of houses, some making weary haste to Anderson shelters, others coming towards them. Mr Goodwin tumbled out from next-door. The wall that joined his house to theirs was half-missing, ripped, obscene. His bed was visible through the blown-out gap, and cream wallpaper flapped like loose skin.

Her house was gone. The sky came all the way down to the rubble. There were no chimney pots or roof diagonals, just reddening clouds and a jagged silhouette, like a boxer's gaping mouth after the knockout punch. She could hear the blare of sirens, children crying, the shouts of the ARP wardens, but all muffled, as if she had cotton wool stuffed in her ears. The house itself – her house, where she'd lived for ever – was a silent hole amid the hubbub. Her stomach churned.

'You two, don't worry, the ambulance is on its way; they'll get you patched up. Now move aside and let us get on with it,' said the voice of a burly ARP warden, as he made shooing actions with his arms. But neither of them moved. They both stood, looking at the place where her house ought to have been.

Other men and women were rushing up, more ARP wardens, fire officers, police, crawling like ants towards the debris of her home. She heard the ambulance draw up behind them and watched as Mr Goodwin was led past them. He was wearing a string vest, no shirt, and his right arm hung limp and twisted. He didn't appear to see her as he passed. She thought, poor Mr Goodwin, he'll have trouble digging his swedes with a broken arm. And then she thought of Dad and Mr Goodwin at the allotment at the weekend, talking about manure and early frost.

The airman tried to guide her into the waiting ambulance, but she broke free and rushed towards the bombed-out house, her shoes catching and tripping her on the uneven pavement. NUMBER THIRTY-TWO said the sign on the skewwhiff gatepost. She stumbled on up the path towards where the front door should have been.

'Mind yourself, love.' A fire officer was beginning to pull

out a charred joist that barred the way through to where the hallway once was. 'Anyone in there? You're all right, we're coming for you,' yelled the fire officer into the wreckage. Nobody answered. He turned to her. 'This is no place for you, young lady.'

'It's her home.' The voice of the airman came from behind; he'd caught up with her.

'They're in the kitchen,' she said to the fire officer.

'How many?' he asked.

'Three – Mum, Dad and my big sister.' Her voice sounded matter-of-fact, as if she was telling Mrs Evans how many ices she'd sold in the interval.

The fire officer shook his head. 'You don't want to see this, believe me, love.' Then he talked over her head, to the airman. 'Take her away and look after her. You both need a bit of medical attention. We'll do our best.'

'No,' she said. 'I'm not going anywhere.'

She could see the fire officer look grimly at the airman. He let out a breath.

'Let her stay. I'll look after her – and I can help,' said the airman.

More wardens and fire officers joined them, tossing bricks aside and peering into the rubble. Through the choke of plaster dust, she worked alongside them: scrabbling, wrenching, pulling, swimming through the wreckage of her home. She didn't feel the splinters, the broken glass, the bruised limbs, as she worked on, reaching out to grasp and chuck still-warm wood and broken bricks. The air smelled strange: hot, acrid, burnt meat. A taste of bile in her mouth, she swallowed it down. Nearby was the airman, breathing heavily, grunting as he helped lift timber and blocks of masonry.

She began to pull away bits of lath from one side, away from where the men were working. Underneath, she saw fragments of terracotta, and earth, and a clump of pulverised flowers, dirty orange. There was the faint smell of crushed chrysanthemums as she reached across to pull out a mass of fractured wood. There were blood spatters underneath. Blood, and then flesh, like the slab at the butcher's: wet and exposed. It was only by the torn scrap of floral cotton that she recognised it as Joan. The rest was a mangled pulp of meaty bones; a sticky mess where Joan's head should have been: crushed, blasted, lost.

She leant in, gulping back the nausea that was forcing its way up her throat. All that was left intact was an outstretched hand. Debris dug into her bare knees as she knelt forward, touching the tips of Joan's fingers. They were perfect: oval nails buffed with the special buffer from the new manicure set, fingernails clean. Vanessa thought that Joan always had such lovely clean nails. And there was the engagement ring: thin gold with little sapphires and pearls. Vanessa held the hand; it wasn't yet cold.

'You're not alone, Joanie,' she whispered. 'I'm here, don't worry. It's Vanessa. I'll look after you.' Plaster dust and ash fell like snow.

On the shattered floorboards next to her, splaying out, lay her sister's ID card, and ATS call-up documents, dusty and blood-spattered. Without thinking, she picked up the grit-encrusted papers and shoved them in her coat pocket. Then she heard the sound of a woman screaming. She let go of Joan's hand and looked round to see who it could be, and realised the sound was coming from her own mouth.

The airman rushed over, pulled her up off the floor and into him, shielding her eyes. 'Don't look. Don't look,' he said.

The scream was replaced by a high-pitched keening, wrenching her chest open: a stabbing, tearing implosion. And then the putrid rush of vomit up her throat, as she stumbled forward, out of his grasp. He caught her, held her hair off her face as the bile upsurged again and again. When she finally came to a shuddering halt, he wiped her face with a clean handkerchief. She tried to stop the feral sounds that were coming from her throat; the effort was like swallowing acid.

'Come on, now,' the airman said, and she let herself be taken away, out of the bombed-out wreckage and onto the road. His arm felt strong and warm and she wanted to just shut her eyes and dissolve into him, to become part of the musty fabric of his uniform. The ambulance had already taken Mr Goodwin to hospital, so they walked a slow stumble together down Western Way towards the first-aid post at the town hall.

'I'm sorry for your loss,' he blurted awkwardly, as they passed the alley that led out to the allotments. She held his arm tight, wobbling and scuffing in the stupid shoes, gulping down the sick feeling.

For a moment, she was outside herself, looking down on

the girl with the cut-up legs and the airman with the blood-ied cheek as they moved slowly down the road, past the alley and the old school playing fields. And it was no longer the alley where she'd been caught being a 'dirty girl' with George, the grocer's boy. And it was no longer the school where she'd been forever asked why she couldn't sit quietly and write neatly like her big sister Joan. It was just a street with a young woman and a young man staggering together like drunken lovers. And then she snapped back inside herself again, with sore feet and wounds that were beginning to sting. At the first-aid post, they were pulled apart, and she was alone.

Years afterwards, she still remembered the smell of disinfect-ant and the sting as the first-aider scrubbed the grit from her knees with a brush. She remembered watching the black pencil line of fake stocking seam run like dark tears down her ankles. She remembered watching the blackout curtains being closed, tight against the night. She remembered looking at the burgundy smear of blood on her good winter coat and worry-ing if the stain would ever come out. And she remembered the throb in her temple and the dislocation and fatigue that pressed down, suffocating. But she didn't remember feeling any grief. She didn't remember feeling anything at all, not then.

After being scrubbed, washed and bandaged, she saw the airman again. She was sitting on a hard wooden chair, drink-ing weak, sugarless tea from a chipped mug. 'They're sending me to hospital to get stitched,' he said, coming out from behind a screen, 'and I have to report back to my unit in the morning. But here's my address.' He handed her a scrap of paper, with scrunched-up writing in pencil. 'Let me know how you are, won't you?'

She nodded, put the paper in her coat pocket, and got up. 'I will – and thank you for everything.'

'It was nothing,' he said, his kind eyes screwing up. 'It wasn't enough.' He looked like he was going to cry.

'There wasn't anything that anyone could have done,' she said, to rescue him. He cleared his throat. She wanted to throw her arms around him, hug him and not let go. Instead, she held out a hand. As they shook, he paused, holding her hand for a moment longer than necessary.

'I don't even know your name – who are you?' he said.

'It's Joan,' the lie slid easily from her bruised lips.

'What are you going to do, Joan?' he said.

She let go of his hand and thrust it back into her coat pocket, fingering the precious documents. There was an angry thudding in her head, and the sick-dizzy feeling tugging at her insides.

'Oh, you don't need to worry about me. I'll be fine,' she replied.

'You'll write, when you're settled, let me know how you're getting on, won't you, Joan?'

'Of course.' She smiled, even though it hurt. 'Just as soon as I can.' She waved him goodbye as he left and tried to keep smiling until the door closed behind him. The young girl volunteer was picking up the metal bowl of disinfectant next to her chair. She looked familiar: tidy brown hair and spots on her chin.

'He's a good-looking boy,' the girl remarked. 'Is he your fiancé?'

'No,' she replied. 'I only met him today.'

After the airman had left she sat down again, drained what was left of her tea and tried to think, but everything was disjointed. Her head ached. She felt so tired. She reached into her pocket and pulled out the papers. First, she saw the airman's details, in his jaggedy hedgehog writing. Her eyes could barely focus, but she saw that his name was Robin Nelson and he was a flight sergeant. A flight sergeant: that was a good rank, wasn't it? Joan's fiancé was an Able Seaman. But that was the merchant navy; she wasn't sure how they compared. She folded the paper and put it away.

Then she turned her attention to the other documents: Joan's ID card, call-up papers and travel warrant. She brushed the grit off them and turned them over on her lap. There was a small, grainy photo of Joan inside the ID card. She looked at it carefully. In a photo like that, you couldn't really tell that Joan's hair was strawberry-blonde. In the photo, it was merely a shade of grey; just like her own mousey hair was in photographs. She checked through the papers again, just as Joan must have been doing when the bomb hit. She was supposed to report to the training camp tomorrow afternoon. The girl volunteer came back to take her mug.

'You're free to go, now,' she said. 'But you're welcome to stay if you've got nowhere else . . .' the girl trailed off, embarrassed concern in her eyes.

'I'm fine,' said Vanessa, stuffing the documents into her pocket and getting up. She winced with the effort, walking as quickly as possible to the door.

'But don't you think you should just ...' the volunteer girl's voice was lost as the door slammed behind her and she went out into the winter darkness.

At first, there was just the blackness and the sound of the wind, and she felt her way along the shop fronts like a blind person, bumping and tripping. Her limbs were heavy with the ache of fresh bruising and raw with the sting of disinfectant. Her head felt leaden. And still the godawful shoes chafed against the tender flesh of her feet. As her eyes became accustomed to the blacked-out night, she noticed a discarded chip paper floating down the street like a ghost and the barrage balloons jiggling like bosoms in the sky. If she kept on walking she'd end up at the police station.

She felt her way along, tripping as she hit the kerb by Howell's Bakery. She was almost at the police station. There it was, a paler wedge of darkness: dark blue against grey with POLICE painted in bold, definite script. Then she hesitated. As she paused she saw the door underneath the sign open. An orange slice of light appeared and two figures emerged. The door quickly closed behind them. The wind had died down slightly and she could hear their voices, although she couldn't make out who they were. She heard 'Alf Tucker' and 'tragic' and she knew they were talking about the bomb on her house. She strained to listen. 'All of them killed?' came the question, but she couldn't hear the answer. Then she heard the sound of car doors slamming and the cough-roar as the engine revved up. She ducked into the bakery doorway, avoiding the luminous fronds of blinkered headlights as the police car sped off.

The police station couldn't have been more than fifty yards away, just fifty paces. But instead of carrying on, Vanessa crossed the street and doubled back on herself. There was a shortcut behind the Red Lion that would bring her out at the tube station.

People stumbled and jostled against each other in their rush to get home, blind as moles, coming out of the Underground into the windy night. She pushed and dodged against the swarm until she reached the steps. Down she went: one-two-three; down-down-down; passing the posters telling her to DIG FOR VICTORY and MAKE-DO AND MEND. At the bottom, the light was a fuzzy yellow and the air smelled of diesel fumes, stale cigarette smoke and exhaustion.

She looked up the long platform. There were bundles of clothing, blankets and cardboard boxes, where people were already settling in for the night. She heard a baby crying and a clink of bottles and the murmuring echo of scores of voices. Groups of people clotted the walls, rustling and muttering like birds. She couldn't see any space for herself, so she walked on, towards the end of the platform, where the train tunnel formed a shocked black scream in the grimy walls. At the far end was a little space next to the wall, beside a couple with a Jack Russell dog. They were sitting on empty packing cases. The dog yapped as she approached. She asked if it was okay to sit next to them. The woman shrugged, the tip of her headscarf wobbling. The man looked up at her. One eye was milky, unseeing in his stubbled face. The dog continued to yap and he kicked it.

She sat with her back against the wall. The platform was hard against her haunches, her legs chilled where they came into contact with the cold concrete. She raised her knees, pushing her skirt down over as far as she could, then she hugged her arms around them, tight. The man and the woman began to argue about money. She accused him of spending it all in the bookies. He said she ate too much and was a nag. The quarrel volleyed on between them.

She tried not to listen, and focused her attention further away. Her head was still aching, a dull pain, and she swallowed down the sick feeling as it rose in waves. All along the platform other people were talking, playing cards, feeding babies, cleaning teeth.

They were interrupted only twice more with the howl and rush of trains and the scuff-shove as passengers hurried past. Then the lights dimmed and the arguing couple spread out a blanket and lay down underneath a torn patchwork quilt. The large clock above the exit gleamed like a full moon. Slowly, its hands inched round. She hugged herself tighter, clenching and unclenching her jaw, waiting for sleep. Later, she heard the man heave himself towards the woman in the gloom. Their argument forgotten, they panted and groaned for an endless five minutes until the man grunted and lugged his body off hers. Then he began to snore.

She could still make out the clock face and concentrated on it, willing the hands towards midnight, so that today would finally be over. She went to sleep at last, with her hands in her pockets, clutching Joan's precious papers safe in her fist.

Chapter 2

At breakfast, Edith's mother looked up languidly from *The Times*. '*Bon anniversaire,* darling,' she said. 'No butter, and Cook's talking about joining the Land Army,' she continued, taking a small bite from a triangle of toast and marmalade.

'Gosh,' said Edie, not knowing what else to say. Today, she really was eighteen. She'd had all the presents and celebrations yesterday. Her parents had decided to hold her birthday party a day early. It was more convenient for them. Pop had 'some important work in town' today, and would be staying over at his club. 'It's just a matter of expediency, doing the whole thing the day before. You don't mind, do you?' Mummy had said, rhetorically, while writing invitations. And today, when she really turned eighteen, it all felt like a bit of a damp squib.

Now Mummy put down the paper and got up, leaving behind a scent of Pears soap and Dior. There was an ivory-handled spoon in the marmalade dish. Edie pulled it out and quickly licked it; it tasted vile. She poured herself a cup of tepid tea from the pot. Through the French windows she saw her mother take out a cigarette, shoulders hunched, one hand cupping the silver lighter. The trees shivered, their bare branches like old men's fingers against the grey sky. The tea tasted like dirty laundry.

Edie got up and walked across to the French windows, following her mother outside. The wind sliced through her day dress and made her eyes water.

'Mummy, may I?' she held out a hand for a cigarette, just as she had held out a hand for the red and green after-dinner sweets as a child. Her mother's cheeks sucked in as she inhaled. Edie noticed streaks of grey in her hair and the lines tracing her eyes and lips, like spiders' webs. Her mother exhaled, the wind ripping the smoke away.

'May I have a cigarette, please?' Edie said in her most polite voice.

'Certainly not.'

'I'm eighteen now.'

'Yes, so you are. Did you enjoy the party? Wasn't it good of the Cowies to make it? Lord knows how they got the petrol.'

'Thank you for the party, and for the pearl for my necklace and the dress,' said Edie, hand still outstretched.

'It all went off rather well in the end, don't you think?' said her mother, inhaling again. Specks of ash disintegrated in the wind. Edie dropped her hand. She'd thought things would be different, turning eighteen, even though she wouldn't be presented at court, of course. But she'd hoped she might be treated as a bit more grown up, at least. She watched her mother and smelled the smoke that was torn from her in the breeze.

Her mother took a final drag and flicked the cigarette butt into a flowerbed. She's forgotten we don't have a gardener to clear away her debris any more, thought Edie. She sighed. Her mother shot her a look, and then disappeared back inside. Edie followed her in, closing the door behind them.

Mummy was already in the hallway, brushing dust off her tweed skirt and getting her coat from the hook.

'I've promised to meet Mrs Carson to discuss what the WVS ought to plan for over Christmas,' she said, picking up her handbag. 'Do come along, darling.'

'No, thank you,' said Edie.

'But I worry about you. What are you going to do all day on your own? Will you go and visit Marjorie? Shall I call her mother?'

'I'm quite tired after last night, actually,' said Edie. 'Would you, send Mrs Carson my best wishes?'

'Yes, of course. And you'll be fine on your own?' She was already halfway out of the door.

'Don't worry, Mummy, I'll be fine. I'm eighteen, remember!'

The front door slammed shut. Edie wandered around the house, trailing a finger along dusty windowsills, remembering last night. What could one expect from an eighteenth birthday in wartime, after all?

There had been a small fruit cake, and she was allowed the tiniest glass of champagne. They danced to the gramophone, except that the music hadn't been anything modern, like Glenn Miller. Marjorie had a Glenn Miller record at her house: the 'Chattanooga Choo Choo'. They used to play it when Edie went over, trying to dance like they did in the films, until they fell over each other, laughing, on the Parquet floor. Marjorie's brother Kenneth had brought the record when he came home on leave. Edie had known Kenneth for ever – well, since she had known Marjorie – and she'd been almost as proud as Marjorie when he joined up and got accepted as an officer in the Intelligence Corps. And the Kenneth she had always associated with conkers and chemistry sets suddenly became something else, and she had half hoped ... but now Kenneth was MIA – missing in action – shot down in a plane over France, apparently. When she'd asked why he was in a plane over France – it wasn't as if he were RAF or anything – nobody knew. And Marjorie had stopped asking her over to listen to Glenn Miller. She hadn't even come to the party. Her mother had called at the last minute to say she had a head cold. So Edie had celebrated with some of the other girls from Queen's College, and they'd danced with each other for the lack of boys – except for cross-eyed Teddy Cowie, who was only fifteen and didn't count. All the boys had gone now. They hit eighteen and – *pouff*! – evaporated.

Edie paused by the hallway mirror and blew on the glass. The cloud of breath condensed on contact, obliterating most of her face, leaving behind just her high eyebrows and a whispering of freckles on her forehead. She pulled away, drawing a heart in the condensation and writing a 'K' in the middle of it. Then, she hastily rubbed it out, wiping her damp fingers on her dress. Buck up, she told herself, sniffing and knowing that she had no right to weep. The grandfather clock ticked on, its painted sunshine face rising genially upwards, as if nothing mattered. Today is my birthday, she thought. I am eighteen, now. I'm not a child. And I'm bored as hell.

She went back into the dining room and looked at the paper. It was the usual mixture of gloom and false hope. She sat down and began to leaf through. The pages were dry as dead skin and the ink came off on her fingertips. There on page five was Churchill's youngest daughter, Mary. She had just finished her training with the Auxiliary Territorial Service. There was a picture of her at a depot in London. She was smiling in the photo, her face soft and pale as dough above the darkness of her uniform.

Mary Churchill had been in the year above her at finishing school. It was Pop who had suggested sending her to Queen's College in London after taking her school-leaving certificate. Of course, going to Paris was out of the question these days. Queen's College was in Harley Street, very near Pop's office. They travelled in together every day, along with Marjorie, who'd also enrolled. As well as French and English literature at Queen's, there were piano lessons and modern dance classes and the dreaded domestic science. Marjorie had had driving lessons, too, but Mummy had drawn the line at that. So while Marjorie crunched gears and learnt about three-point turns, Edie had extra French. She'd had a French nanny as a child, and her maternal grandmother was French, too. Even Madame

Cavelle admitted her accent was spot on, although she never really could get to grips with Molière.

A few times before the summer holidays, they had managed to meet up with Marjorie's brother Kenneth, who was on pre-deployment leave. They went for tea at the Ritz, walks in Hyde Park and to the cinema. Once, during *That Hamilton Woman*, when Marjorie had to go to the loo, Kenneth sat next to her. He put his hand on Edie's knee and then she felt his hot breath on her neck, under her hair. On the screen, Laurence Olivier was kissing Vivien Leigh as if he couldn't stop. Edie slowly turned her face and felt Kenneth's lips move up, over her cheek. They were so warm and soft and they were just about to connect with her lips when they heard the scuffle and jostle of Marjorie's return. Kenneth quickly pulled away and Edie was left breathless in the darkness.

'Golly, have I missed the best bit?' whispered Marjorie, and Edie thought, no, it's me who's just missed the best bit. After that, whenever she looked at Kenneth, his eyes flashed, and there was an unspoken understanding between them that when he came back . . . but then he didn't come back. And she could hardly confide in Marjorie; it would have felt like a betrayal.

Edie went to her mother's sewing basket and took out the little silver scissors that were shaped like a heron. Snip, went the scissors. Snip, snip. And Mary Churchill's faced wavered and slid out from the newspaper. Edie took the rectangle of newsprint and laid it out on the table. The article talked about the recruiting office where Mary joined the ATS, and her work helping out alongside the men in an anti-aircraft unit. It all sounded thrilling. There was a hole in the newspaper now. But with both her parents out, there was nobody to notice, or to care. She checked her watch. The minute hand crawled around like an insect trapped under glass. It would be hours until Mummy got back. Edie picked up the sliver of paper and took it upstairs to her room.

The pink dress lay discarded on the floor, a dying rose, with last night's silk stockings like worms on the scalloped petals. She stepped over it and opened the doors to the wardrobe. On the top shelf was her new handbag, a present from Grandmaman Redette. The bag was boxy, patent leather: glamorous and serviceable. She snapped it open. It was lined with apricot satin, with a little zipped pocket on one side. Edie put the newspaper cutting in the pocket and zipped it back up.

Over by the bed, her piggy bank sat on the bedside table, next to the lamp, and her copy of *Gone with the Wind*. She unstoppered the cork in the pig's stomach and emptied the contents onto the eiderdown. She counted it, put the whole lot into her old brown purse and put the purse inside the handbag. There was more than enough for the train fare, and plenty to spare. She picked up her pocket copy of the Bible, with the green leather cover, the one she'd been given after her confirmation. She never went anywhere without it. She clicked the bag shut, and smiled.

She picked up the handbag and tumbled downstairs to get her coat, fumbling with the bone buttons in the green serge, then grabbed her hat off the peg. Her parents never let her go out on her own. Pop said that once she turned twenty-one, she could do whatever she wanted but, until then, she had to respect Mummy's wishes. They want to keep me locked up in childhood like a caged bird, she thought; they don't want my life to change one bit, even though the whole world is changing around me.

'But I'm eighteen, now, and that's got to mean something,' she said aloud, as she pushed open the front door. The beech trees nodded as she passed, and her shoes crunched on the gravel driveway.

Edie turned right out of Victoria Station. In the newspaper article it said that Mary Churchill had joined up at the Grosvenor Gardens recruitment office. I'm only going to look, Edie thought. I just want to see where she joined up, and after that I might go and have a look at some of the anti-aircraft guns in Hyde Park. Just to see, that's all. And then I'll go straight home, so I'll be back before Mummy.

Her shoes clopped on the pavement. Buses and taxis zoomed past. Her breath made smoke clouds in the wintry air. Across the road, Grosvenor Gardens park was a slice of dusty green amid the greyness. A few brown leaves clung awkwardly to tree branches, fluttering madly, desperate to escape. A woman with a fur coat and a sausage dog on a red lead was walking in the other direction. Edie caught her eye and asked the way to the recruitment office. The dog snuffled at her feet and Edie bent over to ruffle its ears. The woman said the recruitment office was just up the street on the right and smiled. 'Good luck, dear!' she said, before yanking the little dog and walking on. She must think I'm joining up, thought Edie, feeling a mixture of pride and guilt: pride that she should look like the sort of girl who would want to do her patriotic duty, and guilt that she wasn't. I'm just a Mary Churchill tourist, she thought, and then laughed a little to herself, because it sounded a bit ridiculous. She thought about how she'd describe the day to Marjorie, afterwards, when Marjorie was in the mood for company again, and how they could laugh together about the way she'd spent her eighteenth birthday as a 'Mary Churchill tourist'.

She walked briskly, with purpose, spine straight, chin up, chest out, just as she'd been taught in deportment classes – all those afternoons in the dusty studio with a book balanced on her head, trying not to catch Marjorie's eye and giggle. She had always been very good at deportment, although French was the only thing she'd excelled at; she'd won the French prize for her year. Mary Churchill had won the Queen's College French prize the previous year, she remembered. They had that in common, didn't they? Edie sucked in a sigh. Down the curb, across the junction, just missing a grocer's boy with his huge basket on the front of his bike ('Watch your step, lady!' he shouted, veering round her), and up again, alongside the high brick terrace with its important-looking balustrades. Pigeons passed in the pewter sky like tossed handkerchiefs and she worried that her hat would fly off in the stiff breeze.

Finally, she was there. Stone steps led up to the double-doors with AUXILIARY TERRITORIAL SERVICE RECRUITMENT on a discreet painted sign to the right-hand side. So this was it; this was where Mary came to join up. She wondered if Winston or Clementine came with her, or if she came all alone, trotting along from Victoria Station, just like Edie had done?

Edie wondered what it was like inside? Would it be full of barrel-chested sergeant majors shouting at everyone? Or would it just be a case of signing a form and leaving? She paused at the bottom of the steps, looking up at the large wooden doors with the polished brass knocker. As she looked, the door opened to reveal the sturdy form of a woman dressed head to foot in khaki.

'Come in, come in, we're about to begin!' The woman bellowed, gesturing to Edie, who started to climb up the stairs. She could explain once she got there that she was only looking, couldn't she?

At the top, the large woman stepped aside and Edie was ushered into the hallway, eyes adjusting to the half-gloom. The woman closed the door behind her and looked her up and down, as if appraising her lung capacity and general state of health, and finding her wanting.

'If you go to the desk, Sergeant Noakes will take down your details – you are here to join up, aren't you?'

'Yes, of course,' said Edie – it just came out – and made her way across the marble floor to the wooden desk where another woman in khaki was shuffling papers.

Sergeant Noakes, a sharp-nosed brunette, raised her eyebrows when Edie gave her date of birth. 'Happy Birthday,' she said, and then continued ticking items off on a checklist. Then she had to sit on a hard chair next to some other girls and wait for the medical. There was a pasty-faced one called Moira and a mousey one who spoke so softly that Edie never caught her name and a fat girl who chuckled a lot and smelled of chip fat.

In the end, it was quite a lark. She had her medical and her eyesight test. The girl called Moira told her to put her hair up into a high bun just before they did the height measurements. The piled-up hair made her just about tall enough – she didn't need to stand on tiptoes – and was passed 'A1: fit for all duties'. After the medical, they were allowed tea from the urn and a plate of biscuits was passed round, and the girls let her have the last-remaining biscuit as well, on account of it being her birthday. Everyone was very sweet.

Sergeant Noakes told her it would take around three weeks to get her call-up papers and rail warrant. Edie said she couldn't wait.

The train took an age. Something about an unexploded bomb near Clapham Junction. But she had her Bible to read – it was always a comfort. By the time she got home, it was nearing nightfall. Edie walked slowly up the road, dallying, despite the wind-chill, thinking of how she'd break the news to Mummy and Pop. They would be so proud of her, wouldn't they? They would be as proud as Winston and Clementine were of Mary.

Her house looked discouraging under the darkening sky:

the rows of blank windows, two smokeless chimneys and all those thrashing beech trees. For a moment, she wasn't so sure. Maybe she shouldn't break it to Mummy straight away. After supper might be best. Perhaps she should wait until there was that contented pause before the rest of the evening began?

As she pushed open the wrought-iron gates, she imagined Mummy telling Mrs Carson about it: 'Oh, didn't I mention? Edie's joining the ATS. Yes, just like the Prime Minister's daughter. Such a brave thing to do – we are terribly proud.'

She walked up to the front door. There was a light on in the hallway, so Mummy must be home already. In fact, Edie could hear her voice. She opened the front door and went inside and there was Mummy, talking on the telephone, clutching the receiver as if it were a dying kitten that she was trying to revive. At the sound of the front door she looked up.

'Edie! Thank goodness!' She spoke back into the phone: 'Officer, I'm so sorry, but that's her now. Yes, she's just walked in. I'm so sorry to trouble you. Thank you so much. Thank you.' She replaced the receiver back in the cradle as Edie began to unbutton her coat. It was barely five and her mother had already phoned the police to report her missing.

'Where in heaven's name have you been, Edith?'

'Out,' said Edie.

'With whom?'

'With . . .' Edie cast around for ideas, but she was a terrible liar. 'On my own.'

'Where?'

'Just up to town, Mummy.'

'Up to town? On your own? *Mon Dieu!*' A vein appeared in Mummy's neck and the frown deepened between her brows. 'You went all the way to London on your own?'

'Yes,' said Edie. 'I am eighteen, Mummy.'

'I know you're eighteen, for heaven sakes. But you can't just go gadding about and not tell me. You know you should always take a friend, and leave a note, so we know you're safe. You didn't even mention it to Cook. How could you be so thoughtless? Just wait 'til your father hears about this!'

Edie looked at her mother's pained expression and felt a familiar mix of guilt and defiance.

'I'm sorry, Mummy,' she said. Her mother's face began to soften. 'But you go out alone all the time,' she added, watching her mother's features harden again.

'That's different and you know it. You're a young girl and it's not safe and there's a war on, Edith.'

'I know there's a war on,' Edie replied, slipping out of her coat.

'Don't take that tone with me, young lady. What on earth were you doing alone in London anyway?'

'I went to . . .' she looked at her mother's face, chalk-white with anger and worry, and all the love Edie knew she ought to feel was overlaid with a thick layer of resentment. '. . . to Grosvenor Gardens,' she replied as truthfully as she felt she could.

'Well, why on earth would you want to do that?'

Edie shrugged, swinging her coat from one finger. Her mother tutted, sighed and ran a hand over her face.

'Your father spent a lot of money on your party yesterday and I put a lot of effort into organising it, and this is how you thank us? If you wanted to get out of the house you could have come with me. Mrs Carson was asking after you.'

Edie said nothing. Her mother sighed again.

'Well, run upstairs and get changed for dinner.'

Edie did as she was told. When she came back downstairs the curtains had been drawn and there was a fire in the drawing room. She sat close to the fire, hugging her knees and leafing through the new copy of *Harper's Bazaar*. On the cover was a glamorous black-haired woman wearing a red-and-black-patchwork dress, draped over a red chaise longue. She had red lipstick and she was reading a letter. Edie imagined it to be a love letter, like the letter she never got from Kenneth.

Supper was a largely silent affair. The carriage clock ticked away the minutes on the mantelpiece. Mummy talked a little about the cookery lessons she was getting in anticipation of Cook leaving in the New Year. She said that Edie should take some cookery classes, too. Edie played with her rice pudding, making patterns in the goo with the raspberry jam. She was thinking about how to tell her mother about joining up.

'Did you see your father when you were in town?' said her mother suddenly. Edie replied that she hadn't gone anywhere near his club, or his office.

'I just wondered – I thought you might have . . .' her mother's voice trailed off and she took a large gulp of wine.

'I told you. I only went to Grosvenor Gardens,' said Edie.

'I was so worried, Edie. And I thought . . .'

'It won't happen again,' said Edie, quite truthfully.

'That's a good girl,' said Mummy.

After supper they went back through to the drawing room. The fire had burnt down low, so Edie put on an extra log. It was damp and smoked and hissed in the grate. She put up the fireguard and sat down on the hearth rug, leaning her back up against her father's empty armchair. Mummy turned on the wireless and picked up her knitting. Edie idly leafed through the pages of *Harper's Bazaar* once more.

'Did you hear about Mary Churchill?' Edie said in what she hoped was a casual voice.

'What's that, dear?' Mummy had her good ear turned towards the wireless.

'Mary Churchill has finished her basic training with the ATS. She's really helping the war effort, isn't she? It said in the paper that she might even work alongside the men soldiers, on the anti-aircraft guns. Doesn't that sound thrilling?'

'Well, I think it's a scandal,' said Mummy, looking up from the blue wool scarf she was knitting. 'Young women should not be put in that kind of position. Manning the guns, whatever next? It's not right! And have you heard some of the names those girls get called?'

'But not Mary Churchill, Mummy.'

'No, of course not, she's the Prime Minister's daughter and nobody would ever suggest that she ... but even so ... and the uniform is shockingly unflattering, that dreadful khaki.'

'But if Winston Churchill is happy to let Mary do her bit for King and country—' Edie began.

'Well, we all know that Winnie is a law unto himself, darling, but I have to say, there are far more ladylike ways of supporting the war effort. We're making bandages for the Red Cross tomorrow. Why don't you come along?'

'Yes, Mummy,' said Edie dutifully.

It was no good. She couldn't possibly tell Mummy anything.

On the wireless, Tommy Handley made a joke and the studio audience laughed loudly and endlessly. It felt like they'd never stop. Mummy smiled a thin smile and returned to her knitting. The fire crackled and spat. Edie realised that there would never be a good time to tell Mummy and Pop. She imagined the palaver, all the 'no daughter of mine' and 'over my dead body' and realised the sheer futility of telling them at all. She would just have to keep quiet, tell nobody – just for the next three weeks.

Chapter 3

The sound of crying followed Beatrice Smith down the street. Her skin prickled, but she tightened her jaw and continued to look ahead. She kept on walking. It was too late to turn back now. She caught sight of her reflection in the fishmonger's window as she passed. I look like any other young woman, she thought. I could be anyone, anyone at all. Nobody would know the truth. She could still hear the baby. The fishmonger came out in his stripy apron and slapped half a dozen gurnards on the trestle table in front of the shop. He nodded at her.

'Fresh from Brixham today!' he said, loud enough for the people on the other side of the street to hear. A queue quickly began to form in front of the shop. Bea moved on. The scent of fish wafted up the pavement. A truck rumbled past, briefly drowning out the sound of the mewling child. At least it's not raining, she thought.

It had rained all day on her birthday, and almost every day

since. Mrs Morley, the postmistress, came over for tea and brought lardy cake. By the time Bea had shared it out with them all, there was only a small piece left for her. She told herself she didn't mind; she wasn't hungry anyway. The sticky bread caught in her throat and made her cough and cough, until Ma hit her hard between her shoulders and brought her a cup of water. Her eyes stung as they all sang 'Happy Birthday', and Ma gave her the letter from Pa she'd kept hidden. *My little girl, all grown up!* it said, *Enjoy your birthday. All my love, Pa x* and there was a drawing of a bunch of flowers and a big cake and *Sorry it's not the real thing* with an arrow pointing to them. Her eyes were still watering.

'Come on now, girl,' said Ma. 'Your pa wouldn't want to think of you crying on your birthday, would he?'

'I'm not – it's just the lardy cake went down the wrong way,' she lied. She wasn't thinking of Pa; she was thinking of Jock. Maybe Jock's letter was still in the post?

'Come and give the baby a cuddle,' said her sister, Vi. 'That'll cheer you up.'

'I'm not crying,' said Bea, allowing herself to be led in the direction of the playpen, where Baby was sitting up, gnawing on her little fist. She put her arms out to be lifted, and Bea bent over, pulling up the soft bundle of warmth into her arms, smelling her plump newness.

Later, when the others had all had their faces washed and gone to bed, she sat in the kitchen with Ma, sharing a Woodbine. Ma had just bleached the tabletop and the acrid fumes mixed with cigarette smoke as she inhaled.

'Ma, tell me what your eighteenth birthday was like,' she said.

'When I was eighteen, you was a toddler and Charlie was on the way.'

Charlie was the one who'd died from Scarlet Fever before he turned one. Bea couldn't even remember him, even though her ma sometimes talked about him. But then the others came: Violet, May, then John and David, Rita, and after her the twins. Bea had carried and scrubbed and run errands and been responsible for as long as she could remember.

Except for that one time.

She passed the cigarette to Ma.

'Sorry I couldn't get you a present,' said Ma.

'It doesn't matter, really, I know there's no money.'

Bea felt guilty for even having a birthday, knowing it was just something else in the long list of things her ma thought she should do properly, but failed to do at all.

'Here, you finish it,' said Ma, passing over the butt. Bea took a deep drag and watched the tip of the cigarette smoulder like hot coals.

'You still haven't heard from Jock, have you?' said Ma.

Bea shook her head and stubbed the cigarette out into the cracked saucer. She couldn't look at Ma, but she heard her sigh and start talking in a low voice about how Jock probably wouldn't come back, about how whatever he'd promised meant nothing unless Bea had a ring on her finger, about what Pa thought.

Bea looked down at the tabletop, brown-grey and pitted.

She looked at the peeling varnish and the dried-out wood showing through and scuffed it with her fingernail and tried not to hear what Ma was saying.

'We've been so careful, everyone thinks Baby is mine,' said Ma at last.

Bea looked up. 'She's not yours, Ma, she's mine.'

'Ssh, Bea. Quiet now.'

'Nobody's listening, Ma.'

Her ma's voice lowered to a whisper as she continued. 'Nobody must ever know,' she said. 'Your pa thinks it's for the best,' she said.

'Jock said he'd marry me when he came back,' Bea said, her voice sounding loud in the silent kitchen.

Ma reached out her hand and cupped it over Bea's. 'He's not coming back,' she said. Bea looked down. The skin on her ma's hands felt rough. It was chapped and raw from peeling potatoes, putting washing through the mangle, scrubbing the front step. Bea pulled her hand away.

'He is. He promised,' she said.

'Listen to me, girl,' said her ma. 'He is not coming back.'

Bea shook her head, biting her lip. 'But he said—'

'Lads say all sorts of things, girl.'

'Not him, not Jock. He's coming back, I know it. He loves me. He will love Baby. He wants us all to be together as a family. He's a good man, Ma.'

'Bea, you have to face it, he's not coming back. It's been months. I'm not saying he doesn't care, but he might be—'

'He's not dead. I would know, I would have felt it. He is

not dead. He's coming back. He loves me and he's going to love Baby and he is coming back!' Bea ended with a shout.

She knew it was coming. Nobody shouted at Ma and got away with it in this family. She waited for the slap, watched as Ma leant across, lurched towards her. It was harder than she expected and Bea reeled backwards, cheek stinging.

'You shut your mouth, you little slut. Do you want the whole neighbourhood to know?' Ma hissed.

'I don't bloody care who knows,' said Bea.

'Shh, keep your voice down. You won't get another man if you let on she's yours.'

'I don't want another man. I want Jock. And he wants me, he said so.'

Ma said nothing, just shook her head, frowning. Rain spattered against the kitchen window. They stared at each other across the table.

'People are going to start asking about the christening. They're going to expect us to get Baby christened when your pa's home at Christmas. Baby is only six years younger than the twins, and everyone seems to know about my last one,' said Ma. There was barely a quiver in her voice as she referred to the stillborn baby she'd had less than a year ago. Bea had helped then, seen the slithery cord wrapped tight, watched as the grim-faced midwife shook her head and said, 'Sorry, so sorry for your loss, Mrs Smith.'

'I'm not yet forty, so who's to know any different?' said Ma.

I'll know, Bea thought. I'll know that Baby is mine, mine and Jock's. I'll know that she's my daughter, not my little sister and that my whole life is a lie.

'Look at Pa,' her ma continued. 'This war hasn't been all bad. It's an ill wind that blows nobody any good – he's a sergeant now. A sergeant, think of that, Bea. What I'm trying to say is, don't throw your life away before it's even bloody started; don't end up like me.'

'What's so wrong with your life?' said Bea.

Ma pushed herself out of the chair and stood up. Above the fireplace was an old brown teapot with a broken spout. Inside were ration coupons, elastic bands and change for the gas meter. Ma dipped in her hand and brought something out, then passed it to Bea. Bea took the small square of card and looked at it. It was a photo, yellowed with age, of a young woman with a garland of flowers in her hair. The woman had wide eyes, full lips and a beautiful smile.

'That was me,' said Ma. 'That's how I was when I met your pa. He loves me and I love him, but you could say we loved each other a bit too much, and now here I am, like this.'

Bea looked at her mother. She was just Ma, wasn't she? Ma, with the torn apron and capable hands. But now she looked again, and saw the tired eyes, greying hair and the cheeks hollowed out from years of going without so that the children could have their fill. There was nothing left of the smiling girl in the sepia photograph.

'But Baby is mine,' said Bea, holding the photo out for her ma to take. Ma put out her hand and for a moment they both froze: Ma standing, Bea sitting, their only point of connection the old picture caught between their fingertips.

'It's your eighteenth birthday. I'm giving you a better future,' said Ma.

That was three weeks ago. Now Bea turned left into Station Road and quickened her pace. On the wall next to the post office was a billboard with a red-and-blue picture of a woman's face, looking up expectantly, a smile on her glossy lips. There was a big arrow underneath the woman's face. ATS, it said: the women's Auxiliary Territorial Service, recruiting now. Ma had told her the ATS was for good girls, better than working in a munitions factory, like she'd had to. And when Mrs Morley had said something about Bea getting ideas above her station, Ma had silenced her with a look.

The rain-washed streets looked clean in the morning sunshine. Bea suddenly noticed that the sound of the baby crying had stopped and all she could hear was the rush of the London train coming into the station. She shifted the cardboard suitcase into her other hand and broke into a run. She almost didn't make it. The guard was about to blow his whistle, just raising his arm with the red flag, and she thought, well, maybe it's just not meant to be, but then a carriage door opened, right next to the guard and a voice yelled, 'Come on in, we've got room for a little one!'

The guard stopped, his cheeks already puffed, ready to blow, as Bea staggered across the platform, her little cardboard case banging against her leg. The guard, frowning, offered no help. She lugged it up the step and it was caught and pulled inside the carriage. The door slammed behind her. She was met by scores of faces, a wedge of khaki, the train rammed with soldiers.

'Got yourself a live one, Taff!' called a Cockney voice, snickering.

'Take no notice of him. Come over here, love. We know how to treat a girl, don't we, boys?' A different accent: more laughter. Bea looked hurriedly about her.

'Make some space for the lady, will you?' came a calmer voice from nearby. 'Why don't you just perch here for now?' She looked up at the face that matched the voice: a long nose, droopy eyes. He was shoving her case up against the window. 'You're lucky we saw you coming. This is the last train to London today,' he said. His voice was surprisingly low, as if it bubbled up right from the pit of his stomach. Bea nodded and smiled her thanks – she was still too out of breath to talk – and sat on the top of the case, pulling in all her limbs to keep them from touching any of the mass of green surrounding her.

With a screech and a heave the train pulled away from the station. She watched through the window as the town slowly shrank and disappeared, until all that was left were the littered railway sidings and the empty sky. She thought of Baby and tried not to cry. Was she really doing the right thing?

A better future, Ma said. A better future for her would mean a better future for Baby. And of course, there was the money. You'll get her back, said her little sister, Vi. Lots of mothers sent their children away to be evacuated. What's the difference? In a way this is better; at least she'll be with family – she'll be safe here with us. Vi's words went over and over in her head, endlessly repeating themselves to the rhythm of the train: clickety-clack, you'll get her back, clickety-clack, you'll get her back.

Bea swayed and bumped against the side of the carriage corridor. The air was dense with the smell of sweat, smoke and the scent of wet clothes. She looked across through the glass windows into the compartment. Inside, men were sprawled like toddlers, lolling heads and rubber limbs, faces flushed with sleep.

'On your way to London then?' asked the soldier who'd helped her with her case. She looked at him. He didn't look at all like Jock. Jock was shorter, stockier. This man was all gangly and dishevelled, like a daddy-long-legs stuck behind a window pane.

She agreed that she was on her way to London. She knew that he was just trying to make conversation, but chit-chat was the last thing on her mind.

'Sorry about my pals, earlier,' he continued. 'They didn't mean anything. It's just that pretty girls are a bit thin on the ground where we've just been.'

She smiled up at him. She didn't want to hurt his feelings. God only knew where or what he was on his way back from. She knew better than to ask.

'Cigarette?' he held out an open packet of Player's. She leant forward, then paused. 'Go on, I've got plenty,' he said.

'Well, I don't mind if I do,' she said, pulling one from the packet. He struck a match and she breathed in, savouring the warm rush of the first drag. Outside, telegraph poles swooped past and the sun streamed in through the dusty windows. She thought idly how what they needed was a good scrub with strong vinegar and a chammy. In the middle of a ploughed wheat field was a crater the size of a bus, a giant pock mark on the stubbled landscape. She let the smoke curl out slowly between her parted lips, comforted a little by the rush of nicotine and the motion of the train.

It was cold and draughty in the corridor, despite the heaving mass of passengers, and she huddled up, pulling her coat closer around her. It was tight under the arms, and threadbare at the cuffs. She'd bought it with her first wage packet when she left school and took the pub-cleaning job. It was too small; she'd grown since she turned fourteen. But it still looked serviceable, from a distance. She stroked the pale grey fabric with the ball of her thumb as she held the cigarette between her fingers. She'd worn this coat the first time she went to the flicks with Jock: Donald Duck, Pathé News and *Gone with the Wind*, an ice in the intermission and a kiss in the back seat, before the lights came up.

She inhaled again, and flicked the ash onto the floor, then stopped. A thought suddenly occurred to her. This was the coat they put over Baby's cot every night, to keep her warm. Baby would be cold tonight. She'd be cold and it would all be her fault and Ma wouldn't have enough money to buy a blanket, would she? She opened the window a crack and then pushed the remains of the cigarette outside, where it was grabbed by the wind and flung away. The air was icy, biting her fingers. She quickly closed the window, then dug into the depths of her coat pocket to find her wool and crochet hook. The wool was tangled, unravelled from one of the twin's old tank tops, a nasty mustard colour. But it would be warm, she thought. She wondered what to start with: bootees or a matinee jacket? Baby would need to be kept warm.

'Knitting?' said the soldier. Why did he have to keep asking questions? She told him it was crochet.

'My ma does that,' he said. 'Makes all these little squares and stitches them together to make blankets.'

'Oh! Yes, a blanket, of course!' she said, and flushed a little at her outburst.

'You look pretty when you blush,' said the soldier, and she blushed some more, as her crochet hook worked furiously at the looping yellow wool.

She might not be there for Baby, but she could still be a good mother, couldn't she? She could crochet a blanket and send money for food and shoes and, maybe, after the war, when Jock came home, they could all be together, like a real family should.

The fields and empty roads were gradually being replaced by terraced houses, churches and mounds of rubble. The housing got denser, the roads filling with buses and bicycles, and the train rattled on. She'd made six crocheted squares by the time they reached the station. As the train drew in, she gathered her crochet work and put it back into her coat pocket. She got up and caught the soldier's eye.

'It was nice to meet you,' she said.

He grinned. 'May I know your name? I was wondering if you'd like to be pen pals?'

'Oh, I don't think so,' she replied, brushing the dust off her coat. 'I have someone . . .'

'I didn't mean – I just meant to write to,' he said. It was his turn to blush.

'Yes, but, even so . . .' she shrugged apologetically.

'Well, my name's Bill Franks – Corporal Franks – and I'm with 32 Armoured Engineers. Just in case you change your mind.' He reached out through the sliding window to push down the door handle and open the carriage door as the train slid to a halt.

'Well, it was very nice to meet you, Corporal Bill Franks from 32 Armoured Engineers,' she said, smiling as she picked up her case.

She paused in the doorway and looked out over the crowds of passengers scurrying on the concourse, so busy, so purposeful. All those strangers and not a single child – there were no children left, in London. Then she stepped off the train and joined the childless throng. There was no going back: she was one of them, now.

Chapter 4

Vanessa stumbled like a refugee onto the concourse. Getting here had been hell. Crowds eddied and seethed around her as she looked for a sign. A miasma of steam, smoke and London smog hung over the crowded station. She pushed through the throng, butted and jolted like a Dodgem car, until she found the notice board. SOUTHERN RAILWAY: WHAT YOU WANT AND WHERE TO FIND IT, said the painted sign.

Her stomach growled and her mouth felt dry as sand. She'd been sick twice in the night, vomit splashing over the platform edge and onto the dark Tube tracks. She'd had some water from the sink in the station toilets this morning, but nothing else, not since yesterday. Her fingers fumbled in her pockets, but there were no spare coins clinking there, not even a couple of pennies for a cup of tea. She still felt sick, and her head throbbed.

WHAT YOU WANT AND WHERE TO FIND IT, said the sign.

Well, what did she want? She fiddled with the papers in

her pocket, eyes scanning the board. There would be a train to Devon in half an hour. The crowd heaved and milled around her. There was the hiss of steam and the sound of a guard's whistle. Colours swam and bled like paint on tissue paper. She swallowed hard, gulping nausea back down into her empty inside. Why was she here? To say goodbye, that was it. To give her a proper send off, with Mum and Dad. But where were they all?

'Joan!' she thought she heard her mum's voice above the cacophony. As she spun round, the world spun with her, blurring and sliding and out of reach, until the concrete floor was a cold hard slap and then there was darkness . . . and when the darkness went all she could see in front of her was a forest of legs and feet. A small white-gloved hand dangled down in front of her.

'Upsy-daisy!' said a posh voice. The voice belonged to a girl. Vanessa grasped the hand and let herself be pulled up. Now face to face with the young woman, the only thing she noticed was her freckles.

'Thank you,' she said. The world had stopped its wild spinning and was just wavering, hazy at the edges. She reached out and leant on the notice board to steady herself.

'Not at all,' said the posh voice. 'Are you all right, dear?'

'Yes, I'm fine.' Her tongue was thick in her mouth as she struggled to articulate. A taste of bile still in her throat, the echoing rush of station noise and everything swelling, liquid, unfocused.

'You look quite peaky. Shall I get some tea?' the voice continued.

'No, thanks, I'm fine.' She didn't have any money for tea. 'I have to go,' she said.

'Let me get you a cup of tea,' said the voice. 'Honestly, you'd be doing me a favour. I'm going to get one myself anyway.'

Vanessa couldn't focus on the girl's face. Images kept flashing in front of her eyes, like the screen at the flicks when they reached the end of a reel: an airman with his outstretched arms; a mess of bricks that used to be a home; the blank scream of the empty tube tunnel in the darkness.

'I won't take no for an answer,' the voice continued, and the small, gloved hand tucked itself under Vanessa's elbow and led her towards the tea stall in the archway. 'Just lean here a moment and I'll bring yours over,' said the voice.

The pillar felt hard and strong against her back. She was able to focus on the posh girl now: she had coppery hair and an emerald-green hat with a serge coat in the same colour.

'Two teas, please,' the girl said brightly to the dishevelled tea-stall lady.

'That's eightpence, duckie,' said the stallholder, wisps of grey hair escaping from her blue headscarf.

Eightpence for two teas, she thought, daylight robbery. She took the cup as it was handed to her. She clutched it with both hands, wishing they'd stop shaking. The peach-brown liquid trembled as she lifted it to her lips. She felt it run hot and sweet down her throat.

'I put two sugars in yours,' said the voice. 'You look like you need it. I put two in mine as well. I don't normally, but I skipped breakfast this morning. There, is that better? You're starting to get some colour back in your cheeks.' The posh girl was smiling, talking, drinking. She didn't seem to need any response. She talked about the weather, the food rationing, the war – the usual.

Vanessa tried to listen, but the station was full of noise: the chug of trains, the screech of whistles, the clink of china, the hiss of steam, waves upon waves of echoing voices, and inside her head the crash of a bomb exploding again and again. She drained her cup. Her hands had stopped shaking now. The posh girl was still talking, eyebrows jumping up into her pale forehead at every exclamation.

'. . . and poor old Marjorie! He's missing in action, and I said that maybe he's not dead, but they're all assuming the worst and perhaps they're right to do so. I mean, better that than spend months in limbo. But I suppose they must be hoping, secretly – I know I am . . . but, anyway, that's why she couldn't make it to the party, which was a bally shame because, honestly, she was the only person I really wanted to come! Do you know Glenn Miller?'

Vanessa wondered what on earth the posh girl could be talking about. Who was Glenn Miller, and why would this girl think they'd have friends in common?

'No, I'm sorry, I don't. But thank you for the tea. Now I really think I should go,' she said.

'Must you?' said the posh girl. 'It's just that I've got an age to wait until my connection, and, frankly, I could use the company.'

Vanessa closed her eyes and saw clouds of powdery dust,

and red hair, fanned out on shattered floorboards, sticky and matted with blood and grit. She opened her eyes.

'Let me at least get you a refill,' the posh girl continued. 'One for the road, as they say. Or should it be one for the tracks?' She added, and laughed.

Vanessa felt as if her mouth was going to crack with the effort of trying to smile, but she let her cup be taken and refilled. The posh girl passed it back and she said thank you.

The girl clinked her cup. 'Cheers!' she said. 'Shame we haven't anything a bit stronger to put in it. I deserve to get a bit tipsy today. After all, it's not every day you join the ATS!'

Vanessa choked on the too-hot tea.

'Steady on, dear.' The girl patted her on the back.

'Good for you,' she managed, once she'd stopped coughing.

'Thank you. It's all rather hush-hush, actually. Mummy and Pop don't even know I'm here,' she said, winking.

'Where do they think you are?'

'Oh, I'm sure they think I'm at home, sitting next to the radio and knitting, or something equally dull. But I'm eighteen now, and I wanted to do something for my country, just like Mary Churchill. Don't you see?'

Vanessa nodded. She shifted position. Her head was pounding, and all the station noises were crashing waves of sound. Her feet still hurt in her stupid shoes, and her legs were aching and cold. And she was so tired; it felt like the insides of her eyelids had been sandpapered. She yawned, mouth stretching up into her skull.

'Oh, you've set me off,' said the posh girl, also yawning, covering her generous mouth with her gloved hand. 'There's a seat over there – look, where that girl with the grey coat has just left. Shall we sit down for a bit?'

They went over to the seat and the posh girl placed her handbag on the wooden slats. They both sat down and the posh girl crossed her legs. She had silk stockings. And she had a patent-leather handbag that lay between them on the seat. It was so shiny that she could almost catch a glimpse of herself. Vanessa could see the smudged impression of a face reflected back from the glossy leather. It was the face of someone – but it was so hazy and indistinct; it could be the face of anyone at all.

The girl with the posh voice was still talking. There was an ache in Vanessa's temple, and it was as if her thoughts didn't quite fit in her head, like unfolded clothes, bundled up in an old drawer. She pulled her gaze away from the bag and took a sip of tea, looking across into the station. On the crowded platform the guard was waving his red flag and blowing a whistle. The nearest train gave an answering whistle and puffed steam. Another one was pulling away next to it, and further on, trains were coming in, disgorging passengers. She thought about caterpillars. The trains looked like giant caterpillars, the grimy glass station roof a cocoon. She imagined the trains emerging like butterflies, transformed, flying away into the cold sunshine on vast wings like parachutes. Her eyes scanned the mass of people, picking out individuals to focus on. A stout lady in a cherry-coloured hat was waving good-bye to someone inside the nearest train. The girl in the grey coat was getting on, lugging a cardboard case up the steps after her. Further on, a sailor was leaning out of a window and kissing a passionate goodbye to a blonde woman. Her curls shook and she teetered on high-heeled shoes as the train pulled away, leaving her with outstretched empty arms.

An image pushed into her head of a man, running, with outstretched arms, shouting, and then a sudden blankness. She swallowed down the sick feeling and drained her tea.

'Well, thank you for the tea. I'm not myself today, but I do feel a bit better now,' she said, standing up. 'It was nice to meet you ...'

'Edith. My name is Edith, but everyone calls me Edie.'

The posh girl stood up and held out a hand. Vanessa took it. The hand was small, like a child's, but the handshake surprisingly firm.

'Well, it was nice to meet you, too ...'

'Joan,' Vanessa said. 'My name is Joan.'

'Nice to meet you, Joan.'

Vanessa put her cup back on the trestle table and began to make her way back across the concourse towards the tube entrance. She was shoved and elbowed by the crowd as she limped towards the hole where the steps plunged down into the blackness of the Underground. She heard someone calling: 'Joan, Joan, *Joan!*' She thought the voice must be inside her head, like earlier on. She wondered if it meant she was going to faint again. Then she felt a hand on her shoulder. It will be the police, she thought, distractedly.

'These just fell out of your pocket, dear!'

She turned, and it wasn't the police, it was the posh girl – the girl she now knew was Edie. She put her hand out for the papers.

'Thank you,' she said.

'Oh, look, you're joining up, too! Why didn't you say? We can travel up together. That's a turn up for the books, isn't it, Joan? Or should I call you Private Tucker?'

Edie laughed, and this time Vanessa joined in, laughing long and hard, gasping for breath. If she hadn't laughed, she would have cried, and she wouldn't have been able to stop.

The two young women stood in the middle of the crowded concourse, killing themselves with hilarity, as the mass of passengers swirled round them like an irritable river.

'I say, get a move on, will you? You're causing an obstruction!' said a man with a moustache.

'Yes, sir!' said the posh girl – Edie – giving a mock salute. The man tutted and they both laughed harder still.

When the laughter subsided, Vanessa put the documents back in her pocket, shoving them right down to the bottom, next to the airman's address. Then she turned and hooked her arm through Edie's. And as she turned, she left behind her the ghost of poor Vanessa Tucker from number thirty-two: Vanessa the black sheep, Vanessa the orphan, Vanessa with the bad reputation and the disappointing job. At the moment Joan turned away, Vanessa became an insubstantial shadow, stumbling back towards the tube station and back to the place where her childhood had been crushed under falling masonry.

It was Joan Tucker who took Edie's arm and strode back

towards the platform: good, nice, sensible Joan, who was eighteen and ready to do her bit for King and country. The breeze caught her hair and pulled it back from her brows. It felt as if the wind was blowing away the smog and she could see clearly. The train was just pulling into platform five. It was her train, ready to take her to the ATS training camp. Sunshine slanted through the glass roof.

She was Joan Tucker, she was eighteen and she was joining the ATS.

Chapter 5

Please, God, let me get this right. Edie offered up a silent prayer as the drill sergeant opened his mouth. Behind his angry face, at the edge of the parade ground, the sycamore trees beserked. The wind held little flecks of moisture, like spittle spraying on her face. The drill sergeant roared and they moved to the right in threes and marched and wheeled, and this time it seemed like she got it right, like they were all getting it right, finally, like a clockwork machine that had been cranked up into action. For once, her feet and arms did as they were told.

Thank you, God, she thought, standing like a starched collar with the rest of the squad as the sergeant stalked and bellowed in front of them. The wind bit into her bones, but she daren't shiver, and the cold was making her nose run, but she daren't reach into her pocket for a hanky to wipe away the dewdrop that was beginning to form. She'd got it right, they all had. Things would start to get better from now on.

'You pack of tarts had better remember, you're in the army now, and . . .' Would he never shut up? The horrid little man. But surely he was nearly finished. They had done well this morning, and it was almost lunchtime already. They'd been here nearly a week now. Days of drilling and being shouted at and wearing these horrible scratchy, ill-fitting uniforms and the swearing and the dreadful food, and the injections and the aching tiredness. But it was nearly over, wasn't it? They'd proved they could do drill well enough to go on church parade in the morning, and to get some precious evening passes the following week. The worst had to be over. Maybe she'd even get time to write home. He was still shouting, and the wind was slapping her cheeks like an angry nanny.

'. . . I've seen cripples looking better on a parade square. If you lot think you're going on church parade tomorrow, you can think again. Dismissed.'

'I can't believe we're not good enough!' Edie said, spearing a greyish potato with her fork and wiping it in the dribble of brown gravy. 'I thought we did really well out there.'

'We did the best we've done so far,' said the girl sitting next to her.

'And if that's not good enough, I don't know what is. We were all in step, all the way through, weren't we?'

The other girls nodded, their cheeks bulging with boiled beef, carrots and potatoes. All around was the clink and scrape of cutlery and the muted hum of voices as the recruits chewed their way through lunch. Steam rose and hands nursed tin mugs of tea.

Edie put the potato in her mouth and swallowed quickly. It didn't taste good, but she was famished. All morning they'd been out on the drill square in this north-easterly. What wouldn't she give to be able to sink under her eiderdown right now with her copy of *Gone with the Wind,* a large mug of cocoa and one of Cook's special teacakes. But instead, she was here, in the cold, with the shouting and the swearing and, now, not even the solace of church to look forward to. Really, she could cry. She crammed another soggy potato into her mouth and sniffed.

'Anyone have a clue what's on this afternoon?' said Joan, sitting opposite, mashing up carrots with her fork and mixing them in with her potatoes.

'Nanny used to do that for me,' Edie said. 'Sunshine mash, she called it. She always used to make me eat up all my vege-tables, told me they'd make my hair curl like Shirley Temple. That and toast crusts,' she added, poking a piece of meat that was more gristle than anything.

'I'll finish it, if you don't want it,' said the girl next to her.

'Yes, do,' said Edie, handing over her plate. She was still hungry, but she didn't feel like eating; she felt like running away and hiding. Basic training was worse than the first term of school.

'Ta,' said the girl. 'And the answer is, scrubbing. I overheard Corporal Robbins and the troop staffie talking about it on the way in.'

'Scrubbing what?' said Edie.

'I don't know, but I'm sure they'll think of something,' she said, shovelling the remains of Edie's lunch into her mouth. 'They always do.'

This has got to be the final spirit breaker, thought Edie, as they stepped into the denim overalls. Fumbling with a bit of string round her waist, she reminded herself to be cheerful. Did they make Mary Churchill do this as well? she wondered. They were tasked with scrubbing the inside of an empty hangar. There was an enormous concrete floor. They were given buckets of cold, soapy water and old scrubbing brushes with half the bristles missing and told to get on with it.

Dear Jesus, give me the strength to get on with this without complaint. An internal prayer sometimes helped; she tried to think about what He had done for everyone, and her privations just seemed trivial in comparison. What was her suffering in comparison to His? She told herself to buck up, and swung the slopping water bucket to the furthest corner of the hangar.

To begin with, she tried to make the best of it, despite her crushing disappointment about their not being up to scratch for church parade. The girls' voices echoed round the hangar as they set down to work. Someone began singing 'Pack Up Your Troubles' and for a while they all joined in, until eventually the singing dwindled. Then she chatted to the girl next to her, the one who'd finished off her lunch. She was from Kent and her name was Bea. She had about a million brothers and sisters, and her mother took in washing. She showed Edie how to use the brush properly but, no matter how hard she tried, Edie couldn't scrub as well as her. Soon Edie's arms began to ache, and her hands were red and chafed from the cold water and the brush. The hangar was silent now, but for the sound of wet bristles and the scrape of a tin bucket against the concrete. They scrubbed for what felt like hours, until in the end the pain and the rhythm of brushing and the chill wetness became one. She looked at the girl next to her, weary determination in her eyes as she paused to wipe her hair away from her forehead. She had such a kind, sad face. It reminded her a bit of Mary Churchill's: dimpled and doughy. Edie told herself to buck up: no one likes a whinger, least of all a posh one.

At last, the company sergeant major was called to come and inspect, and they stood to attention along the wall, waiting. He threw open the hangar door and walked right across the wet bit that they had just finished. The bottom of his boots were caked in mud.

'You'd better do this bit again. It's dirty,' he said, walking up and down the hangar, and then he began to stride towards the door. Edie heard the sound of one of the other girls beginning to sob.

'That's simply not on,' Edie said, lurching out of line. There was a collective gasp and she caught Bea's eye. Bea shook her head, a worried look on her face, but Edie took no notice. The company sergeant major spun his bulk round to face her, his face beetroot-red, his greasy moustache twitching. 'Now listen here,' Edie continued. 'It was perfectly clean until you walked all over it in your filthy boots. We've all worked really hard and you've ruined it.'

The barrage that followed was worse than she had endured in all drill or room inspections from the previous week. He thrust forwards and the force of his roaring anger pushed her back into line: *just who did she think she was? If she ever spoke that way again . . . letting down the squad . . . letting herself down, letting the country down . . .* his horrid eyes like dirty marbles, his putrid breath as he shoved his shouting face right into hers. She would scrub the entire floor again. On her own. He turned and stalked out.

'Nice one, Lightwater,' said the corporal, handing her a bucket and brush, after he'd gone. Edie realised she was shaking. She could barely hold the bucket handle. The other girls, dismissed, headed outside. Bea touched Edie on the shoulder as she left.

'Chin up, girl,' she said.

And as Edie watched them all file out into the late afternoon, she let a couple of hot tears fall, disappearing softly onto the dampness of the floor. 'Chin up' was what Pop always said when she was sad. 'Chin up, Half Pint,' when she was in trouble with Mummy or Nanny or had fallen off her pony again. She hadn't even told Pop she was leaving. He'd be worried, and Mummy would be frantic. Maybe they'd come and find her and she could escape this horrible place. Maybe Mummy was right; maybe she was better suited to making bandages and knitting scarves for prisoners of war. She turned, eyes blurring with tears, and knelt back down with the brush and bucket. The company sergeant had walked the full length of the hangar in his boots. From outside, she could hear the rest of the squad being shouted at on the drill square: 'Keep yer 'ands still! Eyes front! Hup, two-three-four, down, two-three-four . . .' What was the point? They'd already been told they weren't good enough for church parade, and there'd be no time off next week. They might as well all give up and go home.

The floor was hard and dug into the thin skin on her knees. The water, cold to start with, was icy now. She was shaking still, partly from the shock of the sergeant's anger, and partly from the cold. Her stomach growled; she should have eaten some more of her lunch before passing it over to Bea. Outside, the shouting went on: left wheels and right wheels and marking time. As Edie scrubbed, she followed the squad in her head, moving the brush in time with the squad's footfalls. She had let them all down. Talking back to the company sergeant major. What was she thinking of?

She wiped the tears away with the back of her hand and began to recite the Lord's Prayer under her breath. The rhythm of the familiar prayer mingled with the muffled sounds of drill and the swish of her scrubbing brush. *Our Father, who art in heaven, hallowed be Thy name . . .*

It was dark by the time someone – the corporal – came back and cast a cursory eye over the spotless floor; the company sergeant major not bothering to turn up himself. Then, Edie trudged through the darkening evening to the empty cookhouse. There was a plate of toast and jam and a mug of tea waiting for her. The toast was burnt and cold, and the tea tepid. After she'd finished, she put the plate and mug on the counter and was just thinking about whether to head to the NAAFI for a cocoa or just give up on the whole shebang and go to bed, when she heard the sound of the cookhouse door opening. She turned to look, and there was the company sergeant major. He took off his hat and hesitated, just a fraction, before beginning to walk towards her. Edie didn't know where to look; there was just the two of them in the empty cookhouse, after blackout. She held her breath. What now? Was the wretched floor still not clean enough? How she wished she'd never entered the recruiting office and signed her name in triplicate on their silly forms. How she wished she'd never even heard of Mary Churchill. How she wished she could just go home.

Edie watched the CSM's approaching bulk. His uniform looked more brown than khaki under the dull lights, and his face was no longer beetroot-coloured. He cleared his throat as he got nearer and she braced up, readying herself for the inevitable bawling out.

'Sir,' she breathed, bracing up again, almost unable to speak.

'I thought I'd find you here,' he said. 'Stand easy.' She could see the line where his hat had cut a groove in the skin on his forehead, and the deep furrow between his bushy brows. 'I've got your parents in my office, Lightwater. They've come to take you home.'

'Sir?'

'Your mum and dad. They've been worried sick.' He

rubbed a hand across his head, smoothing down the thinning hair that was slicked down against his scalp.

Edie didn't know what to say. Mummy and Pop were here! She wondered how on earth they'd found her – but then remembered Pop's old friend George Cowie, who was very high up in the War Office, so maybe …

'Why the hell didn't you let them know you'd joined up? We've had the police here as well,' said the CSM, interrupting her thoughts. He let out a sigh.

'I didn't think they'd let me come,' she said.

'I see.' His thumb flicked the rim of his hat.

'So I can leave, sir?' she said. 'I can just walk out?' Could she? Could she really just leave all this behind? Go home now, back to her room, back to Mummy and Pop and Cook and Marjorie and Mrs Carson and quiet nights in front of the fire.

He cleared his throat again. 'Well, you're a volunteer, not a conscript, so if you really feel you have to leave then I think we could find some form of legitimate discharge – your height perhaps – in your case, at least.'

In her case? Had Pop asked George Cowie to pull some strings? Edie looked at the CSM and he looked back at her. His eyes had lost their glassiness. They just looked red-rimmed and tired, like an old man's.

'The thing is, Private, take a look at me. I've been in the army twenty years. The army made a man of me.' Here we go, thought Edie. He's going to tell me to grow up, and try to bully me into staying. 'And I'll tell you this,' he continued. 'There's nothing I'd like better than to be at home right now.'

She thought she knew what was coming next. Something about how everyone was homesick, but that they were all in it to fight Hitler. About how if they all pulled together then they could beat Germany and stop this terrible war. About her patriotic duty. But the speech never came.

'I've got a son your age,' he said, rubbing a large hand across a ruddy cheek. 'Joined up last year, but since he turned eighteen he's been posted. North Africa. I had a letter from him today. He said it's colder than a witch's tit at night in the desert. Excuse my French.' He paused and sighed and Edie looked at his face. There was a nick on his cheek where he'd cut himself shaving. She wondered if he had a wife at home, waiting, keeping his supper warm in the oven. 'Follow me back to my office and you can tell your parents what you've decided,' he said.

The CSM opened his office door and ushered Edie inside. She noticed the cream-painted wooden walls, covered with large charts. To her left was a desk. And suddenly there was Mummy, grabbing her arm.

'Edith Elizabeth Lightwater. This time you have gone too far, hasn't she, Neville?' her eyes flicked across to Pop, who appeared to be reading something on a poster.

'Your mother was very worried, Half Pint,' he said, frowning slightly and swaying as he turned.

'More than worried. I was frantic. Anything could have happened. We had no idea where you were and you didn't even leave a message. How could you be so thoughtless?'

Then her mother abruptly let go and lifted her hands to her face. Her shoulders were jerking, but no sound came out. Edie heard the soft click of the door and sensed the CSM coming in behind her. Pop enfolded Mummy in a stiff embrace, looking awkwardly over the top of her head at Edie. His hair looked very white under the electric bulb. 'All right, old girl,' he said, giving Mummy a pat. The CSM cleared his throat and sat down behind his desk.

'Good set-up you've got here,' said Pop to the CSM. 'Busy?' He was still patting Mummy's back. Her shoulder blades made sharp triangles under her fur coat.

'Very busy,' said the CSM, picking up a fat fountain pen. 'There's conscription for the girls soon – we'll be even busier then.'

'And their training, is it similar to the men's?' Pop continued, as Mummy sniffed and fished in a pocket for a lace-edged hankie.

'Fairly similar. It's modelled on the men's – no weapons training, obviously.'

'Oh, quite. I was an adjutant last time round and I remember . . .'

Pop and the CSM began talking about the military, and the differences with this war. Mummy disengaged herself and looked angrily about. Edie watched, feeling detached, as if the scene was being played out in a cinema and she was just in the front row.

The CSM's desk had a big sheaf of papers and a green-shaded lamp, which illuminated his large hands. He made some comment about junior officers that made Pop throw his head back and laugh. Mummy glowered, searching in her handbag for her silver cigarette case. Edie rubbed her hand where the skin was chafed and raw from scrubbing. One of the other girls would have some Vaseline somewhere, wouldn't they?

'So how's she been getting on?' said Pop, nodding in Edie's direction.

'Apart from the insubordination?' said the CSM.

Pop laughed again. 'Oh, that's in the blood, I'm afraid, old man. When I was in training . . .' and he was off again with another anecdote, while her mother smoked, greedily, her eyes flicking between Edie and the men.

'I'm sorry to interrupt,' said Mummy, eventually, not looking sorry at all, 'but I really think we ought to get Edith home. It's hours back to Surrey.'

'It's all right, old girl, we're staying at the Cowies' country place tonight. Didn't I mention?'

'No, you didn't.' Her mother's voice was like chipped china. 'Meredith didn't say that she and George . . .'

'George is up at Chequers. Something on, apparently. Meredith's about, though,' Pop said.

'How did you know that Meredith . . .?'

'Bumped into her in town,' said Pop, his face bland and open. He reached up and scratched the side of his nose with a long forefinger.

'I see,' said Mummy, sucking in the last of her cigarette.

I may as well not be here, thought Edie. This isn't really about me at all.

'Come on then, Edith, let's get you out of this place,' said Mummy, stubbing the cigarette out in the large brass ashtray on the CSM's desk. 'Do we need to sign anything?'

The CSM cleared his throat again. 'I've checked with the CO, and if Private Lightwater could just sign here and here, then she'll be free to leave,' he said, pointing with his stubby fingers at a piece of paper he was holding towards her across the desk. Edie took two paces towards the desk, within the circle of light that held the three other people in the room. She thought about her connection with each of them: her father, absentmindedly indulgent; her mother with her suffocating, tight-lipped love; and the CSM, who she'd only spoken to for the first time today. Edie hesitated. If she signed now, she'd get into the back seat of the Bentley with Mummy and Pop and that would be it. No more being shouted at. No more six-o'clock starts. No more pointless scrubbing. No more horrible food. No more being humiliated until she wanted to cry. The CSM put the papers down and took the lid off his fountain pen, holding it out for her.

'Edith, will you please stop dawdling and do as the man says,' said Mummy. She was leaning forwards and frowning.

It was hard to see the look on the CSM's face, because the desk light made a triangular patch of light, illuminating the brass buttons on his jacket and the papers on his desk, but leaving his face in shadow. Edith thought about what he'd said in the cookhouse. He'd been in the army over twenty years. He had a son in North Africa. Wasn't that where Bea said her boyfriend had been sent?

'Edith!' her mother hissed. 'We haven't got all night.'

'I'd rather not sign,' said Edie at last.

'I beg your pardon?'

'I'd rather not sign, Mummy. I think I'd prefer to stay.'

'Oh, don't be ridiculous,' her mother snorted. 'Stop playing games, Edith Elizabeth. Sign the paper and get in the car.'

'No,' said Edie.

'Tell her, Neville.' Edie's mother turned to her father.

'Do as your mother says, Half Pint,' said Pop.

'I think I'd rather stay, actually,' said Edie.

'You can't! We've come all this way to get you, and the petrol . . .' Her father made a shushing sound as her mother continued: 'No, Neville, she needs to know what we've been through this last week. How can she not come home with us after all this? Get her to sign the papers now. She's just being selfish.'

'Selfish enough to want to do her bit for King and country?' the CSM said, clicking the lid back on the fountain pen and shuffling the papers.

'Pardon me?' said Edie's mother, as if she hadn't heard. But she had; they all had. The CSM didn't repeat himself. He put the discharge paperwork in a drawer and placed the pen next to the blotter. Edie's mother fumbled with her handbag. 'Where is my cigarette case? I had it just now. Damn!'

'I think maybe we should be getting off, old girl,' said Pop, placing a hand on her arm.

'I'm sorry for your wasted journey,' said Edie. 'And I'm

sorry I didn't write – there hasn't been any time, it's all been so busy, but I will try, from now on, I promise. I hope you both have a nice time with Mrs Cowie – do send her my love,' she added. Edie walked over to Mummy and Pop. Her mother was angry, she knew that, but when she looked in her eyes to say goodbye, what she saw wasn't anger, it was panic. She kissed her mother's downy cheek, smelled the Dior and the soap.

'I'll be fine, Mummy,' she said. Her mother blinked and looked away. Then Pop bent down and she kissed him, too. His cheek was stubbly and he smelled of Imperial Leather and hair oil. 'I'll write and tell you when we get leave,' she said. 'Jolly good show,' he said, and gave her an extra squeeze. Finally, she turned to the CSM, and braced up. He stood to acknowledge the salute.

'Dismissed, Private,' he said, and she moved to the door.

'Well, goodbye then,' she said, pausing in the doorway.

'Goodbye, Half Pint,' said Pop. Mummy said nothing, but her face crumpled, and Edie couldn't look at her, so she went out and closed the door behind her.

Outside, the wind was blowing stray leaves and the clouds were scudding across the scrawny moon. Where to now? Back to the block, to hurl herself on her hard bed and regret her decision, or into the NAAFI with the rest of the squad?

The NAAFI was packed, so full of recruits it was almost impossible to get through the crush to the counter. At last, she got a cup of hot chocolate and a KitKat. The hot drink spilled on her hand as she turned. She felt a tap on her shoulder. It was Bea, asking her if she was okay. She said she was fine. She gulped down the cocoa, enjoying the sticky hotness as it slid down her throat. At the sound of her voice, some other girls turned round, asked her what made her backchat the CSM like that.

'I don't know. It was silly,' she began. Then, seeing more faces turn to look, she continued: 'Well, he was being a bully. And I don't think bullies should be allowed to get away with it, do you? That's what we're fighting this war for, isn't it? To stop being bullied by Hitler. And anyway, I had a prefect just like the CSM at school – Mabel Price she was called – always giving people a hard time for no reason. Honestly, she was just like him, moustache and all.'

The girls laughed, and she realised she was surrounded by smiling faces. She was right in the centre of a group of friends who cared about her, who liked her, and she wasn't alone. Then she saw Joan, her friend from the railway station, swinging towards her group.

'Have you heard the news?' said Bea, as Edie drained her mug and Joan shoved her way in.

'What news?'

'They've changed their minds. After that last drill session this afternoon, they decided that we were good enough for church parade, and we'll be getting evening passes next week.'

'How thrilling!' said Edie. 'And what a surprise.'

'Oh, I'm not surprised at all,' said Joan, who was now next

to Edie. 'I bet they use the same tactic on all the new recruits. It's just a game, Edie.'

Just a game, Edie thought, breaking into a grin. Of course it was. All the swearing and shouting and drilling and scrubbing. It was a game. Play up and play the game! All she needed to do was learn the rules, and she'd be fine, wouldn't she?

Chapter 6

Joan dipped the rag back into the little tin of polish and rubbed it into the brown leather. It slid and stuck, but she kept rubbing until it gleamed. She could smell the wax, feel the soft hide and see how, over the weeks, it had moulded into shape, fitting her feet perfectly now. Nobody took better care of their army brogues than Gunner Joan Tucker.

The first shoe was almost done. She checked her watch: still time to finish off before lights out. She put the shoe carefully under her bunk and picked up the other one. The girl in the bunk above her, Scottish Nancy, had already gone to bed. Both the little coal stoves were lit, making the air smoky, even though the fumes ought to have been carried up the stovepipes and out into the winter night. Washing lines looped round the hut, draped in wet underwear, like bunting. There was condensation on the windows, which would freeze overnight, sticking the blackout blinds down fast. One girl was bathing her feet in a tin bath of salty water, scrunching up her eyes with the sting of it; another was combing her wet hair in front of one of the stoves, hoping to get it dry before the Last Post. It was dripping all over the wooden floorboards. Someone turned up the wireless in the corner when Vera Lynn came on, warbling away.

Joan began to polish the other shoe, dipping, rubbing, carefully buffing, listening to Vera Lynn singing 'We'll Meet Again'. She pushed the rag back into the brown wax, burrowing it right down. The polish was the colour of dried blood.

There was an ache in her temple, and a faint buzzing in her head. It came on like this, sometimes, suddenly, and she'd feel sick and dizzy and forget where she was.

'Joan,' said a voice.

'Joan, do you have any cold cream? I've run out. Joan?'

She looked up. The voice was calling Joan. Was that her?

'Sorry, I wasn't myself for a moment there. What is it, Bea?'

'Do you have any cold cream? I don't like to ask but the NAAFI is already shut.'

'Yes, I've got a ton of it. I stocked up after payday. Hang on a mo.'

She put down the shoe and scrabbled underneath her bed to find the hinged storage box that contained her civvie clothes and her spare jar of Pond's. She passed it up. Bea took it. She was wearing an old brown dressing gown that looked like a man's. Her hair was scraped back under a grey turban. Bea said she'd bring it back, but Joan told her to keep it, repeatedly that she'd got loads more, which wasn't true – but Joan knew that Bea didn't have any money left for toiletries. She sent all her money home. Bea hesitated, standing above her with the cold cream. Joan pushed herself back up onto her bunk.

'Keep it,' Joan repeated. 'You can just owe me a good turn for it.'

'Thank you,' said Bea. 'I'll remember that.' And she went back to her bunk.

Joan went back to her polishing, her head clear again now. From the bed above, Scottish Nancy said she'd heard that the village shop was due to get some cosmetics in. She'd been on kitchen duty and heard it from the woman who delivered the eggs. Suddenly, the whole room was talking about how to engineer a pass to get to the shop before everything had sold out. Joan said she thought the post orderly had a bike and he might let her borrow it.

'Oh, he most definitely will,' said Edie, from the bunk opposite, placing a bookmark between the pages of her Bible. 'I've seen the way he looks at you, Joanie – sheep's eyes across the cookhouse, my goodness. You can be our secret weapon in the battle for glamour, dear!'

Joan laughed and said she'd see what she could do. Then the corporal came round and said lights out in five and there was the general scurry to be ready in time. Edie put away her diary and knelt down to say her prayers. Joan gave her shoes one last caress and put them away.

The Last Post sounded and Joan slipped under the covers, feeling sorry for the bugler, outside in this weather. It was icy even under the mound of scratchy blankets, and there was a draught at the head of the bed where it was flush with the hut wall. The bugler finished and the lights went out and everyone said their muffled goodnights. She put her head underneath the pillow. Then she lay on her hands and pulled her knees right up. She would warm up eventually and sleep would come, and with luck there would be no dreams tonight. Or at least, not that particular dream.

As she closed her eyes, her mind whirled with the shapes of enemy planes, and angles of elevation and her ears seemed to hum with the sound of imaginary aircraft. It was good, being selected for anti-aircraft training. Her head was crammed full of technical information, her body tired from PT and drill. There was no time to stop and think. At nights she was exhausted.

There was a moment, on the brink of unconsciousness, when she was flying, then falling, and suddenly jerked awake at ground rush, eyes wide, blinking into the blackness, panic making her heart thump. But all around was just the soft sighs of sleeping soldiers in the darkness. She slipped her head back under the covers and let sleep catch hold.

Images came and went. Dark shapes blurred and shoved, and her limbs were leaden: she was wading through fragments of terracotta, and earth, and a clump of pulverised flowers, dirty orange. There was blood, and then flesh, like the slab at the butcher's: wet and exposed. And there was the hand: oval nails and a thin gold ring with sapphires. Plaster dust and ash fell like snow. She reached down to touch the fingertips, and heard the sound of a woman screaming. She looked round to see who it could be, and she was awake, sitting up in bed with the sheets a mangled mess. The sound wasn't a scream, it was a moan, and it was coming from the bunk above.

'Nancy?' she whispered. The moan came again, louder. 'Are you all right?'

'Aye, stomach cramps,' came the eventual reply.

'Need an aspirin?'

'I've had one.' The moan again. The bunk moved and creaked, then there was silence for a while. Then the sound again, and the movement from the top bunk. She could see the metal lattice of bed springs bulging down above her where Nancy's bulk quivered.

'Are you sure you're okay?'

'In-di-gestion,' the reply came out in a panted whisper. Nancy moaned again.

Joan pulled her torch from the bedside locker and pushed off the pile of sheets and blankets. The chill air snapped her into alertness. Even the wooden floorboards felt like ice. She climbed out of bed and clambered up to the top bunk, holding the torch in her mouth. The beds wobbled like a tree house, and the torch beam played briefly over all the sleeping forms in the hut and then rested on Nancy, lying on her side.

'Nancy, I'm worried about you.' Nancy just moaned, pulling her legs up higher. Joan could see a rictus of pain on the pale slice of her face visible in the torchlight. She put the torch down and rubbed Nancy's back, underneath the bedclothes. The torch beam splayed out over the covers, making hills and valleys and caves out of the grey blankets.

'Cold,' said Nancy; she was shivering, but her skin was slick with sweat, her pyjamas sticking to her back, the hair at the nape of her neck hot and damp.

'You've had an aspirin?' said Joan.

'Aye.'

'Do you want me to find a medic?'

'No!'

'Okay, how about I get in, warm you up?'

Nancy groaned and Joan picked up her torch and pulled back the covers. She thought she could just give Nancy a hug, soothe her back to sleep. If she'd had an aspirin, and didn't want a medic, then there didn't seem much else to do.

Joan lifted the heavy blankets but as she did so, her fingertips felt wetness. She angled the torch down. Horrified, she saw the sheets were drenched in blood. Nancy's arms were clenched round her stomach, her striped pyjamas wetly clinging. The moan came again, long and loud, and Nancy's tight form quivered. Joan put the covers back.

'I'm going for help.'

Running through the corridors, knocking and calling in the pitch-black. The duty sergeant wasn't in her room. Dark shapes blurred and shoved, and her limbs were leaden: she couldn't run fast enough. There must be someone, some way to get help. Nobody in the ATS accommodation but sleeping trainees, fat lot of good they'd be. She needed a medic, or someone with a telephone. There would be a telephone in the officers' mess, but that was forbidden. She was only a gunner. And she was a woman. And she was in her night-clothes. And it was the middle of the night.

She pushed open the fire door and ran out into the black-ness. The icy drill square stung her bare feet and she felt as if she'd just plunged into a frozen lake. The officers' mess was a white rectangle in the distance, its front lawns chained like necklaces around an aristocratic neck. The windows were black. The stars were out, the moon a silver scythe above the horizon. She ran along the path and up the steps to the door. There was a brass knocker. She grabbed it and rammed again and again and again, until at last she heard footfalls coming closer.

Joan got extra duties for being out inappropriately dressed and being in an unauthorised area, but the troop staffie told her later that the ambulance driver said she probably saved Nancy's life. Acute appendicitis, that's what they said it was. Joan wondered about all that blood. Had her appendix actu-ally burst? The troop staffie didn't answer.

The next morning the whole training camp could talk of nothing else but Scottish Nancy's appendicitis and Joan's late-night foray into the officers' mess. Edie said she'd have plenty to put in her diary about the previous night's excitement, and Bea said it was good of her to give them all something to write home about. Joan was excused from training for a couple of hours, to clean up and get some rest.

How different it was, in the barrack block, empty of the

voices and bodies that usually filled it up. There were ranks of identical bunks, all except hers – she'd had to file a report to the welfare officer first thing, there'd been no time to sort out her bed blocks – which was a mound of bedclothes and coats. As she looked at it she was reminded of something, another pile of clothes and coats and a torn patchwork quilt, chill blackness and the sound of a yapping dog. She felt sick, suddenly. She shook her head, took a deep breath in. She was just overtired, that was all.

Rain drummed on the roof and from outside there was a thin ribbon of singing away in the distance, as the rest of the squad began their route march: 'She'll be wearing khaki bloomers when she comes . . .' There was the vibrating thrum of a convoy of lorries driving into the fuel depot, and some intermittent shouts from the parade ground, but inside it was silent and empty. Someone had already stripped Nancy's bunk and removed her tin trunk from under the bed. The mattress was gone, leaving just the wire netting of the top bunk. The floor around their bunks had been mopped, leaving a dark patch on the floorboards and a smell of disinfectant.

Joan pulled off her shoes and slipped under the muddled covers, looking up at the metal links where Nancy's mattress had been. She could see the crack in the ceiling; the discoloured paint like the face of the moon. Her bedclothes were in a lumpen pile, with her army greatcoat and civvie coat on top, for extra warmth. She fingered the civvie coat. She'd been wearing it the day she joined up, with Edie, before they were selected for anti-aircraft training.

She remembered hot tea, and a cold station platform. She remembered the rickety old steam train, and Edie chatting, sharing sandwiches and seed cake from her shiny handbag. When she got to the training camp in Devon, she'd showed her ID card and call-up papers. Joan Tucker, it said. She was Joan Tucker and she was just eighteen.

Joan looked up to where the metal cage bisected the cracked ceiling into little leaf shapes, the colour of skin. What about before the station, before the train ride? She closed her eyes in an effort to remember. Vertigo. A sheer drop into blankness: the smell of chrysanthemums and something acrid, burnt, a voice shouting 'get down, get down', and the feeling of falling. And that was all. She opened her eyes again. There was a horrible taste in her mouth and her head throbbed. It was no good. She just felt that sick–dizzy–panic all over again. And she didn't want to lie here on her own, with all those unwanted thoughts, like clothes spilling from a drawer that wouldn't shut. She'd go to the NAAFI for a smoke and a brew, until the others came back. There was always someone to talk to there.

She got up and pulled the coats off the bed, smoothed and folded sheets and blankets, shook out pillows, tightened corners, until her bed looked the same as all the others. She hung up her army greatcoat and shook out the folds of her civvie coat. Something fell out of the pocket, a piece of paper. She picked it up, unfolded it. There was scrunched-up hand-writing, in pencil. An image flashed into her mind: a man's face with round blue eyes, a bloodied cheek.

The Gunner Girl

Flight Sergeant Robin Nelson, said the strange handwriting. And there was an address, an RAF camp in Kent. A small memory floated like a bubble to the surface of her consciousness, the musky smell of sweat and fabric and the feel of stubble against her cheek.

Chapter 7

Robin was so tired he could barely speak, and ended up with soft-boiled eggs instead of hard. The mess felt loud and enclosed, as if he were stuck inside a brass bell that had just been rung, reverberating. Quiet. He needed some quiet. His mind flipped and spun in the hubbub, back to the dark, the cold, the immense buzz of the engines, the tip and swerve and Harper's lot ahead of them, suddenly ablaze, a roiling bonfire spiralling away. He breathed in sharply and forced himself to actively look at what was before him: the varnished table, the steaming enamel mug of tea, the oozing, smashed up egg. He tried not to look any further, not to notice the empty chair opposite, where Harper usually sat.

'Who's a lucky boy, then?' A sudden voice, cockney, and a pile of post tossed next to his tea. A small, flat, brown-paper parcel, a gaudy postcard and a letter. The postcard first, a picture of the Blackpool Tower with a beach empty but for a solitary donkey with a small child on its weary back, the message overleaf depressingly short:

Dear Rob, How are you? I've been terribly busy here. I need to tell you that I've met someone else. He doesn't like me writing to you so I'm afraid this will be the last time you hear from me. We did have some larks, though, didn't we? I'll always remember Margate! Pammie x

The parcel, he could tell, was from his mother. He squished it. Another pair of socks, by the feel of it. And probably a long letter detailing her WVS and his father's Home Guard duties, along with news of the shop and details of how many of his old classmates were now missing in action, or worse. It could wait.

But the letter. Beautiful thick notepaper and handwriting he didn't recognise. The postmark said Reading. He didn't know anyone in Reading. He turned it over. On the reverse was a lipsticked kiss. Well, it wasn't from Pam, that much was certain. He looked at the return address. Gunner Tucker, it said. Gunner Tucker? He picked up his knife, slit open the envelope and pulled out the single sheet of notepaper. Quickly, his eyes scanned down to the signature: Joan.

Joan?

His mind corkscrewed and dived, whirling back to late autumn, when he'd been up visiting RAF Hendon, coming through Finchley because of Uncle Len, and there'd been that sudden blast, almost literally out of the blue, except it was already evening, and there was that poor girl, that very pretty girl: Joan.

Joan Tucker.

Chapter 8

'*You put your whole self in, your whole self out . . .*'

Everyone sang along and the army band tootled and crashed up on the dais, underneath the Union Jack and the picture of the King and Queen. It was just the weekly hop, nothing special: checked cloths on the tables, painted rattan chairs, YMCA cream cakes and the dusty shuffle of army shoes on the polished floor. Edie and Bea were on either side of her, holding her hands.

'*Whoa, the Hokey Cokey! Knees bend, arms stretch, ra-ra-ra!*' They burst out laughing as the Hokey Cokey came to a close, and slipped back to their table to grab a swig of lemonade. Joan saw their Junior Commander, Joyce Montagu, being chatted up by Sergeant Taylor underneath a poster that displayed KEEP IT UNDER YOUR HAT and picture of a tin hat. With his square jaw and her golden ringlets, they could have been a couple in a film. As the band struck up 'In the Mood', he whirled her onto the dance floor, and other couples fell towards each other, grasping, shifting and swaying, like khaki ripples in a rip tide.

Bea was pulled away by one of the portly old sentries, and Edie was whisked off by a young second lieutenant who kept manoeuvring her into the tables at the edges of the room. Corporal Jones, the post orderly, appeared at Joan's side, and she couldn't very well refuse. He had sad, bulging eyes, that stayed turned down even when he smiled – which he didn't, much. They joined the throng. His large hand was tight in the small of her back and her head rested against his breast pocket. He was a good dancer, for someone so tall, and it wasn't unpleasant to let herself be propelled around in time to the music and smell the scent of talc and cloth and a tinge of fresh sweat.

'That lipstick looks nice,' he said.

'Thank you for lending me the bike to get to the village shop.'

'You're welcome. Anytime. I mean it, just ask.'

'Thank you.'

She was enjoying being gently pushed and turned, underneath the electric bulbs and the twinkle from the glitter ball.

'I heard about that Scottish girl. They said what you did saved her life.'

'It was nothing,' she replied. And she suddenly remembered that airman: Robin.

'It was nothing,' he'd said, too. She could picture his face, the lips moving, the wash of stubble, the dark red cut on his cheek and how his blue eyes had screwed up, like he was going to cry. She remembered him saying that, being next to him, seeing blackout curtains tight shut, and the smell of disinfectant. His name was Flight Sergeant Robin Nelson, and he was based at RAF West Malling and she'd found his address in her pocket. So she must have been wearing that coat. But where were they? What were they doing there? She thought about the letter she'd sent him – she'd borrowed some of Edie's Basildon Bond notepaper – a short letter, more a series of questions, really. She shifted and twirled with Corporal Jones, remembering the feel of that airman's uniform against her cheek, trying to think beyond his shoulder and face, but it was just a blur. All she could see was the airman's lips, saying 'nothing' and that sad look in his eyes. She knew he was important; she just wished she knew why. Had he got her letter?

'You gunner girls have all got a forty-eight-hour pass, haven't you? Got anything planned?' Corporal Jones voice broke in on her thoughts.

Joan sucked in a breath. She had almost managed to forget about that. Bea had a christening to go to, and Edie was off to a ball with her friend Marjorie. The rest of the troop were going home to their families, boyfriends, pals or relatives. Everyone had somewhere to go, except her. The leave pass ran right from first parade Saturday through to Monday morning – a whole weekend.

'I'm sure something will turn up,' she said nonchalantly.

'I'm supposed to be on duty, but I could try to swap with someone if – if you'd like to go out? But I expect you already have plans?'

She didn't answer him, knowing that he'd take her hesitation as evasion. Of course, she could go out with him on Saturday, but what about the rest of the weekend? She couldn't go home, because she hadn't a clue where it was, and every time she tried to think, there was just a squirming nausea, and the smell of something burnt and the pounding in her head.

They brushed into Junior Commander Montagu, who was being expertly twirled by Sergeant Taylor. 'Yes, the whole troop's off,' Joan heard her saying, 'and won't the camp feel empty without the ATS?' Sergeant Taylor muttered something into her ear and she laughed, showing little white teeth, like a shark's. 'Yes, well I suppose it would have to be something terribly naughty to forfeit leave,' she tinkled, as they swirled past.

Corporal Jones's button was beginning to dig into her cheek. Joan made a decision. 'Why wait until Saturday?' she said. 'You've got a bike, haven't you? Let's hot-foot it down to the village now.'

The dance ended and she pulled away from him. She could see his face clearly, his sad grey eyes widening at her suggestion. It was his turn not to answer.

'You're not turning me down, are you, Corporal Jones?' she said, smiling.

'No, it's just that . . .'

'Well, come on then, get your coat,' she tugged him off the dance floor just as the bandleader announced another Hokey Cokey and everyone else began to form a huge circle.

* * *

They plummeted through the night on his bike, the air an icy river flowing past them. He steered with one hand and held onto her with the other and the bicycle lamp was a feeble wobbling beam, illuminating occasional trees and surprising corners. At last, they tumbled, laughing, into the village pub. Five old men put down their pints to stare in silence. Joan rearranged her uniform and patted down her hair. Corporal Jones cleared his throat and asked what she'd like to drink. Five old men picked up their pints and the darkened corners began to grumble with conversation again. The barman stopped polishing the brasses and regarded them through wire-rimmed spectacles. Joan found a circular table and sat down. As she waited for Corporal Jones to bring her drink, she caught the eye of one of the old men and smiled at him. He smiled back, blackened spaces where teeth were missing. She took out her new lipstick in its perfect gold case and dotted it along her pout, and Corporal Jones came over with half a cider in a lady's glass. He had a pint.

'You make me feel like a bad lad bunking off school,' he said, sitting down beside her.

'Are you a bad lad?' she said, looking sideways at him and sipping her drink. She noticed a flush on his throat. His Adam's apple bobbed up and down as he drank.

'Not really, not until now,' he said, putting down his pint. His smile mismatched with his lugubrious eyes.

'Nobody will even notice we're gone,' she said, patting his thigh. The cloth was still chill and damp from the bike ride.

'Want a smoke?' She got her Player's out of her gas-mask case. He shook his head.

'Suit yourself. Bother, forgot my matches.'

She walked over to where the old men sat, a circle of brown toads, and asked if they had a light. Two of them looked in the other direction, but the one with the missing teeth had a lighter and sparked up for her. She offered her cigarettes round, and even the two who'd ignored her took one. She glanced over at Corporal Jones and gave him a wink. He had almost finished his pint already.

'From the camp?' said the toothless man. She said that she was and that she was very proud to be doing her bit.

'Don't hold for women in the army,' said another man, drawing deeply on his cigarette. He said it wasn't right that women should be out there, that their place was at home. She agreed with him absolutely, she said, but of course all the men soldiers were very busy in North Africa and places, and in any case it was the Home Guard who did the actual firing. The man grunted.

She smiled at him. 'Lets say you lose a sock at home, who is the best person to find it?'

'The missus.'

'Well, socks or enemy planes, it's the same difference. We're spotters. All we do is find them. Like your wife finding your socks, that's all,' she was still smiling, making eye contact with each old man in turn.

'She's right, you know, Alf,' said one.

'Well, I think it's a fine thing, what you girls are doing,' said another.

'I'd like to buy you a drink,' said the toothless one.

'Oh, it's all right. I'm with a pal,' she said, gesturing to Corporal Jones.

'Well, I'd like to buy him a drink and all,' said toothless, beginning to heave himself out of his seat.

'How kind of you,' said Joan, reaching across the table to tip her ash into the ashtray.

The journey back took considerably longer than the journey there. It had started snowing while they were in the pub, a ripped bolster in a pillow fight, downy flakes everywhere and the road slick with ice. Seven times they fell, and seven times they retrieved themselves, giggling. She let him kiss her, but his lips were too cold, and his tongue too large and in any case they started to shiver when they stood still. The snow swirled, and they half rode, half stumbled back to camp. By the time they reached the gates they were soaked through and beginning to sober up. It was impossible to sneak past the sentry with the bike. Of course they were caught, and of course they were told to report to their respective commanding officers first thing in the morning.

'I hardly need tell you how shocked and mortified I was to learn of your behaviour last night.' Junior Commander Montagu stood rigid behind the desk with a look of righteous indignation on her heart-shaped face. Joan looked straight ahead, staring out of the window behind her to where the drill square had been cleared of snow and the sergeant major was already pacing, twirling his baton. Commander Montagu carried on, talking about the disappointment that such a promising recruit – look at the initiative she'd shown with that incident with the Scottish girl – could let herself down so badly: late back to barracks, drunk, with a man. Commander Montagu shook her pretty blonde curls and continued: it was different for the men, she said, they didn't have their reputations to think about, but the ATS, particularly those in a mixed battery, had to be beyond reproach.

Joan thought about Commander Montagu and Sergeant Taylor and the way they'd danced at the hop and wondered whether Commander Montagu was herself 'beyond reproach', but she said nothing, watching the rest of her troop filing out onto the drill square, ready for the final parade before their weekend leave.

'Gunner Tucker, you leave me with no option but to revoke your forty-eight-hour leave pass and confine you to barracks for the weekend,' said Commander Montagu, a little V-shaped frown between her arched brows.

Joan breathed out, feeling her face relax. She didn't have to take leave. She wasn't going anywhere.

'Well, have you anything to say for yourself?' said Commander Montagu.

'I'm very sorry, ma'am. It won't happen again,' said Joan.

'I should certainly hope not. Dismissed.'

Joan closed the hut door behind her and turned away from the drill square. Confined to barracks for the weekend: never had punishment been such blessed relief.

Her shoes slid on the frozen path as she walked away from the HQ block and the drill square and out towards the NAAFI. She could have a brew, a smoke and spend the whole day reading magazines if she jolly well wanted to. Inside the NAAFI hut, the stove was lit, the shelves were full of cigarettes and chocolate, and Ethel was leaning over the counter, staring at the back page of a newspaper, fag in one hand, pencil in the other.

'Tag, you're it,' she said, not looking up.

'Sorry?' Joan had paused near the stove, stretching her hands out to absorb the warmth.

Ethel looked up, her salt-and-pepper hair scraped away from her doughy jowls. 'Tag, you're it, eight letters, last letter "y",' she said, frowning. 'I shouldn't bother with the cryptic ones really.'

'Identity,' said Joan, rubbing her hands and walking over to the counter.

'What's that, duckie?'

'Identity. Identity tag, see? And your identity, "you're it",' she looked down at the paper. 'There, links up with Ypres in your seven across.'

'So it does. No flies on you, duckie,' said Ethel, scribbling in the letters. 'What can I get you?'

'Tea and a copy of *Woman*, please.'

She would have a cup of tea and read a bit of her magazine and then save the rest to read in the long bath she planned to have – as long as she wanted because there'd be nobody banging on the door and claiming it was their turn – and then the whole weekend stretched ahead: forty-eight hours alone, the others all gone. But that didn't matter, did it? Because she was here, and she was Joan Tucker, and she was safe.

Ethel handed over the tea and the magazine. Joan thanked and paid her. The front cover of the magazine had a painting of a blonde pouty woman in an ATS uniform looking side-long at a dark-haired soldier. They looked remarkably like Commander M and Sergeant T at the hop, Joan thought. 'Love is a Mantrap', a complete story by Frances Shields, it said underneath. She'd read that later, in the tub, she decided, sitting down as close to the stove as she could. Joan took a gulp of tea. It was strong and sweet, just how she liked it.

The radio was on, but turned down low, with scratchy news announcements that nobody wanted to listen to. Ethel had gone back to glaring at the crossword, switching between sucking on her fag and chewing the end of her pencil. The door banged open, breathing in a blast of biting cold air. It was Sergeant Taylor.

'Naughty, naughty, very naughty,' he said, grinning and wagging his finger when he noticed her. She shrugged and he swung round to her table. 'Listen, Gunner, you know what they say: "If you can't be good, be careful." Next time, why don't you take a man who knows his way in after curfew?' Then he gave her a wink, before swinging back towards the counter.

'Twenty Woodbines and a Mars bar please, Ethel my darling, and may I say how gorgeous you're looking this morning.'

'Wha'? Oh, right you are, Jack.' Ethel cranked her puffy form into action.

Joan started to leaf through the magazine: how to make your lipstick last longer; ten new ways to cook carrots; the problem pages – they were always worth a look: Worried Blue Eyes, said the headline, but before she could start to read, Sergeant Taylor was at the table.

'You don't mind, Gunner?' he said, as his chair scraped on the floor. It was a rhetorical question. He was a sergeant: she could hardly refuse. The coke stove was behind her, and her neck had started to sweat, but her feet were still icy wet from where the snow had seeped through her shoes on the journey back the previous night. Sergeant Taylor opened his Woodbines and offered the pack to her. She took one. She didn't really like Woodbines: they tasted of old people – but it was easier than refusing. He took out his shiny gold-coloured lighter, and cupped his hands round hers, leaning in to light her cigarette.

'The thing with Jonesey, he's only a nipper,' he said, leaning back on two chair legs and inhaling deeply. 'He doesn't really know his way round yet, know what I mean?'

He was talking about Corporal Jones. She didn't really want to talk about Corporal Jones, or last night. She felt guilty about embroiling him in it, but she'd needed some way of avoiding going on leave, and it seemed like the only way, at the time. Go out, get caught, get confined to barracks: job done. She hadn't really considered the collateral damage to Corporal Jones. She sipped her tea and smoked the nasty

Woodbine, looking at Sergeant Taylor through a lacing of smoke. He held his cigarette in his left hand. He had a gold band on his ring finger.

'So what are you going to do, now you're confined to barracks for the weekend? All alone, without your little pals?' said Sergeant Taylor, blowing a smoke ring.

'Oh, I don't know, I'll be fine,' said Joan, wishing he'd just bugger off and leave her alone. But then, as he was there, maybe he could help? She did feel terrible about embroiling Corporal Jones.

'It was all my idea, you know,' she said.

'I don't doubt it,' said Sergeant Taylor, leaning back and regarding her through an inhalation. His legs were wide, khaki stretched tight across his groin.

'He didn't want to. I mean, I made him, really. I'm only telling you because it doesn't seem fair, him taking the rap when it was my fault. Is there anything you could do, as his sergeant?'

'There's a lot I could do, but why would I?' said Sergeant Taylor, blowing smoke. 'What's in it for me?' His knee was touching hers, and he leant forward. 'I could get him off scot-free, if it was worth my while,' he said in a low voice, looking her in the eye.

Joan pulled away. Did he really mean what she thought he meant? Was this how it worked? She took a long drag, buying time, exhaling slowly. She could hear footfalls outside, little scurrying steps like someone in a hurry. Sergeant Taylor stubbed out his cigarette into the rusty metal ashtray in the centre of the table and tore open his Mars bar with his teeth. He looked at Joan as he did so. She knew that look, the one where the mouth was smiling but the eyebrows were arched upwards, like a cat ready to pounce. The door banged open and the air blasted in.

'Jack – Sergeant Taylor!' It was Junior Commander Montagu, curls sagging from the damp, cheeks flushed. She didn't even acknowledge Joan, who wondered whether or not she should stand and salute or something – officers never came in the NAAFI. 'It's the – er – protocols. I need you in my office at once,' said Commander Montagu. Was it Joan's imagination, or was Commander Montagu's voice wavering, just slightly?

'Yes ma'am,' said Sergeant Taylor, crumpling his Mars-bar wrapper into the ashtray and stuffing the chocolate into his mouth. Commander Montagu flounced out and Sergeant Taylor sauntered after her.

'You want to watch 'im,' said Ethel, when the door banged shut. 'It's 'is wife I feel sorry for.' She sighed and rolled her eyes. 'I'm still not getting anywhere with this blooming cross-word. You want another brew?'

'Please,' said Joan, stubbing out the Woodbine and taking her mug up to the counter. As she reached it, the door banged open again. It was Corporal Jones. They saw each other at the same moment. She noticed him blush.

'Do you want a brew?' Joan said, smiling at him. Why make this more awkward than it needed to be? He nodded and she asked Ethel for another. He joined her at the counter. His eyes looked even larger and glassier than ever, this morning. She could see the little red veins snaking over the white. 'And a couple of aspirin please, Ethel,' he added. He rubbed his head.

'Look, I'm really sorry about . . .' she began.

'Don't be, I . . .'

'What did you get?' she said.

'Confined to barracks. You?'

'Well, I'm here, aren't I?'

'Bad luck – your weekend leave pass, and all.' He looked genuinely sorry. How could she tell him that she got exactly what she wanted?

'Oh, and a Mars bar as well, please, Ethel,' he said.

'I'll get these,' she said quickly, before he could pay. It was the least she could do. 'Is the bike all right?'

'One of the tyres has a flat and a spoke is broken. But it's nothing I can't fix.'

'I'm sorry.'

'It wasn't your fault.'

They both looked at Ethel, instead of at each other, as she came back with the teas and the aspirin and the chocolate. Joan thought she ought to ask him to join her at the table, but she didn't say anything. The enamel mugs were too hot to put to their lips, so they stood at the counter with their fingers curled round. She looked at his big hands, fingernails splayed, like shovels. Ethel was glaring at the paper again. There was a pause as they breathed in the steam for the tea, each waiting for the other to say something.

Finally, he said, 'I really like you,' at exactly the same time as she blurted, 'I don't think it's a good idea if we see each other again.' Then there was an awkward moment when they both stopped, and stared back down at their teas, each knowing what the other was going to say, and not wanting them to say it. Then, he sighed and picked up his mug.

'You okay if I take this with me, Ethel?' he said. 'I've got things to do.'

'You'd better bring that mug back or I'll be having your guts for garters,' said Ethel, chewing the end of her pencil and gazing into the middle distance.

He picked up his mug. 'Well, I suppose I'd better be off.'

'Yes. And I'm sorry about last night.'

'No, don't be. I – I had a good time,' he said, and then he began to walk towards the door. He stopped, halfway, and turned, reaching into the back pocket of his trousers, some of the tea spilling as he did so.

'I almost forgot. This came for you.' He held out a blue envelope. She went over to take it from him. Something must have changed in her expression as she got closer and saw the handwriting.

'From your pen pal?' he said. She nodded, taking the letter from him and turning it over in her hands. *RAF West Malling*, said the return address, in scrunched-up hedgehog writing. 'He's a lucky man,' said Corporal Jones, turning away.

'Thank you,' she said, gratitude and guilt thickening her words. She realised she'd never even asked his first name. 'Thank you, Jonesey.' The door banged shut behind him.

'He's a nice lad, but a bit daft,' said Ethel. 'Now, how about this one: location of cardio-vascular muscle, four letters. I can't make head nor tail of it.'

'Home,' said Joan, carefully folding up the blue envelope and putting it in her breast pocket. 'Home is where the heart is.'

Chapter 9

The scene was laid out like some kind of Nativity tableau: Ma and Pa as Mary and Joseph, and the vicar like the angel Gabriel blessing the Immaculate Conception that was Baby. Bea's brothers and sisters were a gaggle of wise men and shepherds, shuffling about in the front pew and not knowing quite how to behave. And what was she in all this, Bea thought: the donkey?

John kicked David. May told them to stop it. Rita was scratching her head just above her ear and Bea thought distractedly about nits. The twins were tickling each other at the end of the pew. Vi patted some imaginary crumbs off the front of her new coat – new to her; it was Bea's old coat, but Bea no longer needed it, not now she had her huge army greatcoat. Up at the front, Baby squirmed, and the vicar's voice droned on like a wasp in a jam jar. The air was icy.

The church had escaped a direct hit in the Blitz, but a bomb had landed in the churchyard a few months previously, shattering the stained glass on one side of the building. The spaces where there should have been scenes in God's glorious Technicolor were all boarded up. The church was split in half, one side still dancing coloured motes of sunshine and the other a deep shadowy blankness. And in the middle was the font, with Baby.

Beside her, Rita was pinching John. Bea slapped her leg and hissed at her to give it a rest. Then Baby began to wail, as the vicar drenched icy water all down her little red face. Unperturbed, the vicar continued to intone. Bea thought that he must be used to carrying on through the sound of other people's suffering. Baby was sobbing as if her little heart would break. Bea felt an answering tug, and ache in her breasts, and had to sit on her hands to stop herself from reaching out for her little girl.

'Sounds like she needs changing,' said May importantly. Bea told her to shut up. She was thinking about the first time she heard Baby cry . . .

It had been the 21 June, the longest day of the year. The worst of the Blitz was over and for a whole month they'd hardly had to go down to the shelter at all. That night it hadn't got dark until way past nine, and she'd sat out on the front step with Ma, putting off the moment when she had to squeeze back into the little room with Violet, May and Rita.

She and Ma sat together having a cuppa and watching the street turn gradually from amber to grey as all traces of colour drained from the bricks of the terraced houses. Ma got up, wheezing slightly, and said they should go inside. Bea said she wasn't tired. It was true. The baby she was carrying seemed to be controlling everything, keeping her wakeful at night, but filling her with crushing tiredness in the middle of the day.

Her ma shrugged and went inside. Bea stayed on the step a bit longer. The stone was still warm from the heat of the summer day. Far away to the west the sky held the last traces of pinky blue.

Bea pushed her hair out of her eyes. The stars were beginning to come out. She didn't know their names, but she recognised some of the patterns they made. There was one really bright one, low, just to the side of the tall black silhouette of the factory chimney. She wondered if Jock could see the stars from where he was. Maybe he was on duty, or night patrol somewhere. Maybe he was leant up against a sandbag with his rifle, looking at exactly the same star. Why hadn't he written? She couldn't believe he didn't care, not after all the things he'd said. She pulled her eyes away from the star and began to scrabble up; it was an effort to stand with the lump of child inside her.

She'd done what Ma had said and kept it hidden. It'd been easy at first; she hadn't shown for months. Ma's best friend, Mrs Morley, the postmistress, was the only one who knew. She was the one who'd given Bea the dresses, shapeless floral things, years old, and the greying brassiere, with straps that cut into her flesh. Bea wondered what they'd do when the baby came? They couldn't hide it for ever, could they?

She could hear Ma pulling down the blackout blinds inside. As she straightened up there was a tiny clench, far, far down inside her belly. She went inside and closed the front door behind her.

'Ma?'

'Yes, girl.'

'What does it feel like when the baby starts to come?'

Ma looked at her and then immediately went to get water for the big copper, the one she used for boiling linens. Then she began getting kindling and coals together to light the oven.

'Ma?'

'Sit down and have a cigarette, girl.'

'It's your last one.'

'It will help you relax.'

There was no pain at first, just a deep-down strange squeezing, that came and went like a breath. Bea sat down and had just lit the last fag when the sirens started.

'Oh, sweet Mary mother of Jesus!' Ma spat out and disappeared upstairs to wake the others. They all came tumbling down: May and Vi in their curlers, the younger ones half-dressed, owl-eyed and grubby. Ma told Vi to take them all down the shelter. May said what about her and Bea, but Ma said they'd be down as soon as. 'And John, don't you be going near Mr Lavery!' she shouted after them as they traipsed out into the night.

In the silence after the siren, Bea quietly finished her smoke. She got up to put the butt with the others in the tin on the windowsill – there were enough ends to roll a fresh one with the leftover tobacco in the morning. Then she began to rinse the cracked saucer under the tap, wiping away the clogged bits of grainy ash with her fingertip.

'How's you, girl?' said Ma, coming to stand next to her at the sink and taking the saucer from her hands.

'Fine,' Bea shrugged, as another clench tugged inside. She felt like that time it snowed and all the children from the street took trays and sleds up to the top of Bluebell Hill. She remembered reaching the top, breathless, and looking down the long white slope as it fell away beneath her. The old tea tray wobbled and slipped underneath her torso as she began to lie down. Some of the big boys were already off, hurtling downwards, black scribbles getting smaller and smaller, their shouts just tinny wails in the distance. At any moment, someone would give her a shove and she'd be off down the plummeting whiteness and everything would become an uncontrollable blur of rushing cold. But she didn't tell Ma that.

Her ma told her to sit down. So she scraped the chair out from under the kitchen table and sat. She watched her ma: the faded cotton of her weekday dress eddied around her as she flitted about the kitchen, putting the pots away, wiping the windowsill. Bea's stomach clenched again. She thought of rubber bands, pulling tight.

The clock tower chimed ten times and the pain came again. This time she breathed out and shut her eyes. When she opened her eyes the next time, Ma was turning up the lamps.

The clench came again and the next time her eyes opened Ma was taking out the half loaf from the bread crock.

Bea watched Ma take out the toasting fork and go to the grate. Perhaps it was a trick of the light, but Ma looked small as she knelt by the embers, a knotted figure in the flickering light. Until now, Ma had always felt so big: she filled their little house so that no corner of it was free from her authority – or her temper. But seeing her away at the stove, hunched up like that, she looked quite tiny. And Bea felt almost alone. The kettle began to whistle.

'I'll do the tea then,' said Bea, beginning to push herself up.

'You stay sitting,' said Ma. 'Let it whistle a while.' And then she sang a little ditty that had been going round: 'Whistle while you work, Hitler is a twerp; he is barmy, like his army, whistle while you work!'

The pain came again, deeper in. Bea shut her eyes and she was back at the top of Bluebell Hill, staring down the bleak white drop, scared to push off, scared of the treacherous rocks and tree stumps hidden underneath the sleek whiteness.

The whistling stopped and there was a metallic clatter as her ma took the kettle off the hob and Bea opened her eyes to see Ma coming towards her with the toast on a plate. She was smiling with just one side of her mouth. Even her happiness was rationed, partially withheld. From outside came the faraway hum of planes.

Ma put the toast down in front of her with a knife and the dripping bowl. 'Take plenty. It might be a long night,' she said.

Bea dug the knife deep into the white lard. Right at the

bottom was the brown meat jelly, leftovers from the Christmas roast and the payday fry-ups. She could hear Ma behind her, at the sink, sluicing out the warm water from the pot. She could hear the clink of metal against china as Ma added tea leaves and the whoosh as the pot was filled with hot water. Bea's stomach clenched. Harder this time. She shut her eyes and was back at the top of Bluebell Hill, looking downwards, teetering on the edge.

When she opened her eyes again the knuckles on her right hand were white, clutching the knife in the dripping bowl. She pulled out the rich, meaty jelly and spread it thick on the hot toast. When she bit in, some of the meat juice dripped down her chin and she caught it with her finger and scooped it back into her mouth. The clench came again and she stopped chewing, resisting the urge to choke out the mouthful as the pain twisted deeper. When the feeling subsided, she breathed out quickly through her nose and swallowed, feeling the plug of food move down her throat. The aeroplane sounds were getting louder.

The pain came again, swifter this time: gnawing, biting. When she opened her eyes Ma was sat opposite, looking at her. 'It'll get worse before it gets better,' she said. 'Now let's have a look at your leaves.'

Ma poured a little spurt of tea into the chipped china cup with the rose on the front. She swilled it round, concentrating. Bea looked at her. The lamplight threw her features into relief: white and grey shadows – hooded eyes, sharp nose, mouth a tight line of back-stitch, hair like brick dust above her sparse features. Before Ma had Charlie and married Pa, she was a 'canary girl', working down the munitions factory. She said it was the stuff they put in the shells that turned her hair orangey-coloured, and it never went back to normal afterwards. That's what she said.

The aeroplane sounds were closer, louder, like giant blue-bottles. Bea heard a soft thud-thud, like a giant's footsteps. Ma's face went blurry as the pain came again. Closer, deeper in. Bea almost gasped. Then the pain lessened and Ma came back into focus, still concentrating on the teacup.

'Well, my girl, it looks like you're going on a journey ...' Ma began, her voice rising above the engines' drone. There was an almighty thump and the cups rocked in their saucers.

'Jesus, that was close,' said Bea.

'Don't blaspheme, girl,' said Ma, looking down at the cup. 'Oh, that's ruined the lie of them; they're all wrong now – blasted Hitler.'

Ma reached for the tea strainer and poured out the tea properly into the cups. The planes were still loud overhead, but the sound was swerving. They were starting to move away, Bea could tell. She wondered where that last bomb had hit. It was somewhere nearby.

'D'you think we should take a look, Ma? See if we could help?'

'And what? Start digging people out of the rubble? You want to have your baby in a bombsite? Don't be soft, girl. Drink your tea.'

Ma put in two sugars and loads of milk, but when Bea

protested, she said that Bea would need her strength. In any case, there would be more in the morning – extra rations for nursing mothers. Bea hadn't thought of that. The sound of the planes was beginning to fade. Bea prayed there wouldn't be more.

The pain came again. She squeezed her eyes shut and felt her stomach heave as she looked down the slope to the bottom of the snow-covered hill. Someone had come off. There were faraway yells and a splash of red across the whiteness. Black figures clustering like flies around strawberry jam. When she opened her eyes again Ma was gone and Bea was left alone in the half-dark. She wiped the beads of sweat off her upper lip and took a gulp of tea.

The sky was quiet now, but out in the street she could hear the sounds of vehicles in the distance: fire engines, ambulances, someone screaming. Above the cacophony the clock tower chimed. Bea counted: eleven chimes. She took another gulp of tea, draining the cup in one. The corners of the kitchen were dark. The pain came again. And again. Ma came back.

She tried counting in between the pains, but she ran out of numbers. So then she judged it by watching Ma: each time she closed and opened her eyes with the pain Ma had moved. There was a pain as she started to sweep the floor and then another as she was emptying the dustpan, pain as she heaved the water-filled copper over the flames. Another pain came and Ma had disappeared, only to re-appear from the stairwell after the next one, carrying a torn yellow bed sheet and a pair of scissors. She'd rolled up her sleeves and her bony arms looked pale and stringy in the sickly light.

'Here, rip these up and I'll rinse the pots,' said Ma, handing her the torn yellow bed sheet and scissors.

Bea stood up and nicked the hem of the fabric with the scissors, just enough, and then pulled the two sides, tearing them apart with a rush. Suddenly, it felt as if someone had thumped her, hard, right up underneath her ribcage. She doubled over, gasping for breath.

'Knocked the stuffing out of me, that did!' she said, when she could breathe again.

'It does,' said Ma, taking the sheet from her and finishing it off. 'You want to lie down, girl?'

She shook her head. Instead, she stood up. She knew how it would go. She had seven younger brothers and sisters, for heaven's sakes. She'd helped out with the twins. The midwife came that time, and Mrs Lavery: blood every-where and Ma laid up for a week afterwards, and not enough money for Pa to go to the pub to wet the baby's head until after the next payday.

Then it came again: another gut-punch and then another. The copper was boiling and Ma threw in the torn squares of sheeting and took it off the heat. She pushed the kitchen table to one side and put the big brown blanket on the floor, with a pair of old towels on top.

Bea could only watch, she was up and pacing round and round the tiny kitchen, like a caged bear, pausing only for the next thump of pain to pass. Somehow, if she kept moving in between, it wasn't so bad, but she had to stop and shut her eyes when the pain came, winding her, wringing her out. She heard the fire engine and ambulance drive away. The air was hot. Ma kept moving in and out of her peripheral vision: busy, busy. Even between the punches there was now an underlying twisting pull inside and the pain never left.

She thought about Ma's last one. Late last summer. They'd even called the midwife, but it was no good. A little girl, choked on the cord. Not meant for this world, the midwife said, and Bea remembered the sound Ma had made, and the look on the midwife's face. Ma said there'd be another one, after Pa's leave. But there wasn't.

The clock tower chimed, just once this time. Ma kept moving. She kept slipping in and out of focus with each contraction. Bea saw her bleach the kitchen tabletop, clean the insides of the windows with a rag dipped in vinegar, swimming like a fish in the shadows.

Bea slid in between the frozen white hilltop and the roasting dark kitchen, steam from the copper and Ma skittering round the edges of her vision. The pains got worse, longer, deeper, twisting inwards and making her groan. The next time she noticed the clock tower it chimed four times. Underneath the sound of the bells she heard a faint far away thrum as more planes crossed the white cliffs and spewed up bomb alley towards them.

'Ma, I'm scared.'

'Good strong girl like you? Nothing to it,' said Ma, loudly above the increasing volume of the next wave of bombers.

But Bea saw her eyes flick briefly skywards, and her mouth was like a bad hemline: puckered, too-tight stitches.

'Ma, I need the lavvy.'

'No you don't, girl.'

Another agonising shot of pain broke through and a strange sound like a dying animal came from her lips and the pain was all around and inside and like a huge wall she couldn't climb. When it subsided a little, she was left with a shaky ache and said again that she needed the lavvy.

The noise of the planes was loud now. Through the side of the blackout blind, Bea could see little orange flashes and feel the corresponding judder as each shell hit. The cupboards shook. There was a smash as something fell off the shelf in the larder. Ma kneeled down in front of her and swiftly removed her shoes and got her to step out of her skirt and knickers and told her to lie on the towels. The planes were roaring all around and it felt like the whole house was shaking as Ma gently put her fingers up there and felt.

'It's time to push. ' Ma shouted over the bomber's roar. The hurt was bigger and angrier, enveloping her with a rush of pure agony. On it went, the swelling pain all around, a pushing twisting hurt engulfing her and this time it wouldn't stop and Ma said push. She helped Bea onto her heels and she crouched and pushed and screamed and the pain kept hurling itself at her and all around her and it wouldn't stop; it wouldn't stop.

'Push, for Christ's sake!'

'I can't, Ma!' As she said it, her knees began to shake and

give way. The thrum of the planes mingled with the buzz inside her head, right inside, as her body began to jerk.

'You bloody well have to, girl. You are not giving up, is that clear?'

Then Ma came round behind her and hooked her arms underneath Bea's. Bea felt them tight and hard, holding her up. She smelled Ma's smell: sweat and soapsuds. She could feel Ma's taut body against her spine.

'Don't give up on me now, girl. I am not going to lose you and I am not going to lose my baby, you hear? So bloody well push.'

And she pushed and the pain was so high that she couldn't claw her way out and it kept getting worse but she kept on pushing into the pain because her ma was shouting at her not to stop. And the planes were roaring and she was inside the vibrations and the wind was rushing through her as she was off on the tray down Bluebell Hill with the terrifying skyballing downward, pelting onwards faster and faster and louder and louder and the spinning empty jarring pain ripping through as she flew into nothingness.

'Good girl,' yelled Ma, and Bea opened her eyes, and there, between her legs was the sideways head of a little baby, glistening mauve, smooth as a boiled egg with the shell off. Ma loosened her grip from underneath Bea's arms and pushed her down slowly into a sitting position, knees bent upwards, on the towels. Then she went round and sat in front of Bea. The sound of the bombers began to lessen a little.

'Come on now, nearly there,' said Ma, taking hold of the

baby's head and shoulders as Bea pushed again and the little body slithered out purple-blue and slimy in the light from the lamp. Now the planes were a droning hum.

'We've got a little girl,' said Ma, holding the baby up by her ankles and slapping it hard on the behind. The baby began to cry. Her quivering little mouth made an enraged 'O' of surprise as she mewled like a lost cat.

'One last push and you're done, girl.'

Bea grunted, bearing down, and the afterbirth slithered out. Ma singed the kitchen shears with a candle until they were black and cut the cord. Then she wiped the still-crying baby with the boiled, ripped sheets until all the blood had gone, and she wrapped the baby in an old shawl and passed her over to Bea. Bea opened the buttons on her blouse and pulled the little body towards her. The head nodded and nuzzled, searching blindly for her nipple. And then the crying stopped as Bea felt the tiny mouth begin to suckle.

Outside were the sounds of the raid's aftermath: the emergency vehicles; the crackle of fire; the hiss of water; the shouts of the rescue crews. The air smelled like burnt toast. Ma lifted the side of the blackout blind, letting in a flicker of light.

'The Laverys caught it. Pray to God they were in the shelter tonight.'

Bea's legs were splayed and wet. The cupboard doorknobs were pressing hard into her back. Ma began to get busy with water and rags, wiping and wringing and scrubbing. She looked down at the little bald head on her breast and felt an exquisite joy course through her veins. Suddenly, everything seemed like it would be all right. She made a silent promise to the baby: you will be loved, and your father will come home, and we'll all be just fine, a proper family, the three of us together.

Her ma was saying something to her, something about an ill wind that blows nobody any good. Something about everyone being so caught up in their own problems that they wouldn't poke their noses in. But Bea wasn't listening. She was looking down at Baby and feeling like she could stay here for ever, on the hard floor, with the bloody rip between her thighs and this little girl tucked at her breast, so tiny, so perfect: evidence of Jock; evidence of his love.

The all-clear sounded, keening and endless. Ma washed her hands and put the kettle on. The clock tower chimed five times. The door banged open and Vi rushed in, wide-eyed and screeching. 'You're still bloody here, thank Christ. I left the others down there in case you was … I didn't want them to see – we thought you was hit, but you're all right, you're …' She stopped, taking in the scene. 'Bea!' She looked down and Bea looked up: black-haired Vi, with the tear in the lace edge of her nightie and her curlers falling out.

'It's a girl. And as far as you or anyone else is concerned, that baby is your little sister, got it?' said Ma, looking up from her scrubbing. She was taking charge, taking over, daring anyone to disagree. Bea opened her mouth to speak, but all that came out was a sigh. Vi nodded.

'I said, got it?'

'Yes, Ma.'

'You tell the others; if anyone asks, Bea has got flu and you lot have got a new little sister. Are we clear?'

'Clear, Ma,' said Vi, coming over and kneeling down next to Bea. She stroked a strand of hair away from Bea's forehead and leant in so close that Bea could see her eyes begin to moisten as she looked down at the baby.

'She's beautiful, Bea,' said Vi. 'What are you going to call her?'

Bea thought about that night now, as she watched the sunshine splash across the scene in front of her: Ma, Pa, Baby and the vicar.

Ma was in her only decent dress – it was black and old-fashioned and hung loose on her skinny form. Pa was in his uniform; his three white sergeant's stripes stood out importantly against the khaki. They both looked serious, shushing Baby and nodding at what the vicar was saying. Baby had on an outfit that Bea made from an old net curtain. Her monkey face with its tufts of black hair glared out angrily from the wispy white folds of cloth as if accusing them all of something.

When it was finished, they all filed out of the church. Ma and Pa thanked the vicar and put some money in the collection box and then they were all outside in the white-grey winter air. Baby started to cry again.

'Sounds like she's cold,' said May.

'Course she is, the little mite,' said Ma, cuddling her close. They walked quickly up the street, the younger ones griping and trailing at the back until Pa shouted at them to get a bloody move on or he'd give them what-for. The sunshine was a thin and hopeless smear, too high up to make any difference.

Bea had been up early with Vi, making spam sandwiches for them all, and she'd used the last of her wages to buy iced buns, enough for everyone – not even the twins would have to share. Vi fell into step next to her.

'You all right, Bea?' she said.

'Course,' said Bea. 'Why wouldn't I be?'

It was cold in the house, but too early to light the fire, so Pa told the little ones to run up and downstairs a few times to get warm and May went to get Baby's blanket from her cot. It was the one made from the crocheted squares that she'd started on the train: yellow and black and brown, and two soft fuzzy blue ones with the wool that the posh girl had given her – not the best colours for a little girl, but still, beggars can't be choosers. Baby was nodding off, now, as Ma wrapped her up in the blanket.

'Can I hold her?' said Bea.

'I was about to put her down,' said Ma.

A look passed between them and Ma handed over the bundle. Bea looked down at the child's sleeping face and searched for traces of her father there. Did she have Jock's nose? It was hard to tell.

Pa went out to buy lemonade and, when he came back, they had the spam sandwiches and the iced buns and Ma made tea. Pa had a pack of Player's, so they all had a smoke, and then a bit later, Vi lit the fire. Bea's arm was aching from holding Baby all that time, but she ignored the pain.

When Baby woke up Ma took her upstairs to change her, and then brought her back down and mashed up bread and warm milk in a bowl to feed to her. Pa made another brew and they had another smoke and he talked to her for a while about basic training and army life. And it occurred to Bea that maybe what he'd done was a kind of gypsy-switch in his head, and that to him she was no longer his daughter, she was just another soldier, and that was what made it possible for him to keep up the pretence that Baby wasn't hers at all.

Later, Bea played cat's cradle with Rita, even though Rita was too old to be playing games like that and should really have been helping Ma with the dishes. Outside, the light was just beginning to fade and the clock tower in the market square clanged four times. Bea stood up. 'I'd better be off,' she said.

'Can't you stay one more night?' said Rita. 'It's much warmer in the bed with four.'

'I have to be back by first parade,' said Bea.

Rita pouted. Ma put Baby in the playpen and came over to them. Bea looked over to the corner of the room. Baby was playing peek-a-boo with the twins, gurgling and clapping her hands with excitement.

'Valerie is a nice name, Ma,' she said at last.

'I thought you'd like it,' said her ma. 'She looks just like a Val, don't she?'

Bea walked over to the playpen and Baby stretched up her arms as she saw her approach. 'Bye-bye, Valerie,' said Bea, giving a wave. Baby shook a little paw back at her. Bea leant over to give her a kiss. The girl's mouth was dribbling and the kiss a wet blot, but Bea didn't care. 'Bye now, little Val,' she said, waving again, but as she did so, one of the twins popped up again – boo! – and Baby turned away, laughing, distracted.

'I'll walk you to the station,' said Pa stiffly as she pulled on her coat. 'Here, I've got it.' He picked up her case for her. She hugged her brothers and sisters and last of all Ma, but she didn't go back to the playpen where Baby was chewing on an old cotton reel.

Just as she was leaving, Vi rushed up. 'We're all very proud of you, Bea,' she said, giving her one last squeeze. Bea shrugged. There didn't seem so much to be proud of. Army life was easier than home: she had her own bed in the barrack block for starters. And there was always enough to eat; she could eat her fill at every meal without feeling guilty.

Outside, the chill bit hard, even through the thickness of the heavy woollen coat. The streets were empty, save for the odd bike scudding past. It would be blackout soon.

'You don't have to come, Pa.'

'I want to.'

'I can manage on my own, you know.'

'I know.'

They walked along in silence, just the sound of their foot-falls and the occasional rush of a passing bus. The sky was clear and the moon rising, a crescent wrapped in a cotton-wool haze. The frost would set in later.

The platform was deserted except for a young lad with a crate of chickens. Periodically, a feathered head appeared between the wooden slats, squawking sadly. Bea looked at Pa. He had his greatcoat on, too. They looked like a cruet set in their matching outfits. Pa had his beret on, but you could see his dark hair was greying at the sides. His moustache was greying, too. His face looked as if someone had been moulding it from clay, but tired before they finished it off properly; it was creased and pitted, the eyes sunken into their sockets. His breath made clouds in front of his face. There was a high-pitched whistle as the train rounded the corner and then it roared into the station, shattering the quiet with clanking, jarring, hissing, and shuddering to a halt.

Abruptly, Pa stuck out a hand and Bea realised she was supposed to take it and as she did so he stepped in, pulling her closer and patting her hard on the back. He cleared his throat, and sniffed, and thumped harder. Something passed between them then, but she wasn't sure what it was. Maybe it was just a mutual acceptance.

She got on the train and he passed up her case to her. There was standing room only; it was packed with sailors. She stood, between the carriage door and the man with the chickens, and looked down at her pa on the platform: diminished and monochrome in the winter evening.

She thought about her new friends at the training centre in Arborfield, the bustle of barrack life, the warmth, and the food. She thought about the cold little terrace she'd just left behind. And she thought about Baby, gurgling and plump in her playpen. Why had Jock never written?

'Go well,' she saw Pa mouth, as she watched through the glass. He lifted a hand in half-wave, half-salute as the train jerked her away.

Chapter 10

Dry mouth. Hunger. The hunger kept him going, sometimes, when tiredness struck on the return journey – the thought of breakfast. Once, early on, long ago now, his parents had sent a parcel, and it was six of the tiniest pork pies, nestling inside an egg box and a note from his mother: *Dad got these for you. Take them with you, for when you get peckish.* Peckish – like he was on one of their charabanc trips to Torquay. Peckish: he was more than peckish now. He could never manage supper before a sortie.

The light was rearing up behind them as they headed west towards the wedge of darkness. The engine noise reverberated inside his helmet. His fingers were stiff with cold. His head ached. He needed a piss. And he could just about die for one of those pork pies right now.

Just about die.

The sea was beneath them now, grey blankness. Here was where they caught Harper, near enough. You thought you were almost safe once you hit the channel, homeward bound, but they could be sneaky buggers – you couldn't let your guard down. Was Harper thinking of breakfast when they got him? Or was he thinking of Dorothy, at home, waiting and hoping for daybreak?

Missing, presumed dead, that's what they told his parents. Why didn't they say killed in action? There was no body, no absolute confirmation; he might have ditched, swum to shore, how could one be certain, they said. But Rob knew what he'd seen. And he knew the feeling, the clench-dread as the flames fell away – and the guilty prayer: thank you God for sparing me, this time. That feeling came over him every time they crossed the channel home: the mixture of dread and guilt. He'd pissed himself that night, when Harper went down.

Rob blinked, wiped some condensation off the panel with the tip of his leather glove. Skipper barked an order and he responded automatically, checked and re-checked and gave his response. He could have done this bit in his sleep if he'd wanted to: the ennui of the final descent.

Harper: schoolfriend, best pal, dead and gone. But Rob was still here, night after bloody night. He had a nickname in the mess: Bad Penny – he always turned up.

The dawn was crashing down over them like a wave as they crested the white cliffs and England was patch-worked below them. Home, he thought. Home is where the heart is. And he remembered Joan. And he wondered if she'd got his last letter yet.

Chapter 11

'What's that?' – a voice in the darkness, and a violent rattling noise.

Edie opened her eyes, but there was nothing but inchoate shadows and the juddering of the hut walls, and the noise, a terrible fast ratcheting sound. Then she realised what it was: a stick was being run around the corrugated iron of the Nissen hut. Edie sat up, remembering what it meant. 'Invasion alarm – someone put a light on!' she yelled.

'I've tried, they've cut the electric,' came a hoarse shout from across the room. The horrible sound abruptly stopped, and she heard footsteps moving away outside. Then it started again, muffled now, on A–section's hut, across the path from theirs. Edie still couldn't see anything, but a mass of darkened shapes.

'What in Christ's name are we supposed to do?' – the first voice again.

'Battle dress, and then out to the transport,' said Edie,

pushing back the blankets and getting out of bed. All around her she could sense the room lumbering from slumber, but it was quiet except for the sound of quick breathing and the swish of fabric as they struggled into their uniform. Edie pulled off her pyjamas. The night air was sharp against her sleep-warmed skin. Bloomers, brassiere, shirt, trousers, gaiters, boots – it was easy enough to find the right uniform because constant room inspections meant that she knew to within, a quarter of an inch where each item was kept, but her cold fingers fumbled with catches and laces. More haste, less speed, Edith Elizabeth, she told herself. Her heart felt as if it was trying to hurl itself up her throat. Could this really be an invasion?

The rattling noises had stopped completely now, but in the distance she heard the sound of engines spluttering into life: the transport was ready. 'Come on, Gunners, look lively!' – a shout from outside. Edie fiddled with the string on her gas cape, and grabbed her gas mask. Her helmet went on last, chinstrap garrotting.

'Come on, girl,' she recognised Bea's voice, felt a hand tugging hers. At the last minute, she remembered, pulling the little Bible off the top of her locker as she passed, and shoving it into her pocket. At the hut door they paired up blindly, and the corporal ordered them to march at the double all the way to the lorries that were waiting by the camp gates.

Outside, the half-moon was high and bright, the air a sudden burst of sour-cold. They broke into an immediate double along the path, boots crunching on the icy cinders. Their breath rose in steamy clouds, shrouding the sprinkled stars.

As they jogged past the next hut, A-section fell in wordlessly behind them. The path joined the main drag through camp, leading on up a gentle slope towards the exit. The cold air stung her throat but her limbs were warm with exertion, sweat beginning to form at her hairline and in her armpits. Bea was next to her, panting in time to their footfalls. Edie found herself thinking about other soldiers, in different uniforms – jackboots and swastikas – running up beaches, towards white cliffs, their voices barking, harsh and alien, towards pretty seaside towns.

They ran past the parade square and hit the hill. The hill was usually the point where they got shouted at, told to dig deep, push on, and stop fannying about. But this time nobody said a word. Nobody needed to. They kept up the pace, ignoring the breathlessness, the awkward banging of gasmasks, the way their helmets started to slide down as the sweat formed on their foreheads. On towards the waiting lorry, a chuntering black oblong with the headlights turned off, waiting to take them away – but to take them where?

They bundled into the back of the truck, shoved roughly from behind by the corporal. Edie found herself squashed in with the girls from A-section. Slumped up against each other in the darkness, they waited. Her breathing began to return to normal. The smell of sweat mingled with diesel fumes.

There were voices in the driver's cab. Abruptly, the engine was cut. But nobody came to tell them to get out. Still they waited, colder now, without the engine. Her chinstrap was digging right in, and she realised she needed the loo. There were footsteps around the truck, and muttered voices – she couldn't make out what they were saying.

Then she heard Joan from across the lumped-up group. 'This invasion alarm, it is just a drill, isn't it? I mean, it can't be the real thing?'

Half the night they spent out in the truck, until dawn broke and they were ordered to double-back to camp, just in time for the bugler to sound Reveille. Speculation was rife over the soggy toast at breakfast. 'It had to be a drill,' said Joan, swigging her tea and leaning back in her chair.

'But why risk a drill the night before we're posted?' said Bea, chewing rapidly. 'You'd think they'd do it during the course proper, not right at the last moment. I think it was a real alarm, it just turned out false, what d'you reckon?'

Edie pushed her plate away and shook her head. 'I don't know, dear. And I doubt they'll ever tell us, either way.' It had been a calm, clear night, though. And if she were in charge of troop movements, it would be exactly the kind of night she'd pick to send her soldiers into battle, thought Edie, picking up her breakfast things and preparing to get up.

Nobody expected the news that came after first parade. Word was that they'd have most of the day free. The training was complete and their unit was due to be posted in to the anti-aircraft emplacement at Hyde Park that night. The new batch of recruit trainees was due in the following day. But the sergeant major ordered them to march to the armoury.

Edie's fingertips had already turned white by the time they reached the firing range, numb from carrying the rifle all the way there. It was the size of a lacrosse stick, but heavier, the wood slippery-smooth and cold. She didn't like the feel of it, or the idea of it. They'd had all their training on the anti-aircraft guns: spotting planes, adjusting angles, allowing for wind speed and direction. But they'd never actually fired a weapon. Because they weren't allowed: actual firing – of aircraft or enemy – that was a man's job; that was the law.

The grass was frosted on top, but Edie's boots still sank into the tacky mud underneath. The training sergeant hoisted the red range flag up the flagpole; it dipped and swayed listlessly in the chill air. Three magpies fanned out from the bare tree-tops of the woods beyond the range, punctuating the pale grey sky.

'You've proved you know how the big guns work. The Enfield should be a piece of cake,' said the training sergeant, showing them how to load a rifle and make it safe. But they were formed up as a section, and Edie was in the back row. She couldn't see properly. She heard words: *magazine, bolt, safety catch, trigger, recoil.* She tried to focus, but stuck behind the two tallest girls in their section, all she could really see was the edges of their greatcoats, and a slice showing portions of rifle, and the training sergeant's hands, flashing in and out of view. Then he asked a volunteer to demonstrate, and she saw Bea move to the front. She heard more phrases: *Load the magazine – take aim – make safe*; but she still couldn't see what was going on.

'Proper job, Gunner,' the sergeant's voice had a West Country burr. 'Fall back in. Any questions from the rest of you?'

'Yes, sergeant,' said Edie. 'Could you please tell us why we're doing rifle practice?' Her voice sounded high and wavering in the thin air. 'No one said we'd be handling small arms,' she continued, remembering the conversation her father had had in the CSM's office in Devon, about how there'd be no weapons training for the women.

'Any sensible questions?' said the corporal. Someone snorted. 'Thought not. Right, let's get on with it, shall we?'

They had to lie down in threes, on the mud, using sodden sandbags to get the angle of the rifle right. Her helmet slipped down over her eyes. She was shivering – a combination of the cold earth and nerves. Bea was on one side and Joan on the other. The weapon was unwieldy, awkward in her shaking grasp. Bea helped when the sergeant wasn't looking, clicking the magazine into position, whispering hurriedly about the safety catch.

Edie could target. She knew about that, at least, lining up the centre of the distant circle with the protrusion on the end of the barrel and the 'V' in her sights. Her targeting was fine, but she couldn't stop shaking, and there was no feeling left in her fingers. The chill from the frosted ground seeped through her uniform and into her bones. The training sergeant walked along behind them, kicking their legs out into the correct angle.

'Imagine it's his face in the centre of that ruddy target,' hissed Joan, on her left, just before he started to shout.

Ready – aim – fire!

Edie's finger curled round the icy trigger, and she felt the hurl of the recoil, like being thumped, hard, in the ball of the shoulder. She let out a gasp with the shock of it. A flock of sparrows lifted like dust motes at the sound. Behind her, someone laughed. Too much saliva in her mouth, a strange smell, shouting – she swallowed, fumbled with the weapon, felt her boots being kicked back into position on the muddy ground: time to go again.

They had six shots. Afterwards, the training sergeant checked the targets. Bea and Joan had both done well: six hits each. But Edie had missed every single one of them.

When they formed up to march back to the armoury with their weapons, she was called back. 'A word, Gunner Lightwater,' said the training sergeant, and she was surprised that he knew her name. Edie watched the others march back towards the armoury, boots clomping as they hit the tarmac road back into camp. It had started to drizzle. Her rifle slithered in her damp grasp.

'I'm sorry, sergeant,' she said, before he'd even started. She knew she'd get a rollicking for her performance on the range today. Even Gunner Carter had managed four hits. Edie felt she'd let the whole section down.

He didn't reply, watching the others disappear up the road, not even seeming to have heard her. 'Give us a hand with this, will you, Gunner?' he said at last, motioning to the range flag, hanging down the pole like a bloodied bandage. 'Gets a bit stuck in the wet.'

Edie put her rifle down on top of a sandbag and together they walked to the flagpole. She lifted her arms to untie the rope, wincing – the rifle's recoil must have bruised her shoulder – and watching as the sergeant's deft fingers unravelled the soggy cords.

'You're a piss-poor shot,' he said, as the flag finally descended. 'I would have said you needed your eyes testing, except they told me you came top of the course in the spotting. So if you can tell your Junkers from your Messerschmitts at half a mile away, Christ knows why you can't tell your arse from your elbow on the firing range. If it was down to me, I wouldn't even have you as a gunner.'

'I'm sorry,' she said again, but he interrupted.

'Luckily for you, it's not down to me. And, like I said, you're one of the best spotters we've had coming through.'

'Thank you—'she began, but he continued.

'I'm not here to blow smoke up your arse, Gunner Lightwater,' he said, squeezing drips of moisture from the sodden flag. 'I've been told to pass on a message from the CO. As the best spotter on this intake, he'd like you to stay on, help train up the next lot.'

The other gunner girls were all out of sight now. Edie imagined them joking as they tossed their rifles back to the boss-eyed armourer, jostling into the cookhouse for a cuppa, laughing about something or other. Joan would be pulling her fags out of her gasmask case; Bea would be asking the cook what was for dinner.

The sergeant was folding the flag into a neat rectangle. 'As you know, you lot are posted to London. But you can stay on here as an instructor, if that's what you want?' He paused, before continuing, 'It would mean immediate promotion to Lance Bombardier. Keep your nose clean and you'd be looking to rise up quick – we need more female instructors, what with conscription and all – you could be looking at Junior Commander in a year or so.'

Edie thought about Mary Churchill. She was a Junior Commander, wasn't she? She imagined taking tea in the officers' mess with Mary Churchill. She imagined what Mummy would tell Mrs Carson.

The training sergeant was still talking. Edie watched his mouth as he spoke: his moustache was dark brown, smooth like a feather, and one front tooth was chipped. 'Course, it's your decision. But I wouldn't think too hard if I were you. Promotion, regular hours and leave, more pay – it's the life of Riley here. And I tell you what, it's a different kettle of fish on the emplacements. I know where I'd rather be.' His eyes were quick and beady, flicking over her face, waiting for her response. She was still shivering from the cold, her face was wet with drizzle, and the pain in her shoulder was getting worse. 'Tell you what, I'll take your rifle back, and you can swing by the adjutant's office before scoff. Let him know what you decide.'

'Thank you, sergeant,' said Edie, thoughts like a spilled sandbag, spewed messily everywhere – the chance for promotion, but she'd have to say goodbye to the girls, and if she did, would she ever see them again? – 'I'll certainly give it some consideration.'

In the warmth of the cookhouse, she collected the usual rissole, boiled potatoes and carrots from the tubby kitchen orderly behind the counter. Steam rose from the vat of gravy as she dolloped it on top. Joan waved from the table by the window – they'd saved her a seat, even though they were all already onto the spotted dick and custard. 'Gunner Carter says she saw you going into the adjutant's office,' said Joan, as Edie slipped into her seat. 'Were you really in hot water?'

'Not at all,' said Edie. 'He just asked me to take a message to the CO, that's all.' She didn't want to talk about it, not now. 'Could you pass the salt, please?'

After lunch they went back to their hut. Edie sat on her bunk, watching, as all around her the rest of the section were folding carefully ironed uniforms and stashing them into kit bags. I'll miss this, she thought, looking round. The transport was booked for midnight – troop movements always took place at night – and tomorrow it would all be different.

Bea was rolling up a mess of wool and needles into a port-able pile. 'What's the matter, girl?' she said, looking up. 'You're not packing your kit – anyone would think you're not coming with us.'

Edie stood up, plucked her Bible from the top of her locker and tossed it into the bottom of her kit back. She smiled. 'Of course I'm coming with you. What else would I be doing?'

* * *

Edie knew they must be getting close when she could smell smoke in the air. They couldn't see much, through the space above the tailgate, but there was a kind of faint orange glow. Just a small raid, they'd said, only the East End, again. It was all over by the time their truck rumbled in from the training camp in the limpid pre-dawn. The sirens had stopped; the bombers all sped back across the channel. But there was still that sickly glow, and the faint smell of burning – not like the sweet woody smell of the autumn bonfires from home: different, acrid.

She'd tried to sleep on the way, head leant against Joan's shoulder, army greatcoat pulled over her like a blanket. But the truck kicked and jerked through potholes, and they'd stopped for an hour when they heard the sirens in the distance. Everyone got out to watch, leaning against the side of the lorry and looking out over rolling fields towards their capital city, black in the distance. They heard the bombers roar in from the east, and saw odd spots of luminescence, like bright pebbles skimming on an inky lake. There were bursts of upward-shooting flame: the anti-aircraft guns – their anti-aircraft guns – and the sky was diamond dust overhead. They stood, transfixed by the ugly beauty of it all – even Gunner Carter was silent, for a change. Back in the truck Edie couldn't sleep, couldn't stop thinking about the people there, in the houses where those white-orange lights had exploded so prettily.

They fell into each other as the truck swerved and came to a halt. Nobody spoke. There were footfalls outside, and the tailgate fell open. Past the moving shadows of soldiers picking up their kit and preparing to move, she could see the rectangle of space showing Hyde Park Barracks: a checkpoint and a handful of huts, and – a stark black silhouette against the now-lightening sky – the huge Bofors gun, pointing upwards, ready.

Someone elbowed her in the ribs, and a shout came from outside. 'Come on then, let's be 'aving you. Welcome home, Gunners!'

Chapter 12

'Tell wailing Willie to shut up – we're on our way,' said Edie, as the siren keened, and they tumbled out towards the guns. 'It'll only be a false alarm anyway.'

'I don't know, it feels different tonight, don't you think?' said Bea, breaking into a run.

Joan fastened the last button on her greatcoat and trailed along. She didn't feel the urgency. It was like Edie said; it would be yet another night of 'hurry-up-and-wait' in the freezing cold. All that training, and the Blitz over and done with. Hitler was busy in North Africa these days; nothing happened in London. Her gas mask thumped awkwardly against her chest.

'Get a move on, Tucker,' said Sheila Carter, shoving her so hard from behind that she nearly fell down the concrete steps into the emplacement.

'Leave it out,' she said.

'Well, bloody hurry up, then, will you?'

Joan tutted. She'd never got on with Gunner Carter. As she climbed up onto the cold metal seat on the predictor the siren stilled. The Home Guard men were heaving out the huge cylindrical shells in readiness. Sergeant Farr screeched a command, her hot breath forming little puffy clouds in the chill air. Joan didn't know why she bothered to shout out orders; they all knew what to do. They'd been doing it for weeks now – they could set up the equipment and take aim in their sleep if they had to. In any case, like Edie said, it would probably be another false alarm, she thought, zero-ing out the Sperry and wiping the glass with her glove. She looked up. The moon was waxing, bulbous, bouncing along the rooftops of Buckingham Palace in a frosty shroud. Sergeant Farr's torch glinted off the edges of things as she stalked about, checking and barking instructions. Barrage balloons swam like fat silver fish: bloated. The searchlights, miles away, south of river, played like sunbeams in a pool. The sky was silent, waiting.

'Are you all right, dear?' said Edie, beside her on the predictor.

'Fine,' Joan replied. She heard someone nearby give a loud snort. 'And you can shut your trap, Sheila Carter,' she added.

'Quiet,' squawked Sergeant Farr.

Edie patted Joan's knee, but Joan ignored her. The stars were out, far away beyond the roofs and the balloons and the moon. *Second star to the right and straight on until morning.* Where did she know that from?

A splash of memories in the dark pool: a floral-patterned

pinny, the smell of chopped onions on warm hands against her cheek, a bowl of chrysanthemums on a windowsill. No. She pushed her head against the predictor and thrust the memories away. As her head dropped forward there was a clunk – her helmet hit the equipment. She let the tin hat slide right back until she could feel the icy metal against her brow and smell the hard smell. It was so cold it made her temples hurt, but the freezing ache kept her mind in the present.

One of the Home Guard men started whistling 'Leaning on the Lamp-Post'. Sergeant Farr didn't tell him to be quiet. She never said anything to the men; they got away with murder. Another of the men sparked up a ciggie. Bea, standing ready with her binoculars, began to tap her foot in time to the man's whistling. Sheila Carter, on the other side of the predictor, began to suck her teeth. The smell of smoke drifted past.

'Give it a rest, will you?' said Joan. Bea stopped tapping, but the whistling carried on, and Sheila Carter continued to suck her teeth. Sergeant Farr paced past. Joan sighed.

'What is it, Joan?' whispered Edie. 'You've been like this all day.'

'Like what?' said Joan. But she knew full well like what. She'd had another letter from Rob this morning.

Dear Joan

As ever, it's wonderful to hear from you. How are you getting on in Hyde Park?

Flew again last night. Didn't see much on the way out, a little flak was all. Got to target just as the flares were going down. The markers were late, so we had to bomb visually. We saw a few fighters taking off and were chased by one for about ten minutes on the way back, but we managed to avoid him by corkscrewing. We had to alter our course to get out of six searchlights, but didn't see much else.

We were just coming into land when the skipper said the nose wheel was still detracted, so I had to go out and undo the catch, and after a lot of struggling managed to throw it out. It nearly took me with it, but the slipstream blew me back in again.

I was thinking of you a lot, and wondering if I should ever see you again, but strange to say, I didn't feel a bit scared.

Take care of yourself, Gunner Joan Tucker, and know that you are always right at the forefront of my mind.

Your Rob.

'Your Rob' was how he'd signed it. He'd missed out the 's'. Not 'Yours, Rob' but 'Your Rob'. Maybe he just misspelt it? But what if he hadn't? There was all that stuff about his last sortie and wondering if he'd see her again. Your Rob – was he really hers?

She could still barely remember him. And when she tried, she saw his blue eyes, heard his voice shouting 'get down, get down', smelled crushed flowers, burnt air, and a nauseating blackness rose up inside. His letters unsettled her, but she always wrote back, the link between them like a sharp little thread of red cotton, a kite string on a windy day, bound too tight round her finger, always pulling, nagging.

Her gloved hands clenched and unclenched on the wooden handles, ready to turn and angle the barrel on the predictor.

She'd have to stop writing to him. Yes, that was the answer; not get involved. Next chance she had, she'd go out to the Palais and find herself a chap who didn't know anything about her. She could stop the panic she felt every time she remembered Rob's face, and realised that that was all she could remember, that beyond Rob was just an expanse of darkness, and a buzzing in her skull. She could get rid of those feelings if she just got rid of him, stopped writing those stupid letters: a clean slate.

'Joan, if something's bothering you, you can talk to me, you know,' said Edie.

'I'm fine,' Joan replied.

'Everyone, hush a moment,' said Bea, scanning the searchlit horizon with her binoculars. The man stopped whistling and Gunner Smith stopped making sucking noises and Sergeant Farr stopped pacing. They all listened, but there was nothing to hear, just a faint rustle of twigs in the bare trees by the huts and the growl of a night bus passing Marble Arch.

Joan's head was still pushed against the chill of the predictor. She thought about what Rob had said in his letter: six searchlights and a fighter on their tail. Were there girls like them in Germany right now? A Nazi version of the ATS? Helgas and Brunhildes, or whatever they were called over there, shouting commands in German into the chilly night, trying to snatch her Rob out of the sky. Her Rob? Was he hers? No, he wasn't, because she'd decided not to write back, hadn't she? Tonight would be an end to it.

* * *

She felt it first, rather than heard it, a vibration in the metal that was still pressed against her temple. The vibration became a distant hum, getting louder as she listened. She pulled her head away from the predictor. The others had heard it too. Everyone started to huddle closer to their equipment, frowning, readying.

Stand by!

Standing by!

The planes were droning louder now, giant hornets gathering speed towards them. There was the distant whee-crash as the first bomb fell, but it was too far away. The phosphorescent cage of searchlights spun and splayed but there was nothing there, not yet. The buzzing was intense now, more crashes, fiery footfalls, closer and louder. Ah, there was one – the shape of a bomber like a minnow in a pool.

Plane, bearing three-one-zero!

Angle one-eight.

Angle one-eight, bearing three-one-zero!

She pedalled the handles and the barrel manoeuvred into position. A sound in her head, bomber engines thudding, bluebottles buzzing inside her skull.

On target!

On target!

A minnow caught in the net of lights. Sergeant Farr lifted her hand into the air. There was the heave and clunk as the shells were heaved into the gun. A voice tinny and far away.

Ready!

Fire!

The angry shout and recoil of the enormous gun, muffled as if through cotton wool, and everything blanched, momentarily white. Fairy dust flickered in the sky and then with a sudden roar something fireballed earthwards, crashing into flames, south of Chelsea. Livid splash of blood against the sky, smoke gushing upwards like steam. The air smelled metallic, dark, burnt. A taste of bile in her mouth; she swallowed it down. The buzzing roar as more waves of bombers came in. The night roared on, the yells of soldiers and crackle of shells exploding into the night, and the gaping mouth glow as bombs crashed and houses burnt. And the world turned relentless pirouettes and screamed at them.

By daybreak, and the all clear, the spinning slowed and the colours returned, the dawn sky a smear of red on beige. Joan's shoulders ached from pedalling the handles, and her voice was hoarse from shouting. Her stomach churned.

The cookhouse bought a trolley out at first light. The soldiers poured with weary haste towards it. They had sweet tea and jam sandwiches in grimy fingers, leaning up against the sandbags, saggy-eyed and jubilant. The Junior Commander came out, said she'd had a call, the hit was confirmed, the pilot and all the crew dead. There was a cheer at the news, but Joan didn't join in.

In the rush to eat, crow about the night's success and get cleaned up, she slipped away, clutching her enamel mug of tea, warming her fingers through the gloves. The ground felt undulating, unsure. She looked at the glassy morning sky, acid and empty. She thought about Rob. When she'd finished her tea, and her fingers had defrosted, she slid into the hut and sat down on her bed. She had some sheets of paper left in the writing set she'd bought. It was still in her locker.

Dear Rob, she began. It was only once she started writing that she realised how much her hands were trembling.

Chapter 13

Steam escaped from the urn and the air was thick with the clatter and crash of the breakfast dishes and the smell of burnt toast and frying spam. Cooks hollered above the drone of early morning chatter. '*We're out of toast!*' Bea manoeuvred herself into her usual chair in the corner, next to Joan and opposite Edie, her head thick with noise, bleary-eyed and enervated as the rest of the night crew. That had not been a small raid. At the far end of the table Sheila Carter was saying loudly that if Edie had been a bit quicker shouting her bearings then they might have had a shot at the other plane, too. Bea heard Joan shouting at her to shut up. Bea's thoughts were shoving and jostling in her over-tired mind. The raid reminded her of the night Baby was born, and she was thinking about Jock. Was Ma right? Was she stupid to expect to ever hear from him again?

'Post!' yelled Corporal Whitehead, banging open the cook-house door and tossing piles of envelopes out over the tables.

Edie reached up to catch a squashy parcel with her left hand. Her ma often sent presents: little bars of scented soap in wrapping paper; lace-edged hankies; stockings and silk scarves – Edie was generous and shared her gifts with Bea and Joan, who never got parcels themselves. Bea wasn't expecting anything much. Ma didn't write. Vi sent news of Baby Val sometimes, but Vi was busy with her new job in the pub. Joan usually got something from her Rob, but there was nothing for her today. Joan was still exchanging insults with Sheila Carter. Edie was pulling off the knotted string. Bea reached for the margarine and picked up her knife.

'One for you, and the last one for . . . you!' The corporal threw over the last letter, catching Bea's eye. Bea watched it fly. It was a forces airmail letter, and it was headed straight for her. She stopped breathing, dropped her knife, as she watched it flutter like a leaf, almost landing on top of her toast. She caught it in time. Jock? She ripped it open.

My Darling,

Strange to think that you must be in the ATS already. How different our lives are already . . .

Bea stopped. It didn't look like Jock's writing. His looped, sloped left. This was all tight and jittery, like the person writing it was being continually nudged. She read on, but there was no mention of Baby, or any of the letters she'd written.

145

I can finally write to you now my fingers have thawed out. We've been up on the top deck all morning with axes, clearing the ice off the guns so that she doesn't get top-heavy and capsize . . .

The letter continued. Bea felt her shoulders slump. It wasn't Jock. Jock was in North Africa. This was someone else's letter. She scanned to the bottom of the page.

Your ever-loving fiancé, Fred xxx

Inside felt like water swilling down a drain. Stupid. Stupid of her to think it might be Jock. Someone else had a fiancé up in the Arctic called Fred. That was all. She turned the letter over to look at the address. It had originally been sent to the basic training camp in Honiton, then redirected to the technical training base in Arborfield, and had finally found its way here to Hyde Park Battery, trailing some soldier's passage through the system. Who was it? The cramped writing was so hard to read . . .

Joan Tucker, it said. But Joan had Rob. Who was Fred? It was none of her business. Ask me no questions and I'll tell you no lies, that's what Ma always said. Bea quickly re-folded the letter.

'Joan,' she nudged her friend, who was facing the other way, glowering at Sheila.

'Hmm?' Joan turned.

'Sorry, opened by mistake. This one's for you, girl.' Bea handed over the ripped aerogramme. Joan, frowning, took it from her and unfolded it. Bea watched her face as she read.

The frown gave way to a stare of incomprehension and Bea noticed a stray strand of hair on Joan's cheek begin to twitch, rhythmically, as her eyes scanned down. Joan made a strange clicking-gurgling sound and the letter dropped from her fingers and she slipped sideways in her chair. Bea just managed to catch her before Joan began to puke, violently, yellow chunks of bile all over the table. Bea saw Edie's hand reach out, keeping Joan's hair off her face as she vomited again and again. The other soldiers shot up, but Edie and Bea stayed with Joan, ignoring the warm wet stench of it all over everything.

'Better out than in,' Bea said, feeling the roughness of Joan's uniform under her fingertips as she stroked her back. Afterwards, Edie took Joan back to bed, and Bea helped clean up the mess in the cookhouse. The airmail letter was covered in sick and got thrown away. There was no keeping it.

Bea slopped disinfectant on the table and wondered about the sailor in the Arctic who thought he was engaged to Joan. Ask me no questions, and I'll tell you no lies, she reminded herself. So she didn't ask Joan about Fred, not that day; not until months later, when she had to.

Chapter 14

Joan's chest contracted as the train drew in. WANGLED A DAY'S LEAVE. TOMORROW 10.00 AT WATERLOO, was all the telegram had said. She'd had to sweet-talk one of the girls from the reserve troop to swap duties with her; it cost her a new lipstick, too.

The train belched steam. Bodies thrust and jarred against her: beige and black and khaki and navy: colours bouncing and blending and the smell of damp wool and engine smoke. At least it wasn't too cold here, out of the bite of the early spring north-easterly. Her eyes skittered, looking for the smoky blue RAF uniform. Was he behind the man with the bowler over there? No. Or the large lady in the fur coat further up? No. But he might be right at the back, up near the guard's van, if he'd brought a bicycle – but why would he bring his bicycle? Maybe he'd already got out and she'd missed him somehow; maybe he was behind one of those pillars, slicking back his hair and putting on his RAF cap. Was that him? No, no, that man was fair and too tall. She thought Rob was shorter, darker, stockier, but she couldn't really remember.

She looked and looked and the disgorging passengers continued to push past until eventually the doorways were all empty of people and luggage, the train like a discarded snake skin, left behind and empty. A picture came into her head of a schoolbook, a black and white drawing of a snake slithering from its discarded skin. *Snakes slough off their old selves* was written in large text underneath. She remembered that. She tried to envision beyond the book page. A schoolroom, or a bedroom? What did it look like? Who was there with her? Nothing, nobody: empty space.

The guard came out of the van and went along the train slamming the hanging doors. He looked at her as he passed – yellowing skin, face like putty – and she watched him slam–slam–slam those doors like he hated them, like they all had a Nazi stormtrooper stuck behind them. She saw the driver get out of the front of the train, by the platform barrier. He nodded to the guard, stretched, fiddled with his waistband and glanced up the empty platform towards her. When the guard reached him, they exchanged words and both looked up towards her. She felt herself begin to flush.

'Come along now, love, we're closing the barrier,' called the driver.

She opened up her gas mask, took out her old lipstick and dabbed a little of what was left of it on her lower lip. Then she clicked the lipstick back and closed the gas mask. Rob wasn't here.

'It's not a blooming beauty parlour. Get a move on,' yelled the guard. She kept her chin up and walked down towards them. The guard tutted as she drew near. The driver looked pityingly at her. They let her through the barrier ahead of them.

She'd been stood up, but she wasn't about to let anyone feel sorry for her. Opposite the platform entrance the station pub was just opening. Blinds flew up inside, and outside the door a man in a trilby hat and a trench coat was waiting with a newspaper under one arm.

'Oh, there you are, darling!' she called, and ran across the concourse towards him, looping her hand through his arm as she got there. She looked back – the guard and driver were laughing, walking off. In front of her a ruddy-cheeked landlord was just opening the pub's doors. And next to her – she looked up sideways ... the man was looking down at her, puzzled, but smiling. His teeth were nicotine yellow, and one of them was missing. He cleared his throat.

'I don't think I've had the pleasure, love,' he said.

'Are you saying you don't want to buy a girl a drink?' she replied, and he laughed and they walked together towards the open pub doorway. Walking inside was like going into a dark, smoky cocoon.

In the end, she didn't let him, chickened out. Even drunk, she wasn't stupid, and she didn't fancy him at all. He had a hand on her knee most of the time, squeezing intermittently. He tried a bit of a fumble when the landlord was changing the barrels, but some other customers came in, and there were no cloths on the tables, anyway, so people would have seen what he was doing. He said he had to place a bet on a dead cert for the three-thirty at Epsom, and then he'd show her a good time. She swigged down her port and lemon and said that sounded just peachy. When she put more lipstick on, he said she had a kissable mouth, and did she know she was a very pretty girl and she laughed, throwing her head back and tossing her hair, the way they did in the films. He said he just needed to visit the little boys' room and then they could go.

When he was in the Gents', she legged it. She didn't bother with the tube – too obvious in case he came after her, and she hated the bloody tube anyway – and ran all the way down Waterloo Bridge Road, imagining his footfalls behind her, until she reached the South Bank, panting, runny-nosed.

The grey sky and the buildings and the River Thames all swirled and snaked around as she stopped and tried to catch her breath. There was a flight of steep steps down to the water's edge and she trod them with exaggerated deliberation. Everything was still spinning, fuzzy at the edges, and her heart thumped like a kettledrum. The steps were narrow, greenish with weed or mould and she clung to the wet brickwork as she descended. But there was a little beach, with the low grey tidal Thames lapping gently, and she wanted to be there, down on the strand, away from him and everything. The wet sand sucked at her army brogues and she walked across to a sheltered spot by the wall where there was a chunk of rock to sit on. She waited, but she had imagined his footfalls; he wasn't coming after her. Her breathing slowed. Four port and lemons – he probably thought she owed him a hand job at the least.

It was cold, but she was out of the worst of the wind. She sniffed, letting her eyes follow a Thames barge snailing seawards along the estuary. Seagulls arced and screeched. The sand was dull beige, strewn with empty oyster shells and tiny pebbles. Up on Waterloo Bridge, men in bowlers walked with umbrellas and briefcases, and red busses passed and delivery boys on bicycles, and there was the occasional green army truck juddering along. Nobody thought to look down at her thin strip of tidal beach. Her fingers brushed the damp sand. Her head was spinning less, now she'd stopped running.

Mudlarks, wasn't that what they called beach scavengers in London. Here she was, mudlarking about – wasn't much of a lark though. She blew on her fingers to warm them, and took her cigarettes out of her gas mask. The matches kept going out in the wind, but eventually she got one lit, and let the smoke warm and soothe her. She drew patterns in the sand, and looked out at the wide river. The sun came out, briefly, and she shut her eyes in the warmth, nodded off. When she woke up, the water was right up near her toes. Her head was clearer, now. She smoked another cigarette and she heard Big Ben strike four times and thought she should probably move on – the sun had gone in, anyway, a misty clamminess descending.

She climbed back up the steep steps and walked towards Waterloo Bridge, licking her dry lips and struggling forwards against the stiff breeze. She caught the bus back to Marble Arch, going up to the top deck and looking out at places she hadn't even seen before, even though she'd been living in Hyde Park for weeks now: Westminster, Trafalgar Square, the Tower. She'd wanted to do this with Rob, look at the sights, hold his hand maybe. By the time she got to Marble Arch, all she wanted to do was go back to her bunk, have a couple of aspirin and a cup of tea and forget the day ever happened – and forget all about Flight Sergeant Robin Nelson.

Chapter 15

'I'm looking for Gunner Tucker,' Rob said.

'I'm terribly sorry, but she's gone to the station. Do you want to wait?'

He shook his head.

'I'll let her know she had a visitor; who shall I say has called?'

The girl was as tiny as she was posh, Rob thought, looking down at the skinny redhead. 'Rob,' he said. 'Just say Rob came here.'

'Oh, you're Rob!' said the girl, clapping her hand to her mouth. 'But she's gone to meet you at the station – she swapped duties with Margaret Packham. She wasn't at the station? How odd.'

'I was late. I missed the train.' He shrugged. He missed the train. How could he have missed the train? But then again, how could he have rushed off to get the train, leaving Dorothy Harper, in that state. What else could he have done?

His mind flicked back to Harper's widow: black roots were showing in her bleached hair under the headscarf, and her face, make-up free, looked blank and featureless. He almost hadn't recognised her, there at the bus stop. He only had a few minutes to make it across the village to the station. If she hadn't noticed him, he could have walked straight past her; he would have been in time.

'Dorothy?' he said, after a pause.

She looked down, realising that he'd taken a while to recognise her. 'I know, I look different. I don't – there doesn't seem any point in bothering, now.'

She and Harper had only been married a few weeks. The wedding was in the local church. Rob was best man: a nine-carat utility wedding ring, parachute-silk dress, borrowed ermine stole, cardboard cake. They'd all got blistering drunk in the mess afterwards, someone got out the bagpipes, and Dorothy, with her bleached hair and white dress, had looked incandescent with happiness. How long ago was it? Pammie was there, he remembered, and there was snow on the ground.

'How are you?' said Rob.

'How do you think?' she replied. They looked at each other and neither spoke. She breathed in, fiddled with her headscarf, collected herself. 'I'm on my way home. I've just been to see the doctor. I thought that maybe – but he says no. He says it's just, just grief.' Her face contorted as she said the word and he saw tears begin to squeeze out. 'I wanted to have his baby,' she said, putting up a hand, stifling a sob. 'I thought I might lose him – you knew it could happen, of course you did, but I thought that if I had his baby then at least there would be something left of him, something to remember him by,' she stuttered, wiping a silver skein of snot with her gloved hand. Rob felt in his pocket, pulled out a clean handkerchief, and held it out. She took it, but did nothing with it, letting the snot and tears pour as she carried on: 'But there's no baby, there's nothing. There's nothing left at all.' Rob reached out, patted her shoulder and then drew her towards him. His face was in her headscarf. He could smell her hair. The silky scarf was against his cheek. Her shoulders juddered and her face was wet against his neck and he held her and held her and cleared his throat and tried to tell himself that the dampness in his own eyes was from the sting of the wind – because he had to be strong, because where would we be if grown men started breaking down like sissies in the middle of the street, because what would Harper say if he could have seen? And by the time she pulled away, and her bus arrived, the London train was long gone.

'Where do you think she might be?' Rob said, his mind springing back to the present, to the diminutive soldier in front of him.

'I'm sorry,' said the redheaded girl, 'I really don't know, I thought she was with you, but you're welcome to wait – I'll show you to the NAAFI – but then I have to go; I'm on an errand for the Junior Commander and she'll be livid if I take an age. Honestly, she's a bit of a dragon. I'm Edie, by the way.' She held out a hand. He shook it. Her handshake was dry and firm.

'Joan's written to me about you,' said Rob.

'All lies, I'm actually quite nice!' said Edie, grinning. 'Come on, I'll show you the way.'

Rob checked his watch. He couldn't afford to get stuck in town. If he didn't make it back, there'd be hell to pay, and he couldn't let the chaps down. Damn. When would he get another chance?

'I'm sorry, I can't wait. I have to get back, but I just wanted her to know that I came. I didn't stand her up,' he said. 'Will you give her these?' He thrust out the flowers, bought at the station, crushed from the tube journey, already wilting.

'Daffodils. How gorgeous,' said the girl, sniffing them. 'I'll tell her. I'm sure she'll understand, dear,' said Edie. 'You can meet up again next time you get a day pass, can't you?'

Rob wondered when that was likely to be. There was a new boss coming – Harris – everyone was talking about him, rumours about his plans for bomber command. He wasn't expecting leave any time soon. He thanked the redheaded girl and began to walk back to the tube station. The sky was grey and low, moisture-laden and chilly. At the entrance to the tube was a kiosk, selling postcards and cigarettes. The stallholder had caved-in cheeks and a flat cap. Rob bought a postcard with a red London bus on it, just like the one drawing up at the bus stop opposite. As he began the descent into the tube station, he was already planning what to write.

Dear Joan
  Sorry, sorry, sorry! I didn't stand you up. Here's proof that I was in London. Did you get the flowers?

She would understand, wouldn't she?

Chapter 16

'Well, this is romantic,' he said.

'I suppose so,' Joan replied.

The big houses in Holland Park were like toppling piles of meringues and the stars were out overhead. His arm was round her waist. She knew what was coming, but there wasn't much time. She only had a pass until eleven, and she couldn't be late, not this week when she was acting bombardier, while Martha Toogood was away with her sick mother. There were low walls in front of the huge houses, wrought-iron railings all sawed off like teeth. She paused, leant against a gatepost, let him swing round to face her, arms encircling her. The houses were mostly empty, some of them bombed out, with odd slices of chintz wallpaper or gilded balustrade breaking the piled-up shadows. His breath was warm against her face.

'Clear night like this, I suppose I should be worried,' she said, looking skywards. 'Feels like we're due some action.'

'Feels like I'm due some action,' he said, moving closer. She knew what he meant. She found herself wishing he'd just hurry up and get on with it.

'You're a good-looking girl, and I've loved our nights out,' he said. 'Do you mind if I . . .' He didn't finish the sentence because she'd pulled him towards her and her mouth was on his. Momentarily, their teeth clashed in the confusion, and then they found the way. His lips were a little chapped, and his breath tasted of carrots. His hands were stroking her and she could hear the swish of his palms against the wool of her coat. Without breaking the kiss, she unbuttoned it for him, leaving it agape, but then – her ruddy gas mask was in the way.

'Sorry,' she said, pulling away. She ripped the strap of the gas-mask case over her head and threw it down. As it clattered to the pavement, the catch went, spilling the contents into the street. 'Damn it!'

'Let me help,' he said, and they bent down at the same time, foreheads bumping, apologising, scrabbling blindly on the dark paving stones. 'I can't find the mask anywhere,' he said, pulling out a tiny torch and switching it on. The beam was like a child's finger, poking nosily into the gutter.

'Oh, I never carry it,' she said. 'I'm more worried about my lipstick. You can't find Coty for love nor money at the moment.'

She was squinting, found her comb and powder compact, handkerchief. He passed her the lipstick and she thanked him. She was just putting everything back, when – 'Is this yours, too?' he asked. She didn't reply. She was concentrating on the catch on her gas-mask case; it wouldn't fasten properly. She should have responded, taken it from him before he saw.

'It's a postcard,' he said. She looked up. The narrow torch beam played over the card in his hands. The red London bus on the picture a sudden spot of colour, then gone. He'd turned it over, was reading it, the light picking over the handwriting. There was silence as he read the words, then: 'Who the hell is Rob?'

'Shut up, will you?' she said.

'No, I won't shut up. I think I've got a right to know who this Rob fella is.'

'For goodness' sakes, shh.' She tilted her head upwards and to one side, listening. Yes, there it was: a very faint buzz, like wasps circling a jam jar, but far, far away.

She was already running when the siren started, its howling drowning out the sound of the incoming bombers. He caught up with her as she reached the corner of the street and tugged her sleeve: 'Come on, let's get down the tube station.'

'I'm not going down the bloody tube,' she yelled, pulling away from his grasp. The siren wailed on.

He stared at her, slack-jawed and panting: 'You'll get yourself killed.'

'That's my choice,' she replied, shouting over the waves of sound.

He shrugged. 'Suit yourself,' and turned, sprinting off in the direction of the tube. She paused, catching her breath, watching him get smaller and disappear into the street shadows as he ran. He didn't look back.

The sirens abruptly stopped, and she started running again, trying not to trip on the broken paving slabs and shattered kerbstones. She could hear the bombers, an inexorable drone, getting louder with every footfall. If she could just make it back to the battery – she veered off the Bayswater Road and into Hyde Park – not far now.

Don't slow down, she told herself, although her breath was sawing, chest heaving, and the sound of the planes was now so loud it was impossible to tell which direction they were flying in from. Shadows passed her periphery: the big oak trees, bandstand, an abandoned bicycle. There was a sickle moon, like a question mark above Oxford Street, shivering ahead of her as she ran.

She stopped at the first crash, heart leaping, blinking at the sudden flash of light. But she told herself to keep going, judging that it must have hit further north, beyond Regent's Park, and there was only a few hundred yards to go. Her legs felt heavy, but she forced them on, not stopping now, even when the bombs landed nearer and the glare from the explosions meant she was running blind: running, running, through the noise and the night.

She stopped at the battery entrance, reaching for her ID, but the Home Guard man on the gate just waved her through, flinching as another bomb landed, closer still, making the earth shudder.

Joan knew she should go straight back to the hut – their

section wasn't even on duty until the morning – but she had to pass by the emplacements anyway. She hesitated, wrapped in the clamour of it, watching the scurrying shadows of the team on the guns: coveralls and helmets and the predictor swivelling round, gun turret angling up into the darkness, pointing at the mesh of searchlights up in the sky. They were onto one; she could see that. One girl was yelling out the bearings and one of the other girls was using the crank wheel to get the gun on target. *Position Steady!* Staff Farr raised her arm.

Here we go, thought Joan. But instead of the order to fire, there was a flash of incandescence, and a moment later a screaming roar. She was flung off her feet, a sudden hardness as she hit the ground. She pulled herself upright, coughing, and came face to face with her staff sergeant.

'For christsakes, Tucker, you're not even on duty, get back to bed,' Staff Farr shouted, turning angrily away. 'Is everyone all right? Back to your stations then! What's that?'

Someone was shouting, something about Number One being injured. Number One was the old Home Guard man – Arthur – whose job it was to fire the gun. Another bomb fell, the scream and splash of brightness simultaneous with the bucking earth. Joan looked up and saw the fingering search-light beams, still lighting up the enemy planes. But they couldn't fire with a man down, could they?

Joan ran into the emplacement, dodging the predictor and finding Staff Farr kneeling next to Arthur: 'He's conscious. He'll be fine,' she was saying to another gunner, who'd arrived with a first-aid kit. Then she turned, seeing Joan: 'Tucker, what did I say just now. Get the hell to bed, will you?'

'You're a man down,' said Joan.

'I know we're a ruddy man down,' said Staff Farr, pulling a field dressing from the open first-aid tin.

'You can't fire the guns without Arthur. He's the only man.'

'Bed, Tucker.' Staff Farr looked up. There was another blanching thud – further away now – and Joan could see the expression lit up on her pale face: a deep frown cutting her forehead. The planes were still roaring in, but only men were allowed to fire the anti-aircraft gun: that was the law. And the only man they had was Arthur.

'I can be Arthur,' said Joan. 'I mean, we've still got a shot, haven't we?' They both looked up, away to where the search-lights still played.

'You're not on duty, and in any case, it's against the rules,' Staff began.

'If I'm not officially on duty, then I can't officially be doing anything against the rules, can I?' yelled Joan above the roar of another dropping bomb. Staff Farr gave the tiniest of nods and stood up.

'Gunners, at your stations. Predictor on target,' she barked, and the girls were back in action. Arthur, slumped up against a sandbag, holding a blooded dressing to his brow, looked on.

Bearing three-eleven!

On target!

Position steady!

She saw Staff Farr raise her right arm.

Fire!

Joan slammed the metal hatch shut and the shell burst out of the gun turret. High in the sky, a tiny black silhouette against the yellow searchlights exploded into flames and disappeared earthwards.

When the medics finally came to pick up Arthur, Joan slipped quietly away. It was all over by then, anyway, the thundering skies stilled, and the only sounds were of distant fire engines. Staff Farr caught up with her, halfway back to her hut. 'You know we can't possibly say anything about this, don't you?' she said. Joan nodded. 'But thanks to you, we got a hit tonight, Gunner Tucker, and I'll see you right.'

Joan slid back into the hut and fell onto her bunk. Edie was still awake. 'I'm so relieved to see you back safe. We were all worried about you,' she whispered from the next bed. 'What happened?'

'Arthur's injured, but he'll be fine,' she said. 'They got a hit, too.' Joan shrugged off her coat, deciding against getting changed into her pyjamas – it would be morning soon.

'Poor Arthur,' said Edie. 'But good news about the hit. But what I meant was, what happened to you? You were supposed to be back by eleven.'

Joan undid the laces on her brogues and pushed them off. 'I was in Holland Park when the raid started,' she said, getting into bed.

'And what about John?' said Edie.

'Oh, that's all over,' said Joan with a sigh, pulling up the covers.

'But why? You two had been getting on so well!'

'He found that postcard from Rob, in my gas-mask case.'

'You kept it?'

'Well, obviously I kept it, or he wouldn't have found it.'

'You carry it with you in your gas-mask case, all the time?'

'Oh, shut up about it, will you.'

'I don't know why you won't write back to him. He seemed very nice to me.'

'Everyone seems very nice to you, Edie. Even Sheila Carter seems very nice to you.'

'Oh, Joan!'

'Oh, Joan yourself,' she said, bashing out a hole in the pillow.

'Unless you lot shut up, I'll tell Sheila what you said,' came another voice, the new Geordie girl, from across the room.

'Like I care,' said Joan, loudly. She turned under the bedclothes so she was facing the wall.

'Edie's right, you know, girl,' said Bea in hushed tones from the bunk opposite. 'You found a good man, and you let him go.'

'Not you and all,' said Joan. 'I thought you were asleep.' Her eyes were wide in the darkness, the blacked-out barrack pushing irregular shadows against her face.

'Think anyone could sleep through that racket?' Bea said. 'And what are you going to do about Rob?' It's plain as day you still care about him, girl.'

'Will you both just shut up and let me sleep,' said Joan. But she stayed awake in the quiet blackness, thinking about a face with round blue eyes and dark hair, and pages and pages of familiar handwriting and she felt a twisting ache inside, like homesickness.

Chapter 17

'Hop in, girls,' said Pop. Edie got into the Bentley and Joan slid in next to her. It had been an age since she'd been in a car and Edie noticed how the barracks were now sliced up into rectangular portions by the car's windows: a portion of drill square; a portion of Nissen huts; and portions of guns, equipment and green-grey Hyde Park: her life in little pieces. Pop got behind the wheel.

'Used to have a driver, but he joined the merchant navy. Dead now, poor chap,' he said, slamming the door and taking his pipe off the shelf on the dashboard. This was for Joan's benefit. Edie already knew all about the driver, Archie, a small man with a stomach like a pudding bowl and a pointy little nose. She hadn't liked him much. He always looked like he was keeping secrets. But Cook cried for about a week when they heard the news, and even Mummy used to sigh and look pained when someone mentioned his name.

'Are we going straight home or shall we stop off for a spot

of something en route?' said Pop. Edie caught his eye in the rear-view mirror: the familiar dark brows, slash of silver hair, grey eyes, just a little red-rimmed.

'If we eat on the way then it will save Mummy the trouble, won't it?' said Edie, thinking of Cook, now off with the Land Army.

'Quite,' said her father, stuffing tobacco into the pipe bowl.

'What about that little place in Eton that does the walnut cake?' said Edie.

'Righty-ho.'

He struck a match and puffed on the pipe. The smoke was dense and scented. Then the engine growled and with a jolt they were off and suddenly the barracks, the guns, Hyde Park, everything was gone. She and Edie were thrown about like a Dodgem ride, and London passed by in a blur. It was the first time she'd had one of her army pals home. She was a little nervous about it, but Joan didn't appear to have anywhere else to go on leave.

When they pulled into the gravel driveway, Edie noticed a pale face at one of the upstairs windows. But by the time they'd opened the car doors, Mummy was already waiting by the open front door, a frozen smile on her lips. Edie introduced her, and she took Joan's hand.

'How nice to meet one of Edith's army chums,' she said, looking Joan up and down. Then she looked away, biting her lip, and addressed Edie's father, who was locking the car.

'I made lunch,' she said.

'Oh, don't worry about that, old girl. We stopped off at that place in Eton.'

'I have it all ready.'

'Thought we'd save you cooking.'

'But I've cooked. You should have phoned.'

'We'll have it for supper, then.'

Edie ushered Joan inside. Her mother followed them in.

'Is she in the yellow room or the old nursery?' said Edie.

'The yellow. I thought it would be warmer. And last week, we had French soldiers staying in the nursery . . .' she wrinkled her nose.

'Yellow it is,' said Edie. 'Follow me, Joan dear, and watch out for that bottom step. It's been loose for ever.'

Edie showed Joan around the house. It was odd being back, and seeing it through someone else's eyes. With Joan there, she noticed the huge expanse of black and white tiles in the hallway, the worn Persian rug in the study, the carved oak banisters and half-panelled stairs. She also noticed the chill. In their little Nissen hut with the stove, they could get up quite a fug in the evenings, what with everyone squashed in together, but here at home there were high ceilings and long corridors and nothing to fill them but the ticking of the old grandfather clock. Joan's room – the yellow room – was probably the warmest and nicest in the house, with sun streaming in through the south-facing windows, highlighting the yellow roses on the wallpaper and the gold silk eiderdown. But dust motes danced in the sunbeams and there were circular marks on the bedside table from old cocoa mugs. There were cobwebs in the corners.

'Poor Mummy. It's hard without staff.' Edie shrugged.

'It's a beautiful room,' said Joan, spinning slowly in a shaft of sunlight. 'Your house is lovely, Edie.'

Edie said she supposed it was. She'd never thought about it before. 'What was – what was your house like?' she said.

'My house?' said Joan, stopping mid-twirl. Her eyes looked up and away, to a corner of the room, and her expression froze. She quivered, like a flower bud when the stem is being cut from below, and then sat abruptly down on the bed, next to Edie.

'Listen, would you mind if I had a little nap? I'm all in, and this bed does look a whole lot more inviting than my bunk in the hut,' she said. Her voice snipped brightly, but her shoulders had slumped.

'Oh, yes, of course. How insensitive of me. You must sleep; sleep as long as you want. I'll call you when it's dinner time.' Edie got up off the bed and went to the door. She looked back before she left, to where Joan sat, in the same shaft of sunlight, a slight frown on her smooth features, then she went along the corridor to her old room.

Opening the door to her own bedroom was like stepping back in time and suddenly coming face to face with the girl she'd been four months ago. There on the shelf were her books, ranged chronologically in order of reading, all the way from *Mother Goose* (*Les contes de ma mère l'Oye* – it was the French version) up to *Gone with the Wind*, which she'd only just finished before she joined up. She imagined herself on that final day, waiting for the slam of the front door as her mother left, so that she could pack up a few things in the little bag and race to the station for the London train. She'd been so nervous, she hadn't eaten breakfast, and her stomach churned all the way to London. And there at the station she'd met Joan, bought her a cup of tea, chatted with her all the way to the training camp in Devon. If she hadn't met Joan, would she really have gone through with it? Gone and joined up, without telling Mummy and Pop? Or would she have flunked it, got scared and run home? She couldn't be sure. One thing was certain, it was knowing Joan, and meeting Bea, that got her through that first week. She didn't have a clue about polishing shoes or peeling potatoes or mopping floors or even how to iron her own clothes. And now, here she was, four months on, and she could do all of those things, and more. But back home everything was exactly as it was, like a museum to her girlhood. Her old knitted grey rabbit was on her pillow, and her nightie was folded next to it. She went over to the bed and sat down. Outside in the garden the trees were just beginning to get leaves, a colourwash of mint over the spiky branches. The hedges all needed pruning and there were piles of rotting leaves just left in drifts by the fence. Her eiderdown felt unbelievably soft compared to the scratchy blankets in the hut as she threw herself down on the bed. Maybe Joan had the right idea. Maybe just a little nap?

When she woke, the dinner gong was sounding and the sky was pinky-blue outside. She rolled out of bed and tumbled down the corridor to Joan's room, knocking on her door: 'Joan dear, they've just rung the gong,' she called through the keyhole. Downstairs, the fire was lit in the dining room and the vast table was laid for four.

'Can't get any decent claret for love nor money these days,' said Pop, 'so we'll have to make do with gin and lime. If that's all right with you?'

Edie and Joan helped her mother bring the food through. There were boiled potatoes and carrots and a deflated cheese soufflé, along with parsley sauce. The food was warm but withered.

'No steak?' said Edie's father.

'I will not have horse eaten in this house,' said her mother.

'It's very nice, Mummy,' said Edie, taking a mouthful, her eyes flicking between her parents.

'Horse is not nice, Edith Elizabeth. I can't think where you've been eating with your soldier friends, but we won't be having it in this house, thank you.'

'No, I didn't mean that, I meant the cheese soufflé,' said Edie.

'Well, it would have been far nicer at lunchtime, when I made it,' Mummy retorted. Then, turning to Joan, 'I'm very sorry about this, but waste not, want not, you know.'

'It's very tasty, Mrs Lightwater,' said Joan, washing down the rubbery soufflé with a swig of gin and lime.

'Lady Lightwater, actually,' Mummy said, and Edie cringed. Why did she have to draw attention to it?

'Oh, I'm sorry, I didn't know.' Joan flushed, and Edie felt terrible. She should have mentioned – but she didn't want to seem big-headed about it.

'It's quite all right. You can call me Maud, if that's easier,' said Mummy, sipping her drink and making a face.

'I'd still prefer a bit of meat,' said Pop, putting down his fork and reaching for his copy of *The Times*.

'Not at the supper table, Neville!' snapped her mother. Joan and Edie exchanged glances. Edie's father sighed and withdrew his hand.

'So, where was it you said you were from?' he asked, turning to Joan.

'Near Finchley,' she said.

He nodded. 'And do they ride much, in Finchley?'

'Of course they don't ride in Finchley,' her mother interrupted.

Edie saw Joan looking from Pop to Mummy, a withered piece of soufflé hanging like ectoplasm from her fork. Edie's father cleared his throat.

'Yes, well, nobody's riding much these days, what with the war and . . .'

'Everyone's eating the horses,' said Edie's mother, spearing a carrot.

'Oh, don't be like that, old girl. It's only the old nags that end up in the knacker's yard, the ones that are all worn out and half-dead anyway. No harm in wasting good meat. Not when there's a war on, eh?'

Everyone looked at their plates and concentrated on their food, until at last it was done and Edie suggested clearing the plates while her mother got the pudding.

'I'll help you,' said Joan, shooting up and knocking over

her drink as she did so. Joan apologised at least three times, until Edie's father said, 'Do be quiet, it was an accident, you silly filly, and for God's sake, sit down.'

'Don't worry, I'll get a cloth,' said Edie, rushing out to the kitchen. She helped Mummy with the pudding dishes for spotted dick. The custard was only a little lumpy. Afterwards, Pop brought out the port.

'Pass it to the left,' he said. 'Don't lift the decanter off the table.'

Mummy rolled her eyes, and Edie explained to Joan that the whole port ritual was a legacy of his time in the army, last time round. Pop wanted to know what happened to those after-dinner sweets they used to have and her mother replied crisply that they hadn't been available since 1940. Then he lurched to his feet and proposed a toast to the King, so they all dutifully raised their glasses before drinking.

Joan took a sip. 'I've never had it without lemonade before,' she said. 'But it's quite nice on its own, too.'

Mummy gave Edie a funny look, and Edie knew exactly what she was thinking. 'Oh, Mummy, lots of the ATS girls drink port and lemon,' said Edie.

'I'll bet they do,' said her father, downing his glass and looking across the table at Joan.

'I think your friend seems jolly nice, Half Pint,' said Pop when the last of the supper plates were cleared and they moved into the drawing room. He reached for the whisky decanter. 'Anyone else for a tot?'

'I think we've all had enough, Neville,' said Mummy, sitting down in her chair next to the fire and picking up her knitting. Pop shrugged and poured himself a generous two fingers' worth. Edie asked Joan to sit next to her on the sofa, while Pop leant against the mantelpiece, swilling the whisky around in his tumbler.

'I suppose you girls get chatted up all the time at work?' he said. He was facing them both, but looking at Joan.

'Not especially,' said Joan. 'We're really too busy for that kind of thing.'

'Oho, that's as maybe, but no red-blooded male is too busy for that kind of thing,' said Pop, taking a gulp of whisky. He smacked his lips. 'Ah, single malt, nothing like it.'

Edie watched her mother's knitting needles. The more Pop talked, the faster they went: stab-stab-stabbing at the moss-green wool. Outside, the light was fading; there was just a livid gash of pink along the treetops.

'Edith, be a dear and pull down the blackouts,' said Mummy, frowning at the woolly loops in her lap.

'Yes, do, Half Pint, or that Carson fellow will be on our backs – frightful little oik,' said Pop.

'Oh, Pop, he's only doing his job. He is the ARP warden, after all,' said Edie. Joan got up to help her with the blinds and Edie noticed how Pop looked at Joan – looked at all of her. He never looked at Mummy like that.

'His job? I dare say it is, but I know his sort. Give 'em a uniform and they turn into little Hitlers, the lot of them.'

'Neville,' said Mummy sharply, looking up from her wool.

Edie and Joan pulled down the blinds in the drawing room and Edie asked if they should do upstairs. Mummy said, would they be so kind? It was just that she did find it such a chore doing it on her own every day. So up they went, and on the way round all the bedrooms on the first and second floors, they talked about Bea, and Joan's planned visit to see her. Joan didn't seem to have any family to visit on leave. But when Edie asked her about it, Joan just clammed up, and she didn't want to pry.

Edie could hear Mummy and Pop's voices, even from the landing, so they must have been talking quite loudly, but she couldn't catch their words. Then, as she and Joan were half-way down the front staircase, there was an abrupt silence. When they went back into the drawing room, Pop was wiping his face with his handkerchief. There were splash marks on his cravat, too, and his whisky tumbler was empty, lying sideways on the rug. Mummy was standing up, her knitting a tangled heap on the floor next to the whisky glass. Her face was very white and hard-looking. Edie paused in the doorway and looked at Joan. Joan coughed, at which Mummy and Pop looked up.

'Spilled my drink, what a prize clot,' said Pop, finishing mopping his face and picking up the tumbler. Mummy sat down and stared at her knitting.

'You girls want the wireless on? It'll be light music at this time, I shouldn't wonder,' said Pop. Without waiting for an answer he turned on the radio and the strains of the BBC Orchestra filtered into the room. Edie didn't recognise the tune. Pop had turned it up too loud and it sounded scratchy and distorted, but nobody asked him to turn it down.

'Do have a seat, Joan,' said Edie, remembering her manners.

'No, don't sit down, dance! Dance with me,' said Pop, grabbing Joan round the waist. 'All you young fillies like to dance, isn't that right?' he added, pulling Joan in closer. 'I say, you don't get many of those to the pound, eh?' he said, looking down at her chest as he waltzed her away from the chairs and into the space beyond the davenport. 'Your friend is a jolly good sport, isn't she, Half Pint?' he said, raising his voice over the rough blare of music. 'You are a jolly good sport, aren't you, Jeanie?' he said, looking down at Joan.

'It's Joan,' said Joan, but he didn't appear to hear her, just waltzed her faster, round by the sideboard and the French windows. 'My name is Joan!' she repeated, using the same voice she used when calling out bearings on the predictor during raids.

'Yes, that's what I said,' he replied, spinning her over the leopard skin and towards the trophy cabinet. They were going even faster now, and Edie worried that they'd trip. Her father's heel grazed the Wedgwood urn. She saw his hand moving down Joan's back as they whirled past. Mummy continued to sit, staring at the mess of wool and knitting needles as if picking them up was a harder task than she could possibly contemplate. The music was soaring, up-tempo, loud and fuzzy. As Pop and Joan passed by again, she saw, with horror, that her father's hand was on Joan's behind. She saw Joan's face, pink and unsmiling before Pop swooped her away.

Edie walked over to the radio and reached out for the dial. She turned the knob and it clicked and suddenly everything was silent. As she did so, Joan slid away from Pop's embrace. For a moment, nobody said a word. Then Joan took a sharp intake of breath and smiled at Pop. 'It was very kind indeed of you to ask me to dance,' she said, placing her hand lightly on his upper arm. 'But I'm terribly tired. We have had a shocker of a week, haven't we, Edie?' Edie nodded vigorously. 'Would you mind dreadfully if we called it a night?'

'Not at all,' said Pop, scratching his nose. He was red in the face, panting slightly.

Joan turned and walked over to where Mummy sat. 'Thank you, Lady Lightwater – Maud – for the lovely meal,' she said. Mummy merely inclined her head to show that she'd heard.

'Well, goodnight everyone,' said Joan, still smiling, then she left the room. Edie could hear her footsteps racing upstairs.

'I think I'll turn in, too,' said Edie, following her friend. She paused in the doorway. Mummy and Pop were like statues, frozen in position, far apart. 'Goodnight then,' she said. 'And Pop, if you're so keen on dancing, maybe you should dance with Mummy once in a while,' she added, and quickly shut the door and followed Joan upstairs before either of them could respond.

She ran towards the yellow room, not even bothering to knock. 'I'm sorry. I'm so sorry!' she said. Joan was already sitting at the dressing table. Edie saw her reflection, her face covered white with cold cream, like a clown.

'Don't be.' Joan shrugged, starting to wipe the cream off

her face with cotton wool. Edie slumped down on the bed. She'd always liked the yellow room. It was nicer than her own room: cosier. If she'd had the choice, she would have chosen this room as her bedroom. But the choice had been made for her, as it always was, at home.

'Sometimes I wish I was an orphan!' she said. She caught Joan looking at her, through the glass. But Joan didn't say anything; she just carried on wiping off her make up with the cotton wool, until the white cold-cream mask was all gone. 'I shouldn't have said that. I'm sorry,' she said.

But Joan didn't respond straight away. First, she took off her shoes and lay them carefully beside the bed. 'Has it always been like this at home?' she then asked, beginning to roll down her stockings.

'Like what?' said Edie.

'Oh, you know, like it was just now.'

Edie tried to think. 'Well, I suppose I just can't remember the last time Mummy was happy,' she said. 'She's always unhappy and it feels as if her unhappiness is my fault, somehow. I don't know.'

Joan was pulling off her clothes and getting into her striped army-issue pyjamas.

'I can lend you one of my nightdresses if you want?' said Edie.

'That's kind, but I don't think I'd fit, do you?' said Joan, grinning. She's right, Edie thought, bosoms like that would never squeeze into one of my nighties. She looked at the way they pushed up against the front of Joan's pyjamas, straining the middle button. Was that why Pop had been like that with

Joan? And the men at the barracks, too? The phrase 'bees round a honey pot' came to mind.

'Well, I suppose I'd better say goodnight,' said Edie, pushing herself up.

'Oh, don't,' said Joan. 'I'm not really tired at all – I was asleep for most of the afternoon – I only said that because . . .'

'I know,' Edie interrupted. 'Tell you what, shall I make us some cocoa?'

Edie ran down to her room and quickly splashed some water onto her face and changed into her old nightie and dressing gown. Her woolly rabbit was still on her pillow; she picked it up and put it on the shelf inside the wardrobe, next to the hatbox. Then she pattered downstairs.

The drawing-room door was closed and the wireless was on again. She could smell Pop's cigar smoke as she passed. The kitchen was cold. The supper dishes lay discarded on the side, along with the empty gin bottle. She found the powdered milk and cocoa, but not sugar, so she used some of the breakfast honey instead. When she went back through to the hallway, Pop was at the telephone table, holding up the receiver. He had his back to her. The drawing-room door was open, Mummy's chair was empty, and the wireless had been switched off.

'I can't possibly,' he was saying. 'She's already confronted me, and this will blow the whole thing sky high, darling.' He turned, as she passed, put a hand over the receiver. 'Shouldn't you be in bed, Half Pint?' he said, frowning. Then, 'Work,' he added, sighing and rolling his eyes, pointing at the telephone. She nodded, hurried past into the darkness. Who could Pop be calling at this time of night? It certainly wasn't anything remotely to do with his work, whatever he'd said.

She padded up the stairs and along the corridor to Joan's room. Her father's voice was just a low rumble from the hallway. She carried on walking. She pushed open the door to the yellow room with her foot, careful not to spill any of the cocoa on the cream carpet. Joan was opening a packet of cigarettes. She offered them to Edie.

'No, thank you, you know I don't. Anyway, Mummy wouldn't like it,' Edie said.

'Mummy doesn't need to know.'

'I know, but still . . .' she put the mugs of cocoa down on the bedside table. Everyone else seemed to smoke, but she never had, and now it seemed too late to start. She didn't want to make a show of herself, coughing and spluttering the first time.

'Well, you can just share mine if you want,' said Joan, striking a match. Edie sat on the bed next to her and picked up her cocoa. She took a sip; it wasn't half bad, with honey instead of sugar. She watched how the match flame connected with the tip of the cigarette and how the cigarette suddenly hissed and flared orange as Joan inhaled. When Joan breathed out, the smoke swirled all around them. It smelled pungent, grown up.

'I don't know about you, but I'm a bit chilly. Shall we?' said Joan, pulling back the bed covers. They both got into bed together, pillows plumped at their backs and legs just touching under the blankets. Edie put down her cocoa and Joan held out the cigarette.

'You hold it like this,' she said, demonstrating. 'Not like this – you don't want to look like Sheila-blooming-Carter.' Edie giggled. 'Right, now, when you bring it up to your lips, you let them pout – see – like you're about to kiss a boyfriend.'

Edie felt herself blush. 'I've never kissed a boy.'

'Never?'

She shook her head.

'Edith Elizabeth, I am shocked!' said Joan, in a voice that sounded so much like Mummy that Edie couldn't help but laugh. 'Stop laughing and concentrate,' said Joan. 'Bring the cigarette up to your lips and breathe in. Try not to cough. When you breathe out again, do it gently, like you're blowing a kiss.'

Edie took the cigarette and brought it to her lips. She dwelt briefly on what didn't happen with Kenneth in the cinema, puckered up, and inhaled. The smoke hit her lungs like a punch, and she doubled up, coughing for what felt like for ever. Joan took the cigarette off her. When she finally calmed down, she wiped her teary eyes on the sleeve of her nightie.

'How was that?' said Joan.

'Dreadful,' said Edie, feeling sick.

Joan tapped ash onto the china ring tray on the bedside table. Edie didn't want to mention that it wasn't actually an ashtray. 'You have to persevere,' she said. 'It's never great the first time. But before you try again, tell me who you were thinking about when you put the fag to your lips?'

'Nobody!'

'Nobody called . . .?'

'Oh, give over, Joan.'

'Come on, out with it. What's his name?'

'Kenneth.'

'Kenneth, eh? And?'

'And nothing. Anyway, he's MIA.'

There was a pause while neither of them spoke. Joan continued to smoke. Edie heard the chiming clink as the telephone receiver was put down in the hallway.

'Still feeling sick?' said Joan at last. Edie said she was feeling fine now, thank you.

'Right, let's give it another shot. Here, try it like this; open your mouth and I'll just blow the smoke inside. It won't be as strong, so it'll be easier for you to get used to.'

Joan inhaled and then put her face right up close to Edie's and Edie could see her hazel-flecked eyes and the way her lashes curled. Edie parted her lips and Joan blew smoke into her mouth. Their lips were so close they almost touched. Edie breathed the smoke in and this time she didn't cough, just felt it warm inside her and it made her feel swoony. She said she felt giddy, and Joan smiled and said that it would do, the first few times.

'Want to go again?' said Joan, taking another drag. Edie nodded and they shared smoky breaths over again, until the cigarette was finished and Edie felt as if she were floating away. She closed her eyes. She could stay here for ever. Downstairs, the grandfather clock chimed. Edie opened her eyes.

'I suppose I'd really better go,' she said. 'After all, we have to be up for church in the morning.'

'You don't have to. We can top and tail if you want?'

'Top and what?'

'Tail. Your head at that end and mine at this.'

Edie thought that wouldn't be half a lark, but she needed to say her prayers first. It was cold out of bed, and the room was still shifting slightly. She knelt down and closed her eyes and quickly recited the Lord's Prayer under her breath, and then mentally thanked Him for the health of her family and friends and asked Him to please help them all to stay strong and beat Hitler. She knew she ought to do more, but she was desperate to get back under the warm covers. When she opened her eyes, Joan had lit another cigarette and was blowing the smoke upwards in a plume towards the ceiling rose.

'Aren't you going to say your prayers?' said Edie.

'I don't think so,' said Joan.

'Why? Don't you believe?' said Edie, getting into the other end of the bed. Joan just tossed her a spare pillow and she lay down. Their bodies were a comfortable muddle under the bedclothes. Joan stubbed out her cigarette and turned out the bedside light, saying nothing.

Chapter 18

'Goodbye,' Joan called. She doubted whether Edie would hear her through the thick glass windows. Edie waved from the platform, beginning to walk to keep pace with the moving train. She was smiling as she began to jog, but she looked forlorn, like a schoolgirl chasing a missed bus. Edie kept running, right until the end of the platform, and then stood, waving, a redheaded girl in a green serge coat, getting smaller and smaller, until the train rounded a corner, and she was gone.

Joan turned her attention inside. It was pointless trying to find a compartment – everywhere was jam-packed – but she thought she could maybe just sit on top of her kit bag in the corridor. People could still get past if she tucked up her knees. She was about to sit down when a white-faced woman stopped right next to her, and there was no longer any space to sit. The woman held a grizzling toddler on one hip. 'Why don't you look out for the moo-cows, Annie?' she said in a tired voice, pointing outside. But Annie wasn't interested in the moo-cows. She shook her blonde curls and whined.

The cheerless countryside pulled past the grimy windows: grey skies; brown ploughed fields; and charcoal smudges of hedges and ditches. The very motion of the train seemed to echo the War Office's nagging phrase: *Is your journey really necessary? Is your journey really necessary?* Yes it is, thought Joan. Because I'm going to see Bea – and because I've nowhere else to go on leave.

She remembered the last time she was on a train: down to Devon to the recruit training camp. Edie had been with her then, wittering on about Glenn Miller and parties, and piano exams and how she should have gone to finishing school in Paris, but Hitler put paid to that. Every time Edie asked Joan a question about herself – family or school – her mind had gone as blank and empty as the dull skies that were now streaming past the train windows. All she'd known was that she was Joan Tucker and she was joining the ATS. So they'd ended up talking about films, and film stars, and she'd found that she'd known an awful lot about that, funnily enough.

The woman was trying to put the toddler down, now, but every time her little bootied feet connected with the corridor floor, the girl started to chunter again. The woman sighed and Joan gave her a sympathetic look. A fair-haired young man in army uniform came striding down the corridor towards them. Joan shifted back against the window, ready to let him pass. But as he reached her, he stopped. Her eyes scanned his uniform – no flashes on his upper arms, but a pip on his epaulette: a second lieutenant.

'Crowded, isn't it?' he said, pulling a packet of Sweet Afton from his pocket. She nodded. He was standing quite close to her, and the motion of the train meant he kept rocking in, closer still. She wanted to move away, but the woman with the toddler was still stood right next to her. 'Care to join me?' He held out the open packet. He had an Irish accent, she noticed. She was gasping for a fag, but if she shared a smoke with him, he'd take it to mean something. And although he seemed nice enough, she really wasn't in the mood to be chatted up.

'I'm sorry, I don't smoke, but thank you,' she said, hoping he wouldn't notice her nicotine-stained fingertips. She inched away, nudging into the washed-out woman, whose child was still mewling intermittently. 'Would you like me to take her for a bit – give you a rest?' she said, turning to the woman.

At that, the woman smiled, and Joan thought what lovely blue eyes she had, and how she'd be pretty, if she weren't so obviously at the end of her tether. 'Would you mind? Only she's been up half the night, and I'm desperate for a smoke,' said the woman.

'Not at all,' said Joan, reaching out and taking the child. 'You giving your mum a hard time?' she said, smiling and jiggling the little girl, who gave a sudden chortle, and clapped her sticky hands.

Joan turned to look back at the soldier, who was just about to spark up. He took the hint, retrieving the packet of fags from his pocket and offering it to the woman, who said, how very kind of you, and took one. Joan swapped places with the woman, and the soldier lit both of their cigarettes. Joan started playing 'round and round the garden, went a teddy bear' with the little girl's hand. After a few moments, the soldier cleared his throat and said he'd better get on, his stop was due soon, edged past them, and strode off to the next carriage.

'You missed your chance there, ducks,' said the woman, grinning at her and flicking ash onto the corridor floor.

'Maybe,' said Joan, hugging the little girl and looking out of the window. The sky was turning blue in the distance, as the clouds cleared: grey-blue, like an airman's uniform – like Rob's uniform. 'Maybe, or maybe not,' she said, as the train sped on.

'Here we are,' said Bea, stopping outside the door of a tiny terrace. Joan could hear laughter from inside, and music from the radio. 'The door's unlocked. You go on in, they know you're coming. I'm just off to the chippy – the twins finished the bread and there's nothing in the larder.'

'I'll come with you. Let me get the chips,' said Joan.

'No, you're our guest.'

'But I didn't bring anything with me. I feel like I should have brought a box of chocolates or something.'

'You seen many boxes of chocolates in the shops lately? Even if you did have the coupons.'

'Well, let me get the chips, at least.'

'Oh, go on, then. Leave your bag on the step. No one will take it from outside ours.'

The chippy was round the corner, past the pub. There was

no moon. Most people had already blacked out, even though it wasn't quite dark yet. They picked their way over the cracked paving slabs, passing mounds of rubble and gaps in the terrace where the cloudy twilit sky and the wreckage of bombed out houses formed a grey collage of misshapes.

'You got it bad in the Blitz then?' said Joan.

'Who didn't?' said Bea, tramping along beside her.

'Why weren't your little brothers and sisters all evacuated?'

'They tried. We should have been, but Ma wouldn't let them go. She said nobody was taking her babies away from her.'

They walked on, passing the black pub doors, rimmed with amber light and leaking piano music and singing.

'You had a good time at Edie's?' said Bea. Joan nodded. She didn't want to be disloyal. She didn't want to say that Edie's house was both the largest and the loneliest home she'd ever visited.

Inside the chippy, it was warm and light and smelled of hot fat and vinegar. Joan squinted her eyes against the sudden brightness. She began to order nine bags of chips but Bea said that the twins could bloody well share, after all the bread they'd scoffed, so she ordered eight bags from a man with a droopy moustache and a missing tooth, called Mr Lavery.

'You sure about this, Joan?' said Bea, when Mr Lavery had totalled up. Joan smiled and nodded, even though she was thinking, bang goes that powder compact I was saving up for.

Mr Lavery took her money with an air of sadness, and asked Bea how she was getting on in the ATS. Bea said very well, thanks for asking, Mr Lavery, grabbing the hot paper packets of chips and nudging Joan towards the door.

Yesterday's newspapers bled ink all over the chips and stained their fingers as they rushed back to Bea's house through the darkening streets.

Inside, they were assailed by children. There seemed to be faces and hands everywhere as the chip bags were grabbed and fought over. Bea introduced her to them all, but the names swirled and flew and Joan knew she'd never remember them. Voices yelled and laughed and nothing stayed still. Bea cuffed a couple of them for not saying thank you for the chips, and then suddenly everyone fell silent. A figure had appeared at the bottom of the stairs: a wiry, knotted woman. The children melted out of the way as she moved towards Joan.

'It's nice to meet a friend of our Bea's,' she said, wiping her hand on her apron before holding it out. The handshake was tight and swift. 'How do you like your tea, girl?'

As Bea's mother turned to go and put the kettle on, it was as if the room came to life behind her. It reminded Joan of a game from school called Grandmother's Footsteps, where everyone froze when Grandmother turned to face them. Bea's mum had the kettle on the hob and was getting out the tea caddy when there was the sound of a baby crying. Joan saw the mound of blankets in the armchair begin to writhe, and a little foot kick out.

'I'll sort her. You do the tea,' said Bea's mum, walking over to the waking baby. She picked it up out of the nest of covers and brought it over to Joan.

'This is our youngest, Bea's little sister, Valerie,' she said, holding the wailing child.

'She's adorable,' said Joan, looking at the fierce-eyed girl with the wild black curls. When baby Valerie saw Joan, she stopped crying and thrust out a plump paw. Joan took it, felt the little fingers curl like shrimps. Val's face was red from tears. Bea's mum reached down to where an open packet of chips lay on the kitchen table and took one out. The baby abruptly dropped Joan's finger and reached for the chip. Bea's mum broke it in half, blew on it and gave it to Val, who shoved it straight into her wet little mouth.

'She's a good eater,' said Bea's mum. Joan nodded. Then, not knowing what else to do, she sat down at the kitchen table. Bea finished making the tea and brought it over. She passed a cup to Joan but put her own down on the table next to the chips. Then she turned to her mum, holding out her arms.

'I'll take her for a bit, Ma. Give you a break,' she said.

'Not while she's eating,' said her mum, turning away and reaching down for another chip for the baby.

Joan saw how Bea touched the baby's cheek with the edge of her forefinger and stroked it, quickly, while her mum was turned away, and she saw a look of longing flit over her face. Then, Bea sat down opposite Joan and pulled a packet of chips towards her. The fat and vinegar had bled into the type, but Joan could still read what was printed on the crumpled chip paper: GUNNER GIRL DEAD IN PORTSMOUTH RAID, said the blurred headline, the ink bleeding onto the chips.

'Look at that,' she said, pointing. Bea turned the packet of chips round, read the words. She looked across at Joan, but neither of them spoke. Then she cleared her throat and licked the inky grease off her fingertips.

'Let's get down the pub after this,' Bea said. 'Vi's behind the bar tonight, and I could murder a beer.'

When Joan opened her eyes, she couldn't remember where she was. The colours were all wrong; nothing was in the right place. It wasn't the grey-khaki of the Nissen hut or the cool yellow of Edie's spare room, either. Here everything was dark red and brown – she was somewhere else.

She closed her eyes, feeling sick-dizzy, but there in her mind's eye were clouds of powdery dust, and red hair, fanned out on shattered floorboards, sticky and matted with blood and grit. She opened her eyes again, a pain stabbing her temple, and there was a mantelpiece with a broken teapot and a faded print of a vase of flowers, and bare brick walls. She felt nausea rise up her throat. Her head was thumping and she had a raging thirst. It felt like someone was poking her in the behind with an umbrella handle. Thuds and muffled shouts came from overhead. Why was her cheek so cold? And what was that thing poking her? She moved her face away from the chill and saw ox-blood-coloured tiles and an empty hearth. She felt down behind her. It was an umbrella, an unfurled umbrella, still damp with raindrops. She was so thirsty; her tongue clung to the roof of her mouth. Her eyes wouldn't focus properly – everything looked as if it were covered in Vaseline. She pulled her throbbing head up and saw that she was still fully clothed, in her greatcoat, with a blanket of crocheted squares half-covering her legs, one of which was wedged under the armchair. What was that smell? She heard the thump of footfalls on the stairs and pushed herself up quickly – too quickly – everything lurched, including her stomach.

'Lor' what a night! You all right, girl?' It was Bea. Joan shook her head. She appeared to have lost the ability to speak. 'Get yourself out in the lav before the others. I'll get the kettle on,' said Bea, pushing her in the direction of the back door. 'Oh, and give us your coat. I'll scrub it and iron it dry before you get the bus. No one will be able to tell, don't worry.'

No one will be able to tell what? thought Joan, stumbling down the back steps towards the outside toilet.

Maybe this was a bad idea, thought Joan, as the bus swung round. The driver honked his horn at the stray donkey that appeared on the corner. Joan heard it braying over the noise of the engine and watched it clatter off towards an open orchard gate into the green-tipped rows of apple trees. She was late, and she was hung over and she hadn't wanted it to be like this. Last night came back to her in jagged pieces:

'And a gin and lime for the little lady,' the barman calling out.

'A gin and lime for the lady!' Bea mimicking, 'Ain't I a lady, Alfie?'

'Not much of one, from what I've heard.' Vi, behind the bar, nudging the barman, and raucous laughter all round.

'You can shut your cakehole, Violet Mary Smith!' Bea hollering, and Vi blowing a kiss from behind the bar. More laughter, and the sour taste of the gin in her throat.

She remembered that, at least.

Joan was thrown to one side again as the bus hurled around another country chicane. Were there no straight roads in Kent? She swallowed and pulled out one of the humbugs that Bea had given her before she left.

Bea saying: 'Whatever happened to port and lemon?'

'I'm not that type.'

'Like hell you're not.' Bea, crossing her arms. 'Since you dumped Rob you've had a different lad every week, almost.'

'Have not. Anyway, I didn't dump him; he stood me up.'

'You think I'm stupid, girl?'

The bus was half full, mostly with middle-aged ladies with baskets, but there were a few airmen, too. The women were gossiping noisily, but the airmen were all silent, staring vacantly out over the countryside. Joan rubbed her temple, where it throbbed, trying to remember exactly how she came to be here, on this bus. What else had happened in the pub?

Warm and humid, horse brasses on the dark wood and sawdust on the floor. A man in brown lurching past, knocking her elbow – 'Sorry darlin', – eyes swivelling, red-rimmed. 'Lemme get y'another.'

'I'm fine, really.' Her dabbing at the wet patch on her chest, the man looking down at where the drink had spilled. 'No, no, no, I insist, Alfie, get a double for the laydee!' And her laughing and letting him, her head starting to swim, tipping her head back and letting the laughter rip out, as if the vast black skies overhead really didn't exist.

The bus swerved and growled on, until at last they reached West Malling, where all the ladies got off, waddling and clucking up the High Street. The bus carried on. The worn seats had once been plush but were now threadbare and brownish, with circular cigarette burns. Her coat was still damp, but at least the smell had gone. Joan fumbled with her gas mask and found her packet of cigarettes. She went to light one but there were no matches. What had she done with her matches?

'Knees up Muvver Braaaahn!' Spittle flecking against her cheek and the tuneless blaring of the man and linking arms with him and Bea and kicking out her legs in time to the piano. A chair kicked over, the crash of a glass, yelp of a dog. Then the piano plink-plonking the intro to 'When the Red, Red Robin Comes Bob, Bob Bobbing Along' and everyone joining in, and her gaze in an unsteady tunnel vision, like a searchlight, wavering round the room, looking for the missing piece of jigsaw puzzle.

Some of the silent airmen got off when the bus stopped in a lane and the driver called out 'Douce's Manor'. Out of the window, Joan glimpsed a butter-coloured mansion house amid some trees. Now there was just her and a couple of airmen left. The bus rumbled on.

Dropping her arm out of Bea's, not dancing any more, a kind of clench-ache inside: Robin. 'Oh, for God's sake, girl, why don't you phone him? There's a phone box on the corner' – Bea reading her thoughts. 'Because he won't be there, will he? He'll be somewhere over bloody Germany,' spitting the words out, picking her half-empty glass off the table and downing the last of the drink: the sour taste of gin in her mouth. 'There's a bus to West Malling first thing. Phone the camp, tell them to let him know, come on.'

She took out her lipstick. There was almost nothing left in the little gold tube. It was like an empty shell casing. She had to wipe her little finger right inside the gilt case to find a smear of lipstick. She rubbed it onto her lips and pouted, hoping it was evenly spread – she didn't have a mirror. Joan wished she'd had more time to sort herself out at Bea's, but there'd only been that outside toilet, and then she'd had to run for the bus. She felt like death. She probably looked like death. Even if Robin were there, he'd probably take one look at her and regret it. Joan clicked the lid back on the lipstick and put it away.

Out into the cold night. The phone box smelling of wee. A lit match to try to find the coin slot, the coin falling again and again on the wet concrete floor. Bea holding the match, guiding her hand. Different voices, tinny and far away, asking questions: Robin Nelson. Tell him I'll be there in the morning. May I ask who's calling? Vanessa. Tell him it's Vanessa. Bea snatching the phone off her. Joan. Her name's Joan Tucker and she'll be on the first bus from town in the morning. If you could let him know. Thank you.

There were no road signs but the remaining airmen were starting to stir, grabbing kit bags from under their seats. She was thrown forward as the bus lurched to a halt, banging her forehead on the seat in front.

Out of the phone box and into the windy night. The stars swirling and twirling like sparklers and a churning down in her stomach. And Bea asking, Who the hell is Vanessa? And Joan saying I don't know, I don't know, but I think I'm going to be sick.

'Yer 'ere!' yelled the driver. She looked out of the window, rubbing her bruised forehead. The bus stop was crowded with a huge grey-blue mass of jostling airmen. Was one of them Rob? 'You getting off or not, love?' bellowed the driver.

'Yes,' she said, getting up and pulling her bag out from under the seat. As she got off the bus, the crowd of waiting airmen funnelled in like a bole tide. Then the bus sped off and she was left alone at the bus stop outside RAF West Malling. All the airmen had gone. Robin wasn't there. She still felt sick and had a headache and now she was stuck out here in the middle of bloody nowhere. The camp gates were just behind her and she could see the boxy accommodation blocks and the white two-storey control tower. The clouds still hung low, blocking out the sunshine.

I knew this was a bad idea, she thought, looking round. She checked the bus timetable. The next bus was in two hours. She could walk back to West Malling in that time. Well, if Robin wasn't here, that's just what she'd have to do. After all, she'd been on longer route marches in training. She'd be able to get lunch in West Malling and then get the bus back to Bea's. If any cars passed she might be able to thumb a lift. Joan reached a junction and was just trying to remember which way the bus went when she heard footfalls on the tarmac. She turned and saw an airman running towards her, arms outstretched, just like before. Only this time, he didn't shout, 'Get down!' and rugby-tackle her to the ground, he shouted, 'Joan, Joan!'

* * *

They were halfway across the field when the rain started. The first drops were like soft tears, but it soon began to chuck it down. Rob could feel the rivulets running down the nape of his neck and between his shoulder blades as he bent forward and pushed his legs onwards up the slope. They were still hand in hand, but her fingers, wet, slithered from his and they carried on alone, trudging up the muddy hill. They had already been walking for half an hour. Rob thought about cross-country runs at school. The path was beginning to turn slippery underfoot, the brown mud sliding under his boots. He regretted suggesting the walk, but what else could they do? They only had a couple of hours – flight checks started at three. If only he'd known she was coming. He didn't get the message until NAAFI break, and even then, all he was told was that some woman was turning up on the bus, no name. He thought it might be Pammie. That was why he hadn't rushed to the bus stop, had waited to see who got off.

'I'm sorry,' he said.

'It's all right,' she replied, turning towards him, her hair flattened wetly against her forehead. 'It's not your fault it's raining.' Then she looked beyond him, into the grey-green countryside. A crow flew past, battling the weather, looking like an ink splatter across the blurred watercolour landscape.

'Over there,' he said, pointing at the smudged outline of a building, and they both broke into a run. It was the chapel where Harper got married. They reached it together: dripping granite, a tiny spire like a smokestack and a gravel path winding round to the front door. They paused, panting, in the dry space in front of the oak doorway.

'I'm sorry, too,' she said, pushing her wet hair away from her face. 'I'm sorry about just turning up like this. You must think – I don't know what you must think of me.'

'I think you're the sort of girl who deserves more than this. I wanted our first date to be somewhere decent: I wanted to take you somewhere nice in London, that time. But now you're here, and all you get is a trudge through the rain.'

'Well, it's all your fault then, isn't it?' said Joan. 'What are we going to do, put you on a charge?' She looked sideways at him, a half-smile on her lips, and he remembered the feel of her as he'd held her, after the bomb at Western Way.

They were piled in so close to the door that their uniforms were touching all down one side, khaki against blue, damp cloth against damp cloth. He could smell the rain and the mud, but overlaid was the smell of her, the same as it had been that November night. She was soaked through. She started to shiver. Rob put an arm around her shoulders. She didn't say anything; she let it rest there. He felt her lean into him and let his head drop a little, chin against her wet cheek. They stood looking out at the sheeting grey rain, and he could feel the warmth of her against him.

'We need to get you out of the cold,' he said. He tried the brass door handle, tarnished brown in the dark wood. It turned and he gave the door a shove with his shoulder and the door opened. He stood to one side for her: 'Ladies first.'

Joan stepped inside, ahead of him, walking up the aisle,

shoes tapping on the flagstones. He watched her, watched the way her uniform caught the shape of her body as she moved into the dark church. He could hear the rain on the slates and the wind making the timbers strain, but inside was calm: the air was stilled liquid; it had a milky weight to it. There was a soft thud as he closed the door behind them. She waited for him by the front pews, opposite the little altar.

He looked around. It was how he remembered from Harper's wedding. The windows like portholes showing the rain-lashed sky. The altar covered in a cream cloth with a wrought-iron cross on top and burgundy velvet folded next to a pile of hymn books below the carved pulpit. There was a tiny stained-glass window behind the altar: circular, with a leaded red rose.

He caught up with her, stood beside her, sensed her breathing. She didn't turn. Neither of them spoke. The air was like a musty embrace, holding them and silencing them. They were alone, together. After a while he asked if she wanted a smoke.

'Why not?' she said.

He had some in his pocket, but they were damp from the rain. She had dry ones in her gas-mask case. There was something else in her gas-mask case, too.

'You did get my postcard then?'

She nodded, but that was all, and clicked the case shut. 'Player's all right? I've got no matches, though,' she held out the packet.

He took out his lighter, flicked the top open and leant

across. She had to move in close. He watched the yellow flame lick the tip of her cigarette, as she sucked the life into it, grey to amber, her lips parting as she inhaled. He felt himself harden. He pulled away, lighting his own fag, telling himself to calm down. They were in a church, for Christ's sake. When he looked back, she was still shivering, soaked through.

'Cold?' he said.

'I'll be fine.'

'Here. . .' He started to take off his flight jacket, jamming the fag in his mouth as he pulled his arms from the sleeves.

'You're very kind,' she said. He came round behind her, wrapped the jacket over her shoulders like a shawl, thought about how it would feel to kiss the nape of her neck, just there.

'But won't you get cold now?' She looked at him as he came back round to face her. Those eyes.

'I'm used to the cold,' he said.

They stood looking at each other, not touching. They both brought the cigarettes to their lips at the same time: touch lips, suck, inhale, pause, exhale. Their smoke rose up to meet the shadows.

'My pal got married here,' he said. 'I was best man.'

Suddenly, he wanted to tell her. To tell her everything: about Harper, and Harper's wedding, about the empty chairs in the mess at breakfast times, about the fear that never really went away, about the panic that he crumpled and stuffed into a choking hole in his consciousness every single bloody time he set foot on the runway.

He wanted to tell her, so he did, not caring if she thought him a sissy. The words fell like footfalls on tarmac, one after another, until the end of the road. It felt important to say it all, out loud, because he wanted her to know all of him, without secrets. And here was the right place, in this church, where he'd watched his best friend get married, and where he came to pray every Sunday, even though he knew the futility of it, even though he knew it was all just chance in the end.

She listened, saying nothing, but her gaze never left his. When he finished, the air between them was taut and full.

She parted her lips and held out her arms. He put both hands round her waist, pulling her towards him. It felt like the most natural thing in the world. She was right up against him; he could feel her breasts, her thighs, her breath against his neck. His lips moved across her cheek, and the flight jacket slithered to the floor. His mouth met hers. They were suddenly greedy for each other, gorging on tongues. He could feel her nipples hard under the roughness of her uniform and she pressed herself against him and pulled him closer in and his hands were there and there, underneath now, catching on buttons and the warmth of her flesh and the smell of her and the softness and sweet wetness of her.

'Are you sure?' he said.

'Yes,' she said. And he knew she meant it, because this might be their only chance. Because tomorrow might not happen, for either of them.

He lifted her leg so one foot rested on the pew and pushed up her skirt and her mouth was on his, open and wet, and she was tugging at his belt and her hand was on his cock and his thumb was pushing the thin fabric aside and she was so wet and he held himself ready to push into her and she let out a moan and then the rush, the rush of it. No, too soon. He groaned, slumped forward onto her, cock wet and spent already.

'What is it?'

'I'm sorry.'

And he pulled away, did up his fly, burning with shame. She looked at him and he couldn't meet her eye and he thought, no, this is not how it goes. This is not how it ends.

So he slid down, face against the rough khaki, down, underneath her skirt, until his face was there, right there, and he kissed her there, and licked the warm wetness, and she gasped. He carried on until she was shaking so much that she had to lie, on top of the flying jacket, on the cold stone flags as he knelt between her legs, licking and sucking at the sweetness of her until her back arched and she shuddered and her cries echoed out into the empty church. Then he kissed her and held her and didn't let her go.

Afterwards, she fell asleep and he lay watching her, tracing her features with his gaze and committing them to memory: curled lashes, parted lips, damp hair curling as it dried. Her bare legs goose pimpled and her knickers were wet between her thighs. He took off his jumper, covered her legs as best he could. It hadn't been like that with Pammie. They had always been drunk, and it had been quick and furtive, as if he was stealing something. This was different, like a gift.

He took out another cigarette. The lighter flared up in the half-dark. He was cold without his jacket or jumper, but the smoke was warming. Rob blew smoke rings and watched them disintegrate and disappear above the darkened pews. It was silent in the church now. Even the rain and wind had ceased – the storm had blown over. Light suddenly filtered in though the tiny windows: streams of sunshine casting a metallic filigree over the scene. Rob sat still, finishing his smoke, feeling as if he were caged in a net of gold, wishing he could stay there for ever.

Joan was alone at the bus stop. Behind were RAF West Malling and an achingly beautiful sky: high and blue and cloudless, the pale sun just beginning to dip towards the horizon. She wrapped the flying jacket closely to her, turning away and focusing on the knot of lanes that would take her away. He'd gone by the time she woke up, and the sun was streaming in through the stained glass, like boiled sweets in a jar. Her head was cushioned on his flying jacket, his jumper covering her legs. His scent. The taste of him, the feel of him – she shivered, but not from the cold.

The lanes were empty. She shifted from foot to foot, her stockinged toes rubbing against the still-wet leather. Starlings flocked and swirled overhead. In the late-afternoon sunshine, the fields and trees were vivid green, the shadows endless and black. She heard the choke and growl as each of the plane's engines started up on the distant runway behind her. She took a sharp breath in. Rob would be there now; he had flight checks in the afternoon, another sortie tonight. She was alone at the bus stop, but the bus was just rounding the corner and coming to a halt in front of her. It was the same driver from the morning: lardy jowls and brown teeth.

'You've changed,' he said, as she stepped on.

'Yes,' she said, feeling the warm sheepskin against her neck, 'West Malling station, please,' she handed over her money.

'Try not to worry, love,' he said, passing the change in his fat paw. 'Crying won't help him.'

'I'm not crying,' she said. She threw herself onto the threadbare plush seat and opened her gas mask. There were still two cigarettes, but no matches. She'd forgotten she had no matches. But there, a lighter: Rob had left his lighter in her case. No note, but she had his jacket, his lighter. It was silver and it had his initials etched on the front: RAN. She wondered what the A stood for, and stroked the smooth metal with her fingertip. Then she clicked the lighter open and lit her fag, touching her top lip with her tongue, remembering the feel of him, what happened in the church. It had never been like that before, with a boy – with a man. As the bus pulled away and drove on, she watched the RAF base dwindle to a dot, and the engine sounds become fainter and fainter until it was all just a memory. The rain clouds had gone and the sky was clear ahead, eastwards. She wondered if the storm clouds had cleared over Germany, too.

Chapter 19

Bea had arrived home at the same time as the postman. She saw him beetling down from the other end of the street, lanky legs like a stick insect, worrying the too-small bicycle. She was still smiling to herself about Joan, the silly mare. What a state she was in. Lor', she couldn't take her drink, that one: flirting and falling all over the place and telling everyone to call her by a different name. What was it? Vivian? No, not that: Vanessa. Yes, Vanessa, that was it. Still, at least she'd finally got her to get back in touch with her sweetheart. It was too good a chance to miss, what with his airbase being nearby. Bea couldn't understand why Joan messed him about so much. He sounded lovely, her Rob. He was an airman, and she got letters from him almost every day. Not like—

'Someone's popular,' said the lanky postman, as she met him at the front step. He handed her a pile of envelopes. He wasn't so much a postman as a postboy, she thought, noticing the spots on his chin and the bobbing Adam's apple. 'Vi about?' he added, with studied nonchalance.

'Depends who's asking,' said Bea. The postie looked down at her, blinking. 'She'll be behind the bar later – why don't you catch her then?' she added, wondering whether he was even old enough to go in the pub. Come to that, neither was Vi, not that anyone bothered to check. The boy cleared his throat and glanced hopefully to the upstairs window. Bea didn't have the heart to tell him that he was directing his lust towards the room her mother shared with the four little ones. Bea shuffled through the letters in the pile: two envelopes, a postcard and an aerogramme. Who'd send an aerogramme? Pa's unit was still on the east coast somewhere, wasn't it?

'Well, I'd better finish me round,' said the postie, not moving.

'Yes, you better had,' said Bea, wanting to give him a shove. 'I'll tell her you asked after her. What's your name?'

'Oh, no, don't say anything,' said the postie, getting back onto his tiny bike. 'I'll – I'll see her in the pub,' he called out, as he wobbled off the kerb and away. Not if she sees you first, thought Bea, turning her attention back to the pile of post: a bill – overdue, with 'final reminder' stamped on the front in red; Ma would curse her for bringing that into the house. Bea shoved it through the letterbox; let someone else be the bearer of bad news. Next was a postcard from a cousin who'd been conscripted into the Land Army and sent off to Northumberland. It didn't say 'wish you were here' but instead said, 'wish I wasn't here, it's bloody awful I can tell you' – she pushed that through the letterbox, too. There was a fat cream envelope next. She saw Pa's looping script. He'd have enclosed funny cartoons for the twins, most likely. That one went through the letterbox and she heard it land with a plop inside. And then all that was left was the air letter. It was dirty and crumpled, the colour of sand. She recognised the handwriting, slanting to the left, falling back on itself. On the reverse was printed in green 'I certify that the contents of this envelope refer to nothing but private and family matters' and a space for a signature. She looked at the signature: J McBride.

Jock? She held the aerogramme in front of her and turned it back over. The writing seemed to dance about, but then she realised it was her shaking hands, so she rolled it up, small, and tucked it inside her fist. Her Jock. He hadn't forgotten her.

The postie was nearly out of sight, now. Across the street, a ginger tom picked its way over the rubble where the Laverys' house had stood. The sun made feeble attempts to break through the clouds. The whistling fishmonger was undoing his shutters up the other end of the street. Everything was as it should be. Nothing had changed, except this. She tightened her hand on the scrap of paper, holding it safe. I knew it, she thought. I knew he hadn't deserted me. Not my Jock. She could hear the sound of her own breathing: rushing in and out like waves.

Bea walked across the empty early-morning street to the bombsite. Then she scuffed and tripped across the rubble to the place at the back where the Laverys' old outhouse was still half standing, a wall and a mound of slippery bricks. She slid round behind it, in the space where the weak sunshine hit the remaining brickwork. She found a large slab and sat down, with her back to the lukewarm wall and uncurled her fist. Carefully, she unpeeled the gritty edges of the aerogramme. And then there it was, lying open on her lap. She rubbed away the pricking hot tears that came unbidden. She couldn't see to read if she was crying. What did he say?

My darling Bea,

This is the last time I'll write. I have almost given up hope of hearing from you. All the times I write and you never reply, so I've told myself that this will be the last time. I'm doing my best to win this ruddy war as soon as, and get back to you. But for now I'm stuck in this stinking hole and I don't even know if you're still alive.

If I don't get a letter from you now, I'll know it's over. Either something has happened to you, or you've found another man. I don't know which will hurt the most.

Why did you never write? I wanted to know how you was, how our baby was? Did something happen to the baby? I kept thinking maybe you'd been evacuated, after all. But why didn't you write me your address?

Please God, if this ever reaches you, Bea, know that I love you and think about you all the time. I keep your photograph with me, in my breast pocket, above my heart. It's been my lucky charm. We've been in some scrapes out here in [here the word was scribbled out in blue pencil, and Bea realised she wasn't the only one to have read these words – his letter had been censored by his CO], *but your face has kept me safe so far.*

If you get this letter, my darling, know that when I get out of this place, I'm going to make an honest woman of you, and get a proper home for the three of us: you, me and our baby.

Please write, Bea, even if it's bad news. Put me out of my misery.

All my love, forever, Jock.

She re-read it three times, and then let it lie on her lap. The sun sliced yellow through the grey clouds. She heard the sound of a cat mewing. There was a choking inhalation as the first sob came, and then the others tumbled out, a torrent of tears of relief and regret, hot and fast, her breath heaving: Jock. I did write. I wrote and wrote and thought you never wrote back. What happened? Why didn't you get my letters? Why didn't I get yours? But you're alive. Thank God, you're alive.

At last, the tears subsided. She was wrung out and empty. She wiped her nose on her sleeve and smoothed out the letter. One letter going missing was an accident. But all of them? All of them to him from her? And all of them from her to him? She thought back. She used to write and give her letter to Mrs Morley, the postmistress, who came in to have her tea leaves read on a regular basis. Ma knew Mrs Morley well, on account of the leaves, and she never charged her for the readings. Bea thought of them together at the table, talking in hushed voices over the teacups. They were thick as thieves, Ma and the postmistress.

Bea remembered her own eighteenth birthday, back in November. She remembered how Ma had surprised her with a birthday card from Pa that she'd kept hidden. Until her chest got bad, Ma had always been up first in the morning, collecting the post. It was Ma who hid things and kept secrets. It was Ma.

The realisation was as swift and painful as bleach on a cut: giving Baby up, joining the ATS, thinking something had happened to Jock. It was all Ma's doing, wasn't it? Bea looked up and saw the ginger tom tiptoe towards her over the bricks. She groped with the inchoate mass of emotions rising up. But what she was starting to feel wasn't anger or grief at her mother's betrayal. As the cat came closer, she tickled him under the chin and he began to purr. The sensation she had was hard and high in her chest: defiance.

'Enough,' said Bea aloud, but the cat just carried on purring, stretching out in the sudden sunshine.

'Where've you been all this time?' said Vi. The clock tower was striking ten as Bea closed the front door behind her.

'Well, I had to see Joan get on the bus safely, didn't I?' said Bea, pushing past her sister and going over to the stove. She put the kettle on and took one of the glass baby bottles out from under the sink, along with a rubber teat.

'It's already been done,' said Vi. 'Rita took it up ages ago, while you were seeing Joan off. How's your head, by the way?'

'Fine,' said Bea, measuring the white powder from the tin with the special spoon. May came in the back door with a skipping rope and Vi shooed her back out again. The twins were fighting under the kitchen table.

'You look rough as a dog, though,' said Vi, starting to pull out her curling papers. 'Anyway, I'm off in a bit. I'm on early shift today. See the twins don't go down the docks again, won't you?' Bea nodded, waiting for the water to heat on the stove. 'I told you, Rita's already done that,' said Vi, scrunching up the curling papers and tossing them inside the empty biscuit tin on the shelf under the mirror, where the plaster was all cracked.

'Well, I'm doing another one,' said Bea. 'For when I take her out.'

'Looks like rain; I wouldn't bother,' said Vi.

'I can take her to a café if it starts.'

John came through, carrying a vast piece of twisted metal, and Vi told him to take his bits of bomb back outside, where they belonged. She rolled her eyes at Bea, teasing her curls into place. 'Ma won't like you taking Baby Val out,' she said.

Ma can go to hell, Bea thought. Aloud she said: 'How is she this morning?'

'Not up yet. It's bad today.'

'Baby Val up there with her?'

'Mmm-hmm . . .' Vi nodded, mouth full of Kirby grips. Bea poured the warm water into the bottle, fixed on the teat and gave it a shake. Then she tested the temperature on her wrist. 'Ma doesn't bother with that, now, she's almost weaned,' said Vi, reaching for her coat, Bea's old coat, pale and threadbare at the cuffs. 'The others have all had tea and May went out to the baker's to get some bread, so don't listen if they come in asking for breakfast, they've had it. I'll be back at three but can you see if you can get through any of the washing before the rain starts? I don't reckon Ma will be down today; have you heard her chest?' She was pulling on her coat. 'Are you all right, Bea? You're awful quiet today.'

'Probably just a hangover,' replied Bea.

Vi came over and gave her a squeeze. 'It's lovely having my big sister home,' she said. 'We all miss you when you're not here.'

'Even Baby Val?'

'Especially Baby Val,' said Vi, squeezing her tighter. Jock's letter, tucked inside her shirt, was flattened against her flesh as Vi hugged her.

'Vi?' said Bea, as they pulled apart.

'What?' There was so much to say. Jock was alive. Ma had hid his letters. Jock was going to come back and marry her. Baby could be hers again. They would all be together. Vi was buttoning up her coat. 'What is it, Bea?' Vi reached into her coat pocket and pulled out a tiny tin of Vaseline and dabbed it on her lips.

'Nothing,' said Bea. 'You'd better get a move on or you'll be late for work.'

Vi smiled and was gone and Bea was alone downstairs. She could hear the others outside: May's feet tapping out a game of hopscotch and the twins calling to their friends across the alleyway. Rita must be upstairs. She should go up and ask for her help with the washing. Ma would be up there, too, in bed with Baby Val.

The narrow staircase went steeply up into the darkness. There was nothing on the walls and the bricks were damp, the mortar soft, like the wet sand on the strand. Bea trailed one hand against the brickwork as she went up. In the other, she had Baby's bottle. The door to the big room was ajar. Even from the landing, Bea could hear Ma's breathing, like water draining from pebbles. Bea knocked once and pushed the door open. Baby Val was lying asleep in the covers next to Ma, her plump cheeks flushed and her eyelids fluttering in a dream. Ma's hair was loose: stringy ginger streaked with grey. Bea thought of the ginger tom and the broken bricks under the clouded sky. Ma looked tight and tired, the bed too big for her bony form.

'All right, girl?' she said. Her voice was low and hoarse. Then, noticing the bottle of milk. 'She's had it. I've put her down already.'

'I thought I'd take her out,' said Bea.

'It looks like rain,'

'We can go to a café if it does.'

'You got money to burn?' Bea took a step further into the room, closer to the pile of sheets, blankets and coats layered on the bed. Sunlight filtered weakly through the small window. There was the sound of a van droning along the street below. 'She should stay here at home with me,' said Ma.

Bea took another step in. There were dark circles under

215

Ma's eyes and her skin looked clammy. 'A bit of fresh air won't do her any harm,' said Bea, approaching the bed.

'She'll catch her death if it rains.'

'It'll be good for her to get out for a bit.'

'She should stop here, keep warm.' With one more step, Bea was at the bedside. 'Now just you listen to me, girl,' said Ma. Bea bent down towards the still-sleeping baby. 'You're not taking that child anywhere, d'you hear me?' Bea held the bottle in one hand but, with the other, she swept up the sleeping baby in one quick movement, up into her arms. Bea's arms were strong from shifting equipment at the battery, and her movements swift from training. Baby Val barely stirred as she lifted her up and with three quick steps was out of the door before Ma could even begin to push herself out of bed. 'Don't you dare, don't you bloody dare, girl!' Ma tried to shout, but her voice came out as a croak, and Bea was already at the bottom of the stairs.

Rita poked her head out from the other room. 'What's all the palaver?'

'Nothing,' said Bea. 'I'm just taking Baby Val out, that's all.' She grabbed the crocheted blanket from where it still lay, under the armchair, and had reached the front door before Ma even made it to the landing. She looked up as she left, saw Ma's stooping form, leaning on the door jam, glowering down the dark stairwell at them. Then she turned away and slammed the front door shut behind her.

Catch me if you can, she thought, shoving the bottle down in between her and the baby, holding little Val in the gap between her chin and the gas mask, clutching her tight, keeping her little warm head still and safe, close against her chest.

'You're coming with me, girl,' Bea said. Her footsteps were loud on the cracked paving slabs and the sunlight stabbed through the dark clouds as she ran.

'That's where your pa is,' Bea said. Baby was awake now, and Bea had her on one hip, the coloured blanket slung round both of them like a shawl. She pointed out past the hulking shapes of ships and down the estuary, where the water was a flat gunmetal grey. Seagulls swooped and cried, squabbling over scraps on the quayside. The air smelled of brine and diesel, and there was the sound of engines and of men shouting throatily from deck to shore. 'My pa – your granddad – he used to work here, before the war, and this is where your pa sailed from when he went away,' said Bea.

Baby said 'Da,' and swung out a little fist towards the ships and the sea. The sky was dark, clouds purplish, bruised. Bea shifted Baby to the other hip. They should probably get inside before it rained.

When she'd banged the front door shut and started running, she hadn't really thought about where to go. All she'd thought of was getting baby out of there, taking what was hers and leaving. But her footsteps carried her down the hill, down to the docks – forbidden by Ma because of the type of people that could be found there: drunks, tarts and worse. But Bea always felt drawn to the sea, to the places where solid met liquid and everything was possibility and hope. She took one last look towards the blurred horizon before turning away. Jock's letter crackled as she moved, hidden in the space between her shirt and her breast. Baby patted the place where it lay, and gurgled to herself, liking the funny sound and feel of crumpled paper under cloth.

The big Woolworth's was warm and dry. The crocheted blanket was damp, but they'd kept dry together underneath. Bea bought airmail paper and a pen and ink. She had just enough money left for a cup of tea and a little something for Baby. There was an old highchair in the café, with a faded picture of a baby donkey painted on it. Baby liked sitting up, on her own, watching everyone. She fed herself the pieces of ginger parkin that Bea broke up for her, and she guzzled down the bottle of milk.

Bea spread out the airmail paper on the table and dipped her new pen in the ink. She bit her lip, chewed the end of the pen and began to write. The paper was tissue-thin and the ink bled. She wrote as people came and went with sandwiches and tea and biscuits, and the ancient waitress wiped a dirty rag over the tabletops and complained loudly about her bunions. She wrote as the rain battered the windows like a thousand tiny fists and men scurried past in long coats with newspapers over their heads. She wrote as the man on the till smoked a cigarette out back while a queue built up at the counter. She wrote while the sun broke through and a rainbow appeared above the department store on the corner. By the time she finished, the faraway clock tower was chiming four and Baby's head rested on the front of the highchair tray, surrounded by crumbs and an empty bottle.

Bea posted the letter in the box outside the main post office in the High Street and paused, watching the scurrying figures all around, hugging her sleepy little girl in close. What to do now?

Chapter 20

She was about to knock on Bea's front door when she heard the shriek. Then there was a pause before the voices started: 'It's no more than you deserve, going off with her like that.'

'Did you think I'd run away with her?' – it was Bea's voice, muffled through the wood.

'Why would I think that?'

'I don't know; why would you think that?'

'Doncher talk to me like that, girl.'

'Like what?'

'Like you know fine well what. Unless you want another one?' – Bea's mum's voice, threatening.

Joan knocked, then, loudly, calling out, 'Hello, is anyone home?' As if she'd only just got to the door, as if she hadn't heard a thing. The door began to open and Vi's head poked out.

'Well, if it isn't Little Miss Gin-and-Lime,' she said, ushering Joan inside.

Joan closed the door behind her. They were all in there,

crowded into the front room. Bea and her mum were facing each other at the foot of the stairs, Bea holding Baby Val. The other children shadowed the walls and corners of the room, peeping out from dripping sheets slung over the empty play-pen or from behind the lone armchair. Nobody spoke until the baby began to cry and Bea's mum snatched her from Bea's arms, and began to climb up the steep stairs into the darkness, coughing. Bea watched her. From upstairs came the bang of a door closing, and the downstairs breathed back into life. Marbles spilled out across the bare floorboards, windows steamed with condensation, wet washing dripped from chair backs and children squabbled and chattered. Joan saw Vi raise her eyebrows at Bea, but Bea just looked away. Joan stood awkwardly until there was the sound of the kettle whistling on the hob, and Vi asked if she wanted a cuppa and Joan said yes please. At last, Bea turned to look at her.

'Hungry?' she said.

'Yes,' said Joan.

'You can help me make tea for this lot, then,' said Bea. 'Vi's got to get back for her shift.'

'Slice it thin,' said Bea. Joan looked down at the bread: just over half a loaf for the lot of them. She sliced so thin that the centre of each slice was translucent, crumbling. The hard slab of lard would never spread on that, she thought. Bea was pouring water into a large saucepan. One of her little sisters, the one who looked about twelve, was looking out of the window.

'Mr Lavery's got a new walking stick,' she said, turning back, plait twitching like a cat's tail between her shoulders.

'You stay away from Mr Lavery, you hear?' said Bea, counting spoonfuls of tea from the caddy into the pan. 'Look what I got, May.' She held up a tin of condensed milk.

'Cor!' said May. 'Posh tea!' and she ran off to tell the others.

'Get that from work?' said Joan.

'I told someone in the cookhouse something they wanted to hear, is all,' said Bea, scooping the condensed milk into the pan. 'It's nice for them to have a treat, sometimes.'

Joan counted the slices of bread: just enough, so long as someone could have the crust.

'Was he pleased to see you?' said Bea, suddenly, and Joan realised she was talking about Rob.

'Yes,' said Joan. 'We went for a walk. We – we went to a church.' That was all she said, but Bea gave her a sharp, sidelong look, and she felt she must have given something away. 'You?' she said hastily, before Bea asked more questions.

'I went for a walk, too,' said Bea. 'With Baby Val.'

'Nice to spend some time with her?' said Joan.

'Yes. And I caught up with someone I hadn't heard from for a while,' said Bea, staring down at the boiling tea.

'Will you see them again soon?' said Joan.

'I'm sure I'll see them again,' said Bea, stirring the leaves. 'And Rob – when will you see him again?'

'I don't know,' said Joan. And then the windowpanes quivered and there was a roar overhead.

'They're on their way!' yelled one of the boys, and the

others made zooming sounds, running into the kitchen with arms outstretched, round and round the kitchen table making stuttering machine-gun fire and crashing salivery bomb sounds. The engine noises got louder, mingling until they were one huge roar and then there was the thunder as the planes bansheed overhead, like a flock of murderous geese, flying away from the pink-tinted evening countryside, away from the golden skies and the setting sun, right over her head, east and on across the channel and over to Germany. She resisted the urge to put her fingers in her ears. She wanted all of the painful loudness, all of it: one of those planes was Rob's. Round and round ran the noisy boys, as the sound of engines droned away eastwards.

'David, John and Bertie, you get out of it or I'll be giving you what for!' yelled Bea, but they took no notice, running round and round until one of them stuttered machine-gun sounds at the others and they ran in decreasing circles, yelling out and falling, roiling on the threadbare rug by the fireplace. Joan watched the boys scream, falling down onto the floor.

'I don't know when I'll see him again,' she repeated.

'Lord, that's all we need,' said Bea, as the siren started. They were halfway up the street, on the way to the pub. 'Better get down the shelter.' Bea pulled her sleeve and led her through an alley and across a piece of rough ground. Joan couldn't see a thing and trotted blindly, trying to keep up. Bea was swearing softly under her breath. 'Down you go,' she said aloud, stopping suddenly. 'The steps are a bit slippy, so watch yourself, girl.' she gave Joan a nudge. 'I'll just wait up here for the others.'

Joan inched down the damp steps, keeping one hand against the rough brick wall for guidance. She still couldn't see properly, edging down into the tarry blackness. At the bottom, the air was clammy and smelled of old urine. She could just make out a door, and felt for the cool metal handle. She turned it and pushed inside. Was there a light switch? Her fingers fluttered against chipped plaster. Yes, here. She flicked it on and a single bulb cast a jaundiced light into the underground space: cracked yellow-cream paint, bare concrete floor, wooden benches pushed up against the walls, in the middle a broken brazier, spilling ash. Joan went to sit in the furthest corner.

It wasn't long before the door opened and the benches began to fill: women with knitting, a boy with a book, twin girls with a loop of string to play cat's cradle, a bony grey man whittled a stick with his penknife. They nodded at her as they filed in and sat down, but nobody said much. The wood creaked as a fat woman in curlers plumped down next to her. Eventually Bea appeared, trailing siblings. Finally, her mum arrived, carrying Baby Val, and shutting the door firmly behind her. Nobody talked of lighting the brazier, but it began to warm up anyway, once they'd all squeezed in. The air was thick with the smell of unwashed bodies.

'What happened to the wireless?' said Bea, sitting near the door. She pulled her crochet out of her coat pocket, fingers twitching round the red wool; hook flashing dully in the half-light.

'Mr Lavery—' May, Bea's little sister, began.

'You shut your trap about Mr Lavery,' Bea's mum hissed. Joan noticed how her breath wheezed. Someone tutted.

The siren had stopped now. 'Another false alarm,' sighed the fat woman in curlers, 'and my scones'll be ruined.'

But Joan knew it wasn't a false alarm. She always heard the planes before anyone else: a tinnitus-whine snaking closer. She thought about Rob, in his plane. She took her lipstick out of her gas-mask case and the lighter Rob had left there. She used the back of the lighter as a mirror, but her reflection was smudged and dull. She pursed her lips, pouting, hoping she hadn't gone over the edge. She put the lipstick and lighter back, and pulled his flying jacket tight against her chest.

The planes were getting closer, a humming vibration in the stale air. They could all hear it now. Joan saw people tilt their heads to one side, catching the distant noise, but nobody remarked on it. 'Where's Vi?' said Bea, suddenly.

'She'll be in the pub cellar,' said May.

'With Frank Timpson.' Rita snickered.

'Who's Frank Timpson when he's at home?' said Bea.

'Mrs Morley says he's a spiv!' Rita burst out, giggling.

'Vi and Frank, up a tree k-i-s-s-i-n-g,' started May.

'Give it a rest, May,' said Bea, glaring at her little sister.

The fat lady sighed again, shifting on her ample haunches. And the droning of the bombers was louder still. Suddenly, Joan couldn't bear it any longer. She stood up. 'Who's for a song?' she said, brightly. There were a few desultory nods. She forced herself to smile, make eye contact with them. The old man carried on whittling his wood, but the little girls with the cat's cradle clapped their hands. 'I'm no Vera Lynn, so I'll need all the help I can get!' she continued. Anything, anything to drown out the noise of the bloody bombers. 'Everyone know "Run Rabbit Run"?' May and Rita nodded, and Bea looked up from her crochet and smiled. 'Well, come on then, after three . . .' She didn't want to think about Rob, stuck in the sky over Germany, or the enemy bombs that were just about to come pelting down on them. Sometimes having a good time and forgetting about it all was the only thing to do.

'One, two, three!'

Chapter 21

Spring washed over London like a spritz of perfume. Hyde Park had been dug over for communal vegetable patches, and was now lush with marrows and new potatoes. In Kensington Gardens, netted-cane wigwams protected fruit bushes from birds, and the roses were in bloom.

'I say, we could really use some secateurs,' said Edie, sucking a dot of blood from a pricked fingertip.

Joan, holding a half-full basket of roses, laughed, tipping back her fair curls into the sunshine: 'I don't know why you're so set on doing this, anyway, Edie. Isn't it treason or something, stealing royal roses?'

'What, like killing swans?' said Edie, struggling again with the rose stem. 'I don't think so, dear. In any case, who'll notice? We're so tucked away here.' They were almost hidden, far beyond the Peter Pan statue, where a row of fruit canes bordered a hedge of rose bushes. Bumblebees tumbled and glanced off the roses. The sun was shining and the scent was glorious. 'Anyway, Bea deserves a bunch of flowers to cheer her up.'

'Kitchen fatigues are the worst,' Joan said, nodding. 'Last time, I peeled so many spuds, I thought I was going to turn into one.'

'I know – poor thing – and it wasn't her fault, really. She had to catch the post to get that little matinee jacket she'd made for her little sister in time for her first birthday, didn't she? And she was only a moment or two late for last parade.'

'Well, that's Staff Farr for you,' said Joan, swinging the basket.

'Yes, it did seem somewhat harsh of Staff to put her on a charge, just for that,' said Edie, finally managing to release a long-stemmed crimson bloom. She felt the outer edge of a rose petal – soft, like a baby's cheek. 'She really loves her baby sister, doesn't she?'

'She does,' said Joan. 'And, have you ever wondered—' but she didn't complete the sentence because there was the sound of a man's voice from the end of the fruit canes. 'The royal guard, they're onto us!' Joan giggled, whipping a tea towel over the basket of roses so it looked just like a picnic hamper. Edie held the rose she'd just picked behind her back with one hand, and linked arms with Joan. Together, they began to walk away.

As they reached the end of the fruit canes, there was a swishing of cloth against cloth, and the sound of the man clearing his throat. They rounded the corner. Not one man, but two, Edie noticed. No, not two men – a man and a woman. Heavens, had they intruded on some kind of a tryst? The man was pushing a wing of white hair back off his face, the woman smoothing down her skirt. The man was tall, with a long nose. He—

'*Quelle surprise!*' he said, stretching out his arms. 'Half Pint – what the devil are you doing here?' He began to stride towards her. Edie looked beyond him, to the woman: her face was flushed and she was fiddling with a button on her blouse. It wasn't Mummy. 'Fancy bumping into you here,' Pop said, catching her up in a hug. She smelled gin on his breath. 'And your pal, too.' He lunged at Joan, who quickly held out a hand and said, 'A pleasure to meet you again, sir.'

'Oh, nonsense, nonsense, we know each other, don't we, Jeannie? You don't need to "sir" me,' Pop said, kissing Joan on both cheeks.

The woman was still a distance away, rummaging in a handbag. 'Anyone for a smoke?' she said, trotting towards them and holding out a gold cigarette case.

'Ah, Meredith, marvellous idea,' said Pop, turning round as if he'd only just noticed she was there.

Edie was still holding the stolen rose behind her back. She felt the thorns crushing into her palm. She opened her fingers and let it fall softly to the grass. 'Mrs Cowie,' she said, as the woman approached. They touched cheeks and Edie was reminded of the rose petals: scented and downy. 'Joan, this is Mrs Cowie. Mrs Cowie, this is Joan.' They both said, 'How d'you do.'

'May I?' Edie said, indicating the cigarette case. Mrs Cowie said, 'Of course,' opening and proffering. It reminded Edie of the magazine of bullets, from that time on the range, on their last day of training. She pulled one of the smooth white cylinders out. It had two gold bands on the filter. They huddled in as Mrs Cowie produced a slim gold lighter that matched her cigarette case. She lit Joan's and Edie's, but Pop put a hand out to stop her lighting her own.

'Three in a row's bad luck,' said Pop. 'Jerry sees the first strike, takes aim at the second and, if you show him a third Lucifer, then your number's up.' He took his pipe out of his pocket.

'We're hardly in no-man's-land now, Neville,' Mrs Cowie drawled, clicking the lighter again.

Edie inhaled deeply. Smoking still made her feel a bit dizzy. She glanced across at Joan, who winked at her, then looked away. Pop was stuffing his pipe and getting out his matches. 'So Meredith – Mrs Cowie – and I were just out for a stroll,' he said. 'Such a glorious day for it!' Mrs Cowie nodded, lips clamped round her cigarette. Her lipstick was smudged, Edie noticed. 'And what brings you here, Half Pint?'

Edie exhaled. 'Picking roses, that's all,' she said.

'Ah, yes, a rose by any other name, and all that,' said Pop, sucking on his pipe until the tobacco caught, blistering orange, and the blue smoke began to rise.

'Romeo and Juliet,' said Mrs Cowie.

'Star-crossed lovers,' said Pop, looking at her through his pipe smoke. Edie watched as their glance connected. Then they both looked away.

Edie looked over at Joan. 'Mrs Cowie is Mummy's best

friend,' she said, flinging her half-smoked cigarette onto the grass and stamping on it. Joan nodded, and looked thoughtfully at Pop.

'Indeed she is,' said Pop. 'And we were just talking about her, weren't we, Meredith? It's been an age since you two had a girls' night out,' he added, and then cleared his throat, chewing on the pipe stem.

Mrs Cowie looked stonily into the middle distance. 'Maud should come up to town more often,' she said.

'We should really go,' said Joan, touching Edie on the sleeve. 'We've got that thing on later, remember?' Edie nodded, going along with the half-truth. As they left, Pop gave her another bear hug and whispered into her ear, 'There's no need to mention this to your mother, Half Pint – we wouldn't want her getting the wrong idea, would we?' As they were leaving, Pop then called out after them. 'You must swing by the club sometime – bring your pals – they've started letting the gentle sex into the lounge bar, and there's a piano there.' But Edie couldn't bring herself to shout back an acknowledgement. Her jaws felt as if they were bound together with wire, clamped tight and aching.

They walked on past the round pond, where an old man in his shirtsleeves was pushing out a model square-rigger with a large stick. Joan stopped. 'Come here,' she said, wrapping her arms round Edie. 'You do look down.'

'No, I'm fine, dear,' said Edie, pulling away. If she let herself be embraced, she'd only cry, and what use would that be?

Chapter 22

'You can forget about your brew, Gunner Tucker. The CO wants to see you in his office, pronto. And by the look on his face, I'd say you'd better not keep him waiting.'

'What is it, Staff?' said Joan.

'You'll find out quick enough, Gunner. Now look lively.'

Joan ran towards the commanding officer's hut out beyond the gun emplacements. On the way, she passed tubby Billy, leaning out of the back of the Quartermaster's Stores.

'Better get cracking, Tucker,' he said. 'You'll be in it even worse if you're late.'

What? thought Joan. What the hell am I supposed to have done? Thud-thud, thud-thud, she went, onwards until the pounding of her heart was faster and louder than her footfalls. Why did he want to see her? This morning, of all mornings? It was only a hundred yards or so to the CO's hut, but it felt as if she'd just sprinted a mile, and she was sweating like a horse under her uniform. The CO's door was closed. She hesitated, taking off her cap. She forced herself to knock, twice, gasping to recover her breath, and took off her cap.

'Come,' said a muffled voice.

She reached for the door handle. Her hands shook and the metal slithered between her fingers. For a moment, she saw another hand, bloodied, with a sapphire ring on it; the smell of burnt flesh.

'Come,' said the voice again, louder.

Finally, she managed to get the handle to work, opened the door, marched three paces inside and braced up. The CO was shuffling his paperwork. 'The door, Gunner Tucker,' he said, without looking up.

'Sir,' she breathed, and quickly turned back to close the door. In her haste, she pulled it too hard and it slammed. She turned back and braced up again: chest out, chin up, arms rigid at her sides and fists tightly balled. Her heart felt as if it was hurling itself at her ribcage and her breath came in uneven bursts. She waited for the 'at ease' command. It never came. Instead, the CO got slowly up from behind his desk, picking up a brown manila envelope as he did so. Joan heard the swish of cloth against cloth as he moved round the desk and came to stand in front of her. Her eyes were on a level with his Adam's apple: red and scratched from where he'd scraped it with the razor this morning. She could smell his talc and hair oil.

'It has come to my attention, Gunner, that you are improperly dressed for this morning's royal visit,' he began, sounding a bit like royalty himself. What was he talking about?

'But, sir, I—'Joan thought of the hours she'd spent bulling the toes of her brogues, brushing every fleck of dust from her uniform, and polishing the brass badge on her cap.

'Don't interrupt,' said the CO. 'As a result of this infringement, I have been instructed to give you this.' He held out the envelope. 'You may take it.'

'Sir.' She took the envelope. The front was blank. It wasn't addressed to anyone. She looked at it, and looked back up at the CO.

'You might want to open it,' said the CO, 'and, by the way, stand easy.' It was only then, as she looked up into his face, that she noticed a faint twitch at the corner of his mouth. With still-shaking hands, she opened the envelope. Inside were two white-cloth V-shapes, like seagulls on a painting.

'Congratulations on getting your first stripe, Lance Bombardier Tucker.'

At last, she understood, but she had to be sure. 'I'm not in trouble then, sir?'

'Well, you will be if you don't get those sewn on in time for the Queen and Princess Elizabeth, Tucker. Jolly well done.' He reached out to shake her hand. She shifted the envelope into the one with her cap and grasped his.

'Thank you, sir. You nearly had me there, sir,' she said.

'It was Staff Farr's idea of a practical joke,' he said. 'But surely, you didn't think you were really in trouble? Or have you got a few skeletons in your cupboard that you're not telling us about?' He chuckled and his shoulders and eyebrows jigged up and down.

'No, sir, not at all, sir,' she said in a rush.

'Well, keep up the good work, Bombardier,' he said. 'Dismissed.'

'Thank you, sir,' she said, braced up again and turned to go. Outside the door, she put her cap back on and took the stripes out from the envelope. She ran back towards the NAAFI, clutching the white stripes.

'Congratulations!' shouted fat Billy from stores as she passed, and she wondered how he knew. She shouted her thanks and ran on. Ahead, Edie and Bea were just draining their mugs. They rushed forward to meet her.

'Well done, you!' said Edie.

'So you knew?' said Joan.

'Staff just told us,' said Bea. 'Who would have thought the old bird had such a sense of humour?'

'Thanks, girls. I feel a bit bad that you two didn't get made up as well.'

'Learn to take a compliment. You deserve it, dear,' said Edie, kissing her on each cheek as she did so.

'You don't look very happy about it,' said Bea, giving her a squeeze.

'Of course I'm happy,' said Joan. 'Why wouldn't I be?'

But it wasn't happiness that tugged at her insides and cluttered her mind, it was something else: Whose hand had she seen instead of hers when she went to open the CO's door? A smooth hand with oval-shaped nails and a sapphire ring. Whose hand was that?

* * *

The sun was high by the time the royal party arrived. Joan and the girls waited down in the concrete emplacements, which always smelled dank, even on the brightest day. In the distance she could hear the faint throb and growl of the traffic on the Bayswater Road. Six ducks flew overhead and away, on towards the Serpentine. A dog barked somewhere nearby.

'They should be here by now,' said Edie, chewing a nail. 'Golly, I'm nervous, but nervous in a good way, like I used to feel when I was little on Christmas Eve. Do you remember what that was like, and doesn't it seem so long ago now, after everything we've done?'

One of the other girls shushed Edie impatiently. The tension was making them irritable. Joan felt the sweat pricking her underarms, wiped her palms again on her skirt, waiting. At last, there was the sound of three cars drawing up, the pit-pat of feet on the path and the deferential murmur of voices.

'Here they come,' said Bea.

'I can't believe it,' gasped Edie.

Joan waited silently by the entrance to the emplacement and reminded herself what she had to do: first the salute and then the explanation. The footfalls and voices were drawing nearer. There were figures at the steps, descending slowly. Trip-trap, coming closer, down the concrete steps. There was the second-in-command, his face red and shiny; on the other side, Staff Farr, raisin-eyes darting around, in one final inspection, and, in between them, the tiny khaki-clad figure of Princess Elizabeth, her smile a little white 'U' in the centre of her face.

'So I'll hand you over to one of our junior NCOs, Lance Bombardier Joan Tucker, who can tell you all about it,' said the second-in-command, gesturing towards Joan, who saluted. Princess Elizabeth returned the salute. She looked smaller and prettier than she did in photographs. Joan showed her the Sperry Predictor and gave her the binoculars so she could have a go at spotting, not that there would be any bombers flying over at ten-thirty in the morning. The princess asked Joan how big the gun was. Joan said three foot seven inches and the princess said that was jolly big, wasn't it? After that, she asked Joan how she liked the uniform. Joan hadn't prepared for this question. She had all kinds of technical information in her head about the equipment and the hit rate statistics, but she hadn't expected to be asked anything like this.

'I like being in it, ma'am,' she said truthfully, looking into the princess's earnest grey eyes. 'When I put on the uniform, it feels like I know who I am.'

'I see what you mean. Sometimes it's easier, being clothed for the part, like acting a role,' said the princess. The second-in-command was wringing his hands and just about to open his mouth and usher the princess onwards, when there was a drum roll of shoes on the steps and a man in a pork-pie hat and long raincoat barrelled down towards them.

'I'm terribly sorry, ma'am,' he said, bowing in a perfunctory way. 'Would you mind if I just . . .?'

'Not at all,' said the princess.

'Can I take a photo of you with the ATS girl?'

'Of course. Her name is Lance Bombardier Joan Tucker, and we were just having a conversation about how marvellous the new ATS uniforms are, weren't we?' said the princess. They all laughed politely. The journalist nodded repeatedly and pulled out a notebook, making brief scratchy marks, before lifting his camera.

'Give me a nice smile for the *Daily Mail* readers please, Bombardier,' he said. As he pointed the camera at them, Joan heard a buzzing inside her head, like a bluebottle stuck behind glass, and the world seemed to tilt. The camera flashed, Joan turned her head, upwards and away, towards the blue sky.

'That one won't do, you moved. Would you mind if we took another one, ma'am?' asked the *Daily Mail* man, managing a mix of deference and impatience as he fiddled with his equipment.

'Carry on,' said the princess, her U-shaped mouth beginning to droop just a little.

'Now, you're a pretty girl, Bombardier, let's see a big smile for the papers,' he said, and Joan lifted her lips and showed her teeth and the buzzing got louder and everything sheared and there was that smell, the acrid burnt smell, as the camera flashed again. The hot sun was like a crushed orange flower, right above her. She felt herself sway. Joan saw the princess's mouth move, her white teeth, but she couldn't hear what she was saying because of the buzzing noise filling up her skull. The princess looked round and Joan turned her throbbing head to follow her gaze, and there was the Queen, in lavender silk, with her head on one side and a sugary smile set in place, like a piece of fondant icing among the dense fruit cake of uniforms and guns. She'd seen this before: the Queen, flickering black-and-white figures on a screen. A newsreel, somewhere. But where? When? Joan rocked backwards on her heels, feeling nausea rise.

The princess stepped away towards her mother. With her came a phalanx of others: military, press, men in suits, swimming in and out of focus as they approached. The *Daily Mail* man scuttled sideways. The buzzing in Joan's ears diminished, and the world shifted back into place.

'Are you all right?' said Edie, her voice muffled, touching Joan on her sleeve.

'Fine,' said Joan, rubbing her forehead. 'I'm fine.'

'You don't seem yourself, dear.'

The royals had been shunted along towards the Bofors gun, further along the emplacement, and Joan followed behind Edie and Bea, joining the rest of the battery. But Joan could still smell that burnt smell, taste sour bile in her throat.

Some of the other girls showed the royals how they'd track and target an enemy plane during a raid. When the men fired the guns, the Queen said they certainly did make a devil of a racket, and everybody laughed. The *Daily Mail* man and the rest of the press took more photos, but Joan managed to keep out of the way, sliding behind the tall frame of the CO or the chunky metal blocks of weaponry. After that, the Queen said how lovely it had been to meet them all and she and her daughter were swept off by some men in suits back to the waiting cars.

When they'd gone, everyone started talking at once: *Wasn't she lovely? They were both marvellous. Prettier than I expected. So tiny. I didn't expect to have a laugh with them. Didn't think much of that man from the papers. Did I do okay? You were wonderful. They were wonderful. Wait 'til I tell Vi. I still can't believe it!* They fell silent again as Staff Farr returned.

'Well done, all of you,' Staff said. 'Now get back to the hut because there'll be a room inspection in half an hour.'

Bea let out a groan. 'And extra duties for anyone I hear moaning about it,' added Staff Farr.

'Yes, Staff,' they all said in unison.

'Cow,' muttered Sheila Carter, when she was out of earshot.

'You'd think she'd at least let us have an early lunch break,' Edie sighed.

The rest of the troop, disgruntled, began to trudge back to their hut. Joan followed, at a distance, not joining in with the gossip and griping. Something was wrong, but she couldn't work out what it was.

Once inside, they quickly checked their bed blocks and lockers. Joan helped Edie with her hospital corners; Bea got the broom out to sweep the floor. The rest of the girls were folding, polishing and wiping in readiness. There was a knock at the door. 'This room had better be ready,' came Staff Farr's voice.

'That was never half an hour!' whispered Bea.

'It wasn't even half a minute,' said Edie.

The door opened and Staff Farr stalked in, frowning. 'Your room looks fine, ladies,' she said, her eyes sweeping unseeingly round. She made a chopping motion with her hand, partitioning the hut. 'This half will be on duty today and through until sixteen hundred hours Saturday, and the rest of you will take Saturday night until sixteen hundred hours Sunday. I'd love to knock you all off together, girls, but there simply isn't the cover.'

'Thank you, Staff,' said Joan.

'My pleasure, Lance Bombardier,' came the reply, and Staff Farr turned on her heel, and left. As the door closed, the girls looked at each other and burst out laughing: *I can't believe it! She's never let us off that lightly before. Staff Farr's going soft in her old age. Are we really getting a night off?*

'What a day!' said Edie.

'We'll have to make sure we get a copy of the Mail tomorrow,' said Bea.

'Oh, goodness, yes, I'll have to resurrect my scrapbook, with a special page for the picture of our Joanie with Princess Elizabeth. How marvellous, I can't wait to tell Mummy, she'll be thrilled,' said Edie, throwing herself backwards onto her little bed so that the dust puffed out of the blanket.

The other girls began to get changed into their work clothes: trousers and boots, ready for their shift. Sheila said loudly that she preferred Saturday nights off anyway because there was more chance of seeing a new reel at the flicks. Bea was humming to herself and unbuttoning her jacket. Edie was smiling and drumming her legs on the bed. Some of the others were already beginning to disappear out towards the cookhouse.

Joan's head was still aching. She looked outside, through

the little window, where the sky was as blue as sapphires and the sun was a golden circle. She imagined her face in the paper, next to the princess. Princess Elizabeth meets Lance Bombardier Joan Tucker at the Hyde Park Battery, that's what it would say, underneath. She heard again an echo of the buzzing in her ears, and for a moment it felt like the room was contracting, as if she was trapped inside a dolls' house. The sensation only lasted seconds, and then everything went back to normal, leaving just a hollowness in her chest and the clench of a frown. How many people read the *Daily Mail*, she wondered.

'Stop moping, dear,' said Edie, looking across at her. 'I don't know what you've got to be down in the mouth about; your Robin will see you in the paper and he'll be so proud of his pretty, successful girl.'

'You're right,' she said, unable to smile.

'We should be bally well celebrating,' said Edie.

Maybe Edie was right. She should just have a good time and forget about the nagging sensation in the pit of her stomach. Today's paper was tomorrow's chip wrapper: nobody would notice her picture there, and anyway, why would it matter?

Chapter 23

Edie felt the childish urge to skip. A night off, with her pals, after all they'd been through together so far. Inside, she thanked God for all His blessings: for Joan's promotion, for the Royal visit, for the glorious sunshine, and for a Friday in town with her friends. What could possibly be more perfect?

'*Carpe diem!*' she said.

'What's that when it's at home?' said Joan.

'It means seize the day, in Latin,' she replied.

'Oh, give over, Edie, I don't understand half the English words you use, without you bringing Latin into it,' said Bea, but she was smiling.

'Sorry, it's just – I feel guilty for feeling it, what with everything that's going on – but I do just feel really happy.'

'I'll give you something to be happy about, take a look at the lad on the opposite bank, three o'clock,' said Joan, smirking. 'And don't make it obvious, Edie!'

'Why do you always do this, it's embarrassing,' said Edie,

but she couldn't help but look. Just off to the right, across the lake by the lido, a young man was stretching up for a dive. He had on royal-blue trunks and his torso was tanned from the sun and glinting with splashes of water. A lock of blond hair fell across his eyes and he paused to brush it out of the way. Then he reached up again with his arms, pulling all the muscles taut across his chest. For a moment, he waited, arms upstretched, and the light on his hard, young body made him look as if he were carved from sunshine. Then, with a perfect arc and a milky splash, he disappeared under the dark green water of the Serpentine.

'What did I tell you?' said Joan, laughing.

Edie said nothing. She wasn't thinking about the diver, who'd come up for air now and was making a noisy front crawl back to the bank. She was thinking about Kenneth; that last summer, when they'd all been together, before he was MIA. That was how he looked then, just the epitome of youth and health. She couldn't bear to think what might have happened to his perfect body – or where whatever was left of it had ended up.

'What's your verdict?' said Joan.

'Nine out of ten,' said Bea. 'It would have been a ten, but he looked a bit skinny to me.'

'Oh, you like a bit of meat, do you?' said Joan.

'Girls, will you stop it now?' said Edie, suddenly irritated.

'Oh, come on Edie, you must have an opinion. I'm giving him an eight, because I prefer them dark, but you like fair hair, don't you?'

'I'm not doing this. It's – it's cheap.'

'It's only a bit of fun,' said Bea.

'It doesn't seem right. How would we like it if they looked at us like that?' said Edie.

'They do look at us like that,' said Joan.

Edie suddenly stopped walking, forcing the other two into a halt as well. She couldn't bear the way Joan talked about boys. It was all about, well, the sex thing, whatever that was. And Edie thought that there ought to be more to it than that. The way Joan spoke, it just diminished everything, somehow. They should be waiting for the right man, for marriage, shouldn't they?

'Come on girls, let's not row, not tonight, when we've got the whole evening ahead of us,' said Bea, tugging at her arm.

The lad was back up on the bank again now, shaking his wet hair like a dog and reaching for a towel.

'I'm sorry,' said Edie, frowning. 'It's just—'

'No, I'm sorry,' said Joan. 'I was only larking about. You're so pretty, Edie, lots of boys like you, but you always give them the cold shoulder. Don't you want to have fun?'

'Of course I do, but . . .'

'It's that boy from home; Kenneth, isn't it?' said Bea, as they began to walk on. 'You can't forget, can you?'

'Well, you have to,' Joan said, so fiercely that Edie's arm jolted apart from hers. 'You have to leave the past where it belongs – in the past. There's no point mooning about with regrets. You said it yourself: *Carpe* whatsit.'

In the distance, the strains of 'We'll Meet Again' began

from the bandstand and filtered through the watery yellow sunshine to where they stood. A dog barked, and a lonely bus chugged along Park Lane.

'You're right, Joan,' Edie said brightly. 'And in the spirit of that, I'm taking you all to tea at the Ritz.'

'Blimey!' said Bea.

'But we're not paid until next week,' said Joan.

'Pop sent me a cheque,' said Edie.

'What for?' said Bea, incredulous.

'I don't know. It's months until my birthday,' said Edie, exchanging glances with Joan, remembering the day they'd bumped into Pop and Mrs Cowie in Kensington Gardens.

Edie started to walk again, pulling the other two along with her, then, she gave into her whim and began to skip. The others, laughing, joined in.

'What are you like, you silly mare?' said Bea.

'I'm taking you for tea at the Ritz, cocktails at the Savoy, and then we're all going on to a nightclub,' she yelled, breaking into a run as they reached the boathouse. And as they pell-melled towards Hyde Park Corner, Edie clung onto her happiness as if it were a fluttering kite, running with them, high in the blue sky, and threatening to fly away into the summer evening.

'I'm not sure, Edie; this might be the sort of place you like to go to, but it's a bit posh,' said Bea, stalling as they reached the hotel steps.

'Nonsense. We're all in uniform and our money is as good as anyone else's, dear,' said Edie, straightening up.

'Oh, I don't know,' said Bea.

'Come on, don't be wet,' said Joan and they all marched into the lobby. It was just as Edie remembered it: the hush, the opulence; it was almost like entering a church.

'Through there, past the columns,' said Edie. 'Ladies, we shall be taking tea in the Palm Court!'

The maitre d' stood in the doorway to the tearoom, grave as a vicar. Edie thought she recognised his greying side burns and impassive face from when she'd been here before, with Marjorie and Kenneth.

'A table for three, please,' she said and he led them across the polished floor to a small round marble table next to a golden statue of a nymph. The Palm Court was quite busy, with lots of couples in uniform, and a smattering of older women in tweed. There was a buzz of chatter. Above them the huge frosted glass skylight let in the sunshine, and the pink-tipped chandeliers made the air rose-tinted and shimmery. Aspidistras waved as they passed. In the middle of the table was a vase of pink and white roses. The maitre d' held out the little cream plush and gilt Louis XVI chairs and they all sat down, gas masks clanking against the wrought-iron table legs.

'This is a bit better than national loaf,' said Joan, when the cucumber sandwiches arrived, tiny white triangles with the crusts cut off.

'Shall I be mother?' said Edie, lifting the silver teapot.

'You do come out with some funny things, Edie,' said Bea, cramming two sandwiches into her mouth at once.

At the next table, an officer and a young woman in civvies were bent across so that their foreheads almost touched. He was whispering something to her, and all of a sudden she sprang back, in gales of laughter, tossing her chestnut curls.

The maitre d' glided past. 'Could we please have some scones and eclairs as well?' Edie said, catching his eye. He nodded and disappeared behind an aspidistra.

Edie poured the tea, watching it swirl and steam in the cups.

'Sugar?' said Joan, fiddling with the tongs.

'Love and scandal are the best sweeteners of tea,' said Edie.

'Who said that?' said Joan.

'Oh, I don't know, dear, some writer or other,' said Edie. She didn't want them to think she was showing off. In any case, it didn't matter who'd made up the quote, what mattered was who'd said it to her – Kenneth, right here in the Palm Court, all those months ago.

The couple at the next table got up and left. Edie caught sight of them entering the lift together in the lobby. She whispered to Bea and Joan, wondering if the couple had got a room. Bea said of course they had, did you see the way his hand was on her behind as they walked out. Joan said she must be one of those Windmill girls. Edie, scandalised, said that the woman hadn't been wearing a wedding ring. Joan and Bea both looked at her, then looked at each other and burst out laughing. When they had almost reached the end of the pot, Bea poured the last of the tea into Edie's cup without using the strainer.

'Well, thank you, very much!' said Edie.

'It's not for drinking, it's for reading,' said Bea. 'My ma's got gypsy blood. She taught me.'

'Oh, go on then,' said Edie.

Bea swilled the leaves around, squinting her eyes at the cup. The tip of her tongue protruded ever so slightly from the side of her mouth, as if she was concentrating very hard. 'There's a young man, and water—' she began.

'I knew it,' Joan interrupted. 'I knew that lad at the Serpentine was her type!'

Bea ignored her. 'There's a place with music and dancing, but then there's water, and . . . oh, no, not that.' She put the cup down abruptly. 'I'm sorry, I'm sure I wasn't doing that right. Just ignore it. Are there any eclairs left?'

'It's nonsense,' said Joan. 'It's all nonsense. You were just making it up, weren't you, Bea?'

Bea shrugged a little sadly, and reached for the last éclair. 'I'm sorry, Edie,' she said.

'Oh, don't worry about it. It's nothing. It's just a bit of fun. Let's settle up here and go on to the Savoy. I'm in the mood for a proper drink.'

She paid the bill for them all and they tumbled out of the huge glass doors and onto Piccadilly. The sun was lower now and their shadows fell like long strips of ticker tape as their shoes tip-tapped along the grey pavements towards the Strand.

Joan stopped en route to get her lipstick out of her gas-mask case, and reapplied it, right there, in the middle of the street where everyone could see. A group of soldiers spilled out from a side street just in front of them. Their voices were loud, out-of-place, and their uniforms more green than khaki.

'Yanks!' gasped Bea.

'Just keep walking,' said Joan.

There was laughter as they approached, and Edie heard the word 'dames'. 'Say, ladies,' said a voice as they drew level. Joan and Bea pretended not to hear, but Edie felt that it was simply bad manners to ignore them. She stopped. The one who'd spoken was a little taller than her, with corrugated brown hair and a long nose.

'Can I help you, gentlemen?' she said, ignoring Bea's insistent tugging of her arm.

'We're looking for a hotel – what's the name of it, Art?' the corrugated hair said to his friend. The friend, tall, with blonde eyebrows, held a piece of paper up to his eyes. There was a third man, quite short and plump, who said nothing, but grinned at them all with a wide innocent face.

'Savvy?' he said.

'Savoy?' said Edie.

'Could be,' he replied, squinting at the scrap. Edie asked if she could look. On the crumpled sheet, *Moira, 7 p.m., Savoy* was written in a round, girlish hand.

'Yes, it's the Savoy you're looking for. We're headed there, too. We could show you the way, if you'd like?' said Edie. The men agreed, saying they were 'much obliged, ma'am,' and Edie said nonsense, call me Edie, and introduced Bea and Joan as well.

A quick flick over their uniforms told her that they were

officers. So the six of them sauntered along the pavement together. The men were only a little drunk, Edie thought, and really quite pleasant when one could understand what they were saying. Honestly, she didn't know why everyone seemed to have such a low impression of the GIs, and she said as much to Art, who was the tall flaxen-haired one with the piece of paper. Edie glanced across at Joan, who was being eagerly questioned by the corrugated-hair one, whose name was Ron. Joan was feigning disinterest, but a tell-tale finger kept playing with a strand of hair. The short plump one, Hal, was telling Bea about Chicago. Well, why not, thought Edie. It wasn't as if they'd gone out to pick these boys up, they were merely showing them directions, being polite. And they were all in uniform – practically colleagues, for goodness' sakes. All the same, she couldn't help but imagine what her mother would say: going out, on your own in London at night, and picking up Americans! There was something deliciously rebellious about it.

It was a good mile's walk all the way to the Strand. By the time they got there they knew all about Ron, Hal and Art's hometowns and their impressions of England (less than favourable, but couched very diplomatically by Ron as 'You can tell that you folks have had a tough time'). The sun sank lower as they walked, so more and more of the pavement was covered in shadow, and the sunlight showed as little blocks of yellow, that they passed swiftly though and onwards, chatting.

Finally, they reached the Savoy, with its sandbags painted red, white and blue. The doorman looked rather snootily at them as they jostled into the revolving door. Edie found herself in a glassy slice of pie (as she always thought of these spinning doors) with Art. He was quite a bit taller than her, with enormous hands. Close up, he smelled of an almondy cologne. She felt the beginnings of a blush coming on, being in such close proximity, but suddenly the doors had thrown them back out, into the lobby with the others.

Edie was the only one who'd been to the Savoy before (with Pop, for a treat one lunch while she was still at Queen's College. Apparently, Winston used to take the Cabinet to dine there, sometimes, but they hadn't seen them); so she led the way to the grill, with its leather seats, mirrored columns and crimson carpets. Art scanned the room for 'Moira', but she was nowhere to be seen. He looked rather crestfallen, and Edie felt sorry for him, so she offered to look in the ladies' powder room for her.

'What does she look like?'

'She's got red hair, a bit like yours, but not so shiny,' he said. 'And blue eyes.'

'I'm sure we'll find her for you,' said Edie, surprising herself by half hoping they wouldn't. Joan and Bea came with her to the powder room, which had thick cream carpets, full-length mirrors, and a chaise longue. It was empty. Joan took her lipstick out from her gas mask and slicked another layer of geranium red on, and then she took out a comb and did her hair. Bea sank down into the armchair.

'I could live in here,' Bea said, shutting her eyes. 'This lavvy is bigger than our house, back home.'

Edie called out hopefully for Moira, but she wasn't there. 'Well, shame on Moira, whoever she is. If I was Art's date I wouldn't have stood him up,' she said.

Joan smirked.

'No I didn't mean – I just meant that he's a nice young man and he doesn't deserve to be let down,' said Edie. 'I feel sorry for him, that's all.'

'Sorry enough to let him buy you a drink?' said Joan, holding out her lipstick. Edie took it and pouted at her reflection in the glass as she applied the slash of red. She said nothing for a moment, blotted her lips with tissue and reapplied, exactly as she had always watched her mother apply lipstick at home, exactly as she had never been allowed to until she ran away to join the ATS. She ran her tongue over her teeth, just to check there was no lipstick there, and smiled at Joan's reflection in the mirror.

'Yes,' she said at last. 'What's the harm? Let's have some fun. We've jolly well earned it.'

After cocktails at the Savoy, they decided to leg it to the 400 Club, before blackout. They were all rather giddy. The Americans had kept their glasses topped up, and all they'd had to eat were the cakes and cucumber sandwiches at the Ritz. As they ran up towards Leicester Square, they were running towards the setting sun, a dash from navy blue to rose, and she could see the blackout blinds being shut down, one by one, in upstairs windows, as if the city was closing its eyes for the night.

They almost fell down the steep steps to the cellar door. Edie had always wanted to come to the 400 Club. It was mentioned in *Harper's Bazaar*. Mary Churchill came, and the Kennedy girls, before they all hot-footed it back to America. Edie was a little worried they wouldn't be let in. But the Americans were all officers, and, much as she hated to admit it, her accent and her surname held a little sway. The ruddy-faced doorman winked and stood aside.

Inside was a warm fug, the air thick with the scent of Evening in Paris and cigar smoke. Shadowy figures carouselled round the tiny dance floor: some in uniform, but many in tux and long evening dresses, swishing against the polished wooden floor like peacocks tails. The eighteen-piece orchestra played quite low, so you could hear the murmur of voices and the occasional outburst of laughter above closing chords of 'A nightingale sang in Berkley Square'. Art Deco-style fanlights splayed a soft glow over the walls, so that the whole place had a swimming, underwater feel.

'It's just like the movies,' Joan whispered in her ear.

'Come on, let's get a seat,' said Edie, spotting a banquette near the far wall, but, as she skirted round the dance floor, leading the way, Art grabbed her waist from behind, and propelled her onto the dance floor. The band had just struck up the 'Chattanooga Choo Choo'.

'No really, I can't!' she protested, laughing. She had no idea how to do boogie-woogie, or whatever it was called. But he twirled her round and it felt so good, just to be there in the moment, that she found herself joining in. Her hands touched with Art's and they caught, moved together, span apart, and all the time it felt as if the music was inside her, and everything flowed. She caught sight of Joan's hair streaming out behind her as Ron swung her round, and Bea and Hal, jiving, cheek-to-cheek. There was none of the clumsiness there'd been when she'd tried to learn how to do this with Marjorie, all those months ago.

The bandleader announced that the next dance would be a 'gentlemen's excuse me' and Art pulled her in closer. Her cheek rested on his shoulder and she thought again how nice he smelled, and how well he danced.

'You're a very pretty girl, you know that?' he muttered into her hair.

'Thank you, that's very kind,' she answered, rather breathlessly, thinking of nothing except how marvellous it was to be spending her precious night off dancing at the 400 Club with this handsome American officer.

'Excuse me,' a voice cut in and another man inserted himself between them. Art shrugged and gave way. Her new partner was a small, wiry chap in a dinner jacket. He said his name was Mungo, and he bobbed her around with more enthusiasm than skill. Every time he trod on her toes, he said, 'I'm so sorry, but that's the nicest foot I've trod on all evening.' Edie tried to laugh but, by the third time, the joke was wearing thin, and it was a relief when Art cut back in.

Art's face was close to hers and she could see the stubble on his cheek. His breath smelled of whisky. They moved together, perfectly synchronised, as smoky lights and figures twirled around them. When the band struck up the next song, a slow number, she leant into him, dizzy and breathless, laughing with the sheer joy of it. He was holding her tight as the band played 'Goodnight Sweetheart'; she could feel him tense and hard underneath his uniform. His face was nuzzling into her hair, his breath on her neck.

'Shall we go somewhere else, to talk?' she said, surprising herself with her boldness. As they walked off the dance floor she felt his hand slide down her back, towards her behind, and she thought with a thrill about the woman at the Ritz, getting into the lift with the officer.

They found a little table for two in a corner. It was covered with a long white damask cloth. The chairs were so small, and the place was so crowded that their knees almost touched. He motioned to the waiter for two whisky and sodas. She didn't really like whisky, but it didn't seem to matter. All that mattered was the moment. Here she was, all grown up: Edith Lightwater, out in a nightclub with an American officer, drinking whisky and dancing like there was no tomorrow. Art asked if she came here often.

'I've never been here before in my life!' she said, which for some reason struck her as hilarious and she laughed out loud.

'Well, there's a first time for everything,' said Art, taking a gulp from his drink and looking across at her. Beyond him, the dancers still swayed and turned on the dance floor, the waiters slid past with their round, shiny drinks trays and the band began to play 'South of the Border'. They talked about where his unit was stationed in England. She remarked that

Aldershot really wasn't too far from London. He said he hoped he'd be able to make some regular trips into the capital. He looked right at her as he said it, and she hoped that in the dimmed lights he wouldn't see her blush. She could feel the push of his knee against hers, his foot, too.

'I'm sorry,' she said, moving her leg away.

'Don't be,' he said, and his boot contacted with her brogue again. There was a kind of gently rhythmic pulsing of his leg against hers. She felt hot and flustered. Moving away again would seem rude. In any case, there was a crush of people at tables either side, and she couldn't alter her position without jolting someone else. Besides, it wasn't unpleasant, it was just – and then he put his hand on her thigh. She looked across at him, but he didn't acknowledge her. His eyes were on the dance floor. His other hand traced circles around the top of his cut glass tumbler. His thumb began to knead her flesh, massaging the rough fabric into the bare space at the top of her legs between stocking top and knickers. She glanced around. People at the other tables were laughing, smoking, drinking. She wondered if any of the other women had a man's hand on their thigh. Was this just what people did? Is this what Pop did with Meredith Cowie? Art's fingers were moving upwards now, giving her goose pimples.

'I say, it's terribly muggy in here, let's get out and get some air,' she said suddenly, standing up. As she did so, she caught Bea's eye, who was just leaving the dance floor with Hal. Bea shot her a worried look, and Edie tried to smile. But what she felt wasn't happiness; it was an odd mixture of elation and confusion. Art took her hand and led her away.

They didn't go out through the front door but, instead, out of a side entrance that opened out onto a paved area with an outhouse and some little slippery steps that let up to an alley-way. The door closed behind them and they were alone. It was dark now, but the moon was rising, a yellow gibbous, harvest moon, bloated and sickly beyond the jagged horizon and the jostle of barrage balloons. He got out a packet of Lucky Strikes and she held out a hand for one.

'May I?'

'Sure. I didn't realise you English dames were so keen on smoking.'

'Everyone smokes in the ATS,' she said casually, letting him light her cigarette. They both inhaled and looked at each other across the waft of smoke.

She noticed how his big hands trembled slightly as he brought the cigarette to his lips, inhaling so powerfully that the tip of his cigarette glowed like a furnace in the blue shadows. He dropped the butt and ground it out with his heel while she was only a third of the way down hers. He looked at her. There was something different in his eyes, harder, insistent.

'You soldier girls have a reputation,' he said, and there was a sneer in his voice.

'Totally unfounded,' she replied. 'Well, not totally. Some of the new conscripts, especially those really working-class ones—' she began, and then thought of Bea, and felt disloyal, somehow, and faltered. She flicked the ash from her cigarette.

She laughed, a high, trilling, laugh. At that moment, the sirens started their long slow wail.

'We should really get back inside,' she said.

He took the still lit cigarette from her hand and threw it away. It disappeared like a firefly into the night. Then suddenly, both his hands were on hers and his lips were on hers and he was pushing her back and down, onto the slippery steps. His mouth was wet and pushed down hard, bruising her lips as he thrust his tongue right inside. She tried to shove him off, cry out, but his mouth was over hers and he had both her hands in a tight grasp. As she struggled, her feet slipped on the grimy paving slabs and she fell backwards onto the steps, banging the back of her head.

'What are you doing?' she said, struggling, trying to kick, but the blow to her head made everything slur and the words slid sideways and away, her feet contacting with nothing but air.

'I'm doing what you want. What else did you bring me out here for?' he said, dragging her back up so that she was on her feet. She tried to shake him free, but now he twisted her arm up behind her back and shoved her towards the shed in the corner. Inside, she had the impression of crates and boxes, but she couldn't see. He pushed her back and she fell again; hard things jabbed and scraped.

'Oh, come on, don't be a spoilsport,' he said, his breath in her face, harsh and wet, as the sirens continued their mournful wail. Then his mouth was on hers again, that horrible tongue, like a wet snake, curling around inside.

As the sirens fell silent, there was a hush, with no sound except the brush of cloth against cloth as she struggled ineffectually against him in the darkness. She felt like she was going to suffocate. He was right on top of her, pushing her back, pinning her arms with one of his and shoving up her skirt with the other. And she could feel his long, clammy fingers at the apex of her thighs, forcing them apart. She tried to call out, but she was drowning under the pressure of him on top of her. He fumbled with his fly. She tried to use the opportunity to get free, but he was upon her again, wrestling her down, covering her mouth with his wet lips to muffle her cries.

Away in the distance, she could hear the soft thud, thud, as the bombs dropped, like a hammer on velvet. And then it was there, that hard horrible thing, pushing inside her. A pain ripped through. She felt him shove, again and again and grunt, holding her still, and all she could do was repeat, inside her head, the Lord's prayer, thinking that this couldn't be happening, that God couldn't let something like this happen. But then there was a terrific ripping, tearing sound and everything came crashing down, and they landed on the floor as one, with wood and glass and metal strewn over them and he was a dead weight on top of her.

She heard another thud, further away to the west and then there was silence. He lay still. Drool from his mouth slid across her cheek. His grasp loosened on her hands. His ribs pressed against hers; she could barely breathe. The skin of his cheek was moist with cooling sweat against hers. Edie lay there for what felt like for ever, scared that if she so much as flinched, he would start again. It's not happening, she told herself. This can't be happening.

He didn't move. She could feel his breath, warm and rhythmic against her skin, but the rest of him was utterly still. When she looked up beyond the blonde strands of hair, she could see why. A thick plank of wood lay on top of his skull. He was knocked out cold, with the weight of a fallen joist on top of him. She managed to inch sideways. The thing, now soft as a slug, slithered out from inside her as she shifted. His shoulder was jammed against her cheek now, hard as a cricket ball. If she could just push against something – but her feet were trapped underneath his legs, and he was on top of her, melding into her. She could smell his hateful scent of whisky and hair oil and smoke and that sickly almond cologne.

Faintly, in the distance, she could still hear the strains of the orchestra, playing on through the raid. And there was another sound, too: the steady rush of water. The bomb must have hit a water main.

His arms, his legs, his torso, were all over her, like a giant sandbag, pinning her down. There was all that stuff on top of him, the crushing weight of it. The blackness pressed in. The sound of water got louder. Soon she felt a rivulet of cold liquid begin to run through her own hair and down towards her neck. She renewed her efforts, and as she tried to move, the water seeped downwards. The cool wetness began to seep into her ears like worms, curling up and inside. Her uniform blotted up the dampness, drawing it in towards her flesh. She continued to struggled, until the wet from the flooding shed rose up to meet the damp sweat of her trapped body. It was surprising how quickly the water rose. Before long, she was lying part submerged. She could barely breathe, let alone shout for help.

With a heave, she jolted sideways and, suddenly, her cheek was no longer pinned under his shoulder; her head and neck were free. With small, strong movements, she managed to unpin her arm, too, and cast about, paddling the water, until she found something to catch hold of. The door was ajar, shattered by the blast. Her fingers found jagged wood. She ignored the pain and grasped, feeling the splinters dig in, feeling the muscles in her arms shake with the tension. Her body slid through the wetness, an inch, no more, but enough to wriggle her other shoulder free from under him and then to be able to push with her other arm. Pushing and pulling and heaving up and away from the horrid cloth-load of him, until her torso was free and she was half sitting in the rising water. Just her legs. He still had her legs. She twisted and shook but couldn't break free. It was her shoes, her army brogues, stuck fast underneath him. She leant forward in the darkness, feeling with her fingers through the wet, over the curve of his calf, tense under his trousers, into the space between his legs where her shoes were caught. She fiddled with the wet laces, picking and pulling until they loosened. With the shoes undone, she could begin to wriggle out of them, dragging her feet free from under him. With a splash, she was away. She pulled off her stockings like wet seaweed and sat barefoot in the rising tide.

Her eyes, used to the darkness now, could make out Art. His face was sideways, one cheek in the wetness. On top of him were the roof joist and a mess of broken crates and bricks. She sat in the water and looked at him. She looked at the joist. She sat, feeling the water rise up her thighs and watched the little silvery bubbles of air come out of his mouth and into the dark water. She listened to the rushing water sound, and the faraway music, and the little sticky breathy coughs as Art began to breathe in liquid.

The water climbed higher, reaching her buttocks, moving upwards just like Art's fingers had done under the table. She began to recite the Lord's Prayer, just a whisper, barely audible above the sound of water and the gurgling from Art's throat.

Our Father, who art in heaven, hallowed be Thy name
Thy kingdom come, Thy will be done
On earth as it is in heaven

Above the sound of the water and Art's snorting breaths was the mewl of the all-clear. The raid was over.

Give us this day our daily bread
And forgive us our trespasses

The water still wasn't deep, but it covered half his mouth and one of his nostrils now. He made guttural, frothy sounds. His eyelids fluttered.

As we forgive those who trespass against us

Then, just as the water was inside his mouth and one nostril was covered, Art opened his eyes, and he looked sideways at her. But his gaze was glassy and unfocused.

And lead us not into temptation

A loud rasping sound came from his throat: heaving, sawing, urgent. The water foamed at his lips, churning out.

But deliver us from evil

Edie watched as his arms and legs tensed and relaxed in rapid succession. Had he been in open water, they would have been paddling furiously, propelling him up towards the surface. But he wasn't. He was trapped under the debris from the blast in an inch of flooding mains water, which was now covering both nostrils and filling his open mouth.

For Thine is the kingdom

He made a horrible choking sound as the water slid right inside him and his body shuddered, tensed and then relaxed.

The power and the glory

His eyes stayed open, looking at her.

Forever and ever

Amen

Edie sat, pulling her gaze away from his lifeless eyes. Her skirt hung wet, clinging to her bare legs. She brought her hands up to brush the debris off her uniform and noticed that two buttons were missing, ripped from her shirt, which flapped open, showing her brassiere. The distant sound of the orchestra suddenly blared loudly and a door banged nearby.

'Edie,' came a voice. 'Edie, are you out here?'

Chapter 24

Where was she? Bea called again. She wasn't anywhere on the dance floor or up in the lobby. That yellow-haired Yank had disappeared, too. She looked round. The clouds were covering the moon, so it was hard to see; she could just make out some boxy shapes, drinks crates probably. The outhouse had caught the edge of the blast. There was the sound of water, burst main, most likely, but no flames, nothing on fire. So wherever Edie was with that Yank, she was probably okay, wasn't she?

Bea turned, closing the door behind her, and went back into the club. The band was halfway through a rousing version of the Lambeth Walk, and the dance floor was rammed, with everyone desperate to keep the party going and cock a snoop at Hitler. Bea scanned the throng and caught sight of Joan. She pushed her way through the crowd and tugged at Joan's sleeve; Joan was teaching Ron to do the Lambeth Walk.

'Like this, "Oi!"', she cried, sticking out her thumb. Bea felt an arm at her waist.

'Hey, where have you been, stranger?' said Hal.

'Sorry, I just need to have a word with Joan,' she said, shoving his arm away.

'Joan!'

'What?' Joan turned, laughing, cheeks pink. 'These boys were scared during the raid, but I said we don't let a couple of measly bombs worry us. Gunner girls, we're made of sterner stuff than that, aren't we?' she yelled, swaying slightly.

'Oh, you are some dame!' said Ron, falling into her and kissing her neck.

'Cheeky,' she retorted, pushing him playfully away.

'Joan, listen, I can't find Edie,' said Bea.

'Oh, I'm sure she'll be around somewhere,' said Joan, swaying her hips and rolling her eyes at Ron.

'No, she's not. I've looked,' said Bea, feeling Hal's hand snaking round her waist again.

'C'mon, sweet cheeks, why don't you teach *me* the Lambeth Walk?' said Hal. She turned to him.

'I'm really sorry, but I'm worried about our friend. I can't find her anywhere.'

'She's with Art, right?' said Ron.

'She was last time I saw her.'

'Oh, he'll take care of her,' said Hal.

'Yeah, he'll take care of her, all right,' said Ron. The two GIs looked at each other and smirked.

'Hey,' said Joan, frowning. 'That's my pal you're talking about.'

'Whassamatter?' Ron slurred. 'All we said was that Art knows how to take care of—'

'I know exactly what you said. And I know exactly what you meant. But Edie's not like that, and neither are we,' Joan pouted.

'If you'll excuse us, we're off to powder our noses,' Bea said, thrusting her arm through Joan's and dragging her off the dance floor. They made a bumblebee path, bouncing off dancers, finally making it to the Ladies'.

'Oh, I do feel a bit giddy,' said Joan as they pushed open the door. 'Edie, Edie, Edie!' she called, slapping thighs as if trying to find a lost puppy.

'She's not in here. I've already looked,' said Bea. But Joan continued, knocking on toilet doors, calling and laughing, and then she went to the lavvy herself and washed her hands and put on more lipstick and powder. She smoothed her hair in the mirror, and stumbled a little as she turned back around. She's drunk, thought Bea. Joan's drunk and Edie's missing and I've got a really bad feeling about this.

'Joan, drink some water, for goodness' sakes,' she said.

'What?'

'Drink some water, girl.'

'Why?'

'Because you need to sober up so that we can find Edie. I don't trust that Yank she's with.'

'Edie's a grown-up. She can look after herself.'

'Can she?' They looked at each other across the crimson carpet, with the shiny oval mirrors endlessly reflecting. 'Can she look after herself?' Bea repeated.

'All right,' said Joan. She sighed and then put her head

under the tap and took a long draught of water. When she stood upright again, she wiped her mouth with the back of her hand and her lipstick smeared up towards her cheek.

'Oh, look at you, girl,' said Bea. Without thinking, she spat on her hanky and leant across to wipe the red smear away. As she did so, two debs in cocktail dresses swayed in, pointing and giggling. Bea glared at them. Joan didn't seem to have noticed. She was humming along to the orchestra and tapping her foot.

'Listen, Joan, I need you to concentrate,' said Bea. 'We need to find Edie before it's too late.'

'Too late for what?' said Joan, as the posh girls slid past them, giving sly sideways looks. But Bea didn't know for sure. There'd been something wrong in the lie of those tea leaves, something violent. She had a bad feeling about Edie and that GI.

'Any luck?' said Bea, waiting under the potted palm by the stairs. Joan shook her head. 'The doorman says he hasn't seen either of them leave. But they can't just have disappeared.'

'Maybe we should try the side door again.'

'What side door?'

Bea led Joan back round the edge of the dance floor to where the little exit was half hidden behind some stacked chairs. 'Watch out for the Yanks,' she said.

'Oh, they've lost interest. They've found a couple of debs to keep them happy.' Joan gestured across to the other side of the dance floor and Bea caught a glimpse of Hal gazing longingly down the cleavage of one of the posh women who'd been in the lavvy earlier. So much for 'sweet cheeks', she thought. Anyway, I've still got Jock. When he writes back.

Bea led Joan to the little side door. In places like this, there was always a little door leading to the other side, the dirty, practical place where the staff took care of things. She knew that from the pub – the crates had to get stacked somewhere. She quickly checked that nobody was looking, but all the bar staff were busy. She and Joan slipped outside.

The moon was out now, bright as a new penny. She could see the crates stacked higgledy-piggledy and the smashed-in shed. There was water underfoot and a rushing sound. In the distance she could hear fire engines, shouts, and see the smoky orange air where other bombs had struck. But here was just the tumbledown outhouse and the sound of water.

'She's not here,' said Joan.

'Wait,' said Bea. 'I thought I heard something.' A rustle, a movement. It could just have been the sound of some debris settling, but—'

'I can't hear anything,' said Joan. From back inside, there was a cheer, as the band began the Conga. Bea realised she couldn't hear the sound any more. Maybe it was nothing.

'Come on, let's get back inside,' said Joan.

'Shouldn't we just check the shed first?' said Bea.

'Why would Edie be in the shed?' said Joan. But Bea was already walking towards the outhouse, her feet splashing in the water. The door was broken, splintered, partially ajar. Bea pushed it.

'Edie?' she called, so quietly that it was almost a whisper. 'Edie, are you in here?' As she pushed the door further open, the moonlight flooded in, illuminating the scene inside.

'Joan!' Bea hissed. 'Get here, quick!'

Edie was sat in the water, her forehead on her pulled-up knees. Next to her, a mangle of joists and broken masonry, and something underneath it. Edie didn't look up at them as they entered.

Bea and Joan were standing in water. Bea looked down. The moonlight picked out odd strands of yellow hair, floating on the surface, underneath the joist. Underneath, there was an eye: open, glassy. A fishy mouth gaped, but there were no air bubbles. The water was seeping into Bea's shoes, making the toes of her stockings wet.

Edie was shaking, making ripples on the surface of the water, which caught like waves against the dead man's face. Bea went over to Edie and knelt next to her. The water crept coolly over her knees. She put an arm round Edie's quaking shoulders.

'You're all right, girl,' she said. 'We're going to get you home.' But Edie didn't answer and the ripples of water continued to splash up against the man's pale features. Bea recognised him: the bulk, the blond hair. In this light, his uniform was more grey than green, blotted full of water and darkness.

'Come on,' said Bea, but Edie didn't even lift her face. The night was warm, but she was shivering as if they were out in a snowstorm. Bea looked up at Joan, about to ask for help, when there were footfalls from outside, walking along the street towards them. Joan stiffened and put her finger to her lips. Bea held her breath and tried to keep Edie still. The outhouse roof was half caved-in and Bea could see a torch beam playing overhead. The footfalls began to retreat, and Bea breathed out. Her mind was working fast. They had to get Edie back to the battery. They had to get her in and safe without anybody noticing. Suddenly, the retreating footfalls changed direction, returning, getting louder. Then they began to descend the steps down from the street: one-two-three steps down. Bea looked at Joan in desperation. Joan opened the shed door and walked out to meet whomever the foot-steps belonged to. She pulled the door shut behind her.

'Good evening, officer,' Bea heard her say. The answering voice was deep, Bea couldn't hear it properly, but she could hear Joan saying that she'd checked the outhouse and everything was fine. The man shifted over towards the shed door, he couldn't have been more than three feet away from where she sat with Edie in the water. He was just the other side of the broken door. Bea clamped her jaw tight shut and hung on tight to Edie's bony shoulders. The man said good job about that burst main or the whole street would be blaz-ing away like Piccadilly. He and Joan talked about the raid – unusual, it had been so quiet lately – and then the man (was it a police officer or an ARP warden? Bea wasn't sure) noticed Joan's rank, and they talked about her promotion. Stop talk-ing and get rid of him, Bea thought. Then, she realised: Joan was flirting. And the chattier Joan was, the less likely the man was to actually open the shed door. She heard Joan saying something about blue being far more flattering on a man than khaki. Finally, there was the splash-scuff as he moved away from the outhouse door and he thanked her for checking the shed, saying that public-spirited people like her made his life a whole lot easier.

'Not at all, Officer,' Bea heard Joan reply. 'We've all got to do our bit, haven't we?' And the deep voice replied that if the rest of the army were anything like her then maybe the war really would be over by Christmas. Bea listened, astounded. That Joan, she thought, she's got some neck, I'll give her that – lies as easily as breathing. The footfalls went back up the steps and she listened to them echoing further and further away along the street. At last, Joan pushed the door open, and Bea exhaled heavily.

'Good work, girl,' Bea said. Joan shrugged.

'Now we've just got to get her home.'

'But she's got no shoes,' Joan said. Bea hadn't even noticed, but now she looked down. Edie's feet were bare, blue-white under the rising water, which was seeping into Bea's skirt, making the material cold and heavy.

'I'll get her up and you find her shoes then,' said Bea, but Joan didn't answer. Bea looked up. 'Joan?' Joan didn't respond. She was staring down at something. Bea followed her gaze, right down, to where a shaft of moonlight caught the GI's left hand, loose and flaccid under water. A gold band winked on his ring finger.

'Joan,' she said as loudly as she thought was safe, 'we've got no time, we've got to get Edie out of here.' But Joan continued gazing down at the ring on the dead hand. The water moved the fingers and it looked as if they were idling on piano keys.

'Okay, you look after Edie, get her up, and I'll look for the shoes,' Bea said, but still Joan didn't move. Someone will come, Bea thought. Any second now, someone will come and we'll all be for it. She let go of Edie's shoulders and got up.

'Joan!' she said, and reached over and slapped her smartly on the cheek. The swiftness of Joan's response caught her by surprise, a deft punch, hard, just under her right shoulder. Almost as strong as one of Ma's. She staggered backwards, tripped on something and almost fell on Edie.

'That's better, you're back in the land of the living, at least. Now will you stop gawping at that poor chap and bloody well help.' Joan nodded and knelt down next to Edie, while Bea felt about in the dirty water for Edie's shoes. They have to be here somewhere, she thought, fingers paddling in the gloom. All she could feel was the mass of wet cloth and cold flesh of the GI's body, lying still under the wreckage. Bea looked frantically around, but she saw nothing but splintered wood and broken tiles and the body lolling like a sandbag in the water.

'We have to get her out of here; she's going into shock,' whispered Joan.

'I can't find her ruddy shoes, though.'

'Leave them. We'll think of something.'

She heard Joan urging Edie up, and the shuffle-lurch as they made their way outside. The door was pushed shut and it was dark again. She tried one last feel around. The shoes had to be here somewhere, maybe right underneath? As she slid her fingers along the gritty space, underneath the wet cloth and cold flesh of the dead man, she felt something slice her flesh: a shard of glass or metal.

'Sweet Jesus!' she hissed, pulling her hand back and sucking her index finger. The blood tasted warm and metallic. From outside came the sound of a door banging open and the sudden blurt of the orchestra. Joan was out there with Edie, wasn't she? She heard Joan: 'My friend's a little the worse for wear, I'm afraid,' and she laughed. There was an answering murmur and the door banged shut. Bea stood up. Joan was right, they'd just have to leave without the shoes. She pushed the shed door open to leave and the moonlight shone in again on the dead soldier. Bea took one last look at him. Poor sod, she thought, nobody deserves to die so far away from home, whatever they've done. And she thought of Jock. He must have got her letter by now, but he still hadn't replied. How would she ever find out if something had happened to him, thousands of miles away and alone?

It was a long way back from Leicester Square to Hyde Park in the dark. They got lost twice – neither Joan nor Bea knew London as well as Edie, and Edie wouldn't talk, she just hung between them, like a tired child. On the occasions where they bumped into police or ARP wardens, Bea just let Joan do the talking. 'Our friend's not feeling quite herself, Officer,' was the usual line, said with a grin and a wink. By the time they got back to camp, the black sky was already beginning to leach into pale blue in the east, and the moon was just a stern, faraway pebble. The birdsong was sudden and harsh as they staggered up the path towards the entrance, where a Home Guard private was on duty.

'Busy night to be stagging on?' said Joan chattily, as they approached.

'Not as busy as yours, by the looks of it,' said the old soldier, staring at Edie through his wire-rimmed spectacles.

'Our friend's not feeling quite herself,' said Joan, reaching out nonchalantly and patting him on the arm, just beyond the muzzle of his weapon.

'Too many port and lemons, eh?' He chuckled.

'Not at all. She doesn't drink port and lemon; she's not that kind of a girl,' said Joan. 'We were just spending the evening with her father at his club, and she came over a little dizzy, that's all.' The soldier looked as if he was about to ask for their passes, but Joan carried on. 'We would have been back sooner, but her father said it would be madness to come in halfway through a raid.' She smiled, fingering a stray lock of hair at her neck. The soldier grunted, unconvinced, but waved them through.

'What did you say that for?' said Bea, as they were out of earshot.

'What?'

'About meeting her father.'

'We might need an alibi.'

'But why her father? How do you know he'd go along with it?'

'You've met Edie's father, haven't you?' said Joan. Bea nodded. 'Well, then,' said Joan, as if that answered it. 'Blimey, my neck's aching now. For such a slip of a thing, you're a dead weight, Edith Elizabeth,' she said. Edie didn't respond.

Sheila and the other girls were still out on the guns. It would have been a busy night for them – nobody was there to notice Joan and Bea slide in, half carrying their friend between them.

'Come on then, girl,' Bea said as they levelled with the ablutions block. They got her through the doorway and deposited her on the rickety chair next to the bath. Bea put the plug in and turned on the taps. When she turned back, she noticed Edie's feet; they were dirty and covered with little red scratches and blisters from the long walk back. Edie's chin drooped to her chest.

'Look at the state of her,' she said to Joan. 'We need something decent to wash her with.'

'Sheila's got some Lux flakes. I saw them in her locker.'

'She'll never part with them,' said Bea. Joan shrugged and disappeared out into the pale grey dewfall of the pre-dawn. The door clicked shut behind her. Bea drew the bolt.

'Let's get you out of these wet things then,' she said to Edie, but Edie didn't stir. She just sat on the chair, under the harsh yellow light from the bare bulb. Her hair was matted and tangled like seaweed. The sound of the tap running was like the rushing sound of water from the broken main outside the 400 Club. Bea shook her head and sucked her teeth.

'Listen, girl, I'm going to have to undress you if you're not going to do it yourself.' Edie pushed herself up out of the chair, but made no further move.

'Do you want me to do it for you, then?' said Bea. Edie inclined her head slightly, which Bea took to be an assent. With tentative fingertips she reached forwards and began to undo the remaining buttons on Edie's blouse. They caught the cut on her fingertip, making her swear under her breath. They'd need to find spare buttons for this, as soon as, Bea thought, and the shirt itself would need a boil wash. She pulled Edie's arms out of the sleeves and hung the shirt up on a nail in the wall.

There was a knock at the door.

'Only me,' Bea heard Joan's whisper, and slid open the bolt. Joan came in with a cup of white soap flakes, which she threw into the rising bathwater. On the chair she laid two dark green army towels and Edie's striped army pyjamas. Bea reached into the scalding water and swirled the flakes up into bubbles. She decided not to ask Joan how she got hold of Sheila's precious Lux flakes.

Joan looked at Edie, stood shivering still, with her blouse undone. 'Shall I help you?' she began.

'No, you go,' said Bea, whisking the bathwater into creamy bubbles. 'Hop it. Get some shut-eye while you still can. We're on duty in three hours, don't forget.'

'But what about—' Joan looked at Edie and failed to finish the sentence. Edie, standing in the ugly army brassiere, was blinking into the steam.

'I'll deal with her,' Bea said. 'And if anyone asks, she's got flu. Is that clear?'

'Clear,' said Joan. 'But are you sure—'

'Skedaddle,' said Bea, same as she'd said to the twins when they hung about on washing days, trying to 'help'. Joan left and Bea pulled the bolt behind her and turned off the taps. Then she turned her attention back to Edie, who was still shivering, despite the heat from the steam. Her lips were turning blue-ish at the edges, like someone who's been swimming too long.

'I'll take off the rest of your clothes and then we'll get you in a nice hot tub and wash it all away,' she said, touching Edie's arm, where the fine golden hairs were standing on end. 'Let's do your skirt,' she said, and undid the clasp. The skirt almost fell down, barely catching on Edie's tiny, jutting hips. Bea held her hand and helped her step out of it and then hung it up on the nail with the shirt. 'Now, just your underthings,' she said, putting her hands on Edie's hard shoulders and spinning her round so that she could undo the brassiere clasp. It was hard to undo without cutting into the wound on her finger again. She winced, but got it undone and hung it up on the nail with the rest. Then it was the suspender belt, loose on Edie's concave waist. That too, went up on the nail.

Now, Edie was almost naked, her bee-stung breasts and skinny ribs on show. She's just like a little girl, thought Bea, trying not to look. All that was left were her knickers. They were beautiful French satin camis in pale apricot with a cream lace trim. The gusset was ripped. Bea paused.

'Would you like to take them off yourself?' she said, hesitating. But Edie didn't move, or answer, so she knelt down in front and gently pulled down the slippery satin. She was so close she could smell Edie's skin, peppery and floral mixed, and something else, overlaid, dank and salty. There was a smear of blood on Edie's inner thigh. Bea helped Edie step out of the torn knickers and into the bath.

'You can wash yourself, can't you?' she said, but Edie just sat there, so Bea carefully picked up one foot at a time and wiped the dirt away. Edie didn't flinch as Bea picked grit out from a blister. Bea washed each toe at a time, thinking, 'This little piggy went to market, this little piggy stayed at home ... and this little piggy was a naughty little piggy ...' until Edie's feet were all clean. Then she concentrated on Edie's arms, lifting one up and then the other, wiping soapsuds all the way up and under her arms. She scrubbed the back of Edie's neck with a flannel, and wiped behind her ears, just like she'd always done with the twins at home, once a week in the tin tub in front of the fire. Bath times at home she'd always been last. Age order it went, youngest first, every Saturday night. By the time she got her turn in the water, it was always tepid, with a grey soap-sud scum on the surface. Still, she made the best of it, she thought, picking up the empty cup that had held the soap flakes and using it to pour streams of hot water down Edie's angular back. She watched it sluice down like a river between Edie's sharp shoulder blades.

She'd bathed the twins, but Ma never let her bath Baby. Ma said it was a mother's job to bath her own baby. As if Baby wasn't Bea's at all.

Bea sighed, watching the water slow to a trickle and then

dipping the cup in again. She wasn't Baby any more, though, was she? She was Valerie. In the last letter, Vi said she was starting to walk, now. She wasn't a baby any more. Bea sniffed and wiped her nose with the back of her hand, which made it all wet. Edie looked round, with those big doll's eyes, blue and empty.

'Edie, what happened out there tonight?' said Bea. Edie was silent. She blinked, once, and held Bea's gaze.

'He forced himself on you, didn't he?' said Bea. Edie's chin moved down a fraction. Her bottom lip moved and her tongue made a faint clicking sound, as if she were about to speak, but nothing came out but a breath.

'I knew it,' said Bea, shaking her head. 'I knew something was up after I saw those tea leaves. I should never have let you out of my sight.' Bea dipped the cup back into the water and Edie turned away. 'But listen, girl,' Bea said, pouring the hot water over Edie's shoulders. 'It doesn't have to be like that. It's not always like that, really it's not.' Bea carried on tipping the bubbly water over Edie and thought about Jock. She thought about when she used to hold hands with him when they walked along the Strand. She thought of the secluded patch of sunlight behind the ice-cream stall, just off season, when the crowds had all gone home and the estuary air tasted salty and Jock's breath was warm on her neck. She dipped the cup into the water and it came up with foam topping, like ice cream. It was like a bath full of ice cream. Jock had had a rum-'n'-raisin ice, that time, and his mouth tasted sweet and pungent. 'If it's with someone you love, it's like – it's like a blessing,' Bea continued, in a low voice, watching the water glide down. 'You know you said to me that sometimes, when you've been praying and you feel all warm and filled with joy, remember you said that? Well, if it's with someone you love, it's even better than that, girl.'

The water sluiced over Edie's creamy skin, with its freckles like sand. Bea thought about the Strand and the sea wall and the walk that followed the estuary right out to the marshes where there was nothing but waving grass and the mewing sea birds and the blue, blue sky overhead.

'I've got a baby,' Bea said to the back of Edie's head, but Edie stayed facing forward, not moving. 'I did it with a boy called Jock because I loved him and he said he'd marry me when he came home on leave, just as soon as he'd saved up for a ring. But he didn't come back and I had a baby. My ma – my ma pretends the baby's hers. She pretends because she lost one of her own – stillborn, same time I fell pregnant. And she thinks the soul of her dead baby is in mine. She thinks my baby is hers. But she's not. She's my baby and she always will be.'

Bea could hear the break and crash in her voice, like waves hitting the shore. 'She's mine, and one day I'll get her back. As soon as he writes back. As soon as he comes home.' Bea's throat was tight. She dropped the cup in the bathwater and buried her head in her hands. She felt like a piece of paper someone had crumpled up, ready to chuck into the hearth. She rubbed her eyes, and then dipped her fingers back into the bathwater. It was getting cool.

'Come on, girl, let's get you out,' she said, standing up and holding a hand out to Edie. She helped her out of the bath and ushered her into a towel and rubbed her until every droplet of water was gone. Then she got Edie to hold up her hands and slipped the nightdress over her head. She pulled out the bathplug, swirling the water round so that it wouldn't leave a soap-scum rim, then she gathered Edie's clothes from the nail.

The satin knickers, ripped, lay on the floor. They were expensive, beautiful and ruined. Bea sucked her teeth. The water gurgled down the plughole. She thought about that yellow-haired Yank. Should they have tried to do something more for him? What about his two pals? She sighed and reached down to pick up the soiled underwear. It would have to be burnt.

Chapter 25

Joan forced her eyes open as she exhaled. The smoke hung in front of her face like a veil. It wasn't exhaustion that made her eyes heavy-lidded and her head pound, it was concern. Poor Edie. She inhaled again and this time exhaled with a sighing rush.

'Penny for them,' said a voice. She looked round. It was Billy, the store man.

'Oh, nothing, just that Monday-morning feeling, I suppose,' she replied.

'Thanks for giving me your spam and egg,' he said.

'You're welcome. I'm watching my figure,' she said, which wasn't true, but she couldn't exactly tell fat little Billy from stores that the reason she had no appetite was because her best friend had been raped and they'd all left a GI for dead at the 400 Club.

'You're not the only one watching your figure,' said Billy with a leer as he took out his packet of Craven 'A'. She shot him a sideways look. He sniggered and lit up. Joan leant back against the corrugated metal wall of the hut and tried to wriggle her toes in the too-tight shoes; they were her ones from before, black civvie shoes that had never fitted. But there was a reason she was wearing them this morning. Edie had come back the other night with no shoes; her ATS brogues were somewhere in the wreckage in Leicester Square, along with the drowned American.

'You know what, you're right, Billy, I do have something on my mind,' said Joan, continuing to lounge against the metal hut wall, even though it poked hard into her shoulders. 'Have a look at me and tell me what my problem is.'

He narrowed his conker-coloured eyes, appraising her, blowing smoke in rings as his gaze travelled over her body like searchlights. 'Nah,' he said at last. 'No problem I can see.'

'Look further down,' she instructed.

He grinned, enjoying the game, and his eyes lingered over every inch of khaki, all the way down to her ... 'Shoes,' he said. 'What's up with your shoes?'

'Oh, Billy, I've only gone and lost them. These are my old civvie ones. We were out dancing on Friday and I took them off because – well, you know how it is – and then there was that air raid and ... and Staff Farr will kill me, Billy, you know what she's like, don't you?' Joan let the words hang.

'I don't open the stores until nine,' said Billy.

'Can't you make an exception?' she said, turning her face towards him but leaving her body draped against the hut wall.

'It's more than my job's worth,' he replied. 'You think you're the only one with a bastard for a boss?'

'You never know, it might be worth your while,' she said.

'Will it, though?' he said, looking her in the eye and blowing a large smoke ring in her direction.

'Oh, I don't know, might be, might not be.' She shrugged, maintaining eye contact and smiling.

'All right, I'll meet you at the stores in two ticks,' he said. His tongue flicked out briefly to lick his lips and his fag end fell to the ground.

She finished her own cigarette and counted to one hundred before walking to the stores. The morning cloud was low and wet on her face. Her shoes – the wrong shoes – were still full of the pinch and grief of last winter. Every step hurt as she followed the path. The Quartermaster's stores appeared suddenly out of the fog. The door was slightly ajar. She pushed it open a little further and stepped inside. In front of her was the wooden counter and beyond it, darkness. The blackout curtains were still down.

'Billy?' she called.

'Ssh. Shut the bloody door, will you?' She did, and then she noticed the glow of a hurricane lamp, bobbing towards her between high shelves laden with army kit, and Billy's face, greenish yellow and pitted with dark hollows in the lamplight. His shadow bounced and fled down the gap between the shelves.

'Here,' he said, and as he came closer his face loomed like something from the ghost train at the fair. He put the brogues on the counter and she picked them up to look at them, squinting in the dimness. He lifted up the hinged portion of the counter and slid round next to her. She felt a hand on her bum, warm and sudden. She shoved it away.

'Wrong size. I need a three.'

'You? You're never a three, not those plates of meat. You're at least a size six or my name's not . . .'

'I need a three,' she interrupted, holding out the shoes.

'All right, all right.' He sucked his teeth, took the brogues and slid back round, and away, taking the lantern with him.

For a while, she was in darkness again. Billy would want something in return for the shoes, wouldn't he? He'd want to cop a feel, at least. You didn't get something for nothing. Boys will be boys — that's what Edie found out. Joan heard his footfalls getting closer and watched the orb of lamplight growing larger and brighter. Billy plonked the brogues down and she quickly picked them up and checked the size again. Then he was coming back round, a solid shadow, getting closer.

'Thanks so much for this, Billy, you're a pal,' she said.

'Just a pal, Joanie?'

'Just a pal, Billy,' she said, as he inched nearer.

'We could be more than pals,' he said, and for a moment she thought it would be easier just to shut her eyes and let him get on with it.

'You know I've got someone, Billy.'

'But he's not here, now, is he?'

'No, he's not, but I'm not like that,' she said.

'That's not what I heard,' said Billy, and she could feel his breath, damp on her neck. He was an inch or two shorter than her, and the skin on his cheek was smooth and plump, like a boy's. 'It's just a bit of fun, between friends. I've done you a favour, now you can do me one,' he said, warm and close in the darkness.

'I can't,' she said, side-stepping away from him. She checked her watch. 'Blimey, Billy, look at the time. We'll both be late for first parade at this rate.'

He checked his own watch and sucked his teeth. 'You can't blame me for asking,' he said.

'I don't. No hard feelings?'

'All right, no hard feelings,' he said, wiping his nose on his sleeve. 'That bloke of yours is a lucky man.'

She brushed past him as she left, and then paused in the doorway. 'Thanks again, Billy,' she said.

She was so preoccupied with the shoes, and the time, that she didn't notice Staff Farr walking towards her through the mist and all-but ran into her.

'Watch your step, Tucker,' said the staff sergeant, her eyes darting over Joan. 'What are you doing all the way out here at this time?' she began.

'Sorry, Staff, I was just . . .' Joan's mind raced ahead to try to find a plausible explanation.

'Oh, never mind, just get a bloody move on or you'll be late for first parade.'

'Yes, Staff.' She hurried on and banged open the door of their hut. In front of her Bea was just doing up Edie's buttons, dressing her, like a child. Bea gave her a look, round eyes and downturned mouth.

'Sorry I took so long,' said Joan, handing over the new shoes.

'Thank the Lord you've got them, or there'd be some explaining to do,' said Bea, taking them from her. Then, turning to Edie. 'Sit yourself down, girl, and we'll get these shoes on you.'

Edie looked down at the shoes as if they were the first pair of shoes she'd seen in her life.

'Come on, now, it'll be fine,' Bea soothed Edie, kneeling down and taking one foot and guiding it into the brown leather.

Joan watched as Bea slipped Edie's feet into the tiny shoes, and thought about Cinderella – the bit where the Prince finds her and the slipper fits. Then the image was replaced by a memory: craning her head; black all around and in the distance a jewel-lit stage with a prince in blue bending over a blonde-haired Cinderella; ugly sisters were fat men in dresses with gurning faces, throwing sweets into the crowd; laughter; applause. A pantomime – when was that? Who took her?

There was a thumping on the hut door and Sheila's voice, shrill and urgent: 'The reserve team are already forming up, hurry up or you'll let us all down!'

Joan knelt down next to Bea, her fingers weaving and tying Edie's laces. She gave the toes of the brogues a quick rub; they were still dusty from the stores. Bea stood up, tugged at Edie's arm, told them both to hurry up or there'd be hell to pay. 'A three's right isn't it? Do they fit okay?' said Joan, helping Edie up. Edie nodded.

A sound of running footsteps went past the hut. 'Come on,' said Bea, tugging Edie towards the door. 'Your cap!' said Joan, and there was a panic as they searched for Edie's cap and made sure it was placed exactly an inch over her eyes. From outside came the muffled sound of voices and laughter from the drill square, the whole battery assembling in time for first parade.

Bea pulled Edie back towards the door. They were all properly dressed now; they should just make it. As the door opened, the voices on the drill square suddenly went silent. Joan glanced over her shoulder as she followed the others out, and that was when she noticed the letter on her bed.

'Hang on a sec, girls,' she said.

'We wouldn't be here if you hadn't gone back for that letter,' said Bea, snatching a cloth from her.

'We would've been late anyway,' said Joan. 'What with—' she stopped herself. Edie was nearby, looking through the grimy windows at the men playing football on the grass. Joan lowered her voice: 'We were lucky we made it to work at all this morning, with her like she is.'

'It's not her fault.'

'I know it's not her fault, I'm not saying it's her fault, but it's hardly bloody mine, is it?'

'If you hadn't gone back for that letter, though . . .'

'We still would have been late,' said Joan, unscrewing the

top of the vinegar bottle and pouring it onto the string dish-cloth, making the grey strands slickly acidic. She passed the bottle onto Bea, who took it and soaked her own cloth.

'At least we're not being beasted like Billy,' said Joan. They both looked outside to the drill square, where poor Billy was doubling round with his gas mask on, watched by the sergeant major. All four of them had been late for first parade and all four of them were being punished. Joan felt bad about Billy; she hadn't meant for him to get into trouble. She resolved to buy him a crate of beer from her next pay packet.

At the window, Edie was running her fingers along the sill, making a repetitive groove in the thick layer of dust and dead flies. Her lips were moving, but no sound came out. Bea and Joan exchanged looks.

'I'll start on the outside,' Bea said. Then in a lower voice, as she passed by Joan, she muttered: 'You try to get her to talk; you might have more luck than me.' Then she went out through the door. Joan watched her walk along to the far end, saw her begin to rub vigorously on the furthest window with her vinegar-soaked rag.

Joan went over to Edie. 'How about you wipe and I buff?' she said, holding out the dishcloth. Edie looked up.

'Oh,' she gasped, as if the reason for them being here in the cookhouse after hours was a total surprise. Edie reached for the cloth and Joan let go. But the moment Edie grasped it, she dropped it again, with a whispered 'ow', barely more audible than an exhalation.

Edie stared at the cloth on the floor and Joan stared at Edie.

Her face looked brittle, like china. Then she noticed that Edie's fingernails were bitten, right down to the quick, raw pinky-red at the tips. That vinegar must've stung like anything. Joan bent down to pick up the cloth. She put it on the table behind her, next to the vinegar bottle and the crumpled brown paper.

'Edie,' she said, and put out a hand towards her. Edie flinched.

'We're here for you, Edie,' said Joan. 'Me and Bea, we can't change what happened, but we can help.' Edie shook her head, a furrow between her brows, her mouth hard and small. 'It's important to know,' Joan continued, moving closer, without touching. 'Did he . . . when it happened, did he finish? Edie, do you understand what I mean? Because if he did, you might be . . .' here she left a gap. She couldn't say it aloud, not even here, just the two of them, in the empty cookhouse. '. . . and if you are, then we might be able to do something about it, get it sorted. There are people you can go to.' Joan paused, catching her breath. She looked at Edie; her blue eyes were blank and expressionless. In training they'd been made to watch an awful film about VD and pregnancy, and Edie had just said airily that none of it concerned her because she was saving herself for marriage. 'You do understand, don't you Edie? Edie, I wish you'd say something.'

Edie lifted her right hand to her lips and chewed on her already-raw index fingernail, and looked away, out past the footballers and towards the drill square, where the sergeant major was shouting at Billy.

Joan sighed and turned back to the cleaning stuff. 'Okay, look, I'll wipe and you buff, just make it shine, like this,' she demonstrated, 'because Staff Farr will be back to check.'

Edie nodded and took the brown paper from her. Joan pulled the cloth over the glass, wiping off the accumulated dust and grime. Edie followed, rubbing the glass with small round movements until the evening sun began to shine strongly through, turning the skin on their arms pale lemon and warming their faces.

As they worked, their heads were close together and their breath came in little pants. Cleaning the windows took a surprising amount of effort. The sunshine fell in pools on the lino and the air smelled of old gravy and dust, overlaid with the sharpness of the vinegar. Joan's arm began to ache. She moved onto the next window. Bea was moving along, from the outside, in the opposite direction. Soon they'd meet in the middle. She could see Bea cleaning faster than her and Edie put together, her brown hair roll honey-gilded as the lowering sun touched it.

Billy was gone from the drill square now. Joan was glad the sergeant major hadn't been too hard on him. The other lads were still playing football and as she and Edie wiped away the dirt, the smudged figures became clearer. A couple of them had taken their shirts off; their torsos looked hard and smooth, like soap. Someone fell and there were jeers and calls of foul play. Edie still said nothing – she'd been like this since Bea found her outside the 400 Club: silent as the grave.

Bea came in now, cloth in hand, getting another glug of

vinegar. She looked questioningly at Joan, who shook her head. 'You're doing a good job there, girl,' Bea said loudly at Edie, who didn't respond, just carried on rubbing with the brown paper.

Joan was desperate for chatter and noise, the distraction of gossip. 'Join us for a bit, Bea,' said Joan, hoping for small talk. Bea soaked her cloth in vinegar and began to rub with brisk capable movements, her strong arms moving quickly over the glass.

'You see that lad in goal,' she began, but then stopped. Joan urged her to carry on, but Bea wouldn't. 'It's nothing important,' she said, lapsing into quiet. They worked on without talking. Bea was on one side of her, Edie on the other. There was just the faint squeak of wet cloth against glass and the occasional muffled shout from outside. Joan began to sing, just to break the silence, the first thing that came into her head:

'Pardon me boys, is this the Chattanooga Choo Choo? Track twenty-nine . . .'

'. . . boys, you can give me a shine,' Bea joined in.

There was a soft thud and a clatter and suddenly Edie was on the other side of the glass, running past the cookhouse windows and away towards the guns, capless, her red hair flying like a kite tail behind her. Joan and Bea looked at each other.

'I'll go,' said Joan. 'I'm faster.' Bea nodded and Joan was away, sprinting past the whistling footballers and the drill square and the CO's hut and out towards the emplacements. Edie's figure was a tiny scurrying blur in the distance.

Joan was gaining on her but didn't manage to catch up, and she saw Edie up ahead of her, stumbling down the steps to the guns. When Joan arrived she found Edie curled up by the bottom of the furthest gun, rocking backwards and forwards. She ran over. Edie had pulled into herself, a wet pebble wedged into a corner, red hair spilling like damp weed.

Joan stretched out her hand to where Edie's hands clasped tight against her knees. Gritty concrete dug into Joan's bare knees as she knelt forward, touching the raw tips of Edie's fingers. 'You're not alone, Edie,' she whispered. 'I'm here, don't worry.'

Edie was making strange noises, a high-pitched keening, as she rocked backwards and forwards on the hard ground. Joan shuffled closer, put her arms round Edie, tried to still her, but Edie wrenched herself away, lurched on all fours, heaving as the keening was replaced by the guttural choke of vomit. Joan caught her, held her hair off her face as the bile upsurged again and again. When Edie finally came to a shuddering halt, Joan wiped her face with a clean handkerchief.

'It's all right. It's all right,' she whispered into the top of Edie's hair. 'It's all right; you're not alone. I'll look after you.'

Edie's hair was the colour of crushed chrysanthemums. Joan thought about splintered wood and the smell of burning, broken flowerpots and the sound of sirens. She could smell Edie's sick, in a puddle on the concrete next to them, and gulped back her own nausea. The blood thudded in her temples.

She held Edie in a tight embrace, not letting go, and stayed like that while the sun slanted lower and the trees cast long shadows that shivered in the rising wind, and the crows returned to roost in the big oak tree and the footballers finally finished their noisy game. She bit her lip until it bled, swallowing the metallic taste. When the sky began to turn rose-pink over the far away rooftops, and her knees were numb from the concrete, she helped Edie up to her feet and led her gently by the hand back to their hut.

They got back as Staff Farr was doing her final round. She didn't mention anything about the cookhouse windows – Bea must've had to work like billy-oh to get them done in time – but her gaze moved round and rested with Joan, who was just taking off her boots.

'Bombardier Tucker?'

'Yes, Staff,' she stopped undoing her laces and looked up. Staff Farr's eyes were piercing down at her.

'You worked hard for that stripe. Don't rest on your laurels. If you or your girls are late for parade a second time, there'll be more than a little light housework as extras. Is that clear?'

'Yes, Staff.'

Staff Farr stalked out. Joan thought she heard a couple of the girls stifling giggles across the other side. Bea came over and gave her a sympathetic pat on the shoulder and then took charge of Edie, helping her change and laying out her clothes ready for the morning. When Edie and Bea went to the ablutions block together, Sheila Carter came over to Joan's bed. Joan was just slipping on her nightie.

'What's up with your friend?'

'Nothing,' Joan replied, pushing her arms through the

sleeves and emerging from the neck. She wasn't going to share secrets, least of all with rabbit-faced Sheila.

'She used to yakkety-yak like a blooming Bren gun, but since the royal visit she's been all funny with us,' said Sheila, and then the voices of the other girls chipped in: *Yeah, thinks she's too good to talk to us. She's always been hoity-toity that one. Treats Bea like a servant. We should say something to Staff Farr; she's just not pulling her weight . . .*

'No,' said Joan. 'She's not well, that's all.'

'If she's ill, she should go sick. Get some medicine,' said Sheila, hands on hips, fingers like chipolatas.

'No, it's not that, it's . . .' Joan tried to think of something both vague and plausible. '. . . it's bad news from home. She's in a right state about it. Sorry if we've been a bit off with you lot, but we're worried about her. She won't talk, or anything.' At that there were a few sympathetic murmurs from the others.

'So what's up, then?' said Sheila.

'She won't say. It's like I said; she won't talk. Look, I shouldn't say this, you know I'm not one to gossip, but that morning of the royal visit, there was a telegram . . .' she let the words hang, knowing that they'd all draw their own conclusions. It was a lie, of course, there had been no telegram, but what was one small lie on top of the huge messy secret they'd left behind at the 400 Club?

Joan heard the door of the ablutions block bang shut. 'Please don't say anything,' she said.

'Course not. We're not gossips, are we girls?' said Sheila,

and the other girls shook their heads and looked busy when Edie and Bea walked in.

When Joan asked if Edie wanted a final fag, just before blackout, she shook her head. She hadn't smoked since that night, either. The other girls were in bed, reading or knitting. Joan went outside with Bea, in the gap between their hut and the ablutions block and they sucked on their cigarettes and watched the summer evening leach away.

'They were asking about Edie,' said Joan.

'What did you tell them?'

'That she had bad news from home, that there was a telegram, and she wouldn't talk about it.'

'Think they swallowed it?'

'For now, but what are we going to do about her?'

Bea rolled the cigarette between forefinger and thumb and shrugged.

'But what if she's . . .' Joan began, but still couldn't say it.

Bea was silent, not answering, turning away.

'What if she's got VD?' Joan whispered. 'Or worse. What if she's . . .? What if she's . . .?'

'Up the duff?'

'Yes.'

'Girls have babies all the time,' said Bea, still turned away, so that Joan could only see her three-quarter profile, the soft curve of her cheek and the hard ball of her shoulder. Her voice was flat and expressionless.

'But she's not married. I mean, she's on her own, it would be a disaster for her, wouldn't it?'

Bea did not answer or turn back. Joan watched her exhale. In the distance, there were voices, chattering and laughing away up the Bayswater Road. Joan watched the tip of Bea's cigarette smoulder like a small volcano in the twilight.

'What was so important about that bloody letter of yours this morning anyway?' Bea said, at last, throwing her still-lit stub away into the night.

'It was from Rob,' said Joan. 'He's got a leave pass and he's coming to visit. He says he's got something important to ask me.'

Chapter 26

He could see her in the distance, waiting, but she had her back to him. She would be expecting him to be coming from the other direction, but he'd come the other way, because he'd spent half the day in Hatton Garden, talking to the greasy jewellers, parting with three months' wages. The little silk-covered box in his pocket poked against his thigh as he walked.

She was just a muddy figurine up ahead, like unglazed pottery, set against the grey-beige muddle of a summer rainstorm. She didn't have an umbrella, but she was holding something above her head. He broke into a run, shoes splashing in puddles. As he got closer, he could see it was his old flying jacket, held up, sheltering her from the sluicing rain. He thought back to that April day, when he'd left her alone in the church. He'd had some explaining to do when he'd got back with half his uniform missing.

She turned, hearing his footfalls on the pavement. She

came forward towards him, holding the flying jacket higher, and as he got closer, he could see she was smiling. Then he was there, with her, underneath the sheepskin. And they fell together: her lips, her breath, her hair, the taste of her. The sheepskin dropped as she encircled him with her arms. The raindrops were like soft tears. Rob could feel rain coursing down the back of his neck as they kissed. The last few months just melted away – the knotted stomach, the upside-down firework displays over faraway German towns, the biting cold, the nausea, and the endless round of new pals who so quickly disappeared – all of that went away, and none of it mattered. All that mattered was the moment.

'I've missed you,' she said, between kisses, but he didn't answer, found her mouth again, kissed her hard and felt the exquisite anguish of wanting her so much. They held and stroked, fingers slick with wet, gas masks clunked and tangled; he didn't care. He could stay here in the rain in the middle of the London pavement with her for ever.

'Would sir and madam like to step inside?' said a voice beside them. Rob turned and looked. A portly doorman in a top hat, stood underneath a vast umbrella, just at their side. How long had he watched before he said something? His florid face and squinty eyes gave nothing away. Rob said yes of course, and allowed himself to be ushered up the hotel steps and into the lobby, where another uniformed man, hatless, shiny hair thinning on the crown, asked if sir and madam had a room reserved?

Rob caught Joan's eye. With another girl, this would have

been embarrassing, but she just laughed, threw back her head and laughed. Her ATS cap fell off and landed on the polished marble floor, and she let the man pick it up for her. Then she gave him the flying jacket, saying thank you so much, we're just here for tea. He said very well, if you'd like to follow me, madam, and she said, we have a reservation, actually; the name's Lightwater. And as she said the name, Rob noticed the man's body stiffen, ever so slightly, so he walked a little more upright, to attention almost.

'I thought your surname was Tucker,' Rob whispered, as the man motioned them through the doorway into the Palm Court. 'They won't know that,' said Joan, 'but they'll know who Sir Neville Lightwater is.' She winked at Rob, and gave the maitre d' a gracious smile as he showed them to a table for two next to the window. Rob followed, watching her sway easily ahead. Her hair was different, palest gold. There was the plink-plink of a piano and the smell of flowers and gilded edges; everything was pale, muted and discreet. The room was almost empty; a couple of stout ladies at the far end, that was all.

Chairs were pulled out, napkins flapped like flustered hens. His cap was soaking; it left a puddle on the windowsill. He asked a waiter to take it and put it with the coats. The waiter held it as if it were the corpse of a well-loved pet. Joan pulled her chair in a little closer and patted her hair. It was damp, raindrops like seed pearls on the ends. Catching sight of herself in the mirror on the wall behind him, she took a lipstick from her gas-mask case.

'Have you ever actually kept a gas mask in that?' he said, watching as she slicked red over her full lips and rubbed her top teeth once over with her tongue.

'Never,' she said, clicking the gold lipstick lid on. 'If they send in gas, I'll be a goner.' He laughed, and she put away her lipstick.

'I like your hair,' he said.

'Thanks, I fancied a change,' she replied.

The waiter came back, thrusting menus, solicitous. Rob asked him to give them a moment to decide. He scanned the curly writing, but it was all a blur. The box was poking hard against his leg, now he was sat down, nagging. He turned his attention back to Joan. She wasn't looking at the menu, she was looking out of the window, watching the rain pelt down as a green coach throbbed past, making the windowpane shudder. She looked very serious. He asked if everything was all right.

'It's nothing,' she said. 'I'll tell you one day.' And then she smiled and nudged her foot between his, underneath the table. He pulled his chair right forward and she twined her other leg around his. Above the table they were perfectly respectable, but below, they were locked in an embrace. The box, trapped under the tight cloth of his uniform, pressed hard into his flesh.

The waiter came back and Rob said tea for two and whatever the lady would like. Joan said, 'I don't think what "the lady" would like can be found on a cake trolley,' giving Rob a sideways look. And the waiter's eyebrows shot up. 'I do like eclairs though,' she added, and the waiter replied, 'Eclairs for the lady, very good. Will that be all, sir?' Rob said it would and he glided away out of sight behind aspidistras. When he'd gone, they laughed, and Rob reached forward and took her hands in his. There was the pulse of static as their fingers connected. For a while they just sat, looking at each other. Rob was trying to commit again to memory her eyes, the way her bottom lip pouted, the gap between her teeth.

'You looked different in the paper,' he said, and he noticed something pass over her face, like a cloud scudding over the sun. 'You should've let me know – lucky one of the other chaps noticed and saved me a copy.'

'It didn't seem important,' she said.

He asked about the day of the royal visit, and her promotion, and work, and listened to her talk, and watched her eyes, her mouth, the way she looked sideways at him instead of full on. I could grow old with this woman, he thought.

The waiter returned, piling the table with china and cutlery: translucent teacups and plates and cake forks and a vast silver teapot and a cake stand. There was no room for clasped hands.

At last, the waiter left again, and Rob thought, *Now, do it now*, and he disentangled his legs from hers, and pushed his chair out, stood up, pulled out the ring box and then got down on one knee, right there, in the Palm Court in the Ritz Hotel. Because, like his old dad said, faint heart never won fair maid. She was looking down at him: hazel eyes, a flush in her cheeks. He flicked open the lid of the box. He wasn't nervous at all, because he knew what the answer would be. Right from that moment when the bomb fell on Western Way, they were meant to be together.

'Joan,' he said. 'Will you marry me?'

Chapter 27

'Well?' said Bea, the second Joan stepped through the hut door.

'Well what?' said Joan.

Inside the hut, it was thick and warm, dense with the scent of sweat and drying wool. The rain rattled loudly on the corrugated tin roof. Sheila Carter was busy in the corner with the old Singer sewing machine and a piece of striped seersucker.

'Did he pop the question?' said Bea, her face an expectant blob. Joan looked round; the hut was full. It was barrack night and all the girls were busy darning, sewing and mending. Even Edie was rubbing polish on her boots in languid curves, while staring out of the rainy grey square window. The sewing machine fell silent and six pale faces looked over at her.

'Yes, he did,' she said, still standing right next to the door, wishing she could either bolt out into the rain or run to her bed and hide under the covers.

'Oh, I'm so happy for you, girl!' shrieked Bea, dropping her crochet and running over. She hurled herself at Joan, and suddenly Joan was surrounded as all the other girls came over, too. The entire hut was a squealing mass: *Did he get on one knee? Was it very romantic? Did he look nervous? What did the other people think? The ring, the ring, show us the ring!* Her hand was grabbed and Joan looked down with them, and for an instant she saw a different hand, with perfectly buffed oval nails and a thin gold ring studded with sapphires and pearls, and there was a gritty feeling on her knees and a burning smell. That buzzing sound again. But in an instant the vision went, and it was her own hand there instead, with the chipped thumbnail, and the ring had three aquamarines interspersed with two tiny diamonds. Why had she thought they were sapphires and pearls?

How lovely! Look at that, isn't it beautiful? It must have cost him a fortune! When's the wedding Joan? Who's going to be bridesmaids?

Edie came over last, getting up slowly from her bed. Joan saw her pale forehead and burnished hair through the throng. She took Joan's hand in hers. As she did so, she said, 'But Joan, you've got it on the wrong hand, dear.' Joan said nothing, and everyone just looked at her, and for a while there was just the sound of the rain on the roof and Edie's hard little hand holding hers.

'You did say yes, didn't you?' said Bea.

'No, I said I'd think about it,' said Joan. There were mutterings of concern: *Playing hard to get? It's a dangerous game. Make him sweat, I say! You holding out for some matching earrings?*

'Why did you do that?' said Bea.

'Oh, you know, play 'em mean, keep 'em keen,' said Joan, affecting nonchalance. Edie dropped Joan's hand and it felt suddenly cold and empty.

'What are you on about?' said Bea, stepping in close. 'Robin is a good man. Why didn't you just say yes?'

'I know he's a good man.' The faces were looking questioningly at her. Edie had drifted back to her bed. The others were waiting, sensing gossip, scandal, something to talk about at NAAFI break in the morning. Well, she wasn't going to give it to them. 'I don't see why it's any of your bloody business. And I don't know what you're all standing about gawping for.'

The crowd shrank back. Sheila went back to the Singer, pulled her lip over her overbite and fretted with a bit of puckered hem. The others wandered back to their bunks, rolling eyes at each other and muttering under their breath. Only Bea didn't move. 'You don't know what's good for you,' she said sadly. Sheila's Singer began to stutter and hum in the background.

'And who are you, my mother?' hissed Joan.

'You don't fool me. You make out that it's all about lipstick and dancing and gadding about, but if you carry on like this, you'll end up old and lonely,' said Bea, under her breath. 'Rob is a good man and you won't do better.'

'I don't need you to tell me about Rob,' said Joan. 'It's none of your business.'

'Yes, it is. I don't want to see you throwing away your future. I'm thinking of you. Because I'm your friend.'

'Are you?' Joan held her gaze, chin up, eyes narrowed. Bea shook her head sadly and sighed, turning away.

'Oh, Joan,' she said under her breath.

The sewing machine abruptly stopped, and Sheila swore, loudly. Joan looked round.

'Blasted thing,' said Sheila, sucking her finger where the needle had caught it and getting up. 'I give up. I'm going to the NAAFI for a KitKat, anyone else want something?' There was a murmur of assent and a scuffling as girls handed over change and Sheila pulled on her coat and headed off.

Joan went to sit down on her own bed. She should probably get on with something: the strap on her spare brassiere was almost worn through and there was a hole in the pocket of her work trousers. She sat and thought about what she ought to do and looked outside. The little hut window was like a porthole and the rain sluiced down the pane. Joan thought about Rob and his face when she'd left him outside the Ritz. Bea was right; he was a good man. Why hadn't she just said yes? She fiddled with the red stitching on her blanket until an end came loose. She pulled it, it started to unravel and she watched as the stitches undid themselves, thinking back.

She'd felt him move his feet away from hers and watched as he pushed his chair back. It made a scraping sound on the marble floor. Then he pulled a little black box from his pocket and half-knelt down in front of her. There he was, with his dark Brylcreemed hair and his blue-grey air-force uniform, and she thought, blimey, this is like something from the flicks, and she half expected some soaring orchestral music to accompany the inevitable question. Robin – her Rob – looked up at her and flicked open the lid of the box and she looked down at him, with his kind eyes and his crooked nose and she knew that she was going to say yes, because she loved him, and they'd live happily ever after, just like the films. And then he said, 'Joan Tucker, will you marry me?'

She opened her mouth, but as she inhaled, ready to respond, she looked down into the box, at the ring – the gold ring with the blue stones – and the room tilted, and she heard again the buzzing in her ears. Then, instead of saying yes, she said nothing, because her head was full of images of a hand, and a sapphire ring, and little almond-shaped fingernails, and blood and that acrid smell, and the hand still warm and the settling dust. And there was that loud buzzing, filling her ears. Robin looked up at her, waiting. She held onto the edge of the table because everything else seemed to be swerving away.

'Joanie?' mouthed Rob – she couldn't hear him above the fuzzy roar in her head.

She tried again. 'I—' she began, but no sound came out. She looked down at him, but couldn't focus; everything was shifting. Her hand tightened on the tablecloth. She felt the soft cotton under her fingertips and she pulled it tight, and remembered holding onto the edge of a pinny, feeling the cloth like that, when there were strangers in the house. But what house? Whose pinny?

Rob's face was pinkly indistinct, his features smudged. 'Joan, what's the matter?' he said, but she could barely hear him. She looked at him, trying to focus on his face, but his eyes were just full stops and his mouth a dark underscore.

'Joanie?' He leant in. His sleeve brushed her knee. The box was almost in her lap. She looked down at him, his face on a level with her chest, and concentrated on his features until they became clear. There he was, her Rob. He held her gaze without blinking, and she saw a reflection of herself in miniature, like a small ghost on the surface of his pupil, barely there at all.

'I can't,' she said at last.

The buzzing began to lessen, and from outside there was a swooshing sound as the traffic ran through puddles. The rain pattered against the hotel windows. Robin got up off his knees and sat back down in his seat, slamming the open ring box on the table between them. The Palm Court doors swung open and three young women rushed in, laughing and chattering like birds and shaking out raincoats and umbrellas. The waiter hurried over to the smiling women. Joan tapped the handle of her teaspoon, feeling as if she were about to snap.

'I do love you,' she said at last.

'Then why won't you say yes?'

'I don't know.'

'What do you mean, you don't know?'

'Just that,' she searched for the words. 'Just that I feel as if you don't really know me, not really.'

'Don't be ridiculous. I know all about you. You're Joan Tucker and you're eighteen and you're in the ATS and you've just got your first stripe and you're the prettiest, bravest girl

I've ever met and you're my girl and I want to spend the rest of my life with you.' He banged his palm on the table, making the crockery clatter, and the waiter look over in consternation. Robin frowned and picked up the teapot. His hands were shaking.

'But the day we met—' she began.

'I know. And that makes me love you more, because you were so brave then, so very brave, and after all that, I just wanted to look after you, and I still do, for ever. Can't you understand that, Joanie?' he said, spilling the tea all over the lace cloth. He scooped a spoonful of sugar into his cup and stirred like it was a trowel in a bucket of cement. 'What do I have to do, Joanie?'

'Give me time.'

'We don't have time. Anything could happen.'

'I know that,' she said, shaking her head, looking down at the tea he'd poured her. She pushed her foot towards his, under the table, but he pulled his away. The surface of the tea rippled in the cup, the concentric circles criss-crossing and cancelling each other out.

'Joan,' he said, his voice hard and impatient, 'is there someone else?'

'Of course not,' she replied, lifting her eyes to meet his. It was true, but she still felt like a liar.

The rattle of rain slowed to a patter and then a drip, and she was left sitting on the bed with a handful of red thread, and still thinking about Rob's face. Then the door thudded open and Sheila fell inside, back from the NAAFI, face shiny with exertion and rain, hands full of chocolate bars.

'Your fella's in the NAAFI,' she said to Joan, pulling off her coat.

'Rob's here?' said Joan, starting. Sheila nodded, handing out KitKats and change. Joan caught Bea looking at her from behind the sewing machine. 'Cheeky blighter, I haven't said yes, yet,' said Joan, 'but if he really can't wait, I suppose I'd better put him out of his misery.' She could feel a dozen eyes on her as she headed for the door. Outside, she pushed up her umbrella and it quivered above her like a giant flower. She began to walk: best foot forward. Left–right, left–right, past the lines of Nissen huts, grey-brown in the drizzle, like sleeping tortoises. Bea was right: Rob was a good man, and he loved her, and that's what was important, wasn't it?

Behind the wad of rainclouds the sun still hadn't set. A splatter of raindrops fell on her as she passed under the beech tree. She blinked and wiped them away and then she could see the NAAFI in front of her. The blackout curtains were open and there was a little amber square of light on the curved side of the building. Rob would be inside. Would he be propped up at the counter, chatting to Mrs Cripps, or would he be sat at a table with a cup of tea and an open packet of Player's?

Joan's scalp tingled with damp static as she approached. She was almost there now; the hut side curved like an upturned boat. She'd been stupid this afternoon; she shouldn't have let those memories get to her like that. She reached the doorway and took down her umbrella. Then she pulled the ring off her right hand. Her fingers were cold and slippery from the drizzle and the ring slid easily onto her left. She paused to look at it, splaying her fingers. The ring gleamed dully in the twilight.

She pushed open the NAAFI door. The radio was on inside and the big band music flooded out along with the light and the smell of stewed tea and smoke. She looked round. Elsie was behind the counter, flicking a feather duster about and swaying her ample hips to the music. The rest of the hut was empty except for some chap in a merchant navy uniform having a smoke at a side table. She saw his profile: long nose and glasses. The man turned at the sound of the door closing, dropping his cigarette in the ashtray.

She looked round the hut again. Had she missed something? Sheila had definitely said Rob was here. She'd said your fella's in the NAAFI. Joan shifted from foot to foot and made little puddles on the wooden floor. Elsie waved vaguely with her feather duster, the red polka dots on her apron matched her poppy-coloured turban. Steam escaped from the urn. Joan's eyes moved round: the corrugated metal walls, the wooden floorboards, the rickety table and chairs, and the man in the dark uniform. He was looking down at something he was holding, a slip of paper. It looked like a newspaper cutting.

The familiar buzz began to take hold, quietly at first, like an undercurrent to the music. Out of the corner of her eye, she could still see the polka-dotted shimmer and sway of Elsie. Where was Rob? Was this Sheila's idea of a joke?

She tried to focus on something, stem the sick-dizzy feeling rising upwards. She looked at the man's bony hands on the table. One of them was reddish, knotted, fingers curled. In the other, the good hand, he held a piece of newsprint. He was stroking it, flattening it out against the tabletop. Her eyes travelled up from his hands to his face, and he looked at her. He looked familiar, or at least the good side of his face did. The other side was just an angry scrawl, the result of some explosion at sea, probably. But the good side: the serious expression, the long nose. She knew him from somewhere. She saw a change in the man's expression, and his chair scraped back from the table.

'Vanessa, what are you doing here?' he said, picking up the newspaper cutting. 'I came to find Joan. They told me she was dead, but I saw her picture in the *Mail*.'

Chapter 28

'Call for you, Gunner Lightwater,' said the voice, but to Edie it was just another voice, just more white noise. Everything had been white noise recently; nothing made any sense any more.

Bea said, 'Edie, someone's on the phone for you,' and Edie looked up. Their staff sergeant was standing, frowning in the doorway, looking like a bad-tempered games mistress. Edie got up. She followed the stiff figure of the staff sergeant through the veil of drizzle and into the office. It was warm on the inside, and the smell reminded her of classrooms at Queen's College. The staff sergeant left her at the door. Inside, a telephone receiver lay on the large ink blotter on the desk. She picked it up.

'Hello?'

'It's your mother.'

'Hello, Mummy.'

She felt something, then, like the feeling when you look

down after a fall and see blood. Until that moment, it had been like falling from one's mount: a winding pain, everything blanked out – she remembered almost nothing from the night of the raid. But something began to change at the faraway fuzzy sound of her mother's voice down the line.

'How are you, dear?'

'Fine,' she said automatically.

'Mrs Carson showed me the pictures from your battery in the paper. Shame there wasn't one of you, but I thought I saw your friend Joan in one of the shots.'

'Yes,' said Edie, remembering the sunny day, and the photographers and how marvellous Princess Elizabeth had looked in her cadet uniform. Staff Farr had given them the night off, hadn't she?

'And you had that dreadful raid, too,' said Mummy. But Edith couldn't remember the bombs, only the sound of an air raid siren and the feel of cold water on her thighs. 'Apparently the mews caught it, but I haven't had a chance to speak to your father about it,' she continued. 'Have you seen Pop recently?'

Edie remembered how it was Pop's cheque that paid for tea at the Ritz, and then after the Ritz they'd gone on to the Savoy, with those Americans.

'No, I don't think so,' said Edie.

There'd been three of them: Ron and Hal and Art. Yes, that was his name. She'd thought it a strange name, exotic. You didn't meet Englishmen called Art; they were all John or James or Robert or Kenneth. Poor Kenneth – she could barely remember his face any more.

'What do you mean, you don't think so? Please be clear, Edith Elizabeth, either you have seen your father, or you haven't.'

It felt as if something was opening up, like water breaking through a dam, or a sudden rush of blood from an arterial cut. She remembered seeing Pop and Mrs Cowie, among the roses in Kensington Gardens. Mrs Cowie's face like an upturned flower, Pop's tie loosened, top button undone, face pink. Then, a couple of days later, a cheque in the post, from Pop. How long ago was that?

'I've been busy with work,' she said into the receiver.

'Indeed,' said Mummy, and Edie could imagine her expression, at the other end of the phone. 'He's not been home for an age,' she added. 'I've tried calling the town house, but he's never there, and he's impossible to catch in the office.'

'I expect he's been busy, too,' said Edie, thinking about Mrs Cowie, the flush in her cheeks, the smudged lipstick. And then thinking of that American, Art – breath smelling of whisky, and her own lipstick smeared over her wet lips.

'I daresay,' said Mummy.

'Why don't you come up to town, Mummy? I haven't seen you in an age,' said Edie. Mummy said how impractical it would be. She had all her WVS commitments; she couldn't let Mrs Carson down, what with everything so busy at the moment. 'We could have a picnic in the park,' Edie continued. 'Like we used to, remember, with Marjorie sometimes, and – and Kenneth.'

'Surely, you're too old for picnics in the park,' said Mummy, her voice sounding tinny and far away. 'You're not a little girl any more.'

'No,' said Edie. 'No, I'm not a little girl any more.' There was a silence then, just the hiss and crackle of the phone line. Then a click. They must have been cut off.

When she was little, Nanny had always taken Edie to see Mummy after her bath and before her evening cup of milk. Mummy would be getting ready for dinner. Nanny would drop Edith off at the door to the dressing room. The open wardrobe was a forest of satin and tulle. A rope of pearls hung from the cheval. The glass-topped dressing table had three joined-up mirrors on it: a triptych of Mummy. There were crystal bottles and jars with powder, rouge and mascara, and bottles of perfume with puffball spritzers. Outside, the sun would be lowering, Turkish-delight pink, suffusing the room with rose-coloured light. Mummy would ask Edie about her day, and read her one of the stories from the big Perrault book: *Cendrillon* or *Le Petit Chaperon Rouge*. Back then, Mummy and Pop always had visitors: men in dark suits with cigars, and women who flitted like moths. Mummy would hear their cars in the drive and break off mid-sentence, giving Edie a lipsticked kiss on the cheek before wafting off downstairs. And Edie would be left among the silks and the furs, with nothing but her reflection and a half-read French fairy tale for company. She'd have to finish the story herself. She felt like that now.

After she'd replaced the receiver back in its cradle, Edie stood for a while in the empty room. If she could go back home now, crawl under her covers, with a book and a torch, would she be happy again? Would this horrible ripping, tearing feeling go away?

Staff Farr was nowhere around, so she switched off the light and shut the door. Outside, the rain had stopped. It was almost dark: purple shadows and sighing trees, the crescent moon just beginning to emerge from the retreating clouds. She should go back to the hut, sort out her locker, clean her teeth, and say her prayers. But there was a sound, behind the next hut, some low voices, a scuffle of feet. Edie walked round the side of the building. She was so bound up with the sudden onslaught of memories that had begun to resurface that it didn't occur to her to feel scared. The ineffectual moonlight just picked out the edges of two figures, standing close together.

'Hello, there!' Edie called out.

'Edie?' came the reply. It sounded like Joan. That was all right then. Edie began to walk towards them, thinking about offering congratulations – it seemed as if Joan and Rob had sorted out their lovers' tiff.

'Oh, Joan, dear, sorry to interrupt. Hello, again, Rob.' She wondered if he'd still remember her from that day back in early spring when he'd come looking for Joan on camp.

'Who's Rob?' It was another man's voice.

'Oh, I'm terribly sorry, I thought you were—' she stopped herself. She must have been mistaken.

'No, Edie, please, it's fine.' It was Joan. But there was an edge to her voice. 'This is Fred. Fred, this is Edie.'

Edie couldn't see very well. The chap was side on. Joan turned her head, looking as Edie approached. It was hard to tell, in the twilight, but there was something taut, anxious about her.

'I don't believe we've met,' said Edie. 'But any friend of Joan's is a friend of mine.' She held out a hand. The man took it. His handshake was swift and bony. Up close, she could see that one side of his face was pitted and scarred. They stood like three corners of a triangle. Edie looked at Fred, and at Joan. Joan was biting her lip, and her hair was all messed up. Something wasn't right.

'I'm so sorry to interrupt, but I thought I'd better remind you about the rule,' said Edie, thinking quickly. 'There's a rule about no visitors after dark, so I'm afraid you'll have to leave now, Fred.' He didn't move an inch. He was staring at Joan. With the damage to his face, and in the near-dark, it was impossible to make out his expression, but Edie could hear his breath: sharp hissing bursts, as if he had a blockage in his airway. 'The thing is, Staff Farr normally does the rounds about now, and she does tend to make a fearful fuss about it,' she continued. Still he didn't shift.

'I'm sure you wouldn't want Joan to get put on a charge because of your being here so late,' said Edie. He laughed, at that: a short snort, with no mirth in it whatsoever. There were footfalls in the distance, as the bugler went out onto the parade ground. Joan began to walk away, tugging at Edie to follow.

'It was nice to meet you, Fred,' Edie said as they left. Fred didn't answer, didn't move but, as they were a few feet away, he called after them.

'You owe me, Vanessa,' his reedy voice ribbonned up the cinder path towards them. 'I'll be back to collect my dues, sometime soon.'

Edie looked back. He was watching them. He watched them all the way back to their hut. But Joan didn't turn. She strode forwards like it was a route march. At the hut doorway, she ushered Joan in first, slamming the door shut behind them. From outside, the bugler began to sound the Last Post. Why had that strange man called her Vanessa? And what was that about collecting dues?

Inside, the girls asked Joan how it went. She laughed and said it was just a wind up. She said it was just some loony, nothing to do with her. And Sheila Carter said that the chap had said he was Joan Tucker's fiancé. Why would he say that? Joan said maybe he just saw my photo in the paper the other day. But as she said it, she gave Edie a quick look, and Edie knew she was to say nothing.

After she'd brushed her teeth and got into her striped pyjamas, Edie knelt down to pray. The floorboards were hard under her knees, and the air a suffocating fug. She pressed her sweaty palms together, feeling burdened down with secrets: Pop's, Bea's, and now Joan had something to hide, too – and on top of it all her own, dark secret, the one she was just beginning to remember. Give up your troubles to Jesus, that was the advice. But her thoughts were an inchoate mess, and she couldn't even begin to find the words.

'God help us all,' she muttered under her breath, unclasping her hands and crawling into bed.

Chapter 29

'Oh, where has your father got to?' said Lady Lightwater, smoothing out the wrinkles in the tartan travel rug. 'Be a dear and help me with the hamper, will you, Edith?'

Bea and Joan helped Edie unpack the wicker basket and lay out the porcelain plates and yellow checked napkins. There were crystal tumblers, too, and miniature salt-and-pepper shakers. There was more in that picnic basket than they had in their kitchen back home, Bea thought.

'Those hens Mrs Carson gave me have finally started to lay, so we've got egg-and-cress rolls, and scones with jam and cream, and when I was cleaning out the larder the other day I found this, among other things – heaven knows what Cook actually did all day, the larder was downright filthy, although I do miss her seed cake,' said Edie's ma, pulling out a dusty bottle that read ELDERFLOWER CHAMPAGNE 1938 on its peeling label. 'Spare sugar to make fizzy pop – those were the days,' she sighed. 'Now where is Neville, he promised to be here at twelve thirty sharp.'

Bea sat next to Edie on one of the velvet cushions. The sky was huge, endless. The leaves of the oak tree above them were dusty splodges of green against the blue. A little boy squeaked along the path on his trike, followed by a hard-faced nanny in a black uniform. Bea wondered who he was, why he hadn't been evacuated, why the nanny hadn't been conscripted. Sometimes it seemed as if there were different rules for the rich, who never seemed to mind farming out their children while they were off arranging flowers or whatever they did. Bea thought she might've liked to have been a nanny, if things had been different. She'd looked after all her brothers and sisters all right. Ma used to rely on her, especially with the twins. Funny how she'd been able to look after all of them except her own. Baby Val was the one Ma kept to herself. Bea hadn't seen her since April, months ago. Jock still hadn't written back.

Shop girls were sunning their bare legs on the seats near the pond, and on the bandstand a four-piece struck up 'We'll Meet Again'.

'If I hear that song one more time I think I'll vomit,' said Joan under her breath.

There were no clouds. The world was all chopped up: a slice of blue sky; a slice of yellow sunshine; a slice of green grass. Joan was pushing the cuticles back from her nails. Lady Lightwater arranged the rolls in a basket lined with one of the napkins. Edie looked into the middle distance, eyelids fluttering. Nobody spoke. Bea thought that they must look like a picture she'd seen on a posh biscuit tin

once: ladies taking in the sun on a perfect summer's day.
Except they weren't in crinolines and parasols, they had
scratchy khaki uniforms and gas masks instead. She shifted
on her cushion. It was so hot and airless that she was sweating horribly. She thought about where Jock was – probably
even hotter, out there in the desert.

Lady Lightwater got out her cigarette case. She offered
them to Bea and Joan who each took one, thanking her
politely. Finally she offered the open case to Edie. Edie looked
at the cigarette case, and looked up at her mother, and shook
her head. Her mother shrugged and put the case back in her
handbag. The sun beat down through the oak leaves. Bea
could feel beads of sweat forming on her upper lip. Some lads
were playing cricket over near the battery. A woman was
pushing a bicycle towards Kensington Gardens. Down by the
bandstand, a couple had begun to dance. The sun was white
and relentless. There wasn't a breath of air. Bea lit her cigarette. As she exhaled, the smoke looked like mist lying on the
little domed roof of the bandstand.

'Lovely spread,' Bea said, looking at the food, breaking
the silence.

'Yes, well, I thought Edith deserved a treat, after the royal
visit and the raid and all that hullaballoo. I saw you in the
paper, dear,' Lady Lightwater said, nodding to Joan, who
smiled glassily and tapped out her cigarette ash on a tree root.
'I hear you all had a bit of a time of it, you poor things,' she
continued. Bea stiffened. She looked at Edie, who was looking away, biting her lip. Joan slowly opened her mouth, her

full lips looking as if she were just about to take a bite from a peach. Bea held her breath.

'Well, yes, Lady Lightwater – Maud – we hadn't had a raid for such a long time that I have to admit it was rather a shock,' Joan said. Bea exhaled, feeling the breath catch in her throat. Let Joan talk.

'And were you all on duty that night?' said Lady Lightwater, pulling a stray piece of tobacco off her lips where it clung to her lipstick. Edie, Bea and Joan looked at each other, as Lady Lightwater flicked the tobacco away onto the grass. None of them had really spoken about that night. If they didn't talk about it, they could almost forget about what had happened outside the 400 Club. Almost.

'Hmm?' said Lady Lightwater, as if Joan had answered and she simply hadn't heard. The three girls looked at each other, eyes wide. 'Cat got your tongue, Edith?' she said, flicking ash on the parched grass beyond the rug. At that moment, there was a 'Hulloooo' from the distance, and Bea looked up to see Edie's father striding towards them from the direction of Bayswater. He was carrying his jacket and his turn-ups swung as he walked. Bea had only seen him once before, when he'd come to pick up Edie and Joan back in April. She'd forgotten how tall he was.

'Ah, what a sight for sore eyes!' he said as he approached. Bea thought he looked like one of those kestrels you some-times saw up on Bluebell Hill: beaky nose, arched brows.

'So glad you could make it, Neville,' said Lady Lightwater, checking her gold watch.

Edie, Joan and Bea stood up. Lord Lightwater said, 'Jeanie, I remember you,' and Joan didn't bother to correct him, and he kissed her on the cheek. Bea introduced herself as Beatrice Smith, and flushed when he kissed her on the cheek, too. It didn't seem right, kissing someone you'd only just met. The only other man who'd kissed her was Jock. Sir Neville briefly grazed his wife's face with his own before turning his attention to Edie.

'And how's my Half Pint, then?' he said, stepping forward, arms outstretched towards her. She held out her right hand. 'Oh, don't be silly, Half Pint, I'm not going to shake hands with my own daughter,' he guffawed, and enveloped her in a bony embrace. She struggled free. He raised an eyebrow and took out his pipe from his pocket.

'Sit down, everyone,' said Lady Lightwater. 'We've been waiting long enough.' She handed the elderflower champagne to Edie's pa. 'Do the honours, darling.'

'Well, this is nice,' said Lady Lightwater, as they sat, chewing silently on egg-and-cress rolls. 'Isn't it nice, Neville?' He nodded. He was looking across to where the shop girls were hoiking up their skirts and dabbling their toes in the pond. 'I was saying to the girls that I thought they deserved a treat, after the royal visit, and that frightful raid,' Edie's mother continued, dabbing at the side of her mouth with a napkin and leaving red lipstick marks on the cloth.

'Frightful,' said Sir Neville, through a mouthful of egg-and-cress.

'Well, thank God you didn't catch it, Neville. It must have been so close to the town house. Margot said the end of the Mews was totally obliterated. I know you had to work late but you must have been home by the time it started? I do wish you didn't have to work so many weekends at the moment. Were you at the town house, darling? You can't still have been at the office at that time?'

He took a large swig of elderflower champagne and scratched his nose with his forefinger. 'No, no, I wasn't at work,' he said, wolfing down the rest of his roll.

'You were at the town house?'

He shook his head, chewing on the roll. He's using it as an excuse not to answer, thought Bea, noticing how he avoided his wife's questioning gaze as she continued her interrogation.

'You can't have been still dining at that hour – or were you? Which restaurant do you prefer, these days? Margot says the Savoy's gone a bit downhill recently?'

Edie's mother's questions seemed innocent enough. She could just have been making small talk. But Bea noticed the way she leant forward, how sharp her eyes looked, how small her mouth, and how Sir Neville seemed suddenly extremely hungry, reaching for another roll before he'd even finished off his first. Bea caught Joan's eye. There were no flies on her – what she'd said to the gate guard that night was dead right. Edie's father needed an alibi just as much as they did.

'So, were you at the Savoy, Neville?'

'Well, the fact is, old girl—' he began.

'He was with us,' Joan interrupted. Everyone stopped

eating and turned to look at Joan. 'Don't you remember, girls,' said Joan, lassoing Edie and Bea with her gaze. 'We'd been out to celebrate the royal visit and then we went on to see your father at his club, didn't we, Edie?'

Bea chewed rapidly on her food, trying not to make eye contact with anyone. Ask me no questions and I'll tell you no lies, her ma always said. But she saw Edie look at Joan.

'Oh, come on Edie, you can't have forgotten already?' said Joan. 'Remember, we bumped into that friend of your parents' on the way there. What was her name again? M-something, wasn't it?' Bea looked up, couldn't help it. She had to know. What would Edie say? Edie looked blankly back at Joan.

'Oh, I wish I could remember,' Joan continued. ' We saw her just coming out of the club as we got there. Very pretty, dark hair in a bob. May? No, that wasn't it,' said Joan, staring deep into Edie's eyes. 'What was it, Edie, you must be able to remember? That woman? Bea, can you remember her name?'

Bea swallowed a dry lump of bread. 'Meredith?' she said, understanding at last where Joan was going with this.

'Meredith?' said Lady Lightwater sharply.

Sir Neville cleared his throat and scratched the side of his nose again. 'Ah, yes,' he said. 'So you did. What a splendid surprise it was to be invaded by a battalion of the gentle sex at that hour. We managed to find a nice tot of Russian vodka to steady our nerves after the raid, as I recall.' He was looking at Joan.

'Oh, yes, that's right!' said Joan, throwing back her head and laughing. 'And Edie had rather too much. We had to practically carry her back into camp, didn't we, Bea?' She looked over at Bea, who nodded and reached for the last roll. 'I tell you what, we were so late back, we were lucky not to be put on a charge, but with everything else going on that night, the guard hardly even noticed!' She laughed again, and Edie's father joined in, loudly. Lady Lightwater looked from one to the other and brushed some crumbs from her lap.

'You didn't mention, when I phoned,' she said. 'Neither did you, Edith Elizabeth.'

'Oh, for heaven's sakes, old girl, there's a war on. I hardly need bother you with the minutiae of my social life, you're far to busy with all your WVS stuff to need to know my entire diary details, eh? And I expect Half Pint was up to her ears in army nonsense. Too busy bulling her boots to remember what day it is, I'll warrant!'

Lady Lightwater smoothed an eyebrow with a forefinger. 'Well,' she said at last, 'would anyone like to make a start on the scones?'

'It was good of your ma to treat us,' said Bea, as they wandered back towards the battery. Edie didn't answer.

Bea squinted against the glare. The air smelled like baked pastry. She licked her parched lips. She slid an arm through Edie's and Joan joined the other side, so that they walked three abreast along the straight path back to the battery. They were soon in step: left–right, left–right (*Face front, Gunner Smith, stop anticipating*). The rhythm carried her along. Her scalp felt itchy with sweat. Nobody mentioned the lie.

Left-right, left-right, they carried on along the dusty path towards Speakers' Corner.

'What's that?' said Joan, pointing. They paused. A dark car was parked at the battery entrance, figures scurrying like ants. Nobody answered Joan. There was a beat, and then, without speaking, they all set off again: left-right, left-right, towards the battery, towards the waiting police.

Chapter 30

'Tucker!'

'Yes ma'am.'

'You're in next.'

The door opened and Bea came out. She walked straight past, without so much as catching Joan's eye.

'Bombardier Tucker,' came the voice from behind the door. She got up and took two steps towards the door, pausing and turning to look at Edie, who was still sat waiting her turn. Face white and eyes huge. Joan gave her the tiniest nod.

Inside, three men were ranged around the big desk in front of the window. One, a crooked silhouette against the light, was busy scribbling on a notepad and barely looked up. Another larger man motioned for her to sit down on the small chair that had been placed in front, and at a distance from, the desk. The third man sat in the middle, his fingertips just touching, so that his hands made an empty triangle above the blotter. The caustic afternoon light glared through the window behind them; their faces were in partial shadow, like smudges on a copybook.

'Good afternoon, Bombardier,' said the man in the middle. His voice sounded matter-of-fact to the point of boredom. 'We've just been talking to Gunner Smith about the events of last Friday, and we'd like to hear your version. You've heard about the dead GI?'

Joan nodded.

'There were other fatalities during that raid, of course, but the Americans seem to think there are some – how shall I put it – inconsistencies with the GI's death. We're putting together a full investigation for their military police.'

He coughed. Joan shifted in her seat. She tried to see his eyes, but they were in shadow. She couldn't tell his expression. Had Bea remembered what they'd said to the gate guard, that night? The scribbling man looked up from his notebook, pen poised. The sun was striking in, right at her. She squinted, waiting.

'So, Bombardier, can you tell me everything that happened to you from the time you left the battery in the afternoon, until you arrived back in the morning. In your own time.'

Joan nodded. Her chest felt tight, and her breath came in little gulps. She forced herself to breathe deeply. 'I left the battery with Gunner Smith and Gunner Lightwater,' she began. The man at the desk folded his arms and sat back in his chair. The man with the notebook began to scribble. The larger man breathed audibly and fiddled with a fountain pen. 'We went together for tea at the Ritz, and then on for cocktails at the Savoy – we were celebrating because I'd just been made up, promoted, you know, and there'd been a visit from the Queen and Princess Elizabeth earlier that day.'

She stopped. The man in the middle nodded at her to continue. She rubbed her eyes. She could feel perspiration pricking under her arms, down her back, sticking her skin to her shirt, between her thighs. She uncrossed her legs and re-crossed them. The silence hung like a blanket.

The man nodded again, lifting his eyebrows. 'And?' he said.

'And we met three American officers on the way to the Savoy. We had drinks with them at the Savoy. And then we left, just before blackout; it must have been about ten thirty.'

'You left with the Americans and went onto the 400 Club?'

'No.' She felt her face flush.

'No, you didn't leave with them, or no, you didn't go onto the 400 Club?'

'We went to see Gunner Lightwater's father at his club.' She said the name of the club. The lie was hot in her mouth. It felt like an air raid siren, loud and warped. After that, the rest followed easily. 'To be honest, Officer, I was quite tipsy. My memory of the evening isn't as clear as it could be. If you need to know more, why don't you ask Gunner Lightwater's father?' Let him lie. Sir or not, she knew his type. He was used to lying, wasn't he?

'Her father's name?'

'Sir Neville Lightwater. You can contact him through the Prime Minister's office, if it's urgent,' she said. The three men exchanged glances.

'Thank you, Bombardier. That will be all.'

She steadied herself on the chair back as she got up. The door looked further away than it should be. It seemed to retreat away from her. But it was only a couple of steps, wasn't it? Two steps and she'd be out of here: left-right. Her hand was already on the door handle.

'Oh, one more thing, Bombardier.'

She turned back, fingertips still on the doorknob. 'Sir?'

'What size shoe do you take?'

'A five,' she said. 'I take a size five.'

'Thank you, Gunner. Write that down, will you, Fanshaw. Bombardier Tucker takes a size five shoe.' He took a large handkerchief out of his pocket and wiped his forehead with it. 'You may go, Bombardier.'

As she opened the door, she saw Edie still shrunken in the chair. Staff Farr barked at her to get up. There wasn't a moment to say anything as she was ushered past, out into the aching sunshine. She heard the door close as Edie went inside. And Joan could only hope she'd done enough to protect her friend.

Chapter 31

Bea was thinking about Jock again as she came past the back of the ablutions block. Her eyes were sandy with lack of sleep, but there was something she needed to do before she could rest. Some hand washing: the type you didn't send to the laundry with your uniform – a little blue bag with blood-stained bloomers inside. The army-issue pads were all right – better than the rags she'd used back home – but what if you came on halfway through your shift, on the gun emplacement, in the middle of the night? You couldn't exactly tell those old Home Guard lags that you had to go AWOL to get your sanitary protection sorted. So she had to wait, feeling the blood seeping warmly, slowly into her bloomers. And when the shift was over, wash everything out, before the stain set permanently.

She was trying to remember Jock's face when she told him about the baby. She remembered how she noticed she hadn't had the curse for a few weeks, longer than usual. But even though she knew what that meant, it felt as if she didn't say anything about it then it wouldn't be true. When Ma asked, straight up, why she hadn't been boiling her rags, and whether she was up the duff, Bea just said yes, because she'd known all along, really. And Ma slapped her so hard she fell over, bashing her cheek against the hearth. It was too late to get Jock to marry her, because he was sailing that day, but Bea wasn't worried. She knew how Jock felt about her; the wedding could wait until his return.

Down at the docks, before he left, she whispered it in his ear, and he'd looked surprised, but pleased. She tried to remember his face now, how he'd looked when she told him, and they said goodbye: his freckles, his little sparky eyes and sandy hair. The blink of surprise when she told him about the baby. But she couldn't capture his image properly. It was like when someone moved in a photo: smudged and unclear. Still no letter; was she stupid to hope? She stood and watched from the docks as his ship sailed, and she saw him on deck, waving. And she waved back, feeling like she was a piece of tissue being slowly torn in half, as the ship sailed away up the estuary.

As she turned the corner, she saw two figures spring apart: Billy – fat little Billy from stores – and Joan. She looked at Joan, and Joan looked back, chin up, as if daring her to say anything. Billy tipped her a wink. Bea looked away and hurried on. It really wasn't any of her business.

The water was tepid, which was good. About blood temperature was right, otherwise it would only set the stain. If only she had some salt. Still, a good scrub with carbolic soap should do it. Oh, Joan. What about poor Rob?

All the other girls who'd been on duty with them last night were already in bed, including Edie, who was scrunched up under the covers, despite the heat. Edie had been late for duty that night, missed her tea and all. They'd covered for her, and she'd turned up looking washed out, saying she'd just stayed in church too long. She didn't seem right, though. But then, she hadn't been right since that night. At least she was talking again, now. Bea heard the ablutions door open and looked in the mirror above the sink. It was Joan.

'It's not what you think,' said Joan, before Bea even opened her mouth.

'I never said anything,' said Bea, rubbing soap on the stain.

'Edie said the police asked about her shoe size, and we can't risk it, that's why.'

'Do you think the police called her pa?' said Bea.

'They've got nothing on us.'

'No, but have they? Why were they here if they didn't think . . .' Bea's voice trailed off. Just seeing a copper made her feel guilty, even if she hadn't done anything.

'If they had anything definite, they wouldn't be round here asking questions, sniffing about and – don't look at me like that, Bea.'

As Joan was talking, Bea couldn't help thinking of what she'd just seen her doing with Billy. What was she playing at? 'But why Billy, Joan?'

'Like I said, the shoes. We can't have them finding out about the shoes.'

'And Rob?'

'What about Rob?'

Bea thought, if I had what you have, Joan, I wouldn't treat it like it was nothing. I wouldn't throw it all away on fat Billy from stores. If I had what you had I wouldn't even be here; I'd be in my own home, with my own little girl and a good man who loved me.

'Is it because you worry that if you say yes to Rob and admit you love him, then he'll get killed, too?' Bea's words came out before she thought. She was too tired to remember to keep it buttoned. Joan just looked at her.

Bea looked away, down the sink, where the blood was seeping slowly from her underwear: pink clouds, sunset. She found the gusset and rubbed some more of the yellow carbolic soap into it, then she picked up either side and began to rub it against itself, quick and hard, until the soap bubbled through the fabric and the bloodstain began to fade. After a while, her hands got tired, and she dipped the bloomers back into the water. She looked up and Joan was still there, staring at herself in the tiny mottled mirror.

'He's got nothing on me,' Joan muttered.

'Who?'

Joan blinked, and quickly licked her lips.

'Nobody. I mean, the police. He's got nothing on us. They've got nothing on us,' she corrected herself.

But Bea could tell she wasn't talking about Edie. There was something else, wasn't there? And then she thought about Edie, late for duty, pale and strained. And now, huddled up under the covers, despite the heat. There was something up with her, and all.

'What about the other thing?' said Bea, as if Joan could read her thoughts.

'What other thing?' said Joan abruptly. 'I don't know what the hell you're on about. There is no other thing!' And she turned away then, so Bea couldn't see her face in the mirror any more.

'What are you doing here, Joan?' said Bea, at the reflection of the back of her head.

Joan held up her wash kit. 'I came on just before duty, didn't I? Lucky I had a pad in, just in case, I knew we were due, but I still need a wash.'

'You said "we".'

'Of course I said "we" because we always come on at the same time, don't we, you, me and Edie.'

'But Edie's asleep, isn't she?' Bea looked at Joan's reflection, saw her eyebrows shoot up.

'Oh. You mean—' Joan began. Bea nodded. 'Oh, heck. Do you think she knows?'

Bea shrugged. 'Give it a couple more days; she might just be late.' But Bea didn't believe it. Like Joan said, they always came on at the same time, ever since basic training. And in any case, there was something different about Edie, she could tell.

Joan went into the bathroom with her wash kit. Bea heard her turn on the taps. Bea sighed, thinking that it would take more than Joan copping a grope from fat Billy to sort this mess out. She wrung out the bloomers and pulled the plug. The pink scummy water gurgled and hissed down the plughole. Then she rinsed the bloomers under the tap until the water ran clear. She would hang them up on the stove in the hut. It wasn't lit, this time of year, but they'd dry quick enough in this heat.

She went back to the hut and found Edie, curled up small, like a knot under the covers. Bea thought about how she'd helped Edie after that night, undressing her and washing her. That bird-like body wasn't big enough to fit a baby in; it would break her. Poor Edie; poor little rich girl. Bea hung up her bloomers. They dripped onto the wooden floor making a pat-pat sound. Then she quickly stripped and fell into her own bed. All around were the sighs and creaks of half a dozen sleeping soldiers, exhausted after their night staring into the darkness.

As Bea pulled the covers up under her chin, she was thinking about hot baths and cheap gin and wire coat hangers that had been straightened out, blunted at one end and blackened at the tip. She thought of the gurgling sound as the blooded pink water eddied and sucked down the drain.

Chapter 32

'We need your help,' said Joan, as soon as the secretary closed the door behind them. There was no point beating about the bush, was there? Sir Neville unfolded himself behind the rosewood desk and walked round to meet them halfway across the vast wood-panelled room.

'Half Pint!' he said, bending down to embrace his daughter. She stayed rigid as a china doll in his embrace. He straightened up and kissed Joan on the cheek. 'How lovely to see you, Jeanie,' he said. He smelled of cologne and pipe smoke. 'And you, too,' he said kissing Bea. She flushed. 'To what do I owe this unexpected pleasure?' he said.

Joan and Bea looked at Edie, stood between them, but she simply stood there, eyes fixed on a vase of lilies on the windowsill, as if they were the most fascinating things in the world. Joan nudged her bony ribs. Edie blinked, inhaled as if to speak, but then stopped.

'Well, well, well. Tongue-tied, Half Pint?' he said, smiling.

Sir Neville picked up his pipe from the desk and stooped down to empty it into the waste-paper basket. Joan shifted uneasily. It wasn't meant to be like this. They'd come to give Edie some support, that was all. She had to be the one to tell him. But it was like she'd gone back to the state she'd been right after that night at the 400 Club.

He opened a tin of Golden Virginia and began to fill the pipe bowl. Joan caught Bea's eye above Edie's head and raised her eyebrows. Bea frowned and pursed her lips. What now? Edie was looking at the flowers again. Outside the window, the row of houses opposite were yellow-grey in the morning sunshine and there was a tiny triangle of blue sky wedged above a roof edge.

It was already uncomfortably hot. The sash windows were all open, but not a breath of air stirred the leaves of the lilies in the vase. There had been flowers like that at the Ritz: urns of lilies, pots of aspidistra. And roses on the teacups, she remembered, when Rob had asked her to marry him. She still hadn't given him a response, couldn't find the words. She twisted the gold ring on her finger. She should tell him. She would tell him, just as soon as they'd sorted Edie out. But tell him what?

Edie's father finished filling his pipe. He tamped down the tobacco and got out his Swan Vestas. He lit the pipe, chewing on the stem and exhaling clouds of thick, bluish smoke. 'Is it about cash, Half Pint?' he said at last. 'You girls spent all your wages on gin and lipstick already this month and need a bit of a loan, hmm?' He was stooping over slightly and looking into Edie's face. Edie coughed but stayed stood rigid, as if to attention.

'No, it's not that, it's—' Joan began.

'I'm talking to my daughter, not to you,' he said. There was something hard in his tone. It made Joan think of the sound of boots on a parade square. He'd stopped smiling now. Joan felt her cheeks redden at the rebuke.

'Come on, Half Pint, out with it. There's got to be some reason for you to turn up at my office at ten past nine on a Monday morning, and clearly you haven't come here for a spot of chit-chat.' But Edie showed no sign of even hearing him.

He straightened up and puffed at the pipe some more. The phone rang in the outer office and Joan could hear the clipped tones of his secretary telling someone on the line that Sir Neville was unavailable just now. He paced in front of them, like a decorated officer inspecting the enlisted filth. Joan's feet felt damp in the thick lisle stockings. The edges of her brogues were beginning to dig in. She swayed slightly on the balls of her feet. He paced past and turned on his heel. She saw one side of his face pass them, and then the other, and she noticed how he had a wavy line, a vein snaking up into his temple on one side. And Joan thought about that merchant-navy man: Fred, he'd called himself. She thought about his face, one side livid red, burnt away. He'd called her Vanessa. He'd said he was Joan's fiancé. And when she'd told him she was Joan, he'd got angry, whispered threats, called her a fraud. But she'd got rid of him, hadn't she?

Sir Neville stopped in front of Edie. He was frowning, now. 'I haven't got all bloody morning. You girl soldiers might not have much more to think about than where your next pair of silk stockings is coming from, but some of us have more pressing things to attend to. Now, come on, let's get this over with. How much? Cash or cheque?' Joan saw a solitary tear begin to well up in Edie's right eye, but she didn't even blink it away. Slowly it ran down her pale cheek and lodged in the corner of her lips. 'Oh, I don't have time for this,' barked her father, and stalked back to his desk and sat down. 'Come back when you have something to say for yourself. Pat will show you out,' and he had his palm over the bell that he used to summon his secretary.

'No!' said Joan.

'I beg your pardon?'

'We need your help. She's in trouble,' said Joan.

He snorted, his hand still hovering over the bell. 'What kind of trouble?' There was silence inside the room. From outside came the cough of a motorbike engine starting up. Inside, the air was hot and thick. Joan opened her mouth to speak, but Edie's father put up a hand to silence her. He puffed on his pipe. 'What is it, Half Pint?' The pipe smoke hung in the air between them.

Edie finally stopped looking at the flowers and turned her gaze onto her father. She shook her head and then looked down at her feet. Bea watched as two tears fell, one-two, down onto the Persian rug.

'What kind of trouble?' said Sir Neville, leaning forwards

across the desk. Bea gave Joan a panicky glance. 'Not *that* kind of trouble. Tell me I've got the wrong end of the bloody stick. Not that kind of trouble?'

Edie raised her head and then inclined it slightly, a half-nod, an acknowledgement. Sir Neville stood up abruptly and strode over to Joan. 'You let her get into trouble.' His face was up close, sudden purplish-red, and Joan thought again of Fred, breathing vitriol into her face: 'Who the hell do you think you are?'

Joan flushed, opened her mouth to reply, but Sir Neville stopped her before she had the chance. 'Oh, stow it, Bombardier. I couldn't be less interested in your petty excuses.' He took another puff of his pipe and glared at Bea. 'And you. I hold you just as much responsible as her,' he said. Joan saw that Edie's shoulders were shaking and she moved to put an arm round her, just as Bea did the same, and they stood, arms around her quaking little form as her father fumed in front of them. He went back to the desk and picked up the phone, asking to be put through to Mrs Cowie. There was a pause.

'Ah, Meredith, so sorry to trouble you this early. Ungodly, yes . . . well, some of us have to work, I suppose, to keep the rest of you in Molyneux frocks and so forth . . . Yes, yes, of course, but listen, I have a small favour to ask . . . No, I'd love to, of course, but not that; it's actually rather serious. It's Edith. She's in trouble . . . No, what I mean is she's got herself into trouble . . . Yes, *that* kind of trouble . . . Christ knows, but of course I can't be seen to . . . Surely you can get your hair done another day? Meredith, this is my daughter, not some port-and-lemon-swilling officer's groundsheet, for Christ's sake.' At this, he looked pointedly over at Joan. 'The Mount Royal is perfectly decent. But for heaven's sakes, not Vitane. I don't want her going the same way as the Pickwoad woman ... Yes, ghastly business. Well, thank you, Meredith. I do appreciate this, old girl.' He hung up.

'Right then, Half Pint, you can say goodbye to your pals now. Mrs Cowie is on her way here. She'll sort you out.' Edith looked at him.

'Mrs Cowie?' said Joan.

'Yes, Meredith Cowie. This is woman's business. I can't possibly be involved. Not in my position. I've already had the police asking questions about the night of that raid—Oh, don't worry, I didn't breathe a word to those self-important little oiks. But I can't have anything else, you understand?'

'But what about Edie's mum?' said Joan.

'Her who?'

'Her mother. Your wife?'

'Oh, we needn't bother Maud with this. Better that we don't tell Mummy, eh, Half Pint?'

Edie was still shaking. Joan gave her a squeeze. She thought about the little baby fluttering in Edie's belly, the baby that was about to be sucked out in some hotel bedroom. 'Can we stay with her?' said Joan.

'Certainly not. It will only arouse suspicion. In any case, shouldn't you be getting back to your unit?'

'But she'll be all alone,' said Joan.

'Not at all. Mrs Cowie will be there. Now, come along,

girls. Say your goodbyes.' He talked like it was the end of a tea party. Joan looked at Bea above Edie's head.

'But what will we tell our OC?' said Joan. 'We're all on duty again tonight.'

'Oh, isn't it obvious?' said Edie's father. 'I thought all you girls knew the score. She's got acute appendicitis, of course: emergency hospital admission. I'll ask Pat to sort you out with something official.' And Joan remembered Scottish Nancy, that time, in training: blood all over the bed sheets and the midnight flee to hospital. Appendicitis, they'd said, then.

They dislodged themselves from Edie as he picked up the phone and issued instructions to his secretary. As his secretary ushered them out, Joan turned back and caught a glimpse of Sir Neville walking back over to Edie, his arms outstretched. 'Chin up, Half Pint,' he said. 'Pop will sort this all out, you'll see.'

And she heard Edie's voice, suddenly crisp and clear. 'I do wish you'd stop calling me Half Pint.'

Chapter 33

Mrs Cowie tutted and checked the little gold wristwatch again. Her lips made a moue of irritation.

'You can go, if you want,' said Edie.

'No, I promised your father,' said Mrs Cowie.

Edie was sitting on the end of the bed. The bedstead was iron, with knobs at the corners. There was a claret-coloured bedcover that matched the carpet. Opposite the bed the window was open, to let in some air, but it was still too hot, oppressive in the high-up hotel suite. She could hear the whine of traffic from far below, and see the top of the spire from the nearby church. Mrs Cowie started to pace, muttering something about how the least one could expect was for people to turn up on time when you were paying that kind of money for their services. Her black bobbed hair shook as she walked, and Edie was suddenly reminded of Wallis Simpson – 'that American hussy who stole our king' as Mummy put it.

'Why did Pop ask you to come?' said Edie.

Mrs Cowie looked up sharply. 'Your father is a very dear friend,' she said.

'And my mother? Is she a dear friend, too?'

'Well, that goes without saying.'

Does it, thought Edie. She could feel the bedsprings underneath her. It would not be a very comfortable bed to sleep on. But then, she wasn't here to sleep, was she?

Outside, the pale green church spire speared the chalky sky, and inside, Meredith paced. She paused. 'Try not to worry,' she said. It was the first acknowledgement since they met up at Pop's office earlier of what was actually going on. 'It's really quite straightforward, in the right hands,' she added.

How would you know, thought Edie, and then she remembered those hushed telephone conversations about 'work' that she'd overheard when she was home on leave. Edie watched Mrs Cowie, trotting backwards and forwards between the cheval mirror and the door.

'Did you come here for yours, too?' said Edie.

'I don't know what you're talking about!' said Mrs Cowie, flushing and speeding up.

Edie thought about how she'd ended up here, in one of the furthest rooms from reception, in this second-rate hotel in Bryanston Street, waiting, with her father's mistress, for the illegal abortionist to arrive. It was Bea who'd noticed that she hadn't got her curse this month, and Joan who'd made them go and see her father about it. She'd felt stupid, that she hadn't even known – but nobody ever told you these things. How was one supposed to know? Mrs Cowie had been summoned to whisk her off, as if they were going to nothing more important than a trip to Harrods. They took a taxi to the Mount Royal Hotel. The ancient moustachioed receptionist showed studied disinterest as Mrs Cowie booked Edie in under the name of Mrs Lionel Jones.

Edie watched as Mrs Cowie paused in her pacing to regard herself in the cheval, smoothing her skirt and hooking a stray hair behind her ear. Then she checked her watch again. Edie wanted to ask her what was going to happen. How did they get the baby out? Would it hurt? But it was another one of those things that it was impossible to ask.

She thought it strange that a baby could be growing inside her. She knew it wouldn't look anything like a baby now. She thought about the baby dolly in her old dolls' house in the nursery – it was just a china face sewed onto a rectangular little cushion thing, wrapped in cloth, like a pin cushion with a face. She thought of the baby inside her like a pincushion, to be stuffed with pins until it deflated and disappeared. Would the doctor have to cut her open? Or did they just suck it out somehow? Anyway, it wasn't a baby, was it? It was a situation; it was *that* kind of trouble, something that had to be *sorted out*, at great expense.

Edie sighed. The room was too hot and perspiration pricked at her armpits, under her heavy army shirt. But she could feel gooseflesh on her forearms, and she shivered a little. I must be scared, she thought, acknowledging the fear without actually feeling it. Still Mrs Cowie paced. Outside, the sky was duck-egg blue, the church spire verdigris. Inside was stuffy, the low ceilings capturing every drop of moisture, and the air was thick with humidity.

At last, there was a knock at the door. Mrs Cowie almost ran to open it. Edith stood up as Dr Bloomberg came in. He wasn't at all as she'd expected. She had imagined someone with a severe expression and a white coat and stethoscope, but Dr Bloomberg was a middle-aged man with a pink cheeks and a grey suit, carrying a Gladstone bag. He took off his hat and placed it on the occasional table and put down his bag and shook Mrs Cowie's hand. Mrs Cowie introduced him to Edith, but not by name. She said, 'And this is the young lady I told you about,' and the doctor put out his hand. Edith took it; it was warm and clammy, with pudgy fingers.

'I do apologise for the delay,' he said, but gave no reason for his lateness. His face was blank, clean-shaven and expressionless, like blancmange. There were little dark pink lines where the rim of his trilby had been, but underneath his bald head was peach-coloured and shiny. 'Please arrange for hot water and fresh towels while I prepare,' he said, and went through to the ensuite bathroom. Edie heard him turning on the taps. Mrs Cowie called room service.

'It's quite all right; they're very discreet here,' she said to Edie as she hung up. And Edie nodded and looked out of the window to where a dove-grey cloud was beginning to form behind the spire.

Dr Bloomberg came out of the bathroom. Meredith stood with one hand on the cheval mirror frame, biting the inside of her lip. 'Well,' said the doctor. 'How many weeks is she gone?'

'I'm not sure,' said Mrs Cowie, and turned to Edie. 'When did you last have the curse, dear?' The doctor and Mrs Cowie were both looking at her, waiting for an answer. Edith felt flustered; it was such a personal question. Nobody talked about such things, ever.

'Come, come. I'm a doctor. I need to know.'

'Just tell Dr Bloomberg, dear.' Edith thought back. It must have been a couple of weeks before the royal visit, she supposed. Mrs Cowie and Dr Bloomberg discussed how long ago that was, Mrs Cowie counting out the weeks on her fingers. Her fingernails were dark red, like the hotel carpets.

'Good,' said Dr Bloomberg, nodding importantly in Meredith's direction. 'You've caught her early. It shouldn't be too problematic at this stage.' He began to roll up his sleeves.

There was another knock at the door and a muffled voice called out, 'Room service.' Mrs Cowie called out to say leave it outside, and they all waited as the maid's footsteps retreated down the corridor. Only when they heard the ping of the lift did Mrs Cowie open the door and bring in the trolley. On it was a huge ewer steaming with hot water and two neatly folded claret-coloured towels. They matched the carpet, and the shiny satin bed cover.

Dr Bloomberg opened his bag. 'Perhaps you should refresh yourself before we begin,' he said. It was more of a statement than a question, but Edie didn't really understand what he meant. She looked over at Mrs Cowie, who was making shooing motions with her hands, ushering Edie towards the ensuite. So Edie got up and went into the bathroom. Mrs Cowie's head appeared round the door.

'Just go to the loo and wash yourself *down there*,' she whispered, gesturing. Edie nodded and locked the bathroom door. Her urine stung and the water in the toilet bowl was yellow. She took off her shoes and the hateful lisle stockings and khaki bloomers. She hung the bloomers and stockings on the towel rail, not knowing what else to do with them. She took off her skirt and lay it over the edge of the bath. She filled the tiny sink with lukewarm water and used the hotel flannel to soak herself, down there, as she'd been told. And she rubbed her pubic hair with the soap, lathering it up. The soap was already soft, used. She thought of the doctor's chubby pink palms all over it. She wiped off the soapsuds with the flannel. It made a wet patch on the floor, so she covered it over with the bath mat. The tiny window here was frosted glass and the church spire just a sliver of pale green.

There was a knock at the bathroom door. 'The doctor is ready for you,' said Mrs Cowie.

But I'm naked from the waist down, thought Edie. He can't see me like this. She quickly put on her skirt, but she left the bloomers and stockings hanging limply from the rail, like game waiting to be butchered.

She unlocked the door and went back into the bedroom. The doctor turned to look at her. He was fiddling with a long orange latex tube. There was a basin of water at the foot of the bed. The sheets had been pulled back and a bath towel placed over the middle of the mattress.

'I don't want to ruin your uniform,' said Dr Bloomberg.

'Take your skirt off, dear,' said Mrs Cowie.

Edie looked at them. Surely, they didn't expect her to just strip. The doctor was putting one end of the tube in the basin. The water was cloudy. The tube had a sort of round blob in it. It looked like one of the puffball spritzers on Mummy's perfume bottles. The doctor turned his back and took something out of his bag.

'Come along,' said Mrs Cowie. Edith fumbled with the catch on her skirt and it slid to the floor, exposing her. Mrs Cowie motioned for her to get onto the bed, so she did. The towel was scratchy under her buttocks. Mrs Cowie pulled a sheet over her middle, but bunched it up, so it barely covered her thighs. She half sat, looking down at her legs thinking distractedly about how her toenails needed trimming.

The doctor still had his back turned to them. He'd taken off his suit jacket and his braces cut into his shirt. There were dark patches under his arms. It looked like he was wringing his hands. The air smelled suddenly sharp: surgical spirit, she thought. That's good. It means he's clean. He turned back and picked up one end of the latex tube. It had a white end. It reminded Edie of a duck's bill.

'Lie back and lift up your knees,' he said.

As she lay, Edie heard the bathroom door open and close and the lock click. Mrs Cowie had shut herself in the ensuite. Edie was alone with the doctor. She turned her head on the pillow; outside, the sky was darkening, the clouds building up behind the church spire, purple and lumpen. Dr Bloomberg's hand was warm and sticky, pushing open her thighs underneath the thin cotton sheet. She could smell the surgical spirit, and soap, and the smell of his sweat. She couldn't look. Then there was the thing, hard and probing, there. She didn't mean to, but she kicked out.

'Keep still, now, there's a good girl.' He talked to her as if he were talking to a horse. And his hand was on her again and the thing was there and she couldn't help it but she lashed out and he tripped backwards. He made an 'ouf' sound as he fell. And then said, 'Good God!' quite loudly. She heard the sound of the bathroom door being opened.

'Is everything all right?' said Mrs Cowie.

'Can you please control your daughter?' said the doctor, brushing himself down and picking up the tubing again.

'She's no daughter of mine,' said Mrs Cowie and slapped Edie, hard on the cheek. It stung. Mrs Cowie said, 'Don't be a silly little tart; you've caused your father enough trouble already. Have you any idea how much this is costing him? Just lie still and let the doctor get on with it.' And outside, the sky was now bunching up beyond the church spire and the sun had gone in.

Then someone held her knees apart and they put the thing there, right in, all the way in, and it hurt like it had done outside the 400 Club and they kept saying. 'That's it, be a good girl now. It doesn't hurt, does it?'

But it did hurt. It hurt as the hot water shot up the tube and hit her womb like a lead weight and everything ruptured and gave and the air was taut with pain as her stomach contracted and heaved and the bed groaned and everything was hot and wet and full of hurt and the wetness spread like the bed was blotting paper and the pain went on and on and the towel was claret-coloured like the carpet and someone patted her hand and said, 'There, there, that wasn't too bad, was it?' And she wanted to say, yes, it was too bad; it was all too bad – it was all bad and there was no goodness left, but she couldn't talk at all. And then someone propped her up and made her take a tablet in water and they stabbed a needle in her arm and everything began to go soft and blurred at the edges, and she heard the doctor say, 'It started so nice, but it looks like rain, now.'

And the spire in the window turned charcoal and then darker and then the voices all went quiet and it was black.

Chapter 34

The little gold ring on her right ring finger winked in the sunshine as Joan rubbed a second coat of oil into the gunmetal. Cleaning the predictor was one of the jobs she didn't mind. There was something satisfying about getting every blackened speck out of the corners, and re-oiling the whole thing until it gleamed. She liked the rhythm of it, and the feel of the metal under her fingertips. She and Bea had been working together, but Bea had just been called off by Staff Farr to take a telephone call. Joan decided to take a break, dropping her cleaning rag down next to the oilcan.

Joan closed her lids against the hot sun and leant back against the concrete wall. She listened to the other girls talking as they tackled the Bofors in the next emplacement. They were discussing a new film out at the flicks, called *First of the Few* and the reserve troop were all planning to go and see it on their next evening pass. That dishy David Niven was in it, apparently. It was all about Bomber Command.

She thought about Rob. She still hadn't given him an answer. She thought of his face, as she looked down, after he'd asked. That look he had. It made her feel all wrong. Bea said she should have said yes straight off. Joan didn't know why she hadn't; except there was that dizziness and the buzzing noise and it didn't feel right. She would have phoned or written to Rob that night, but then that chap turned up in the NAAFI, calling her Vanessa, saying that he was Joan Tucker's fiancé. He said his name was Fred. He said they'd got engaged before he went off with the arctic convoys last year. He thought she was dead, he said, but he saw her photo in the paper and came to find her. He said, 'Funny, Joan, you look exactly like your little sister, Vanessa.' And he pushed his face right into hers. When she thought about him, she felt sick. Thank God, Edie had turned up. Joan told everyone he was a nutter, just some poor sailor back from the North Sea, not right in the head, obsessing about a girl in the paper. But she recognised him. She knew his name before he told her. And when he said, 'Vanessa' like that, it was like someone pulling back the elastic on a cata-pult, ready to hurl.

But he'd gone away, hadn't he? He'd gone. Maybe he was just a nutcase. He probably wouldn't come back. What she needed to do was have a good time and forget all about it. Maybe Bea could help? Maybe they should go to the flicks with the others? She opened her eyes and turned round and began to say, 'Hey, how about . . .' forgetting Bea wasn't there. But someone else was. It was Billy who was standing so close;

he must've sidled up while she had her eyes shut. His thigh was right next to hers.

'How about it? Any time, just say the word, Tucker,' he said, grinning, pulling out a packet of Craven 'A'. She shifted away.

'I'm sorry, I thought you were Gunner Smith,' she said.

'Nope. Just me. Just little old me,' he said, offering the packet to her. She hesitated, then took one. The match flared and she inhaled and the smoke was as hot and dry in her mouth as the midday air behind the guns. 'How's tricks?' said Billy, slipping a hand familiarly behind her waist.

'Not here,' she muttered through an exhalation.

'Quartermaster's on leave,' said Billy.

The group of girls cleaning the Bofors gun broke into uproarious giggles. Where was Bea? Where was she when you needed her? Billy's hand began to slide downwards. His fingers made a pointed shape, which he shoved under her arse and in, down there. Goosing, that's what they called it.

'No, Billy,' she said under her breath, moving sideways.

'I'm on me own in stores for the rest of the day,' he said.

The gemstones on her ring flashed in the light, as she brought the cigarette to her lips again. 'I'm with Rob,' she said, and inhaled deeply.

'That's not what you said the other week, when the coppers was here.'

'That was different,' she voiced through the smoky exhalation.

'I kept me trap shut for you.'

'Thank you. I'm grateful, really I am.'

'How grateful?'

How could she get out of this without making a scene? Where the hell was Bea? Billy was back again, his fingers probing and feeling downwards from the base of her spine, under her arse.

She took a drag on her cigarette so that the tip was really smouldering, flicked the ash off and rolled it against the wall, so that it was a little white-orange cone of heat. She held it in her right hand, listening to the other girls, just out of sight in the next emplacement. Someone was talking loudly about the new junior commander who was due in post, wondering if they'd get someone decent this time. Nobody had liked the one who'd just left. Good riddance to bad rubbish – Joan recognised Sheila Carter's voice. Casually Joan let her hand fall, still staring ahead. Billy was so close that the burning tip of her fag contacted with the cloth of his trousers, at the top of his thigh, near his groin.

'Ow, what did you do that for, you silly bitch?' He jumped away. There was a little black singed circle on the khaki trousers.

'Sorry,' said Joan, dropping the fag on the concrete and grinding it into the dust with the toe of her boot.

'These are new issue and all,' said Billy.

'I said, sorry,' said Joan, not looking at him, still looking ahead. She could just glimpse out of the top of the emplacement. A figure was walking up the main drag: a man striding towards them. He was too far away to see what uniform he had on, but he was getting closer by the moment. He walked quickly, eyes fixed straight ahead, eyes fixed on her. Her chest contracted as she realised who it was.

Chapter 35

Rob saw her way before she noticed him. Some lad was chatting her up, it looked like. But he'd gone now. There was always some lad. It wasn't her fault, he thought. He'd have given it a go, if he was in Hyde Park Battery, if he was down on the guns, instead of up in the sky, dodging flak. He glanced round to say as much to that merchant-navy chap who'd been on the bus with him. Strange bloke. Awkward talking to him with that huge burn on his face, hard not to appear to be staring at it.

The tube was closed and the bus from Victoria had been full; they'd ended up sitting next to each other. Rob hadn't wanted to talk, not to anyone, but the navy chap had started, saying he was off to meet his girl in Hyde Park Barracks, and Rob had admitted that he was also on his way there too. Rob watched London trail past, lit a cigarette, listened mostly, tried not to stare at the angry burn on the man's face. 'I'm taking her to a posh hotel – lucky she'll still have me, like this,' he gestured and Rob was forced to look at the indecent rawness of it.

'Explosion?' said Rob.

The man nodded. 'Convoys – Archangel.'

'Bad luck.'

'Could've been worse. At least I made it back. I made it back to my girl.'

But Rob didn't respond, because he was thinking about Joan; thinking about what he was going to say to her. The two men got off together at Queensway and began to walk through Hyde Park, along towards Speaker's Corner. The air was hot; desiccated leaves hung limply. Clouds were beginning to pile up like lumpen sandbags.

'What's your girl like?' said the merchant-navy chap. And Rob was forced to describe Joan, her pale blonde hair, and the gap in her front teeth.

'You got a photo?' and Rob said no. She'd never sent a photo. She'd never sent a photo and it was too late now. After that, neither of them spoke, and there was a kind of uneasy comradeship as they strode together towards the battery. At the gate, Rob was waved through – no one ever questioned bomber command these days – but the other bloke was stopped, his documents checked. Rob walked on ahead.

Now, he looked back, to say something to the navy bloke, but he'd disappeared. Not that it mattered. He could do without an audience for what he needed to say. There she was. He swallowed, throat dry.

He was always seeing her in the distance: waiting in the

summer rain for him outside the Ritz; at the bus stop at West Malling in the spring; halfway down Western Way on a cold autumn evening. He was always running to get close, to catch her. But not this time. This time he walked. He could see her more clearly as he got closer, the outline of her against the edge of the hut. Jesus, but he still wanted her, even now. He thought of that time in the church: her lips, her flesh, the scent of her hair.

She'd seen him too, now. She took a step forward, faltered, held her ground. He kept walking. If she ran to him, then what? If she ran to him, covered him with kisses, begged for forgiveness, said yes, and yes and yes. Would he change his mind? He thought of the first letter, with the lipstick kiss on the back. And all the times he'd crossed the channel back home and it was her face, pulling him like a magnet, back home, back to Blighty. No. No, it was too late.

She stood and waited. As he got closer he could see her hair curling out from underneath her cap, the pout of her lower lip. He thought about the big pile of letters from her in his locker, still smelling of the scent she sprayed them with. He thought about taking them with him on his next sortie, opening the hatch over Germany, letting them scatter like snow on the enemy.

There were girls at the next emplacement, gathering their things up. There was nudging and pointing at his approach. He walked slowly down the steps. Closer still and he made eye contact with her. He almost hesitated. It wasn't too late, was it? Yes, it was, he told himself; it was too late the moment in the Ritz where she paused when he proposed. It was too late when she couldn't bring herself to say yes. The last few steps were like walking through sinking sand. He forced his legs forward. All he wanted to do was hold her, catch her up feel her lips on his.

'Rob?' she said. She bit her lip, looked at him.

'Who did you think it was? Another one of your fancy men?'

'No. I knew it was you.'

'I've come for the ring,' he said.

She nodded. 'Of course,' she began to pull it off the finger of her right hand. He watched her hand twist and pull, her face sideways so he could see the smooth curve of her cheek, the escaping lock of blonde hair. His throat ached, battened-down grief stabbing his jaws.

'Here,' she held it out. He put his hand out to take it. Their fingertips touched, he fumbled. It dropped onto the ground and they both bent down, heads touching as they grappled for it. She found it first, wiped it on her skirt, and gave it back to him. He hated himself for wanting to clutch at her fingers as the ring passed between them. He wanted to catch her hand and hold it and hold it. He stuffed the ring in his pocket, cleared his throat.

'I'm sorry, Rob,' she said in a small voice.

He hadn't meant to question or whine. He was trying to be a man about it. 'Why, Joan?' He couldn't help himself.

'I didn't say "no",' she said.

'Don't toy with me.'

'I'm not – I didn't mean to.'

'You didn't even bother to phone or write.'

'It wasn't like that. It's complicated,' she said, but she didn't continue, did nothing to explain.

'What makes you think you can just lead a chap on like that and drop him?' She opened her mouth to respond but he cut in. 'I know you better than you know yourself. I would have done anything for you, Joan, anything. You'll regret this. You'll regret this for the rest of your life, because I'm the only one who really cares, who really knows you.'

'But you don't know me,' she began.

He ignored the crack in her voice, clenched his fists and let his humiliation fly. Three months' wages for the ring, a week's wages on that stupid uneaten posh tea, and a humiliating journey back to Kent in the rain. And for what? Enough. No more being wrapped around her little finger.

'I think I understand all too well. Got yourself a nice ring and hoped I would bugger off and die somewhere before you'd have to go through with it, didn't you?' Anger ripped out, making him shout. 'Who the hell do you think you are, Joan Tucker?' She didn't respond.

He thought he'd feel better, once he'd said it, but he couldn't look her in the eye. He was dimly aware of the girls by the table, silently gawking as he turned and left. This is what I set out to do, he thought. I've lost Joan, but I've kept my self-respect. Plenty more fish in the sea, that's what his old dad would have said. He trudged out towards the gate. There was no sign of that odd naval bloke. Plenty more fish in the sea and pebbles on the beach. The ring clinked against the small change in his pocket. He thought about Harper's widow, and Pammie up in Blackpool, and the new brunette in the typing pool in headquarters, but Joan's face kept swimming into his consciousness, saying sorry in that small voice. A cloud passed over the sun, turning the path from gold to grey at a stroke.

He'd done the right thing, hadn't he?

It was over. Goodbye, Joan Tucker.

Chapter 36

The darkness pressed in on Bea's eyeballs, a stark contrast to the vivid outdoors. It was hot as the kitchen on a boil-wash day and the air was still and thick. It smelled sweetly pungent: sweat and bodies and soap and talc. One girl sighed and muttered in her sleep, turning on the creaking springs. At the far end, someone snored.

Bea's mind went over everything again: Staff Farr beckoning her away from the guns to take the call, dust puffing away from her footfalls and the air dry in her throat. Staff had held the office door open for her. 'It's your sister Vi on the line,' she gestured to the telephone on the desk. 'I'll let you have some privacy.'

Vi's voice had been crackled and small: 'Oh, Bea, thank the Lord, she took her time finding you, didn't she? I haven't got much change. It's Ma, Bea, she's really sick this time and it looks like hospital. I can't get through to Pa, but they said they'd tell him. It's her breathing. She can't seem to get enough air in, and the doctor said . . .' The pips went and then the line went dead. Bea replaced the receiver back in its cradle. It clicked. And then there was stillness. The air was thick and dense. Bea stood still in the quiet hut. Ma sick. Pa uncontactable. Vi on her own with the others, and her job in the pub. Who'd be looking after Baby?

Staff said she'd see what she could do to help. She said don't worry about going back to the guns, just go and get some rest.

Now Bea needed to sleep. They were on duty again later – the stupid new eight-hours on–off routine. Her lids were heavy and there was a throbbing ache at her temple, but her thoughts whirled and shoved. Even with eyes closed in the blacked-out hut, sleep refused to come. What about Baby? Who's going to take care of Baby? Vi would be busy with her job, Rita was all right, but she'd be back in school any day now, and so would the others.

Then, from outside, footsteps, a voice: 'You'll come over here if you know what's good for you. Vanessa, I'm warning you.' Vanessa – that was what Joan called herself, that night when they went drinking, wasn't it?

'Sod off, Fred.' A voice, thick and sullen – but it sounded like Joan.

'You can't get rid of me that easily, Vanessa.'

'I've told you. I'm Joan.' So it was Joan. But who was the bloke? Why was he calling her Vanessa?

'You still haven't told them?'

'Why should I?'

'Didn't you listen to a word I said, last time? No, you never were one for listening, or for knowing what's good for you, Vanessa.'

'It's Joan.'

'Joan, then. But if you're Joan, then we're engaged, and you won't mind me doing this.' There was a scuffle and something thudded against the side of the hut. Bea sat up in bed. What the hell was going on? The voices continued.

'You little bitch.'

'Like I said, sod off, Fred.'

'I'll sod off then, but you're coming with me.'

'Why would I do that?'

'Because of what I'll do if you don't.'

'What can you do, Fred? You've got nothing on me.' And Bea remembered what Joan had said in the ablutions block: he's got nothing on me. Then she'd corrected herself, said she was talking about the police. Was she talking about this Fred chap? But who was he?

'If you're Joan Tucker, then you're my girl, and you'll come with me. But if you're Vanessa, then you shouldn't be here at all. You're just seventeen. And I think your command-ing officer would be very interested to hear that. So what's it to be?'

'You wouldn't.'

'Wouldn't I? Think about it. What have I got to lose? I've booked us a room in the Mount Royal. It's only over the road, just past Marble Arch. Posh. Just the kind of place you'd like, Joan.'

'What do you think I am? Bugger off and get yourself a Piccadilly Commando.'

'I don't need one. I've got a fiancée. I've got you, Joan.'

'I'm not . . .'

'Just now you said you were.'

'For God's sake, Fred. I'm not your tart.'

'No, you're my fiancée, aren't you, Joan Tucker? That's what it says on your ID papers, doesn't it?'

'I'm engaged to someone else.'

'No, you're not. You're engaged to me. And you promised me if I got back home safe from Archangel you'd do this. I've got it in writing. I've kept all your letters, kept them safe, Joan.'

That lad's not right in the head, thought Bea. There was more scuffling. A muffled grunt. 'I'm not going with you. You can't make me,' said Joan.

'I think I can. And you know why. We'll walk out arm-in-arm, like lovebirds, and I'll have you back in time for your duty. Just do your duty to me, first. Come on; don't make a fuss, Joan. We're engaged, remember?'

There was silence for a moment, and then footfalls moving away into the distance. Bea tried to process what she'd heard. 'Joan?' said Bea. 'Joan, are you all right?' But Joan didn't answer.

Bea pushed herself up, scrambled out of bed and to the hut door. There was a rush of sunlight as she pushed it open. 'Joan?' Bea repeated, looking round, but her friend had already gone. There was birdsong from the tree, and the distant shouts from the other gunner girls, practising their drills on the emplacement.

'Shouldn't you be getting some rest?' came a voice from beyond the end of the hut. 'You're on duty again later.' It was Staff Farr, on the path passing the hut entrance.

'Yes, Staff,' said Bea.

'But while I'm here . . .' Staff Farr crossed the dusty grass and came over to her. 'I've sorted out that administrative matter with the pay office,' she said, holding out a manila envelope. 'Here, an advance, so you can help out your family. But no leave yet, I'm afraid, we're a man down as it is, what with your friend's *appendicitis*.' She raised an eyebrow at the last word. 'Well, I'd better be off, due to meet the new Junior Commander,' said Staff Farr, turning to go. 'Oh, and,' she reached into her breast pocket and pulled out a piece of paper, 'this came for you just now in the second post.' She held out a small crumpled air letter towards Bea, and Bea reached out to take it. She recognised the handwriting.

Chapter 37

At Marble Arch, Joan stopped. As they walked out of the battery, she'd caught sight of Billy, tried to show with her eyes that she needed help, but he just looked deliberately away. A black car ground past, sending choking petrol fumes. Fred still had her arm twisted up behind her back.

'I can't do this,' she said. Above Marble Arch, the sky was grey, furrowed clouds, like a headache in the sky. 'It's not right,' she said. She looked at Fred. She could only see the one side of his face – the good side. 'You understand, don't you, Fred?' she appealed.

He let go of her arm, turned, faced her full on, so she could see the join where the burnt flesh met the saved: tentacles of red, clawing at clear, cream flesh across his cheek, his nose. 'Of course,' he said. 'I'll walk you back now. I'll walk you right back to your CO's office and we'll tell him that it's all a mistake, you're not my fiancée; you're not Joan Tucker.'

The traffic swirled and buzzed. She felt herself rock on the balls of her feet. 'No, we can't do that.'

'No?' only the good side of his face showed any expression. The world was spinning, blurring. She stumbled. He caught her, held her elbow. 'Have it your way,' she said.

'Oh, I intend to.' He held her elbow, and she let him guide her, underneath Marble Arch, like a church entrance, and across the street, through the slovenly afternoon traffic.

She concentrated on the moment, trying to ignore her rising panic. One foot in front of the other, left–right, face front, over the road, up the kerb, beyond the rubble at the end of Oxford Street and on behind into Bryanston Street, past the church with the green spire like mould, the delivery vans and the discarded paper bags. How could she get out of this? There was a smashed milk bottle on the pavement, flies delighting in the sickly smell of gone-off milk. *No point crying over spilled milk.* Who said that? She thought of a floral pinny, flour-covered hands, and a kind voice. *No point crying over spilled milk.*

Fred still had her elbow. It doesn't matter, she told herself. He can do what he wants, and then I'll leave. So what? A few minutes of him heaving and groaning on top of me, that's all. Then it will all be over, and I can go back, back to being Bombardier Joan Tucker. But an image came into her head of an unshaven man with a milky-blind eye, and the feeling of cold concrete under her thighs, and the lumpen-thump of bodies under a torn quilt and the moon-faced clock with its hands stuck at midnight.

'Nearly there,' said Fred, grasping her elbow tighter and steering her up the street. 'Told you it wasn't far, didn't I?'

He propelled her up the stone steps and into the entrance, past the tubby doorman, who looked away as they passed, and then on again, up a wide varnished wooden staircase that opened into a vast cream marbled lobby, with low-slung stained-glass lampshades like Christmas baubles, and a lugubrious receptionist with a grey moustache. Fred said that he had a reservation: Mr and Mrs Cripps. The receptionist handed over the room key, without making eye contact, muttering that it was top floor, far end of the corridor. The key was attached to a circular wooden fob. The cream paint was chipped. Three-four-seven, it said in faded black lettering.

Fred shunted her in the direction of the lift. She could feel bruises beginning to form where his fingers dug in. The lift pinged and the doors slid open. A woman in a tight pink frock swept past, smelling of old perfume and sweat. She didn't acknowledge them. Nobody looked at anyone else in the Mount Royal Hotel. Everyone looked the other way.

Fred let go of her arm once they were inside the lift and the doors had closed. She could hear him breathing, panting like a dog. She felt her heart sink as the lift rose. The walls were mirrored, and she took out her lipstick from her gas-mask case and quickly slicked on a coat of summer geranium.

'My Joan doesn't wear paint,' said Fred.

'This Joan does,' said Joan. The lift stopped and the doors opened.

'Get out,' said Fred, shoving her ahead of him. The

corridor was low, dark and endless, like a tunnel with no light at the end of it. The air was dank and smoky. The crimson carpet muffled their footsteps.

'In here,' he said, as they reached the end of the corridor. He fiddled with the key in the lock. The door opened to reveal a tiny room, almost filled with a double bed with a red eiderdown. There was one small window. The curtains were open, and in the distance she could see a grey-green spire, almost touching the bruised mass of clouds. She went inside and heard him close the door behind him. He didn't even bother locking it, before he had her up against the wall.

'Joan, I've waited so long for you,' he said, but as he looked at her, his eyes were unfocused. He was pawing at the buttons on her uniform, muttering: 'Why did you stop writing, Joan? Why did you stop? I kept all your letters, and then you stopped. You didn't stop loving me, did you?'

The air shivered and there was the faraway rumble of thunder. His hand was on her breast, now, his face in her neck.

'They told me you were dead. But I found you again, in the paper. All that time we spent apart. But it doesn't matter. None of it matters, now we're together again, like you promised.' The air was thick. Her head throbbed. 'Joan, why aren't you wearing the scent I bought you for your birthday? And your hair – what have you done to your beautiful hair? It used to be the colour of sunrise at sea – remember I wrote you that – but you've bleached all the colour out. Why did you do that, Joan, when you know how I loved it?'

There was an insistent humming in her ears, muffling his

words. Her throat was sandpaper dry. His lips were on her skin, his long fingers probing inside her bra. Joan shunted him forwards, towards the bed. The quicker she could get this over and done with, the better. He stood by the end of the bed, gazing at her with that strange look. She thought she could smell chrysanthemums. There was a faint flash, and a pause. The thunder was louder this time, closer in. Soon the storm would be right overhead.

'Come on then, Fred,' she said, looking into his eyes. 'Come on now; there's a good lad,' she talked to him like a child, and she started to unbutton the fly on his trousers. He looked down at her hands, fumbling with the catch. She could see the point in his face where the burnt flesh met the good, like port seeping into milk.

'Where's your ring?' he said.

'What ring?'

'The engagement ring I bought you, Joan, where is it?'

She looked down to where he was looking, at her left hand, outstretched. And it seemed to her that for a moment she could see an engagement ring: thin gold with little sapphires and seed pearls, and for an instant her nails weren't chipped from shifting clunky army machinery, they were perfect ovals, buffed, fingernails clean. Joan always had such lovely clean nails, she thought, because of that new manicure set she got for her birthday. She brought her right hand across meet the other; it wasn't yet cold.

She glanced away. There was a flash and a deafening crack. Then she heard him: 'Get down! Get down!' He pushed her back onto the bed, pinning her down. His knee was in her groin. The buttons on his jacket dug into her. In her face, the damp-cloth-sweat smell of his clothes. The suffocating weight of him on top of her and her skull whipping back against the bed board. She tried to breathe, couldn't, shoved at the weight on top of her. A button grinding into her cheek; acrid smell in her nostrils. They rolled together, slow motion wrestlers. A sound in her head, deep and painful: bomber engines thudding like bluebottles buzzing inside her skull.

She bit down hard on flesh until she felt the metallic warmth of blood. There was a blinding flash and the sound of someone screaming. She turned her head to see where the noise came from. It was him, clutching a bloodied cheek, howling feral noises. She wrenched free. And then the acid rush of vomit up her throat, as the bile upsurged. She tried to stop it; the effort was like swallowing acid.

'I'm not Joan. I'm Vanessa!' she yelled, above the roar and crash. 'I'm Vanessa!'

Chapter 38

A man shoved past her as Bea reached the hotel doorway, drenched already in the sudden storm. She noticed his face, fleetingly, as he passed: livid red on one side, and dripping blood, like a freshly picked scab. He was in a merchant navy uniform. 'Watch yourself, pal,' she said, but he ignored her, breaking into an uneven run as he hit the corner with Oxford Street, then disappearing into the sheeting rain. There was another crack of thunder.

She caught the eye of the fat doorman, who held out his giant umbrella and rolled his eyes at her. 'Dunno why he was in such a rush to get away, he's only been here about ten minutes,' he said, then caught himself, cleared his throat, and looked away across the street.

'Was he here with a girl?' said Bea, thinking of Joan, thinking of how the hell she was going to find Joan.

'I couldn't possibly say, madam,' said the doorman, who had suddenly regained his professional demeanour.

'It's a friend of mine. I'm worried about her,' said Bea. 'Some lad said he was taking her to the Mount Royal, but I don't think she wanted to go with him,' she said.

'I'm afraid it's not hotel policy to give out information about the guests,' he said snootily, still looking out into the middle distance, where the gutters were gushing grey water into the drains. She moved a step closer to him. She could see his thinning hair, black streaked with grey, slicked back greasily across his shiny forehead under the cap. Was that a touch of rouge on his cheeks? He smelled sweet, like spilled cider. She'd heard about the staff at some of these posh hotels: what went on with young cavalry officers and waiters, in basements and broom cupboards.

'I suppose it's more than your job's worth to say anything?' she said. The doorman cleared his throat, nodded imperceptibly. She felt the advance wage packet, fat in the manila envelope in her pocket. It was meant for doctors' bills, for Ma: a whole month's wages, ahead of time. 'How much is your job worth?' she said.

His eyes flicked quickly up and down the street. There were a couple of people sheltering from the storm in the church doorway, at the far end. Other than that, the place was empty. Rain drummed on the awning. The doorman cleared his throat. 'A guinea,' he said.

'A guinea?' she said. 'I'm only a bloody soldier, chum. I'm not one of your hoi-polloi.'

'All right, then. Three shillings.'

'Two.'

'Go on then, two.' Bea pulled two notes from the wage packet and slipped them into his palm. He quickly stuffed them into his trouser pocket. 'Top corridor, far end, don't know the room number, but that's where Mr Simeon puts all the t—' She could tell he was going to say 'tarts' but he stopped himself – '. . . type of clientele,' he finished.

There was the sound of a car drawing up. A large black Ford stopped at the kerb and a chauffeur in a grey uniform rushed round with a black brolly and opened the rear passenger-side door. Bea glimpsed a stockinged leg and the hem of a powder-blue skirt. 'Thank you, and enjoy your stay at the Mount Royal,' the doorman said loudly, ushering Bea inside.

She didn't notice at first, because it was dark up in the top corridor, much darker than it had been in the mirrored interior of the lift. She stepped through the doors, noticing only the serried ranks of bedroom doors, like a row of gravestones, grey oblongs stretching away into the darkness. She wiped the wet hair off her brow and walked forwards into the gloom.

'Joan?' she called out hesitantly. Nobody answered. What to do? Knock on each bedroom door individually? What if Joan wasn't here at all? The doorman hadn't actually said . . . Her feet made no sound on the burgundy carpet, as she began to walk down the corridor.

'Joan?' she tried again, louder this time, but still there was no response. She was thinking about what had happened with Edie; how they'd noticed too late. Not Joan, too. Not again. She began to run down the corridor, calling out Joan's name. But the doors all stayed shut and silent, and the corridor was empty. At the end was a fire door, and the corridor turned to the right, another empty row of blank doorways leading off into the gloom. Bea paused; caught her breath.

She thought again about what that bloke had said to Joan outside the hut. What was it he'd called her? It was the same name she'd used when she got drunk in the pub, on leave. What was the name?

'Vanessa?' she called out, louder still. There was a murmur from the very far end of the corridor. A pile of shadows lurched into life.

Chapter 39

'Vanessa!' someone was calling her. She thought the voice must be inside her head. Her eyes swam. The carpet was like lava flow. The voice called again. She hadn't imagined it, then. She looked up. A young woman in uniform was walking towards her.

'It *is* you,' said the woman, she had an accent – not cockney, Kent maybe? – and a round, concerned face, bending over. She looked familiar. There was a hand on her shoulder.

She nodded, shifting position. Her head was pounding. 'Yes, it is me,' she replied, but the words were thick, like gobbets of dough plopping unchewed from her lips. She had her back against a wall. All around were doors, doors shut tight, unseeing eyes.

'What the hell did he do to you, girl?' said the woman, bending over her, touching her arm.

'Fred? Nothing. It's Joan he wants, not me,' she replied.

'Well, you're safe now,' and the woman knelt down beside

her, put an arm round her shoulder. The woman's arm was on hers, khaki on khaki – she was in uniform, too, just like the woman. It made no sense. Her mind groped in the murk. 'What are we going to do with you, Bombardier Tucker?' the estuary accent rolled like a river round her.

'Bombardier Tucker?'

'That's you, girl. Bombardier Joan Tucker, ATS. Deary me, you're not yourself at all, are you?' The woman's voice was soft and kind. The buzzing had almost stopped. There was a vile taste in her mouth. The woman took out a clean hankie and reached forward to wipe her face. 'Need to get you looking presentable before we can go back,' she said. 'Come on, let's be 'aving you.' A hand outstretched in front of her. She grasped the hand and let herself be pulled up. The ground shifted and lurched. She bashed into a bedroom door as she struggled to get up; the door opened.

'I didn't order room service,' said a tired-sounding posh voice.

Chapter 40

When Edie woke up, the room was empty. Mrs Cowie had left a note, on the bedside table with a phone number, and an old copy of *Harper's Bazaar*. It was the one with the red-and-black-patchwork-clothed woman on the cover, the same one she'd read the day she joined up, Edie remembered. The letters of Mrs Cowie's neat rounded handwriting swam about on the paper, like goldfish in a bowl.

Eventually, her head began to clear. She got up to go to the loo; the water in the bowl was pink, afterwards. She'd been left spare pads, so she changed them, wondered if it would be safe to have a bath. Then she went back to bed and leafed through the old magazine, but the glossy photographs of smiling women held no interest. Next to her half-empty water glass was a copy of the Bible, bound in dark red leather, with gold embossed lettering on the cover. She picked it up. The pages were tissue-thin, the typescript small and cluttered: sinners who begat sinners who begat and begat and a furious

God who spat fire and seemed to delight in suffering. There was a tugging pain in her abdomen. She looked up. Outside, the church spire was a dull lichen colour, probing the pregnant clouds. Was that thunder?

'Buck up, Edith,' she said aloud, pushing back the bedcovers. She ran a bath, as hot as she could bear – well, it could hardly make things worse, could it? Her skin prickled, mottled pink in the scalding water. There was a red swirl in between her thighs, like the wool Bea crocheted with. She thought of crochet hooks, and probing fingers, and listened to the storm brewing outside. The skies had darkened, the church spire a burnt spike against clouds of ash, and a gust of wind rattled the sash window.

There was an immense flash, she saw the bright streak hit the spire, and then a deafening boom, like the bomb strike at the 400 Club. Just like the bomb that night.

She hadn't meant to cry, but there it suddenly was: strange guttural gulping sounds, and saline splashes into the pinky bathwater. There was a kind of choking heat, that rose up from inside her chest, coming out as tears and mucus, and that wounded-animal yelping noise. At the next thunderclap, she gave way completely, letting out a yell – not of pain this time – but of rage, and beat her fists again and again against the sides of the bathtub. Outside, the storm slammed, and rain battered the windowpanes and Edie screamed and hit out, hating them all, and hating herself.

As the storm died down, her tears slowly ceased. She got out of the bathtub and dried herself on the sandpapery hotel towel. She washed her face in cool water from the tap, not looking at her reflection in the bathroom mirror. There was a dull, twisting ache in her lower stomach. She put her clothes back on, wishing she had something clean to change into. She went back into the bedroom, wondering what the hell to do now.

And then there was a knock at the door. She hadn't ordered room service, but she opened it anyway – and there were Joan and Bea.

'Come in,' said Edie, ushering them both inside. She quickly smoothed down the eiderdown, thinking about blood spatters on the sheets underneath. She motioned for them to sit. Outside, the thunder was a fading sigh. Inside, the air lukewarm, empty.

Bea was red-faced and worried-looking. Joan had a button missing from her blouse, and mussed-up hair. Her lips were pale and puffy, without their customary slick of red. Bea guided Joan in, sat her down on the bed and brushed the hair from her eyes. Everyone seemed to be avoiding looking at each other, or saying anything. Edie could hardly bear it.

'Tea?' she said. 'I think we could all do with a cup of tea, don't you?' She dialled zero on the black Bakelite telephone next to the bed and asked for a pot of tea for three please. Then she sat down on the bed next to Bea. The springs creaked. They were all facing the window, staring out onto the pale green isosceles of church spire set against the clearing clouds. Raindrops still dawdled down the windowpane. 'Shouldn't be too long until they bring it,' she said, thinking about how quick room service had been with the hot water and towels, earlier.

Edie began to worry at what was left of the nail on her right index finger. Bea swatted her hand away: 'You'll only make it worse, girl.' After that, nobody spoke. They just sat, staring at the retreating storm clouds, waiting for room service to arrive.

At last there was a knock at the door. Edie got up to open in. She took the tray from the little rat-faced girl and brought it in, putting it down on the occasional table, where Dr Bloomberg had put his equipment. It hurt when she bent over to put the tray down. It still hurt, deep inside her abdomen. She straightened up and closed the door.

When the tea had brewed, she was Mother, like she'd been at the Ritz. Only nobody suggested reading the leaves, this time. The teacups had scarlet roses on them, with thorny stems. Edie thought of blood clots and sharp needles. She handed out the cups and sat back down on the bed next to Bea. She felt a clench in her stomach and held the warm teacup there, letting the heat of it ease the spasm.

It wasn't that they didn't care about each other, or that they didn't know what to say; it was the reverse of that, Edie thought. They knew too much, cared too much. There was this enormity of unspoken sentiment, filling every corner of the tiny hotel room.

'Looks like your pa did a good job with the coppers, girl.' It was Bea who finally broke the silence. 'Staff told us the inquiry's over.'

Edie nodded, sipping her tea. So nobody would ever know the truth about what happened outside the 400 Club. Nobody except the three of them here, in this room, bound by silence. There was a rapid clink of china against china. Edie looked across at Joan. Her hands were shaking, cup rattling, splashing tea into the saucer. The air still smelled faintly of surgical spirit.

'Joan, are you all right, dear?' said Edie. But Joan did not respond until Bea touched her on the arm.

'Joan,' said Bea. 'Edie asked you a question.'

Joan started, as if stung, and more tea spilled into her saucer. 'Pardon?'

'Edie asked if you was all right, girl.'

'I'm fine,' said Joan. But she was still trembling.

'Is it Robin?' said Edie.

'Who?'

'Your fiancé?'

'He's gone,' said Joan, dully.

Edie went round to the other end of the bed to sit next to Joan, putting her cup down on the bedside table, next to the Bible. She put an arm round her friend. 'Is it because of that Fred chap?' she said.

'How do you know about Fred?' said Bea.

'Same as you, I shouldn't wonder,' said Edie. 'He seemed like a nasty piece of work to me.' She looked at Bea, who still had that harassed expression. Then she looked at Joan, who turned away, eyes glazed, saying nothing. Enough, thought Edie. We simply can't carry on like this.

She withdrew her arm from Joan and sat down on the threadbare burgundy carpet, turning her back on the stupid church spire and facing her two best friends. She shifted until she was comfortable, reached for her teacup, took a sip and then began again. 'Very well,' said Edie, looking at Bea. 'What about you? What are you going to do about your baby?'

'Your what?' said Joan, blinking.

'Her baby. Oh, come on, Joan. Surely you knew, dear?'

'Baby Val?' said Joan, slowly. And Bea nodded, mouth puckering, like she'd just swallowed some foul-tasting medicine.

Edie took another sip of tea, little finger outstretched, just as she'd been taught. 'I've been doing some thinking, while I've been incarcerated here,' she said. 'Nanny always said things would all come out in the wash. Well, girls, I have a feeling that today is laundry day.' She put down her cup on the carpet and knelt up, quite close, so that she could see each of their faces, eyes on a level with her own. Bea drained her cup. Joan bit her lip.

'It strikes me that the time for secrecy is over,' she said. 'We owe each other a debt of honesty, at the very least. What is said today stays inside these four walls, but here it is.' She took a deep breath, before continuing. 'I've watched a man drown, and I did nothing to try to save him. I've had an illegal abortion, right here in this room.' At this, Bea started forward, reaching out. 'No, I'm fine. Let me finish.' Edie waved Bea's comforting arms away. 'You, Bea, have an illegitimate child who you've been forced to pretend is your sister. And you, Joan – you're not really Joan at all. Your real name is Vanessa.'

As the words spilled out, a sense of calm washed over her. There it was, out, and the ceiling hadn't come crashing down. The other two sat on the bed, with their teacups and their taut expressions, and Edie said: 'Well, what have you two got to say for yourselves?' They both stared at her.

'Ma's sick and I've had a letter from Jock,' said Bea at last.

Chapter 41

Bea felt nervous, she had to admit. Edie's idea was good; it made sense. But the thought of meeting Lady Lightwater again made her palms sweat. It would all be posh, and she wouldn't know the right things to say or anything.

'What did he say, again?' said Edie, as they traipsed along the village High Street, past the baker's and the post office. Bea didn't need to take out the air letter and re-read it. She already knew it by heart.

'He says he's got a shrapnel wound. They've patched him up and they're going to send him home. He says we can get married as soon as his ship docks,' she said.

'Well, that's splendid. Isn't that splendid? You always said he'd write; you never gave up hope, and now this. Shall I tell Mummy that you're engaged?'

'You can say what you want,' said Bea. She didn't care. Nothing mattered, because her Jock was on his way home.

'Well, then, I'll just tell the truth. Honesty is the best policy,' she said.

They carried on walking, and they passed a village green, with a pub called the Barley Mow, and the shops fell away to houses, and the further they walked, the larger the houses became, and the longer the driveways, and the higher the front gates. Edie was almost like the old Edie again, chattering away, pointing things out, waving at village acquaintances. But there was something different about her, Bea thought. She was harder, somehow. It was like gobstoppers: when you suck them, there's layers and layers of lovely sweetness, and then, right in the middle there's the aniseed. It was like that with Edie, Bea thought, the layers of sugar had been all-but stripped away, leaving behind this hard little seed.

It began to mizzle. The sky was grey all the way down to the treetops and a fine mist drenched them as they walked. From the opposite direction a vicar came, hunched and black on his bicycle. 'Good morning, Miss Lightwater,' he called out. His bicycle wobbled as he lifted his hat. Edie returned the greeting, but when he'd passed she frowned a little, and walked on faster.

'Blast this weather,' Edie said.

But Bea didn't care about her damp clothes or the way the weighed-down tree branches dripped on them as they passed. She wasn't thinking about the weather. Shrapnel, Jock wrote. Bloody hurt and all, he'd said. She imagined him, laid out in a gritty tent, air like an oven and the sand blowing in and the sting of iodine. Bloody hurt and all. He said they'd get him on a ship as soon as. He had a bit of a fever, so they were waiting for that to clear up. He said don't you worry; the buggers missed me meat-and-two-veg so I can still give you a wedding night to remember. He asked, did she know anyone with any parachute silk for a dress? They'd sort it just as soon as he was able to walk again. He said he wanted to walk her up the aisle and out of the church and to meet his baby girl. He said leave the ATS, I'll take care of you now. That's what he said. The air letter would be getting wet in her breast pocket. It didn't matter. Nothing mattered, now he was on his way home.

From behind them came the growl of an engine. It sounded like a truck, and Bea automatically stuck out her thumb. The noise grew louder, and in her peripheral vision she noticed a dark green shape. There was the honk of a horn. She looked up.

'Where to, ladies?' The conker-haired driver poked his head out of the cab. He had a harelip, and it made his voice sound fuzzy.

'Oh, only about half a mile up the road, before the hill to Old Windsor,' said Edie.

The driver said he was dropping off some girls up that way anyway and gestured at them to get in. The back of the truck was covered with green canvas. A hand reached out and flung away a cigarette end. They walked down and inside was a group of faces, pale blobs under the canvas.

Edie got in first, reaching her foot up high onto the tow bar and swinging her other leg over the tailgate in one swift movement, as if she were getting on a horse. As Bea began to follow her, the truck started up again. There was a scramble and she almost lost her footing, but hands grabbed and clung and she was pulled inside as they jolted away.

Bea sat on the truck bed, against the tailgate; she looked up for a seat, but there wasn't room anywhere. Young women in funny uniforms were perched all over piles of canvas-covered equipment, reminding Bea of the way pigeons clustered in Trafalgar Square. There wasn't an inch of spare space. Edie was wedged in next to her, already chatting and smiling, but Bea couldn't understand a word she said. They were all speaking French. The truck lumbered on.

Edie turned to translate: they were all French soldiers from the Down Street Barracks in London. They had leave, but obviously couldn't go home, so were sent instead to visit various friendly British families. 'One of which is mine – *quelle coïncidence*!' she finished off, patting a blonde French girl on the knee. Then Edie went back to speaking French. Bea didn't mind. She was thinking.

How would Jock feel about the plan that Edie had come up with? Edie said they should just present it as a '*fait accompli*', whatever that meant. It would be nice to settle down away from the town, with grass and flowers, for Baby. Surely Jock would be all right about it? But Edie still had to talk to Lady Lightwater . . . Bea felt her palms sweat again.

They would have rolled into each other as the truck came to a halt, but they were already so tightly packed that there was no room for movement. Edie got out first, still chattering in French, and five of the girl soldiers followed her, stepping right over Bea. Bea got out last, heaving herself over the tail-gate and dropping down onto the road. The driver beeped his horn and they waved their thanks as the truck rumbled away up the wooded lane.

'Well, here we are then,' said Edie. Bea looked up. In front of her were a massive set of wrought-iron gates, beyond them a gravel drive, rose bushes and the vast cream façade of a house with more windows than she could count. '*Allons-y,*' said Edie, lifting the latch and striding up the drive. Bea, last through, clicked the gates carefully shut behind them, bringing up the rear. She looked at Edie, leading her gaggle of Frenchies up the drive. She looks like a troop commander taking her men into battle, Bea thought.

Edie rang the bell and said something in French and all the girls laughed and then Lady Lightwater appeared in the front doorway, and there was cheek-kissing and introductions, and Bea hung back, looking at the unweeded flowerbeds and the spiders' webs on the window ledges. She stood on the bottom step as all the palaver went on beyond her and looked down at her feet and noticed that the steps were filthy, really filthy. The first thing I'll do, she thought, looking down at the mud and the mould, the very first thing I'll do if it all turns out, is to give these steps a right good scrubbing.

Chapter 42

There was never going to be a good time to broach the subject, thought Edie, pulling cups and saucers out of the cupboard.

'I don't know why you didn't phone first,' Mummy was saying, and Edie replied that if she'd phoned it would have spoiled the surprise. The truth was, she hadn't been quite sure what to say on the phone: I'm bringing my friend Bea to see you because . . . no, it was much better to ask in person. She pulled the last cup from the cupboard. It looked a bit dusty inside, so she gave it a rinse under the tap and asked Mummy for a tea towel.

'They're all dirty,' she replied. 'I had such a bother getting the sheets aired and ironed for this French onslaught, and I've been helping out almost every day with the mobile canteen, and doing the Red Cross POW parcels with Mrs Carson when I have a spare moment and there just never seems to be the time. And your father's never home. Never. His work

The Gunner Girl

seems to keep him in London all the time these days. Not that he'd help with the laundry, I'm not saying that, but you know . . .' she trailed off as she lifted the kettle off the hob. She'd overfilled it, and it spilled scalding water down the front of her dress. 'Damnation!' she thumped the kettle down on the work surface.

Edie put the wet cup down on the draining board and went over to where her mother stood, glaring at the kettle as if it were an SS guard.

'Poor Mummy,' said Edie, patting her on the shoulder. 'You're lonely and you need help.'

'And where, pray, is one supposed to get help these days? The world and his wife are conscripted!'

Edith let her hand stay, lightly touching her mother's jutting shoulder. 'I've got an idea,' she said, 'if you'll just hear me out.'

'There's no time for ideas now, Edith Elizabeth. We've got an army of free French to feed and water, not to mention your ATS chum. Where's she sleeping?'

'Oh, we're not staying, Mummy. We've got to go on to Kent this afternoon. We just dropped by.' Edie let her hand fall, and went back to the table, laying out the cups and saucers ready.

'You just dropped by?' said Mummy. Edie nodded. 'Well, *they're* here for three weeks. Three weeks! And there's another lot coming along after that. I couldn't really say no, could I? I've said they'll have to do their own cooking. Only no horse. I will not have horse eaten in my house,' said Mummy, and sighed.

She pulled the tea caddy off the shelf. 'I am remiss, Edith. I'm sorry, I haven't even asked how you are?' She began to scoop leaves from the Twinings' tea caddy into the big cream teapot, the one they used for the beaters when it was shooting season. Her lips moved as she silently counted the scoops.

'Fine,' said Edie. 'I'm fine, Mummy.'

'You look peaky. Are you eating properly?'

'I have been a little off-colour,' said Edie.

'And one for the pot,' said Mummy, putting in the last scoop and lifting the kettle. 'What's been the matter?'

Edie paused, as the water from the kettle began to sluice into the teapot. Honesty, that's what she'd said to the other two. It was important to be honest.

'Well, I got myself into a bit of trouble.'

'What do you mean, trouble?' said Mummy, concentrating on the stream of boiling water.

'You know, *trouble*,' said Edie. Her mother stopped pouring, put the kettle down; she was facing the wall, but did not turn. Her spine looked like a knife-edge under the tight dress.

'And the trouble – are you better now?' she said at last.

'Yes, I'm fine.' Edith cleared her throat. 'Pop helped.'

Mummy picked up the kettle and began to pour again. The steam swept up, clouding her. She finished pouring and put the kettle down. She did not turn to look at Edie.

'Your father didn't say ...'

'We didn't want to worry you.'

'I see.' She still hadn't turned round.

Out with it, Edie thought. Truth will out. Don't flunk it now. 'Mrs Cowie was very kind, too.' Edie thought she heard a sharp intake of breath.

'Meredith?'

'Yes.'

There was silence. Mummy's hand fluttered up and smoothed her hair. Then she leant forward with her hands on the work surface, as if exhausted. Edie waited. At last, her mother straightened up and turned round. Her face was as blank and smooth as the side of the teapot.

'I must thank her, next time I see her.' Edie nodded. It was done. 'Well, then, better get on with this, I suppose. I wish I had some coffee to offer them,' said Mummy, looking angrily at the teapot.

'I'm sure they'll be fine with tea,' said Edie.

'And I don't have any lemon, either. The Continentals don't take milk with tea – they have lemon. I can't remember the last time I even saw a lemon.'

'Mummy, there's a war on. They won't mind.'

'I know full well there's a war on, young lady. But that's no reason whatsoever to let standards slip,' said Mummy. And they both knew she wasn't talking about the lack of coffee or lemon for the tea.

At that point, Bea came into the kitchen, rubbing her palms on the sides of her skirt. She bobbed her head to Mummy and smiled a little nervously.

'Do you have a dustpan?' she said.

'Whatever do you need a dustpan for?' asked Mummy.

'Sorry to mention it – it's only that I found a dead mouse in the fireplace and I thought that . . .'

'A mouse? Oh, dear God, get rid of it at once. I'll find the dustpan. Where is the blasted dustpan? For heaven's sake!' She began banging cupboard doors. Bea walked over to the sink and looked underneath.

'I've found it, Lady Lightwater, don't trouble yourself,' said Bea. She also found a basin and a scrubbing brush. She filled the basin with the rest of the hot water from the kettle and added some soda crystals, and then disappeared with them and the dustpan.

'Thank you so much, Bea, you are a dear,' Edie called after her.

'Was she in service, before?' said Mummy.

'I think she was a cleaner for someone,' said Edie. 'Oh, did I mention she's leaving the ATS? She's getting married as soon as her fiancé gets home – he's got a shrapnel wound and they're sending him back. They've got a baby girl. Her mother has been looking after the baby for them. Anyway, she's looking for work and a place to stay.'

'Is she?' said Mummy. Her face gave nothing away. They looked at each other over the pile of teacups.

'Yes. And you said you needed help.'

Mummy pursed her lips and ran her index finger over one eyebrow, smoothing it down. 'She seems like a very competent young woman, but I couldn't possibly have a baby in the house.'

'You had those evacuees, before they decided to go back.'

'That was different. And anyway, those children weren't born out of wedlock.'

'She would be married before she came here. She'd stay in the ATS until her wedding. So the baby wouldn't be, you know.'

'But even so . . .' her mother began.

'She's very quiet, and a really hard worker, honestly Mummy, you'd hardly know she was here. Just until the end of the war. Please.' Her mother looked down and away, and Edie thought she'd flunked it. To her, it had seemed such a straightforward plan. Mummy needed help. Bea would need a place to stay. A perfect match. But Mummy didn't seem to think so. 'You can't carry on like this,' said Edie, giving it one last try. The sweep of her gesture took in the streaked window-panes; sink full of unwashed dishes, crumbs on the work surfaces and footprints on the flagstones. 'Can you?'

Her mother looked up, finally looked directly at her and shook her head. It was a tiny, controlled movement. 'No, Edith,' she said. 'I can't carry on like this.'

'Well?'

'We'll need to clear it with your father,' she said at last.

'I'm sure he'll agree,' said Edie. 'He'll do anything to keep you happy, Mummy.' Her mother shot her a look, but nothing was said, sucking in a breath, as if she were inhaling an invisible cigarette.

'I'm sure he will,' she said on the exhalation. 'Now, where are those buns? I bought buns this morning, but where have they all gone?'

'I've got them,' said Edie. 'I've already plated them up for you.'

'Well, you seem to have everything under control, Edith Elizabeth,' said her mother.

Yes, Edie thought to herself; yes, I think I do. But there were still a couple of things left to get sorted by close of play.

Chapter 43

'Business or pleasure?' said the gate guard as she showed her ID card. Without his thin ginger moustache he would have looked about twelve years old.

'Business,' she said. She wasn't going to take any of his cheek. Unfinished business, she thought to herself, walking past the barrier. The white control tower was an art deco wedding cake in the distance, at the far end of the RAF camp. She turned back towards the pubescent guard. 'Where's the sergeants' mess?' she said.

'You won't be allowed in,' he replied, looking her up and down. 'It's senior NCOs, men only.' He reminded her of someone, from before. Something about that skinny swagger, and the way he talked to her tits instead of her face.

'Can you direct me to the sergeants' mess, please, Aircraftman?' she said, emphasising his rank. She might be in a different branch of the armed forces, but she knew full well that a bombardier outranked and aircraftman, and so did he.

'Over there, by the parade ground,' he muttered. She nodded her thanks.

It was just off the main road into camp: a new-looking brick building, rust-coloured under the blanket of grey cloud. The camp was bigger than Hyde Park Battery, almost like a small town. Figures scurried in and out of buildings, like wisps of smoke. In the distance, aircraft engines purred. The air was thick with humidity and the tarmac road glistened wetly as she crossed over to the parade square. She looked up at the ranks of blank windows, all blacked out to daylight. Of course, they'd all be asleep, if they'd been out on a night sortie.

She walked across the empty parade square, looking up. The windows looked back, unblinking. Which one was his? If she'd known, she could have chucked gravel up to wake him, like the boys from school used to do at hers, until Dad came out with his belt unbuckled and threatened them with a thrashing. How she'd laughed, peeping out of the curtains as Frank Otterwell and Larry Parsons went high-tailing down Western Way with Dad roaring after them in his vest and braces. She remembered that, now, after everything that had happened with Fred, in the hotel. She remembered other things, too: she used to work at the cinema; her dad was in the police; people whispered about her and George, the grocer's boy, because of what happened that time up at the allotments. Her name used to be Vanessa. Used to be?

She was at the bottom of the steps now, and she felt dizzy looking up. Maybe it was the clouds moving behind the rooftop, but the mess looked as if it was swooping, and there was a buzzing hum. Probably just the planes on the runway, she told herself. She closed her eyes and took in a deep breath. She had no expectations. She owed Rob the truth, that was all. And she wanted to see him, even if it was the last time.

'Can I help you?' – a voice at her elbow. She opened her eyes. The voice belonged to a woman in a WAAF uniform, brunette hair showing underneath her cap. Her lips were very pink. Was that lipstick? Did the air force allow women to wear lipstick at work?

'I'm looking for Flight Sergeant Nelson,' said Joan.

'Is it really urgent?' said the woman, frowning. 'Only, I don't want to send someone barging in there to wake him up after the night they've just had, not unless it's, you know, life or death stuff. Is it?'

'Is it what?'

'Life or death stuff?' The woman was looking at her, her slanty grey eyes glowering.

'No, but . . .' Joan began.

'Thought not. You can wait, if you want. There's a NAAFI just over there,' she gestured up the road, in the direction of the control tower.

But I've come all this way to tell him. It's important he knows, because then he'll understand, and even though it won't change anything, he should know the truth. He deserves the truth, she thought, looking past the woman and back up at the blackened windows.

'But I'm his . . .' Joan began, moving forwards. The woman

caught her arm, just above the elbow, and she held tight, fingers like little claws.

'His what?'

What was she? Not his fiancée, not even anyone he knew. He thought he knew Joan; he didn't even know Vanessa existed. 'Nothing,' she replied.

'Well, I'm sorry, but I really can't let you wake him then, unless . . .' she turned her attention back to the woman's face. There was a different look on it now. The frown had gone. There was something else there. What was it? Panic? Concern?

'What did you say his name was, your friend?'

'Robin. Flight Sergeant Robin Nelson.'

The woman suddenly loosened her grip, and her face relaxed. 'Rob Nelson – he's fine. I saw him at breakfast. Thank God.' The woman let go of her arm. 'So don't worry.'

'I've got to talk to him,' she said.

'I can't let you. We can't afford to have the men tired out before they even begin, not now, not with everything that's going on, don't you see?' The woman's lips moved slowly, enunciating every syllable.

'And who put you in charge?' she said. 'I haven't come all this way to be given the brush off just by some . . .' she scanned the woman's uniform to look for a badge of rank – she was probably only an aircraftwoman – but her eyes caught sight of the wings. She stopped speaking, catching herself in time. The woman was an officer.

'If they're tired, they're more likely to make mistakes. And they can't afford to make mistakes,' the woman said. She wasn't frowning now. She just looked sad, exhausted.

She looked up at the windows – he was up there some-where, her Rob. Was he still hers? Could he be hers again? But the flight officer was right. She couldn't wake him up, just to tell him. Not if he was flying again tonight. She sighed. 'Then could I leave a note for him, ma'am?'

'Of course. And I promise I'll see he gets it just as soon as he gets up. Do you need paper?'

The flight officer took her across to the headquarters building. As they opened the office door, a black Labrador bounded out, and licked her hand. She ruffled his ears, and asked his name.

'Vertigo. I know, silly name. Not my choice,' came the reply. 'He belonged to – to someone else, but he's not here now, so, well, you know how it is. But he's a good boy, aren't you, Verti?' She stroked the top of his head, and there was a look on her face – it reminded her of the way Bea had looked that time, when Joan had seen her stroke Baby Val. 'Right, paper, pen, envelopes. I'm just off for a meeting, so I'll leave you in peace. Just leave the note on my desk and I'll see he gets it before flight checks,' said the woman.

She thanked the flight officer, who left with the dog trot-ting at her heels. Then she sat down and picked up the pen: *Dear Rob, You must hate me, and I can't blame you, but there's something you need to know. There's a reason why I couldn't say yes. The problem is, I'm not who you think . . .*

It wasn't as hard to write as she'd thought; she kept it brief.

She told the truth about how she stole Joan's call-up papers, about how she was really Vanessa, just seventeen, not even old enough to join up yet. She even told him about Fred, her sister's fiancé, and what he'd tried to do, and what she'd done to him, in the Mount Royal Hotel. The words came easily, little hard, bright chunks of sentences, like those wooden blocks that toddlers play with. It was just like a two-year-old building a tower: this happened, and this happened, and this happened, block upon block upon block. It was easy enough, now she could remember everything. But then, when it came to sign off, she got stuck: *So, now you know everything but I don't know how to finish this letter. Do I sign it Vanessa or Joan? I don't know. I don't know how it's supposed to end* . . . and the tower of blocks came tumbling down.

That was all she could do. No love, no kisses, no name. She folded up the stiff paper and found an envelope, licked and sealed it. On the front, she wrote *Fight Sergeant Robin Nelson – urgent*. She got up, placed the letter on the desk and prepared to leave the tiny windowless office. She noticed a mirror compact, left behind, next to the blotter. *Darling*, was engraved on the front. She thought of the sad look the officer gave when she stroked the dog. She clicked the mirror open and looked at her own face; her features crowded into the small silver circle. There were mauve smudges under her eyes, and her lips were dry and pale. She put the mirror down, opened her gas-mask case and took out her lipstick. Then she applied it, carefully colouring in the moist, red bow. There, that was better. She snapped the mirror shut, and put it back in the same place as the letter, between the blotter and the telephone. She put the lipstick away and checked her watch. There didn't seem anything more to be done. She turned to leave. As she reached the door, she stepped back, quickly, inhaling as if there was something she'd forgotten to say. She reached for the sealed envelope and planted a kiss on the reverse. It looked like poppy petals.

'Get what you came for, Bombardier?' said the sarky ginger gate guard as she left. She could see the green country bus pulling up at the stop outside the camp gates. If she hurried up, she'd catch it, and be back in time to meet the others. She paused and fixed the gate guard with a look. George, that was who he reminded her of – George the grocer's boy.

'Oh, why don't you just sod off, you void coupon,' she said, and stuck two fingers up at him as she walked past.

'You can't do that, I'll get you put on a charge. I know who you are,' he screeched after her, unable to leave his post.

'I don't think you do,' she called back to him. 'I don't even know myself!' and she started to laugh. She saw the bus and ran for it, laughing long and hard, gasping for breath. If she hadn't laughed, she would have cried, and she wouldn't have been able to stop.

Chapter 44

Bea could hear Ma's rasping breath from the halfway up the stairs. The front door banged shut below her. Edie and Joan were taking the others out for chips, just to give her and Ma a couple of minutes. Bea had given Vi the advance on her next month's wages. The doctor was on his way. And they couldn't miss the train back to London or they'd all be AWOL. There wasn't much time.

The air in the stairwell was still and solid, she felt as if she were pushing through it, swimming up to the surface. At the top step she paused and took a breath, noticing the crumbling bricks on the unpainted wall. There was red dust all over the floorboards. Vi didn't have time to clean, what with her job and all. But Rita and May could help – she'd have to say something to them after. The house was in a right state. No wonder Ma could barely breathe, what with the dust and the cobwebs and –

'Bea.' She heard her voice as a whispered exhalation. There was a bubbling in-breath, and there it was again. 'Bea.'

The Gunner Girl

Ma was waiting for her. She was propped up against the bedstead. How small she looked: shrunken. Bea remembered the time when the twins brought back that dead frog they'd found in the alley. It had dried out in the sun, and its skin was all shrivelled up, clinging to its tiny bones. She thought about that dead frog as she looked at Ma, sitting up under the thin sheet.

The little window was slightly ajar, but still a bluebottle thudded and buzzed ineffectually against the pane, unable to escape. Ma's hair was plastered wetly against her head, the ends snaking out over her damp nightdress. She patted the bed and muttered something. Bea couldn't hear, but she understood she was to sit down. The room smelled. What was it? Not just dirt, although that too – the sheets needed a boil wash – something else, sort of sweet and mucky at the same time. Ma's face was waxy pale, covered in a sheen of sweat, but she was shivering. The bedsprings creaked as Bea sat down.

'Doctor's on his way,' she said.

Ma's eyes were large and dark. She gulped in breaths, wincing with the effort. The fly bumped again and again against the glass. Bea took Jock's letter out of her top pocket and tossed it down on the bedcovers in front of Ma.

'I got a letter from Jock,' Bea said. She looked at Ma, and saw a flicker pass over her face, like a cat's paw ripple on the estuary on a calm day.

'You know I don't read good, girl,' Ma said, the words sawing from her dry throat. Her lips were dry and cracked, but her skin looked damp. There were beads of sweat on her forehead.

413

'I know. But you recognise his handwriting, don't you?' said Bea, feeling anger rising in her chest. 'Don't you, Ma?' But Ma turned her head away, looked towards the window, the fly and the drizzled afternoon. Sounds from the street carried up: footfalls, laughter, a honking horn in the distance. 'I'll tell you what he says,' said Bea. 'He says he's coming back for me.' Ma did not turn back. 'He's wounded, and they're sending him home to get better and as soon as he's back we're getting married,' Bea continued. Ma's breath was loud, scraping up her throat and into the empty air. The tendrils of dirty hair were quivering against the withered skin of her neck. 'And we're coming to get Baby back,' said Bea. But Ma kept her head turned. 'Did you hear me? Jock's going to marry me and I'm leaving the army and I'm taking Baby back where she belongs.'

'Over my dead body,' came the barely audible reply.

'Yes, over your dead body,' spat Bea. Ma's head swivelled back and the two women looked at each other.

Ma swallowed and exhaled. 'I did it for you, girl,' she said.

'For me? Lying about Jock, making me join the army, taking my baby away – how is that for me?'

'I knew he was going to get hurt. I saw it in the leaves. I thought he wasn't coming back,' Ma's face was crumpled with the effort of speech. Exhausted, she let her head fall back; it clunked against the metal bedstead.

'The leaves lied, Ma,' said Bea. 'The leaves lied. Jock's coming back, and we're going to be together as a family and there's nothing you can do to stop us.' She swept the letter up.

It was damp and all the ink had bled. She put it back in her pocket. 'We're getting married and we're getting our baby back and I'm going to work as a housekeeper for Lady Lightwater, and Jock is going to be her caretaker and Baby will grow up in a nice big house in the country with flowers and trees and ponies and clean, healthy air.'

'I was trying to protect you,' her mother whispered.

'From what? From happiness? You think I don't deserve to live happily ever after?'

'But the leaves said – I was doing right by you, girl.'

'You took away my baby.'

'I gave you a chance, a chance for a future, girl,'

'I don't want your bloody future, I want my baby. I just want my baby back.'

'I was looking out for you.'

'I don't want you to look out for me. I want you to leave me alone.'

Ma shook her head. 'I know how it ends, girl.'

'No, you don't. Because there's nothing in them leaves. I'm in control now; I decide what's going to happen. And there's a future for me and Jock and Baby as a proper family, without you, without all this.' She gestured round the shabby little room, with its bare floorboards and unpainted walls. The bluebottle finally found the gap, buzzed free and all that was left was the sound of Ma's uneven, painful breaths: in-out, in-out.

There was a knock at the front door. 'That'll be the doctor,' said Bea. She got up and smoothed down the bedcovers where she'd been sitting. There was a dirty cup on the empty packing case next to the bed. Ma saw her looking at it and reached for it. The knock came again. 'Coming!' Bea yelled down. Ma passed her the empty cup. There were tea leaves swirled round inside like mud spatters. Their fingertips touched as the cup passed between them. Then Bea turned away.

'Mind your step on the way,' Ma said as she left. And Bea, running downstairs to open the door for the doctor, running down as she had done hundreds of times before, thought it was an odd thing to say – Ma had never told her to mind her step before.

Chapter 45

They'd all come to give Bea a send-off, except Vi, who'd waited behind with the doctor to sort out the details of getting their mother taken into hospital. The doctor said there was a chance she'd pull through, given the proper care. Bea said Baby would be fine to go back home with the others: Rita and May could hold her hand – it was only round the corner and she was a good walker, now. And there was enough money to pay for a babysitter, too, just for a few weeks, until everything was arranged with Jock and the wedding.

Yes, thought Edie, watching Bea hugging her goodbyes to her flock of siblings, it was all working out rather well, really. She could just about hear the train in the distance, a far away chug-chug. Soon they'd all be on their way back to the battery, all three of them together. Of course, technically, she was still off sick with appendicitis, but the other two had to be back, and this would be the last train to London today.

Joan hadn't talked much about Rob. She'd said she hadn't

been able to see him, and her face had that closed, hard look. She said she'd left him a letter, though, which was something. Edie hadn't given up on Joan's story having a happy ending too, in time.

The clouds had lifted and it was a clear evening, the sun lengthening their shadows, like ribbons across the platform. The blackberries were ripening on the bushes in the sidings. And she thought, suddenly, of blackberry picking with Marjorie and Kenneth, at the end of the school holidays. Kenneth was talking about joining up, joining the Intelligence Corps, like his father, and she'd jokingly said something like 'Intelligence, with your grades? Are you sure?' and he'd pelted her with blackberries – purple blobs all over her poplin blouse, Mummy had been furious, and Cook had made blackberry and apple crumble. And later, Kenneth had joined the Int Corps and then ... but that was so long ago now.

What about you, then? A little voice nagged inside her head. Bea's going to get her dream and Joan still has a chance. What about Edie? Is there a happy ending for Edie, too? Edie sighed, looking at the noisy, messy bundle of Bea's family over by the waiting room. No. What mattered now was to move forward, somehow. Maybe happy endings were for other people.

Suddenly, Baby Val slipped out of the knot of siblings and toddled over towards her. 'Little minx,' Edie said, catching her and scooping her up.

'Don't you go running off, girl, it's not safe!' yelled Bea, untangling herself from her brothers and sisters.

'It's all right, I've got her,' called Edie, lodging Baby Val on one hip. She smelled of chips and carbolic soap and warm babyness. I let them kill mine, thought Edie, kissing the nest of curls on the top of Baby Val's head. I let them push me and shove me and suck it out of me. Edie clenched her jaws tight and swallowed hard and looked over Baby's head to where the two train tracks merged into one and told herself to buck up.

There was a droning hum overhead and, looking up, she saw the V-formation of Lancasters heading out east, away from the train tracks, across the English Channel. Joan was stood alone at the far end of the platform, watching silently as they passed. She looked and looked, until the planes were out of sight and all that was left was a vibration of disappearing sound. Poor Joan, thought Edie.

Baby Val slapped Edie's cheek with her soft little paw. 'Ma, Ma,' she said, pointing. Edie looked. She was pointing at Bea, who was picking her way along the platform, past a mass of kit bags and towards a group of soldiers. Did Baby know already? Edie wondered. Had she already been told that Bea was her ma? Or was this just baby speak? No matter, it would only be a matter of weeks, maybe less; Jock's ship could dock any day now. Edie watched Bea treading carefully over bags and piles of discarded coats.

'I know you – it's Bill Franks, isn't it? Corporal Bill Franks of 32 Armoured?' she heard Bea saying. A gangly looking soldier stood up, grinning and said it was Sergeant Bill Franks these days and they began chatting and gesticulating and Edie heard something about 'my fiancé' and 'my baby girl' and pointed across to where Edie stood holding Baby Val, and the train tooted, coming through the tunnel.

Edie looked along the platform and people were starting to pick up their bags and say their final goodbyes and the group of soldiers were all getting to their feet, and, way up at the end of the platform, Joan was still staring away at the empty sky, and Edie thought she really should go and get Joan because if they missed this train, they'd really be in hot water when they got back.

Baby Val was wriggling and saying 'Ma' and Edie didn't mean to, but she was looking at Joan and not taking enough notice and Baby Val wriggled free. Edie tried to run after her, but there was a tangle of soldiers with kit bags in front of them and Baby Val tottered between their legs and away. Edie shouted, 'Val!' after her, but she didn't stop. There was the sound of everyone talking, saying goodbye, and the rushing growl of the train getting closer. Again, Edie shouted, 'Val!' Tried to push past the throng and catch her, and this time Bea looked round, and saw. Edie shoved through the cluster of soldiers, shouting again, but Baby Val didn't stop or turn and her little legs moved surprisingly quickly. Bea looked round and saw her little daughter running, running, and the train was pulling in. Heads turned in idle curiosity at the kerfuffle. At last, Edie found enough space between passengers and ran after Baby Val, yelling at the top of her voice. And Bea was there in front of her, yelling Val's name, catching up with her little girl, arms outstretched, grabbing, right at the edge of the platform as the train was screaming in. And Bea had almost caught her baby girl, when someone shouted, 'Mind your step!' and Bea tripped and was over, down on the tracks and someone else snatched up Baby and the train screeched to a halt, but Bea was down and the train didn't stop in time and the station went quiet as they heard a dislocated screech and then silence.

Edie stopped running. There was the hiss of steam and the train doors began to swing open and Edie shouted, 'Stop! Everyone, just stay where you are!' She caught sight of the guard, white-faced, on the platform edge. 'For God's sake, man, don't just stand there, call an ambulance!' she shouted. She shouted even though she knew, they all knew, that there was no point.

And Baby Val, held tight by a stranger in uniform, pointed down by the edge of the platform and said, 'Ma?'

Chapter 46

'Come!' said the voice. One RMP opened the door and the other yelled at them to quick-march inside. The RMP yelled 'Halt!' and ''Shun!' when they were in and they stood, shoulder to shoulder, waiting for the inevitable.

Joan could feel Edie, rigid and trembling beside her. She held her breath. They were really for it, now. AWOL: absent without leave. They'd be court martialled, surely? The CO was sitting behind his desk and a young woman was standing beside him. It must be the new junior commander the other girls were talking about, she thought. She could hear Edie's breath coming in little bursts.

'Thank you, I'll take it from here,' said the CO. 'You can wait outside.' The RMPs left. The CO's chair scraped on the lino as he stood up. The junior commander looked at them. She had mousy hair and a pale doughy face, like – she suddenly remembered that newsreel, that day, before it all started – like the Prime Minister's daughter. She had a faint squinty frown on her wide brow. Outside, a sudden gust of wind made the tree branches patter against the window like someone trying to get in. The CO glowered. He cleared his throat, and they waited.

'Well, I hardly need to tell you the severity of your offence,' he began. The phone rang, trembling through the dead air. The CO nodded at the junior commander, who picked it up.

'Hyde Park Battery, Junior Commander Churchill speaking,' she said. So it *was* her. There was the muffled scratchy sound of the voice at the other end of the line. 'Is that something I can help with?' said Junior Commander Churchill. The CO tutted. There was more muffled chat from the phone. 'Perhaps he could call you back?' said Mary Churchill. The sounds from the telephone were louder this time, but she couldn't make out the words. Mary Churchill nodded and put her hand over the mouthpiece. 'He says it's urgent,' she whispered to the CO.

'They always say that. Just get rid,' the CO hissed back. She took her hand off the mouthpiece

'I can take a message. May I ask who's calling?' she said and then almost immediately pulled the phone away from her ear. There were the sounds of tinny shouts from the receiver.

'He says he wants to talk to the organ grinder, not the monkey,' she said, no longer bothering to whisper or cover the mouthpiece. 'It's Lord Mountbatten, by the way.'

The CO immediately took the phone from her. Joan watched his expression change from irritation to panic as he answered the call. 'Hello, yes, sorry about that . . . I see. I'm in the middle of ... yes, I understand, but ... right away? Of course. I'm on my way.' He hung up and shook his head. 'I say, it never rains but it bloody well pours.' He picked up his cap and his fountain pen from the desk. 'You'll have to carry on, Commander. You know my views on this incident.'

Mary Churchill said, 'Yes, sir' as the CO stormed out, slamming the door behind him.

'At ease,' said Mary Churchill as soon as the door closed. She and Edie moved their right legs wider and shifted their hands behind their backs, their chins lowered half an inch. Mary Churchill walked out from behind the desk and stood squarely in front of them. 'Well, this is a terribly bad business. You have jeopardised the reputation of the battery, if not the entire ATS,' she said severely, her small teeth like pearls in her soft mouth. She stopped talking for a bit, then, and paced up and down in front of them. Eventually, she stopped, and sighed. 'Oh, stand easy, for heaven's sakes,' she said, and they unclasped their hands and relaxed their legs.

Mary Churchill pushed herself up so that she was sitting on the edge of the CO's desk, legs dangling like a schoolgirl's. Her hair was honey-edged in the sunshine, just like Bea's. Just like Bea's used to be. The wind in the trees was louder than the traffic on the Bayswater Road and the twigs tapped and tapped and they waited and waited. Would they be sent to military prison? How long for? Lord, what a mess.

At last, Mary Churchill spoke again: 'I understand you have both just lost a colleague and a very dear friend.' They both nodded. 'Nevertheless, this is a very awkward business.' She sighed again, loudly, like a horse. 'You should never have been there, and you certainly should have at least contacted your unit immediately after the incident and returned to work.'

'But the family needed us,' said Edie. 'There wasn't anyone else there to help—'

'I know you, don't I?' Mary Churchill interrupted Edie, who nodded. 'Queen's College?' Edie nodded again. 'I seem to remember you did French with Madame Cavelle, too?' She turned and picked the charge sheet off the desk and checked the name. 'Edith Lightwater. Oh, yes, Neville's girl, now I can place you.' She put the sheet down. There was another pause, and Joan watched as Mary Churchill's eyes flicked up above their heads and she pursed her lips.

Afterwards, the two RMPs marched them to their hut: confined to barracks pending a preliminary hearing scheduled for the afternoon. Passing faces stared. The air smelled clean, rain-washed, a bit like gin. The wind whipped a stray strand of hair into her mouth and she spat it out.

Inside, the hut was empty, half dark, despite the uncurtained windows. Joan sat down on the bed next to Edie. The bedsprings creaked underneath them. Edie's Bible lay untouched on the locker top. The air was musty and thick with things unspoken. But there was nothing to say. They were guilty as charged.

She remembered a Sunday afternoon, before it all started. Dad would've been at the allotments, Mum in the kitchen, her big sister out with Fred. And she'd sat alone in the still air of the front room, carefully balancing a deck of cards, gently up-up. Then the desolation when Mum opened the door, and

425

a gust sent the whole house toppling over the tabletop, and she knew she'd never be able to build a house of cards like that, not ever again.

She sighed, patted Edie's thigh, next to her on the hard bed, remembering everything that had happened over the last few days. It was Vi's voice that stayed with her. 'My sister,' she'd howled. 'My big sister.'

'It wasn't your fault, you know,' Joan said aloud. And she wasn't sure if she was talking to Edie, or to herself.

There was some muttering from outside the hut and Staff Farr came in. They both stood up as she entered. Staff Farr opened her mouth as if to say something, paused, closed her lips, took another step forward, and then began. 'I've just received a call,' she said. 'From the deceased's sister.' For a moment, it was impossible to understand what Staff Farr was saying. Who was 'the deceased'? Bea – she was talking about Bea. Bea wasn't a person any more. She wasn't the smiling, ever-hungry, comforting presence in the next bunk; she was merely 'the deceased'. 'Violet Smith,' Staff Farr continued. 'She asked me to let you both know that Jock arrived safely and he's taken the baby to his mother's, for now, while he convalesces. She said she thought you'd want to know.'

They thanked Staff Farr, expecting her to leave immediately, but she didn't. She took one more step forward. The staff sergeant's face had a different look from usual, the frowning brow replaced by something else. Her lips were pressed shut, and they peeled slowly open to speak, like someone steaming open an envelope. 'I don't blame you, girls,' she said in a low voice. 'I don't blame you, and I'm prepared to say as much in a court martial.' She took a step back and said, in a louder voice: 'The Junior Commander has also asked me to inform you that you may get yourselves something to eat, and you are then to ablute and smarten yourselves up in preparation for the preliminary hearing. You will be in works dress, of course.' Then Staff Farr turned on her heel and left. There was muttering again outside the door, and the sound of footfalls moving away.

Joan turned to look at Edie, who'd sat back down on the bed, head in her hands. 'At least Baby Val's with her dad now,' she said to Edie. But Edie didn't answer, because she was silently weeping. Joan sat back down next to Edie and stroked her back, the cloth of her uniform rough against her fingertips. She was thinking that in the last war people had been shot for desertion. They were hardly likely to get off scott-free, were they? They'd been told to get some food from the cookhouse before the hearing. Who knew what the food would be like in military prison? she then said to Edie, tugging her to her feet. Edie replied that she wasn't hungry, blowing her nose on a lace-edged handkerchief and muttering that she didn't think she'd be able to keep anything down.

'Tea then, just a cup of tea?' she said, pulling Edie towards the hut door. She pushed it open. Staff Farr must have sent the RMPs off on a break. They were nowhere to be seen. The wind was beginning to die down, and the mid-morning sunshine slapped full into their faces as they walked down the cinder path towards the cookhouse. There was the distant clatter-splash of breakfast cutlery being rinsed under the outside tap, and someone's reedy whistling of 'A Nightingale Sang in Berkley Square' carried on the breeze. Sheila Carter was puffing up the path towards them, lugging a crate of tools.

'That fella's back,' she panted, squinting at them as she drew level.

'What fella?'

'The one from before – your fiancé,' she said, shoving past. 'In the NAAFI.' Sheila waddled off. The sunshine suddenly hardened, and Joan felt cold.

'I'll check for you,' said Edie, reading her mind, shoving her hankie in her pocket.

Joan watched Edie scurrying ahead, past the cookhouse and on towards the NAAFI. Edie's hair was escaping from her cap, her head dipping as she ran. It reminded her of how Edie had run off that day when they were cleaning the cookhouse windows. She remembered how Bea had had to finish the windows for them. Oh, Bea.

Edie's frame got smaller with distance, then paused and faltered by the NAAFI entrance. The door opened and a handful of girls spilled out, and Edie disappeared inside. Joan looked at the group of girls who came scudding up the path towards her. They were newly posted-in. She didn't recognise any of them. They passed like a khaki sandstorm, trailing looks and whispers in their wake. Word had got out, of course. It always did.

She thought of Laurel and Hardy, at the flicks. 'Look what

a fine mess you've got me into!' said the fat one, and the skinny one scratched his head, looking stupid. The ground tilted and all her edges blurred and she was back there again, where the air smelled of stale smoke and she hadn't got the right change for the ices, but she didn't want to go back to the office to ask, and get her arse felt up by Mr Evans and these bloody shoes, how they squashed her toes. When would it be home time? There was the sudden flashing ahead as it came to the end of the reel. Then the screen flickered and went dark—

'It's him!' A posh voice, suddenly.

She blinked her eyes open, took a gulping breath, and told herself to focus, but the path felt soft as quicksand and the air was already beginning to hum. She looked down the snaking grey path and saw the NAAFI door begin to open and the figure of a man emerge. The sunshine struck the side of the man's face; it was livid red on the left-hand side. He was carrying a piece of paper.

'The Junior Commander,' said Edie, pulling her sleeve. 'Mary will know what to do.' Joan let herself be tugged away, in the opposite direction, towards the CO's office.

'Yes, Brigadier, I think she's the right sort,' Junior Commander Churchill was saying into the receiver as they entered. 'Shall I send her over? Very well. Goodbye, sir.' She clicked the receiver into its cradle.

'What is it now, for goodness' sakes?' she said, scribbling a note down on a piece of paper. 'I thought you'd both been given instructions to prep for your hearing?' She began to rootle through desk drawers, not looking at them.

'The thing is, ma'am,' Edie began.

'Oh, where does he keep the envelopes?' Mary Churchill interrupted. 'Here – what a silly place to have them. Yes, Gunner, what is it?'

The office smelled of school. It smelled of the schoolrooms where she'd been asked why she couldn't just sit still and write neatly like her big sister.

'It's Bombardier Tucker,' said Edie. 'You see, she—' Edie faltered.

There were crunching footsteps getting louder as they approached, up the cinder path. Mary Churchill folded the paper and put it inside the envelope. 'Get on with it,' she said, licking the envelope and pressing it shut.

The footfalls stopped outside the door.

Closing her eyes, Joan saw clouds of powdery dust, red hair fanned out on shattered floorboards, sticky and matted with blood and grit. There was a burning smell in the air. She opened her eyes, sucked in a breath, and watched as Mary Churchill wrote something on the front of the envelope and pushed the lid back on her pen.

'Spit it out, then,' said Mary Churchill, looking up. There was a knock at the door.

Bile in her throat, and everything swelling, liquid, unfocused.

'One moment, please,' Mary called out. 'Perhaps Bombardier Tucker could speak for herself,' she said, getting up.

Images flashed like the screen at the flicks when they

reached the end of a reel: an airman with his outstretched arms; a mess of bricks that used to be a home; the blank scream of an empty tube tunnel in the darkness.

And then a voice. She heard someone calling: 'Joan, Joan, *Joan!*'

With an effort of will, she opened her eyes, back in the room.

'I'm not Joan.'

The knock came again. 'I beg your pardon?' said Mary Churchill.

'At the door, that knocking. It's a man called Fred. He was my sister's fiancé. My sister died when our house was bombed. She was Joan. She was Joan Tucker. I'm not – I'm not anyone, really.'

'*Mon Dieu,*' muttered Mary Churchill. The knock came again, more insistent. 'You'd better come in then,' said Mary, and the door began to open.

Chapter 47

Edie watched how Joan flinched as Fred entered. Apart from glimpsing him just now in the NAAFI, the last time she'd seen him it had been twilight, and she hadn't fully appreciated the extent of his burns. The whole left-hand side of his face was like red wine mopped up with a crumpled napkin. She tried not to stare.

'How can I help you?' said Mary Churchill.

'This girl is not who she says she is,' said Fred, gesturing at Joan. His voice was gravelly. Whatever had happened to him must have damaged his throat, too. He thrust out his hand. He was holding a large piece of cream paper, folded. Mary Churchill took it from him without comment, opened it and read. Edie glimpsed angular black lettering, dates and lines.

Mary Churchill cleared her throat and placed the paper down on the CO's desk behind her. 'Thank you for drawing this to my attention. I shall see that this is dealt with in the appropriate manner,' she said. 'You may go.'

But Fred took a step forwards. 'I don't think you under-stand, ma'am,' he said, breathing heavily. 'This girl is an imposter. She shouldn't be here. She should never have been here, she—'his words were slurring, jostling into each other.

'I see that. And as I said, I shall ensure that this is looked into.' Mary interrupted. 'Now, if you don't mind, I need to be getting on . . .'

'Something has to be done, don't you see?' Fred carried on. 'She's stolen my Joan. She's taken her. I've got nothing now, nothing. She's mocking the memory of my Joan; she's laugh-ing at me, and what I went through. She's a silly little tart and she needs to be punished. Punished for taking away my Joan.' It would have been less frightening if he'd shouted, Edie thought, if he'd yelled and writhed like a drunkard. But his understated rage had them all transfixed. 'She was never going to amount to anything. She knew that. Her sister's death was an opportunity. The Joan you know doesn't exist, should never have existed. This isn't Joan. This is Vanessa. And you need to send her back to where she came from.'

As he carried on speaking, Edie noticed Mary Churchill reach behind her and pick up the telephone on the desk. She mouthed something into the receiver, but Edie couldn't catch it, because Fred had moved closer towards them now, still talking.

'Look at this.' He pointed to a scab on his cheek, a curved bite mark, a burgundy crescent on top of the scarlet skin. 'You did this, Vanessa. Little bitch. You're a thief and a liar and a cheat.' His face was close in now, cream skin and red burns fighting a violent struggle as he spat out his words. He was so near that Edie could smell Fred's breath: pungent, like rotting fruit. She saw Joan rock backwards on her feet. But Fred wouldn't stop, pushing forwards, insisting that Joan was a liar, a tart, and worse, and then he was talking about sea ice and diesel fumes and the heat of the air when the engine room is on fire, and how Joan had promised to wait, how he'd come back all that way to find her. He carried on and on, until Joan began to stagger backwards, as if his very words were thumping her in the gut. Edie watched as Joan turned pale, began to slump.

'That's quite enough!' Edie said, starting forward, reaching out to help her friend. She hadn't noticed Mary Churchill move away behind them, silently opening the door. Suddenly, the RMPs were there, grabbing Fred's arms, pulling him away.

'Take him to Queen Alexandra's,' said Mary Churchill, 'he needs help.'

It seemed strange that Fred didn't resist the two military police at his shoulders. He just kept on talking, about 'his' Joan and how she'd been taken, and about the ice and the flames and the smell of death. As Fred was shunted to the door, he kept looking at them, kept on saying those quiet, horrid words. Edie could feel his eyes, even as she struggled to hold Joan upright.

'You're nothing, Vanessa,' he said, as he was bundled away and the door slammed shut.

Joan's head lolled, and Edie could no longer hold her weight. She watched, horrified, as Joan slid down onto the floor and began to twitch, gutteral sounds escaping her slack mouth. She knelt down next to her friend, but could do nothing more than hold Joan's head in her hands as she writhed, eyes wide and unseeing. Edie heard the door slam, and Mary Churchill was there beside her.

'She's having an epileptic fit,' Mary said. 'Help me get her into the recovery position.' Together, they shifted Joan's pulsing body into a lumpen 'S' shape on the floor. Edie asked what else they should do, but Mary said just wait, and make sure she doesn't choke. Saliva was beginning to drip out of Joan's mouth onto the lino. She was making a strange ticking sound, and her head was jerking. Mary went to call a medic.

There was the scuffling from outside as Fred was shoved up the path, and inside, Joan's throaty ticking sound. Edie kept her hands around her skull, cradling it like a newborn. It felt like for ever before the fit finally stopped. Joan opened her eyes, unfocused, and let out a brief cry of panic.

'Ssh,' said Edie, stroking her hair off her face. 'It's all right, dear. You're not alone,' she said.

A first-aider came and checked Joan's pulse and said she seemed fine but that she should probably get herself checked out by a doctor before returning to duty. Edie thought it strange, nobody seemed bothered: shouldn't Joan go to hospital? But the first-aider made a tutting sound and said no one would thank her for clogging up the wards with someone who'd just had a bit of a funny turn. They helped Joan up into the chair and brought her a glass of water. She said she only felt a bit woozy, but Edie had never seen her so deathly pale.

'You know what this is,' said Mary, when Joan seemed a little calmer. She held up the piece of paper Fred had brought, as Joan sipped the water, white-faced and silent. Joan shook her head. 'Have a look,' said Mary, passing it over. Edie, standing behind Joan, saw the fluttering cream sheet, with its important black writing. *Death certificate*, it said. *Joan Chastity Tucker.*

Chapter 48

'She's in the CO's office. They've just taken her fiancé to the loony bin and she'll be in the clink this afternoon for going AWOL,' said the fat girl, grinning at the thought of the slab of juicy gossip she'd just doled out.

'Thank you,' said Robin. 'Thank you for letting me know – erm –'

'Gunner Carter,' she replied. 'Sheila, if you like.' He smiled his thanks again. Was it his imagination or had she actually just tipped him a wink. No matter. He had to find Joan. There wasn't much time. There was the sound of talk from inside the hut, and he paused at the door, not wanting to eavesdrop, but not wanting to interrupt, either. His fist was clenched, ready. From behind him, on the distant emplacements, came the shrill shriek of a gunner shouting orders, blaring out the voices from inside the hut. He let his fist fall, three times.

'Who is it, please?' came the voice from inside.

'Flight Sergeant Nelson,' he said. 'I'm here to see Joan—'

he didn't have the chance to finish his sentence before the door was flung open from the inside. He could see her there, sitting inexplicably in the CO's chair, sipping a glass of water and holding a sheet of paper. She looked up as he entered, and her face was pale, make-up free – she looked about thirteen years old, like a schoolgirl, sitting behind her desk, studying an impenetrable piece of algebra. She looked at him as if he were a ghost, as if seeing him here was a total surprise. But she must have got his telegram?

The red-haired girl – Edie, wasn't it? – closed the door behind him. Nobody spoke at first. They all just looked at him, as if him being there were a mystery. But he'd sent the paperwork days ago, and the telegram just this morning, before he cadged the flight with the WAAF woman to RAF Redhill.

'You got the form, and the telegram?' he said.

'I'm sorry, I don't know what you're talking about,' said the woman officer standing next to Joanie. Joan's hand was shaking, he noticed. She put the glass of water down, and it slopped onto the blotter on the desk. What was it that fat girl had said about her being on a charge or something?

'I got your note, Joanie,' he said. 'And I sent a request for leave for us to get married straight away. Didn't it arrive?' Joan started, dropping the piece of paper she held in her other hand. But she didn't get up. 'I understand,' he continued, looking at her, wishing there wasn't the expanse of floor and desk and other people between them, wishing they were alone, like they'd been in the church, all those months ago. 'What you told me doesn't change a thing. I want to spend the rest of my life with you, whatever you damn well call yourself.'

He turned his attention to the woman officer. 'I sent the paperwork, but I couldn't get leave until now. I telegraphed, earlier. I thought you would have received it.' Joan was chewing her lip, looking like she wanted to say something, but couldn't. 'I don't know when I'll be able to get leave again,' he said. Whatever Joan was in trouble for, whatever had happened, he wasn't leaving now. Not this time.

The woman officer sighed and smoothed her hands over the front of her skirt. 'I'm terribly sorry you've come all this way for nothing, but your fiancée is on an AWOL charge. There's to be a preliminary hearing this afternoon,' she said.

'But—' he tried to interrupt, but in her soft, definite voice, she carried on. 'It is a shame, but I have no record of your request for wedding leave for Bombardier Tucker. You know, paperwork gets mislaid or destroyed all the time, in wartime, and although I sympathise with your situation, there it is,' she said. 'Now, if you wouldn't mind, Flight Sergeant—' she indicated to the door.

He shook his head. 'You can't do this,' he said. 'I don't know when I can come back. I don't know if there'll even be another opportunity. This is it.' He turned to Joan, now. 'This is it, Joanie, the last chance.' He took three quick steps towards the desk. He could see the piece of paper that Joan had been reading. It was a death certificate, a death certificate for Joan Tucker. But it didn't matter that she wasn't Joan. It didn't matter who she was. He loved her anyway, despite everything, because of everything.

'Now, Flight Sergeant, don't make me call the RMPs again,' said the woman officer, reaching for the telephone. But then Joan suddenly did something that made the officer stop, hand on the receiver.

Joan picked up the death certificate from the desk and ripped it, right across the middle, and then again and again, until all that was left were tiny shreds, which she let fall, like confetti, into the metal waste-paper basket beside her. Then she stood up, turned to the officer. 'You said it yourself, paperwork gets mislaid or destroyed all the time in wartime,' she said. 'I'm still your Joan,' she said, turning to him, now. 'I'll always be your Joanie.' And she began to walk out from behind the desk.

The woman officer dropped the hand that was reaching for the telephone and instead placed a restraining hand on Joan's shoulder. 'I'm afraid I can't let you just—' she began, as Joan shrugged her off, continuing to walk towards Rob.

'It's about time,' said Edie. Rob had almost forgotten she was there. 'I mean timing. When did you write requesting marital leave, Robin?'

Days ago, he replied, but they were a few men down, and he'd had to keep flying. Edie said that Joan had been AWOL since then, since the night he'd posted the form; that's why she was on a charge.

'But you can't be absent without leave, if you're actually on leave, can you, ma'am?' said Edie, looking across at the woman officer.

The officer looked back, her face slowly clearing. 'Oh, I see what you're driving at,' she said. She let go of Joan and began to search around the desk, flinging open drawers until she retrieved a blue slip of paper, which she began to write on.

'Oh, yes, that ties in nicely,' said the officer. 'Good thinking, Gunner Lightwater.'

In the meantime, Joan had come to stand right next to Rob; there was a line of static contiguity where the edge of her uniform brushed his. He could smell her hair. He ached for her, as they both stood and watched Edie and the officer, heads bent over the desk, upper-class accents chinking into each other as they filled in a form.

'Leave to get married, back dated by seventy-two hours,' said the officer at last, holding up a blue slip of paper. 'Bombardier Tucker, it appears that you haven't been AWOL; you have been on wedding leave. I expect to see you on parade first thing tomorrow, with a marriage certificate and a ring on your finger. Is that clear? Last I saw of the padre, he was walking his dog by the Serpentine, so quick sticks, you might catch him before lunch,' she said.

Robin let Joan out of the hut first and held the door open for her friend Edie, but the officer called her back. '*Un moment, s'il vous plaît*, Gunner Lightwater,' she said. 'I haven't finished with you, yet.'

Outside was like coming up for air after a long spell under water. He felt in his pocket among the keys and small change.

'Catch!' he tossed the ring, and the sunlight made it sparkle as it flew towards her. She caught it and smiled at him.

The fat girl was coming the other way, this time with an armful of gas masks, trailing rubber straps like the tails of small animals. 'Blimey, how many fiancés have you got, Gunner Tucker?' she said.

'Just the one,' said Joan, slipping the engagement ring onto her left hand. 'And it'll be Mrs Nelson, from now on, thank you.'

Chapter 49

Edie thought she'd be able to go back for her things. It didn't occur to her as she got into the staff car that she was turning her back on the ATS for ever. She hadn't even had a chance to say goodbye to Joan. When Mary Churchill called her back in to the CO's office and explained that she wasn't on an AWOL charge either, because she was still officially off sick with appendicitis, and when they'd had that hurried conversation in her rusty French, she'd still thought that there would be time to pack up, say *au revoir*, at the very least. She'd wanted to see Joan and Rob get married. But the war machine had other plans, it seemed. The last time she'd been in a car was in Pop's Bentley, back in the spring. How things had changed, in those few months since.

'War Office, is it?' said the driver. She had some kind of northern accent, but Edie couldn't be certain quite where she was from. Her dun-coloured hair was tucked into a tidy hair net at the nape of her neck.

'Please,' said Edie. The driver was one of theirs. The car jolted into gear and they pulled away. Edie looked into the wing mirror, seeing the battery diminish in size behind them, until the guns were just matchsticks and the soldiers nothing but scurrying beetles. Ahead, the cream and grey slabs of London buildings loomed. At Hyde Park Corner, they turned onto the Mall, and the barracks finally disappeared from view, replaced by Buckingham Palace, flagless and severe.

Edie wondered where the Royal Family were today: Windsor or Sandringham maybe? Perhaps Princess Elizabeth was away with the ATS cadets, wiping her royal hands on grubby coveralls as she learnt how to change the oil in an army truck on her vehicle maintenance course. Edie looked down at her own driver's capable-looking hands as they manhandled the gearstick. What was it Marjorie had called it? Double de-clutching? Edie thought that if she'd taken driving lessons with Marjorie instead of having extra French tuition at Queen's, then maybe she'd have become a driver too, instead of – instead of what? She really had no idea what was in store for her.

As they accelerated up the Mall, she looked past her driver's snub-nosed profile to the tree-lined pavement and beyond: streaming red buses, black cabs and cyclists interrupting her view of St James' Park. Pop had told her once about some schoolfriend's uncle who'd spent the three days before the last war – 'the Great War' he called it – weeping by the lake in St James' Park. It was guilt, Pop said. The chap was something high up in the government and he'd seen what was coming and not been able to do a thing to stop it. Edie thought she knew now how that man must have felt.

They were halfway towards Horse Guard's Parade when the driver suddenly slammed on the brakes. A funeral cortège was pulling out of the junction with Marlborough Road, on the left. It was a proper old-fashioned funeral: blinkered black horses with oily haunches and plumes of black and purple ostrich feathers, quivering. As it turned in front of them, she could see through the glass window of the carriage, see the coffin. It was very small, white, with a wreath of pale pink roses on the lid.

The driver misinterpreted Edie's stifled gasp. 'I know, we'll be stuck for blooming ever behind this lot,' she muttered. But Edie wasn't thinking about the delay in reaching the War Office; she was thinking about what happened in the Mount Royal Hotel, outside the 400 Club, and on the train tracks of a station in Kent. Three deaths, all down to her, and a mass of guilt that pushed up against her ribcage and choked up her throat. Three deaths, and no forgiveness. *Dear God*, she began her reflexive internal prayer, but consciously stopped. You cannot beg for pardon, she told herself.

The driver tutted, drumming her pudgy fingers on the steering wheel. The black carriages and dark-suited mourners poured out in front of them and Edie thought of how Bea's funeral had been: the straggle of stunned siblings in that meagre, bombed-out church. Her mother was in hospital, by then. Her father, delayed travelling back from his unit, missing the service and only making it just in time for the burial.

He'd pumped their hands, sorrow hollowing out his face, as he thanked her for her support. How she'd hated that. Being thanked for something that was all her fault.

The driver revved up behind the final mourners. Edie looked down at her hands, twisted together in her lap, bitten fingernails, skin red-raw from over-washing. She couldn't seem to stop washing her hands these days. Lady Macbeth's got nothing on me, she thought, sadly.

'I hope you're not in a rush,' said the driver, as the car began to inch forward. 'I'd overtake, only I don't want to scare the horses.'

'An extra minute or two won't hurt,' said Edie.

'You won't get put on a charge or anything?'

'I very much doubt it. Anyway, what's the worst they can do? Pack me off to the Continent to fight Jerry on my own?'

She remembered that comment, years later. She'd only said it to ease the tension, make the driver feel better about the situation. Still, many a true word spoken in jest, isn't that what they say?

Outside on the pavement, a huge gust of wind whipped up the tree branches into swirling green dervishes and passers-by held onto their hats. Suddenly, Edie could bear it no longer. 'It's just over there, isn't it?' she said, pointing right past the driver's face, towards the junction with Horse Guards Parade. 'I'm sure I can find my way from here.'

'I'm supposed to take you all the way,' said the driver.

Edie looked at the slow sway of the funeral cortège and felt as if she couldn't breathe, as if the swathe of black and purple was reaching right back into the car and suffocating her. 'Oh, who's to know?' she said brightly. 'I'll nip out and you can do a U-turn and give yourself an extra ten minutes' NAAFI break.'

'You're sure?' said the driver, coming to a slow halt.

'Absolutely,' said Edie, fixing her cap firmly on her head and reaching for the latch. 'You don't need to worry about me, dear,' she said, opening the car door and stepping out onto the kerb. 'I know exactly where I'm going, now.'

Chapter 50

'It's not going to be much of a honeymoon for you,' said Rob, as they got out of the tube.

'It's more than I deserve,' she replied.

'Don't be daft. We'll do something proper when this is all over. Torquay, maybe – used to go there every summer when I was a nipper – there's some grand hotels along the front.'

'Torquay it is.'

'And then we'll settle down. Dad wants me to take over the butcher's, but I've got other ideas.'

'I don't get to make sausages, then?'

'You get to do whatever you damn well please. You can spend the day filing your nails and shopping for frocks, as the wife of a successful motor manufacturer. Me and Harper, we made a whole business plan – his old man's got a garage, so he knew a bit about the business. The engineering that makes planes fly faster will also work for cars. There'll be opportunities once the war's over, you'll see,' he said.

'Once the war's over,' Joan repeated. It sounded like the end of a fairy tale.

They were going up the steps now. Up-up-up, past the posters telling them to BE LIKE DAD, KEEP MUM and THIS IS YOUR COUNTRY, FIGHT FOR IT. The sunshine was waiting for them on the top step.

Rob asked if she was all right and she said 'fine', even though there was a shaky feeling deep inside as they stepped out of the darkness and into the smothering warmth of the late afternoon sunlight. She tried to take a deep breath in, but it felt as if a fist were clenched around her lungs. She faltered, felt for Rob's hand.

'You don't seem too chipper. Shall we get you a brew? There's a café over there.'

Joan shook her head, but the Red Lion was opposite the station, and Rob said maybe something stronger, to celebrate? She'd never been in the Red Lion before, what with Dad being a copper. She couldn't risk pretending to be eighteen, like some of the other girls. She hadn't drunk alcohol at all, before joining the ATS.

Joan scuffed across the street. The wind had died down now, and this heat made her feet swell up. It felt like her army brogues were half a size too small. They chafed at her heels. The Red Lion looked the same, with peeling black paint and the red-and-gold sign. There was a black A-board outside, proclaiming *Today's Special* in smudged chalk handwriting, and a hanging basket beside the door, spilling bizzie-lizzies from the moss. Rob let go of her hand, stepped aside and held the door open for her to go in first.

The pub was empty, tomb-dark after the glare outside: crimson, brown and black, smelling of the sweet dank smell of old beer soaking into carpet and stale smoke. She sat down at the first table, next to the window. There were little tablets of stained glass with the brewery name back-to-front in red and green and yellow. Outside, blue skies showed above the rooftops and the bizzie-lizzies swayed.

'Gin and lime?' Rob called from the bar. She nodded, smiled.

'Large one?' she nodded again.

Joan looked at him there, the handsome airman at the bar. He'd taken his cap off and a lock of his dark Brylcreemed hair fell over one brow. He shared a joke with the puffy-faced barman and smiled his lopsided smile. That's my husband, she thought. I'm going to spend the rest of my life with that man. It felt as if she'd taken off her usherette's tray and stepped right into the cinema screen.

Rob came back with the drinks and sat down opposite her. She twined her legs round his. 'Thank you,' she said, taking her drink.

'Pleasure, Mrs Nelson,' he replied. 'I got you these as well,' he tossed over a packet of pork scratchings. 'Wedding breakfast.'

'You know how to treat a lady.' She smiled.

He winked. 'No expense spared.' And they laughed, a little, at the shared joke. 'Tell you what, though, when this is all over we'll do it properly,' said Rob. 'Champagne, huge cake – my Mum will love making the cake – and you can have an

amazing silk dress, with a train that goes right out the door.'
He reached for his pint.

'When this is all over,' said Joan, wondering when that was
likely to be.

'To us,' said Rob, clinking her ladies' glass with his pint pot.
'To the future.'

'To us,' she agreed, feeling like she was trying to catch
something in the wind, like a falling leaf always spinning out
of reach.

When they finished their drinks he asked her if she was
feeling better and if she still wanted to go through with this,
and she said she was and she did. The shaky, fluttery feeling
was still there but at least she could breathe properly now. She
told him she just needed to go and powder her nose.

The Ladies' smelled of urine and bleach. There were ripped
copies of *Reader's Digest* in lieu of toilet roll, slippery and
sharp as she wiped herself. She washed her hands with the
tiny sliver of greying soap in the sink. She patted her face
with her damp hands and pinched her cheeks to make them
pink. You couldn't get rouge for love nor money at the
moment. Bea used to get beetroot for them before a night
out – she had a friend on kitchen duty. Beetroot juice worked
pretty well, if you did it right.

Bea, she thought, looking at her reflection in the glass and
pulling her lipstick out of her gas-mask case, how pleased
you'd be for me today: my wedding day. They'd found the
padre having a quiet smoke by a weeping willow. They'd just
had to grab two witnesses from whoever was available, so

they'd ended up with Sheila Carter and Billy from stores. Bea would have laughed at that, she thought: Sheila bloody Carter and fat Billy as my wedding witnesses.

Joan put on two coats of Californian Poppy. When she came out of the loos and back into the saloon, Rob was back at the bar, taking their glasses back to the barman, and he turned to look at her, and she paused, returning his gaze and for a moment they were both silent, staring, as if it were the first time they'd ever clapped eyes on each other.

They walked arm in arm up Western Way, past the allotments. The air was hot, and the gin made her head swim and her mouth taste fruity, as if she'd been eating pear drops from the sweet shop on her way home from school. She looked down at the pavement and tried to avoid the cracks, but her footsteps were way too big, these days. They were getting closer, now. Still arm in arm, they carried on up the road, and the too-tight shoes made her wince at every step. There was a green bus, and a woman on a bicycle and a rag-and-bone man with his horse and cart. The horse looked skinny and lame.

Do they ride much, in Finchley? I will not have horse eaten in this house! Where are you now, Edie? Where have they sent you? Will I ever see you again?

Left-right, on they went, a slow march along the dusty pavement, where the shops gave way to houses: modern semis with clipped privet hedges and overblown roses spilling petals into the street. Most of the little front lawns had been dug over, with fruit canes, runner beans, marrows and peas, just like Dad had had at the allotment. Who had his allotment now? she wondered. A woman came out of the front door of number fifty-eight: grey hair, string bag full of lettuces. Was that Mrs Gladwell? Joan looked down at the pavement and sped up, and Rob kept in step with her.

Fifty-eight, fifty-six – she heard Mrs Gladwell's footsteps cross the street behind them and fade away into the distance. It wouldn't be long before they reached number thirty-two. Number thirty-two Western Way. They were going back to where it all began. Two trucks lumbered past and an army dispatch rider sped in the opposite direction. She saw a string of blonde hair escaping from the motorcyclist's helmet as she passed them. That's one of ours, thought Joan. They walked on in silence. And she could see it, up ahead, the cavity in the fascia of semis. As they got closer, she could see that some of number thirty-four was still standing, but number thirty-two was gone.

It shouldn't have been a shock, but it was. Somehow, here in summertime, she'd half expected to see the white pebble-dashed walls and the bit of black gabling and the blue polka-dot curtains at the upstairs bedroom window, and the black front door with '32' in polished brass letters and the doorbell that went 'ping-pong' and Mum waiting in her pinny with floury hands from making pastry, and opening the door and saying, 'Oh, here's that nice young man we've heard so much about. Come in and I'll put the kettle on. Your father will be home for his tea, soon.' But instead, there was a mound of rubble and a hastily painted sign in black on a broken plank that said, BOMB SITE – KEEP OUT. Plants had begun to grow among the fallen bricks: dandelions with downy heads floating away and some kind of vine that crept and smothered over everything. The front gate was still there, swinging on a hinge like a dallying schoolboy. And the pavement was still broken, tree roots exposed like bare knuckles.

She stood and looked at the empty sky and the mess of her broken home underneath it. Rob put his arm round her: warm. She could smell him and feel him. Her eyes cast round the scene. Up the street a bit, just there, that was where he tackled her to the ground. And over there was where he found his RAF cap. She never had managed to get the blood-stain out of that old woollen coat, not even with bicarbonate of soda and an old toothbrush, like Bea told her to. She moved closer into Rob, needing him to be the still centre in the spinning circle rush of memories.

'We don't have to go in, if you don't want to,' he said.

'I want to,' she replied. She broke free from Rob's embrace, turned the KEEP OUT sign face down and pushed through the broken gate. She could feel Rob just behind her as she picked her way towards the remains of her home. The front path was smashed apart. All that was left of the lawn was a few little triangles of green showing between the bricks and rubble, and the weeds, shoving through, taking over. There were splinters of wood with black shiny paint near where the front door should have been. She had to clamber over fallen joists and broken blocks of masonry. Shards of broken glass blinked, catching the sun like jewels hiding in the rubble. Her shoes caught and her ankle twisted on the jagged mass of bricks, but Rob was behind her. He'll catch me if I fall, she thought, and carried on. At last she was there. There where she'd found Joan. She could still see the patch of lino with a dark brown stain. That was where she'd taken Joan's hand, the perfectly manicured little hand with the sapphire engagement ring. And just there, not two feet away, that was where she'd found the call-up papers and the ID card.

She sat down, sat amid the bricks and the plaster and the shattered glass and wood splinters and old, dried blood and remembered the noise and the hand, still warm, in the ash and the grit and the dust, that night. Oh, Joan. I miss you. I miss you so much, my big sister. My perfect big sister.

'They got the wrong one,' she said. 'She was the good one. It should've been me, here, not her.'

'Don't say that, Joanie,' said Rob, trying to put his arm round her. She shrugged him off.

'I'm not Joan,' she said. 'I'm Vanessa. I'm an usherette and I'm a stupid little tart who will never amount to anything. I'm not real. You've married a fraud, Rob. You've married a bloody ghost.' And a sudden gust of wind took her words and hurled them, down the street and away. And Rob looked on, saying nothing, waiting.

She saw the drops fall, splashing onto the dust. It can't be raining, she thought distractedly. There's not a cloud in the sky. But then she put a hand up to her cheek, and felt the hot tears and watched them fall, down onto the broken masonry.

And from somewhere deep came a tearing, ripping her throat and her chest.

She didn't know how long she cried for, or how long Rob sat, waiting, watching, patiently. He didn't move until her howls subsided to sobs and her heaving chest slowed and he silently passed her a handkerchief.

'I'm sorry,' she said, wiping her eyes and blowing her nose, still not making eye contact with him.

'You've nothing to be sorry for, Mrs Nelson,' he replied, and she could hear that his voice was thick. He cleared his throat. He put his hand on her arm again, and this time she didn't shrug it off. He began to kiss her, gently, on the nape of her neck, and his lips were soft and his breath was warm. And she noticed how there were poppies growing around the base of the Anderson shelter, as she turned to return his kiss.

Acknowledgements

Thank you to each and every one of you who helped with this book.

You know who you are – thank you. xxx